Like a Fading Shadow

Antonio Muñoz Molina

Translated from the Spanish
by Camilo A. Ramirez

Farrar, Straus and Giroux
New York

Farrar, Straus and Giroux
18 West 18th Street, New York 10011

Printed in the United States of America
Originally published in Spanish in 2014 by Seix Barral, Spain, as *Como la sombra que se va*
English translation published in the United States by Farrar, Straus and Giroux
First American edition, 2017

Library of Congress Cataloging-in-Publication Data
Names: Muñoz Molina, Antonio author. | Ramirez, Camilo A., 1985– translator.
Title: Like a fading shadow : a novel / Antonio Muñoz Molina ; translated by
Camilo A. Ramirez.
Other titles: Como la sombra que se va. English
Description: New York : Farrar, Straus and Giroux, 2017.
Identifiers: LCCN 2016050908 | ISBN 9780374126902 (hardback) |
ISBN 9780374714161 (e-book)
Subjects: LCSH: King, Martin Luther, Jr., 1929–1968—Assassination—Fiction. |
Ray, James Earl, 1928–1998—Fiction. | BISAC: FICTION / Literary. | FICTION /
Historical.
Classification: LCC PQ6663.U4795 C6613 2017 | DDC 863/.64—dc23
LC record available at https://lccn.loc.gov/2016050908

Designed by Jonathan D. Lippincott

Our books may be purchased in bulk for promotional, educational, or business use.
Please contact your local bookseller or the Macmillan Corporate and Premium
Sales Department at 1-800-221-7945, extension 5442, or by e-mail at
MacmillanSpecialMarkets@macmillan.com.

www.fsgbooks.com
www.twitter.com/fsgbooks • www.facebook.com/fsgbooks

1   3   5   7   9   10   8   6   4   2

My days are like a fading shadow; and I am withered like grass.

—Psalms 102:11

1

I awake inside his mind; frightened, disoriented from so much reading and researching. As if my eyes had opened in an unfamiliar room. Angst from the dream lingers. I had committed a heinous crime or was being pursued and condemned despite my innocence. Someone was pointing a gun at me and I could not run or defend myself. I could not move. Before thoughts can fully form, the secret novelist inside us all is already plotting stories. The room in shadows was concave and the ceiling low like a cave or basement or the skull that holds his brain, his feverish mind, exhausted from reading and solitary thinking, with all his memories, his physical features, the images of his life, his heart palpitations, the propensity to believe he had contracted a fatal disease, cancer, an angina, the routine of hiding and fleeing.

I woke up and for a moment I forgot where I was and I was like him, or he himself, because I was having a dream more his than mine. I was in shock that I could not recognize the room where I had fallen asleep just two hours earlier; was not able to remember the position of the bed in relation to the window and other furniture, or my location in a space that was suddenly unknown; I even struggled trying to remember what city I was in. This probably happened to him often, after sleeping in so many places while on the run, thirteen months and three weeks, five countries, fifteen cities, two continents, not to mention all the nights in different motels and boardinghouses, the nights curled, shivering against a tree, or under a bridge, or in the backseat of the car, or on a bus that smells of tobacco and plastic and arrives at the underground parking of a station at three in the morning, or that night he was so anxious, flying for the first time, paralyzed by fear, looking out through the small oval window into that dark abyss, the surface of the ocean shining like wet ink under the moonlight. (He would fly overnight once more, crossing the Atlantic in the opposite direction; this time in handcuffs and fetters; dozing off against the window, in a dream where the handcuffs transformed into vines and the weight of the fetters was the mud where his feet were sinking.)

•

My dream could have been his and, in any case, has everything to do with him, although he did not appear. I have spent too many hours immersed in his life, days on end since I arrived in Lisbon. It only takes a few seconds online to access the archives containing detailed accounts of almost everything he did, places he visited, crimes he committed, prisons where he was held, even the names of women who slept with him or shared a drink at a bar. I know the magazines and novels he read and the brand of salted crackers left open and half-eaten in a rented room in a boardinghouse in Atlanta where his name never made it to the register because the owner was too drunk to ask for it. Photocopies and scanned pages of old files list every article of clothing he took to a dry cleaner in Atlanta on March 30, 1968, and picked up the morning of April 5; or the forensic report on the trajectory of the bullet he fired the day before, April 4, in Memphis, from the bathroom of a boardinghouse, resting the barrel of a Remington .30-06 rifle on the windowsill; or a declaration from the plastic surgeon who operated on the tip of his nose in Los Angeles; or the copy of a fingerprint left on a mail order clipped from a photography magazine.

Even the most secret lives leave an indelible trace. At that time, advertisements in magazines often included mail order forms. The vastness of reality produces equal measures of astonishment and insomnia. It is amazing how much you can learn about a person and still never truly know him, because he never said what was most important: a dark hole, a blank space; a mug shot, the rough lines of a facial composite based on disjointed testimonies and vague memories. He survived on instant coffee, heated with a submersible heating element, powdered milk, canned beans, and French fries dipped in mustard or Kraft salad dressing. He frequented the cheapest diners and ordered his burgers with extra onion, bacon, ketchup, and cheese. He ate his fries by the handful. Some remembered him being left-handed, others were certain he always used his right hand to sign and smoke. In some of the police descriptions he has light brown hair; in others, black and graying on the sides. He had a small scar on his forehead and another on one of his palms. People remembered him smoking, holding the cigarette in his right hand, which displayed a gold ring finger with a dark green stone. But he was not a smoker and did not wear rings. A ring could be one of those details that make you easier to remember and identify. He never got any tattoos.

I stayed up late searching his tracks through the vast sleepless memory of the Internet. When I finally turned off the lights, my eyes burned from staring at the computer for so many hours, and my head turned with dates, names, and trivial events—a modicum of reality that was hard to imagine someone making up. In prison, to stay in shape, he learned to walk on his hands and do complicated yoga postures in the small cell. He could gain or lose weight easily. To the end, he took Polaroids of himself regularly: with sunglasses, without them, with eyeglasses, always foreshortened, never in profile because profiles were too distinctive, even after the nose surgery, also never directly from the front, as the big ears would surely set him apart. He would send different photos of himself to contacts in pen pal clubs, thinking this would confuse the authorities when they started looking for him. In a hospitality school in Los Angeles, he learned how to mix one hundred twenty different cocktails. For several months, he took a locksmith correspondence course offered by a school in New Jersey. Among his papers, they found a brochure about all the advantages of a career in locksmithing. When he was nine or ten, he would wake up to his own screams every night. He dreamed that he was blind. He tried to wake up and open his eyes, but he still couldn't see because he had fallen into another dream of blindness. He was scared of falling asleep, scared of his nightmares. He did his best to stay awake through the night. In the dark, he could hear his father and mother snoring, both drunk on a bare mattress, using old coats as blankets. On straw mattresses across the dilapidated floor, his siblings huddled together, covered in lice and bedbugs, hungry, trying to keep warm during those winter nights in the one-room house, breathing smoke from the old wood-burning stove.

•

I have learned so much about him that sometimes I feel like I am recalling his own memories, places he saw where I've never been: the Nevada desert on the highway to Las Vegas, the cobbled streets and low houses of Puerto Vallarta, the echoing corridors of a prison with stone walls and towers and Gothic vaults, the silhouette of the Lorraine Motel seen in the distance from a window in a bathroom, a putrid room in a boardinghouse surrounded by empty lots and heaps of trash, in a neighborhood on the outskirts of Memphis. I have decided I have no choice but to travel to Memphis. I have written down the address of the hotel in Lisbon where, forty-five years ago, he spent ten days while on the run. I googled the name and learned the hotel still exists and it is only fifteen minutes away from here. In this moment, a figment of my imagination suddenly becomes a tangible reality. I have woken up from a dream of hiding, danger, shame; a dream that could be his and that has without a doubt instigated my urge to discover him, to stay up late researching, fighting off sleep, hypnotized by the laptop's glow, leaning on the desk where I have been working for a few days, long enough to create a habit, in successive layers, the desk and the apartment, the street, the corner I see from the window, the streetcar that brakes as it goes downhill and rings a bell, the roofs of the city, the decaying walls of the buildings, the balconies with broken windows on the higher floors, the name I have not said with such purpose in so many years, Lisbon.

•

My window faces the back of an abandoned building. Not much sunlight comes in. I can see a glass gallery and iron railings worn by humidity and rust. Beyond a broken door frame, a corridor extends into the dark and carries out the constant cooing of pigeons. The birds have colonized the abandoned building. They go in and out through the broken windows. Weeds grow between the tiles on the gallery. On my side, ruin has not encroached although our bedroom is only a stone's throw away. The building where we are staying was restored recently; it has the appeal of new amenities and the solidity of old architecture, thick walls, ample spaces. The gangrene of decay and collapse advances quickly in old cities by the sea. The building where the pigeons live and the rainwater seeps in through the cracks is the failed inverse of this one, it is that part of the city that the elements are claiming back. We have made this side our home in just a few days. High ceilings, airy rooms, sturdy floorboards creaking under our steps like the deck of a boat. The bed is big, the sheets are clean and pleasing to the touch, the pillows plump, the soft light from the lamps filters through paper spheres textured like thin parchment, your presence beside me and on the mirror, in the half-light you like to create, closing curtains, turning off lights, leaving some of the doors slightly open. Regaining a sense of familiarity, detail by detail, the horror of the nightmare begins to dissipate.

•

I feel my way through the walls. Leaving the dark bedroom allows me to escape the dungeon of sleep. I stand disoriented in the hallway, reaching a wall instead of the door I anticipated. My brain is not used to guiding my steps blindly. My imaginary map of the apartment is now out of sync. Nothing comes easier to me than the feeling of being suddenly lost. A sound behind me makes me turn: the refrigerator fan starts and the space begins to recover its true configuration. The world is a moving maze of signs, electric shocks, sound waves, brief flashes of light in the dark. The brain re-creates it entirely in its hermetic box, locked within its vault of bone. He believed that it was possible to guide from a distance the steps and actions of someone who has been hypnotized, order them to murder, plant a bomb, or rob a bank.

My hand now slides down the carved wooden doorway to the living room, and from this, like a fossil, I reconstruct with certainty the space in the dark, the desk to the right, the sofa to the left, and in front, the window facing the street. The dilated retina collects scattered light to complete the tapestry of perception, returning to it its three dimensions. The wind must have closed the window shutters. As my hand runs along the edge of the desk, my fingers touch the keyboard and the laptop turns on, a white beam of light suddenly illuminates the room. He liked using a typewriter. He had learned typing while serving a two-year sentence at Leavenworth federal prison in the mid-fifties. Somewhere in his vast file, there is probably a receipt of purchase listing the brand of the machine. He threw it from the car window while driving at full speed from Memphis to Atlanta, hearing or imagining police sirens in the distance. The typewriter, a Super 8 camera, a projector, several empty beer cans—he threw them all and watched them fall through the rearview mirror. I have the list of everything he took in the '66 Mustang with Alabama plates; in the blue gym bag he dropped along with the rifle before escaping; and what they later found in the trunk and the floor of the car, down to the bits of facial hair and dried foam on the blades of the disposable razor. I now know by heart the sequence of aliases he used and abandoned as they served their purpose, like old suits left behind in a hotel closet. I see his figure take shape before me, his shadow, his entire biography, composed of these minute details, one by one, like broken tiles in the mosaic sidewalks of Lisbon.

•

It is a spring morning and I am walking on one of those sidewalks, Fanqueiros Street, with my map of the city and a piece of paper with some directions from Google Maps. I left the apartment without saying where I was going, with a feeling of secrecy and shame. The first steps in creating a story often feel childish, and in this case, I wasn't even there yet; I had just embarked on a search without a destination. I walk into a stationer with the intention of buying a notebook. I find one that I like very much and realize that I had been to this same shop just a year ago and bought an identical notebook in which I wrote only one thing, a date, December 2. I walk past ghostly fabric stores, closed-down shops still displaying calligraphy from half a century ago; stands with wilted vegetables sold by Nepalis or Pakistanis; doors that smell of humidity and neglect; facades of dilapidated tiles; forlorn people standing by the entrances to their empty shops; pharmacies with marble counters and wooden shelves; clothing stores that become more contemporary as I approach Figueira Square, with its bronze king on horseback, surrounded by buildings with sunken rooftops overrun by weeds.

I see the narrow display window of a doll hospital I first saw twenty-six years ago. The square remains identical, the old streetcars, the soft morning sun of November, and that unmistakable scent of freshly baked bread and roasted chestnuts briefly dissolves my grasp of time. How strange is the sudden realization that I am the man with the graying hair and beard reflected in that window. But it is even stranger to have been that young man, back then, so much younger than I thought I was, father to a three-year-old son and a baby just born, my face probably unrecognizable to those who only met me recently, so nervous, so restless, lighting cigarettes and inhaling smoke with deep breaths, armed with a notebook and a map, just like I am this morning, and ignorant of what is to come—his destiny, your existence. What he and I have in common, this and that morning, almost thirty years ago under the same timeless light of this city, is that we walk through Lisbon searching for ghosts, his more fictitious than mine. The ghost I chase walked these same sidewalks, walked across this square, and turned that corner, João das Regras Street. It gives me chills just to look at the sign.

In a book, in a news article, the name and number of a street do not matter much, they are superfluous details. But being close to this place, and knowing that I can approach it, infuses wonder and reality in what was previously almost fiction. João das Regras Street, number four. As I walk up Fanqueiros Street, I imagine arriving at the Hotel Portugal, pushing the revolving door with gilded edges, treading the worn carpet, perhaps sitting on an armchair in the low light of the lobby. Just entering the hotel would anchor my speculations, making tangible everything that until now belonged only to dreams and the light sleep that followed my readings.

I have read online reviews by recent guests of the hotel. The rooms are small, the facilities outdated, and from dawn till night-time, on the lower floors, you can hear the trains in the nearby metro station. He stayed in room number two on the first floor. There is an old dresser with a mirror and a marble ledge opposite the bed. I saw a photo of the room in the June 1968 issue of *Life* magazine. It must have smelled of old wood and dust when he opened the drawers. A hotel maid said he kept the room tidy. He slept badly and the train vibrations probably aggravated the insomnia. The surrounding build-ings are tall and the sunlight that floods the nearby square does not reach João das Regras Street. I walk along, looking for number four, but I reach the end of the street and it seems the number does not exist. The world I was about to enter has vanished. I see an old hard-ware store with all kinds of keys, locks, and padlocks on the shelves. He would have seen it too, when crossing the street, with all the familiar tools from his locksmith course. The hotel sign, between the two rows of balconies shown in photographs, is nowhere to be seen. I ask a waiter standing by the entrance to a bar and he points to a facade covered with scaffolding and tarps. The old Hotel Portugal closed down and the building is now empty and under construction. It will become a luxury hotel.

2

He looked pale as a ghost when he stepped out of the shade of the arcades, instinctively moving away from a policeman in a blue uniform who was walking toward him, gun in holster, folder in hand, more of a clerk than a policeman, with a large stomach protruding over the belt. He glanced at the pistol, though his eyes barely moved, and stepped aside. No one would have thought it was an abrupt motion, and in any case he was one of many moving under the arcades, people in and out of offices: posters on the large doors, windows with iron railings, the clicking sound of typewriters.

Typing nonstop, first names, last names, parents' names, birth dates, addresses. They ask for information without looking up, typing on their forms, hitting the keys hard for crisp type on the carbon copies. They write things by hand on index cards with stapled or glued photos that end up in file cabinets. Identity card number, driver's license, passport, social security number, inmate number, length of sentence. When they make a mistake, they stop the machine and fix the letter or number with a small brush and white-out, then blow so it dries as quickly as possible.

•

The sun beat down harshly on his white skin and sandy hair, making it look lighter and more sparse despite the parting to the side, which made his face look longer and younger. On the passport, he put 1932 as the year of his birth though he had been born in 1928. A man's age depends largely on whether he visualizes himself young and strong or old and weak, said Dr. Maxwell Maltz. Others will see you the way you see yourself. They will step on you if your face begs to get stomped on. They will chase you if you look like a fugitive.

The streetcar tracks, crisscrossed on the cobbled pavement of the square, gleamed under the sun with a moist sheen. There was a light humidity in the air, all the more noticeable when you looked into the distance, beyond the square, at the sea, or maybe it was a very wide river, extending above a low silhouette of hills and houses. It was a humidity saturated with smells, reminiscent of New Orleans or Saint Louis or Memphis, but not as thick. The river or the sea did not have the mud color of the Mississippi. Montreal's river was also so broad you could not see the other side. Vast rivers and iron bridges in the distance, docks, warehouses, hissing locomotives, the promising wailing sounds of the boat sirens. On the winding rails, the red and yellow streetcars advance and their old wood frames creak as they wobble from side to side. He stopped, as one of the streetcars passed, and put his sunglasses on. He had practiced the move many times in the mirror. Women thought he looked refined. He would take the sunglasses from his breast pocket and in one continuous motion unfold the frame and bring them to his eyes. But he still blinked too much when he performed the opposite motion and this ruined the desired effect. When he practiced he tried to control his blink reflex. It was hard to notice how light his blue eyes were because he seldom made eye contact. He considered buying contact lenses to change the color of his eyes.

The passing streetcar blocked him from view as he squinted at the light. Seconds later, the sunglasses were on. He was able to catch a glimpse of himself on the moving window, anonymous among the crowd waiting to cross the street, taller than the rest, five feet eleven inches. A dirty window vibrating like the rest of the vehicle, an old machine approaching its end, slow and worn-out, the yellow paint damaged by the heat and humidity, covered in signs and old ads faded by the sun. Some of the windows did not have glass and the passengers leaned out on their elbows as if they were in the windows of their house.

Everything in the city was old and dilapidated. The signs on the government buildings and the uniforms of the officers guarding the entrances, the tables on which functionaries wrote, the typewriters, the file cabinets where documents were stored. In the offices of the Ministry of the Overseas, there were old world maps hanging on the walls. He had asked with difficulty how long it would take to get a visa to Angola, and the functionary had stared at him from behind the typewriter and placed his cigarette on an edge of the table covered with burns. Angola was the name of a Portuguese colony in Africa and also a prison in the American South. The functionary asked for his nationality and suggested he come back later to speak with the person who dealt with those requests. The office was filled with stacks of files and wall maps and it had high ceilings covered in filth. The functionary's desk was next to a balcony facing out to the river or sea. As he waited for the functionary to finish taking note of his case, he saw a large cargo ship moving on the water. Atop a pile of worn registry books, a small fan turned slowly, barely disturbing the heat in the office.

•

At the center of the square, there was a statue of a king on horseback, an immense plume of feathers adorning his helmet. The king and his royal horse stand on a marble pedestal in which an Asian elephant and another horse are carved. Asian elephants have smaller ears than their African counterparts and it is easier to tame them. On a cover of *Man's Life*, in full color, an angry elephant wraps its trunk around a half-naked woman and lifts her up just as a white hunter shoots his rifle to save her. Through swamps and jungles, the Asian elephants splash the muddy waters as they move, obeying the orders of handlers who use bamboo sticks. The handlers are called mahouts. *Mahout* is an extraordinary word that most people don't know.

The hooves of the royal horse trample over bronze snakes. On the sides of the pedestal, the horse and the elephant also trample over terrified people. A seagull settles on the feathered helmet of the bronze king. The spurred boots hang to the sides of the horse's stomach, ready to thrust into the animal and crush whoever comes under its hooves. The king never looks down. In the prison farms of the South, the guards patrol on horses and support the butts of their rifles on the sides of their saddles; they wear wide-brimmed hats and sunglasses instead of helmets with feathers. The new trend is to humiliate white prisoners by forcing them to share their dormitories and tables with black people. As he advanced through the square in a straight line, he stopped for a moment under the long shadow of the statue, surrounded by white light, the sky, and the sea or river that looked amber behind the dark lenses. The shirt collar was tightly buttoned. There would be a red mark when he took the tie and shirt off and looked at himself in the bathroom mirror. He would fold his trousers, hang the jacket, then go through the pockets and empty them. The Laundromat receipts with his name and the drop-off and pickup dates, letters signed with a different name, his name before coming to Lisbon, before going to London, the one he used while hiding in Toronto before his first flight. In one of the pockets, he kept a newspaper clipping with an ad for cheap tickets to African capitals. The piece of paper is now laminated and on display inside a glass case in a museum in Memphis. In the television news, fires from riots glowed in the night skies of American cities and illuminated the dark faces of those breaking store windows with rocks and bats, looting and running down the sidewalks covered with broken glass and cars on fire. It was wise to rip the receipts into tiny pieces and flush them down the toilet. It was also important to rub the fingerprints off any surface you touched.

•

He felt the roar of the engine during takeoff, the hollow feeling of fear in the pit of his stomach, his face turning even whiter, his hands gripping the armrests. He took the BOAC flight from Toronto to London on May 6 at 10:30 p.m. "Easy, man, it's all good," said the fat man next to him with a mocking tone. The same man had already humiliated him by explaining how to fasten his seat belt even though he had not asked for help. He did not move for fear of unbalancing the plane. He felt the urge to slap a child who was running down the aisle. The plane picked up speed and he sank into his seat, half closing his eyes.

Shrink back, close your eyes, remain still, hold your breath—it does not matter, they can still find you. But not always. In prison, he hid inside a bread cart, under a tray of warm rolls. Legs tucked in, his forehead against his knees, breathing through his mouth, the musty smell of the two pairs of trousers he was wearing, one from the prison uniform, the other for outside.

A fakir can go without breathing for a long time using auto-suggestion. He heard voices nearby, the sound of the wheels on the concrete floor, then a starting engine. The warm smell of the bread combined with the cool air of the outdoors. His heart felt like a beating drum pressing against his knees. His stomach hurt and he thought he would get diarrhea. Autohypnosis can give you complete control over bodily functions. He did not know when he would eat again so he had wolfed down twelve fried eggs in the kitchen when no one was looking. He had also stuffed twenty chocolate bars in his pant pockets, his shirt, and a small toiletry bag. The bread tray warmed his head. A guard lifted the metal lid of the cart when the truck stopped at the last checkpoint, but he had made himself even smaller and had focused all his energy on sending hypnotic waves to the guard so this one would not look under the bread tray.

•

But now, inside an airplane, seat belt already fastened, he could not run. The fat man extended his hand and introduced himself, first and last name, then a nickname. How calmly people pronounce a name when it's the only one they've had. They never hesitate, not even for a second, never have to worry about misspelling it. He would draw even more attention if he ignored the man. He unclasped the armchair and extended his hand, avoiding eye contact despite the proximity. Your face will be forgotten faster if they never see your eyes. The large hand squeezed his, soft and sweaty, very pale. You are less likely to leave fingerprints if you use less force with your hands. Even better if you put small bits of tape, cut into oval shapes, on your fingertips.

He had not done this before picking up the rifle, leaning the barrel on the windowsill, and pulling the trigger. He repeated in a low voice the name he was still getting used to. Sneyd. He said it quietly, barely separating his lips, hoping that the man would mishear it and be less likely to recall it later. The noise of the engine drowned their voices. "Schneider?" said the man, cupping his ear, perhaps trying to be funny. The man's large size made him feel even more cornered in his seat.

He said he owned a bakery chain in Toronto and was going to London to visit his daughter, who was studying economics. Amazing how people share details about their lives without being asked. But sometimes it is useful and you can incorporate them into your persona, add a profession or business, and practice your story. He said he was a publicity manager at a publishing house. He had read this title in a newspaper he found while waiting at the gate. For a second, he had considered saying that he was the head veterinarian at a zoo.

But his favorite occupation was merchant sailor, the pilot on one of those cargo ships that navigated through the Mississippi, from Saint Louis to Memphis and New Orleans, from New Orleans to Havana and those small islands of the Caribbean with white beaches and palm trees like in the travel magazines. Pilot, first officer, head chef, bartender. Long watch shifts on deck, hands on the wheel, sunglasses under the visor cap, a white captain's shirt with his rank insignia displayed on the shoulders. Sailboats and luxury yachts appeared often in the color ads of magazines.

People will believe anything you say. But lying requires focus and this time he was nervous and fatigued, so he decided to stay quiet after the lights were dimmed. The first thing James Bond does, after taking his seat in an airplane, is light a Morland cigarette with his polished Ronson lighter and ask for a double martini, dry.

Suddenly, it seemed like the plane was not moving. The fat man had fallen asleep, and was now snoring with a newspaper covering his face. He removed it carefully and examined it from beginning to end. The photo wasn't that big; they were not even highlighting it. It was an old mug shot, just from the front, the same they had used before. Blurry, badly printed, even harder to see in the dim light of the cabin. One ear larger than the other; a prison crew cut; and the old name, the first one, now as disconnected from him as the face in the photo, with the shade of a beard and the frightened yet defiant eyes of a prisoner. The newspaper said he was probably dead. His accomplices or instigators had executed him to prevent him from giving away their names and information.

•

Suddenly the light came on and the stewardesses started serving breakfast. Daylight filtered in through the oval window. He had barely closed his eyes. The hands of his watch marked one o'clock. The newspaper was now on the floor and the page with his photo was folded neatly in one of his pockets. The less the authorities knew, the more they had to make up. A Cessna had taken off from a clandestine airstrip in the Florida swamps, taking just one passenger to Cuba. Although it was dark when he removed the page from the newspaper, he was careful to look around him and make sure the stewardesses were not looking. The captain announced they would be landing at Heathrow Airport in thirty minutes and the temperature in London was sixty-four degrees Fahrenheit. Passengers should ready their passports and customs declarations. He looked at the form the stewardess had given him a few minutes before. It felt like an impossible task. Next to him, the fat man wrote quickly, filling the boxes with capital letters, name, date of birth, country of citizenship, home address, address in the UK, flight number and airline, departure airport, passport number.

He carried the revolver in his back pocket. James Bond kept his Beretta in a holster made of antelope skin. Why ask for all those details in a form if most are already in the passport? Ramon George Sneyd. Born in Toronto, Canada, on June 6, 1932. The name was misspelled in the passport. Sneya, not Sneyd. His own fault for having filled the application so hurriedly at the travel agency. His hand had been shaking. He could feel the sympathetic yet condescending look of the travel agent. The fat man sucked on the cap of his pen while copying the number from his passport. It was disgusting that just a few minutes before he had asked to borrow the pen.

For some reason, the fat man now seemed suspicious of him. Some people are born snitches. They have never been in prison. No one has pushed them against a chair with their hands tied behind their back. They have never been cornered in a prison shower, curled naked on the concrete floor, covering their testicles as they are beaten with a rubber baton. They have never been offered a reduced sentence, or a cell with no roaches or rats, in exchange for information or a memorized testimony for some judge. But they are snitches all the same, born that way, it is instinctive to them, it is amusing, they choose to do it. "I knew there was something odd about this guy from the first time I saw him. I greeted him and he did not reply. I asked him things and he would not answer, like he was trying to hide something. He said his name was Schneider, but I saw him write a different name on the form. Of course I recognize the face. I won't forget it as long as I live. That stare." They will take his photo and he will be smiling like a hero. A one-hundred-thousand-dollar reward. Plus all the money they will pay him to repeat his lies for a magazine, for television, covered in makeup, so full of himself, shaking hands with the TV host, calling him by first name as if they were old pals. They all tear their clothes and cry for the dead man, the hypocrites, indulging in their hatred for the assassin, but just give them an opportunity to benefit from the situation and they will happily take it.

•

The king's marble head, with its feathered helmet, faced the sea, river, whatever it was. The proud face was turned slightly to the right. The air smelled of the ocean. A cargo ship with a high prow, and a hull that looked freshly painted black, was approaching the shore. There were tall yellow cranes on the deck. A name was painted on its side: *Jakarta*. Jakarta is the capital of Indonesia. Kuala Lumpur is the capital of Malaysia. The capital of Mongolia is Ulan Bator. His schoolteacher had been shocked to learn that he knew the names of countries and capitals, the altitude of mountains, and also many important dates in history. That teacher did not hide her repulsion for him and used to laugh at him in front of the others. He would go to school barefoot or wearing his father's old boots, several sizes too big, and the old man's coat with the sleeves rolled up. Before he could enter the schoolhouse, the teacher inspected his head for lice. If he had any, she would turn him away.

Twenty-nine thousand thirty-five feet is the height of Mount Everest. Ottawa is the capital of Canada. South Africa has the richest diamond and gold mines in the world and they pay very high salaries to white men who are experts in the use of weapons and can guard the black miners. In Biafra and Congo, a white mercenary is a hero.

In winter, his father would break the floorboards and feed them to the woodstove. He started using the roof shingles when there was no more floor. He had already cut all the branches from the few trees on the barren land where he had once hoped to start a farm. The plot ended up becoming a junkyard. At night, he urinated or vomited in one of the buckets that collected water from the roof. His father eventually used the planks from the bunk beds where he slept with his siblings. After that, they slept on the floor, covering their heads so they would not suffocate from the wood smoke.

The capital of Australia is Canberra. In prison, he earned a small income renting out old westerns and novels about aliens, also magazines with black-and-white photos of nude women and color covers where they were being attacked by wild animals. He also rented a deck of cards with photos of nude women. They would be wearing some colonial ornament: a *salakot*, a leopard skin, a spear.

He read *Reader's Digest*, *Time* magazine, the medical encyclopedia, *National Geographic*, old and outdated issues that made it to the prison library. He had read every James Bond novel multiple times. He received *True* magazine every month, filled with stories about sailing voyages and safaris in Africa; tiger-hunting expeditions in India; places to get lost in the islands of the Caribbean or the Pacific, off the coast of Mexico; the sensual women of Tahiti wearing nothing but loincloths; falconry; sightings of alien spacecraft.

In *Dr. No*, James Bond wakes up on a Caribbean beach and sees a naked woman from behind; she is only wearing a leather holster. Falconry is the art of hunting with domesticated falcons. The technical term for an alien saucer is *unidentified flying object*. He read books about yoga and hypnosis, and memorized columns of words in alphabetical order to improve his vocabulary. According to the National

Investigations Committee on Aerial Phenomena, NICAP, interplanetary vehicles have long observed the Earth. He learned the meaning of acronyms, no matter how long and difficult. He stared at the photos of glaciers and distant beaches and memorized their names so he could imagine himself there after his escape. Puerto Vallarta, Acapulco. Dream beaches on the Pacific.

The capital of Rhodesia is Salisbury. The capital of Angola is Luanda. There is also a war in Angola and they need mercenaries. Brazil has no extradition treaty with the United States. He came home from school one day and his mother had used half the pages from this geography textbook for the woodstove. The rest of the book ended up on wire next to the toilet. In Rhodesia, a white man is still a white man who is proud of his race and ready to take up arms and defend his country's freedom at any cost.

•

Did the functionary at the Ministry of the Overseas look at him too closely? Now he remembers a folded newspaper on top of the stack of files. But he had no choice, he had to return to that office. Thankfully, the functionary spoke English. He seemed pleased with his control of the language, but his accent was strange. Understanding people in this city, making yourself understood, was a torment, a nuisance, like going in circles, misunderstanding after misunderstanding, gestures, words without meaning. These people spoke with obscure words and barely opened their mouths to pronounce things. He couldn't even understand the name of the city when they pronounced it. Words were shortened to a whisper.

At first, he felt completely disoriented, not understanding what people said. How did he miss that detail. No matter how well you plan something, it always turns out differently. It was like living in a fog that did not disperse, a thick fog of sounds from this people, with their shifty eyes and sallow faces, their narrow foreheads, their short bodies, their mistrust. It was like finding yourself in the middle of a conspiracy as the only one who is not involved.

In the Ministry of the Overseas, the functionary was looking at his passport, not noticing that the cigarette he had put down was beginning to burn the edge of the table. Nothing puts them in a hurry. He remained standing behind the counter, getting more nervous, worried by how long the functionary was looking through his passport, a small pencil behind his ear, saying things in that indecipherable language, then in his strange English. Return tomorrow, he finally heard him say, pointing at the clock with his nicotine-stained finger. He turned around, already in a panic, as was often the case when he felt people were holding him up on purpose. But he had his escape route. He never went inside a building without observing all the possible exits. He left, cursing at the man in English. He was walking down a hallway lined with metal cabinets, when he heard someone calling him from behind. He stopped. The functionary wanted to give him something. It took him a while to realize what it was: *Senhor, or seu passaporte.*

•

The ship cruised slowly from right to left, from one corner of the square to the other. The vast square extended all the way to the water, where the bronze king was looking. He could see a few sailors on the deck. One of them was leaning on the railing, looking at the city he was leaving behind. The sailor held something in his hands: binoculars. He had left his pair inside the bundle of old clothes he used to wrap the rifle after the shot. And later he had dropped the bag with the clothes without thinking, feeling his hand unclench the handle, realizing his mistake as it was happening, but already too late to take it back.

With some effort, he discerned that the man on the deck was actually an officer. He had a flat black cap with golden embroidery, and was wearing a white shirt. Perhaps the look on his face was one of arrogance, pitying those who stayed in that dull, ruinous city. Perhaps he could see, through his binoculars, the pale man in the black suit, tie, and sunglasses, standing very close to the water, on the first step of the marble staircase where waves were splashing.

In the rush to escape, he had dropped the bag with the rifle and the clothes, after firing the one shot, after running down the hallway that smelled of urine and bleach, down the stairs, and out the door to the street where dusk was already setting. He remembered his right shoulder recoiling but he could not remember the sound of the explosion. It was as if it all had happened in silence, devoid of reality, that's how he remembered it.

He did not remember much else about that moment, except that it was like looking at it from outside. From outside and far away, from the safe distance that the binoculars transformed into a secret proximity. The salesman had assured him that the rifle could bring down a deer from a distance of three hundred meters. A deer or even a charging rhinoceros.

Like watching a movie or squinting to look into one of those machines at the fair: he saw the man step out of his room onto the balcony, stroking his face as if he had just shaved, the same black face from the photographs and TV programs, the wide cheekbones and slanted eyes, the skin shining with sweat.

It was strange to see him in person for the first time, to study his every feature. A breeze blew the curtain behind him like the sail of a boat. The contrast with the white flapping curtain defined the figure of the man even better. He ran his hand over his face and leaned on the rail. He was saying something, smiling. His lips moved silently. He had an unlit cigarette. The white cuffs and the gold ring and watch were bright against the black skin.

Across the street and the parking lot, in that disgusting boarding-house, in that bathroom covered in shit—him, balancing in the tub, trying to get steady. The footprints would get on the grimy surface. Grease, metal, the smell of the rifle pressed against his face, combined with the stench of the place, urine and vomit fermenting in the heat.

Someone was knocking on the door and shaking the handle. Probably one of the halfwits or alcoholics who resided in that place. In a nearby room, the sound of a television combined with the noise of a couple yelling, two drunks arguing about something. After her fourth or fifth kid was born, his mother began drinking so much she would often pass out on the floor after falling from her rocking chair. She breathed heavily against the dirt floor; the floorboards were long gone, burned in the woodstove. She had four more kids after that. Had she lived to see him now, she would not recognize him. Dark suit and tie, sunglasses, alligator shoes, good manners. This was the new him. She died of cirrhosis at the age of fifty-one. Being in prison was the perfect excuse to miss the funeral.

•

No one could possibly know where he is right now. They assure the public that they are on his tracks, that there is no way he could have left the country. They lie. Thousands of federal agents analyzing every clue, fingerprint, hair caught in a comb, a signed receipt for the hunting rifle, the binoculars, several boxes with bullets, even empty beer cans and tags from the dry cleaner. The bullets were not sharp enough to pierce through the tissue and bone and leave a clean wound. Whatever they say, any clue they have is no more useful than the old skin of a snake long gone into a muddy riverbank. The rifle, the bullets, the car, the transistor radio, the suit he left at the Laundromat under his old name. The transistor is the only thing he actually misses. He had kept it tight between his legs as he hugged his knees inside the bread cart. The smell of the fresh rolls reminded him that it would be long before he ate again.

If only he had the radio now, perhaps he could listen to a program in English. If they gave him the visa to Angola, he would leave in the boat that looked like the *Jakarta* and was still moored in the harbor.

Angola, what an exciting word, like Rhodesia or Mozambique. On the covers of *Man's Life* magazine, men with tanned, athletic bodies saved beautiful women from danger: natives wearing feathers, leopards with huge fangs, snakes coiling around their thighs. In the dark backstreets by the harbor, the bars where you could find prostitutes and sailors were named after distant countries or states in America. There were daily lists with the names of all the arriving and departing ships, other ports and destinations, names that unleashed his imagination like the old maps in the schoolhouse, exotic names like *Mozambique, India, Beira, Sofala, Angola, Luanda, Patria, Veracruz*.

Some of the alleys never saw the light of day and their neon signs blinked at all times. The sign for the Texas Bar featured a cactus and a cowboy hat. There was also a bar called Alabama. How strange to find that name here. As soon as he was back in the hotel, he would look for the two Portuguese colonies in Africa. He kept buying maps and newspapers, even though he was running out of money. He had taken the steps down to the water, lost in a vision of the passing ship and the silhouette of the officer on the foredeck holding a pair of binoculars. Beyond the marble steps, there was a stone ramp covered in slippery algae. The tide had risen and the water now washed over his shoes. Two columns flanked the stairway. A seagull was perched on each one.

•

The receptionist at the Hotel Portugal tried to look him in the eyes as he gave him the room keys, but he looked away, mumbling what could have been a greeting. The eyes convey the unique identity of a face. The photo on the passport showed the Canadian traveler wearing glasses like those of a professor or a lawyer, the same glasses he wore the night he checked in at the hotel. Sometimes he wore the other pair, his sunglasses. When he returned and took them off, after many hours under the sun, his eyes were bloodshot.

There was something asymmetrical about his eyes, similar to the ears. One ear was larger and hung lower than the other. The receptionist tried to practice his English but the new guest could not understand or maybe he could not hear well. He nodded or shook his head, always looking down or to the side, biting the corners of his mouth as if he were in pain. What little he said was incomprehensible, except when he needed to know something, like how to get to the South African embassy and also the Canadian one and the port and where to buy newspapers in English.

The newspapers under the arm added to his dubious professorial look, especially the night he checked in, the one so evident in his passport photo but less so in person as the days went by. An impostor who falsified his diploma or was caught having an affair with a student. A funeral director whose breath reeked of alcohol. Those who saw him in Atlanta on April 5, early that morning, more than twelve hours after the shooting, said he looked like an insurance agent or a preacher.

He locked himself in the hotel room and read all the newspapers in bed. On the bedside table: a hypnosis manual, the spy novel *Tangier Assignment*; a study guide for the correspondence course on locksmithing; a book with a large title across the cover, *Psycho-Cybernetics*. On the floor: scattered British and American newspapers and a page from a Portuguese paper with the list of all the ships coming into and out of the port. In a drawer of the little table by the window: travel brochures for South Africa with the names of cities underlined and the margins filled with calculations for expenses, always small amounts, and currency conversions from dollars to escudos. On a sheet of hotel stationery, he had practiced several signatures: Ramon Sneyd, Ramon George Sneyd, R. Sneyd, R. G. Sneyd, Ramon G. Sneyd. Not a single call or visit in ten days, not one letter or postcard sent. He received a letter from the Rhodesian mission in Lisbon, his name and the hotel address neatly typed on the envelope. The next morning, the envelope and the letter, a brief, official notice, were in the trash can.

•

One night, one of the first, the receptionist was dozing off when a loud laugh came through the revolving door. A young woman walked in, wearing heavy makeup, a tight, low-cut dress, and high heels. She staggered, walking on the old carpet. The pale-faced guest followed her, with a serious expression, wearing professorial glasses, a dark suit, cigarette in hand. The woman, somewhat taller than him, took his arm and whispered something in his ear. He nodded. She took the cigarette from his hand. He had been holding it while she retouched her lipstick. He broke away from her and straightened his posture before approaching the reception desk to ask for his key. He briefly looked the receptionist in the eyes before looking down, as usual. His eyes seemed smaller, very blue, almost colorless, clouded with alcohol. He displayed the oscillating confidence of a drunk who is about to fall. A very pale drunk, one ear bigger than the other, a pointy nose with a reddened tip, the tie crooked but very tight, a prominent cleft chin. A professor who was caught coming out of a peep show or a sex shop, a perverted mortician.

The receptionist gulped and said in English that guests were not allowed to bring women to their rooms. For a moment the guest looked him straight in the eyes, with a gesture of surprise or maybe a slight smile, like someone who is not fully in control of his facial muscles. There he stood, baffled, as the woman cursed at the receptionist in Portuguese. She pulled him by the arm, telling him in English that she knew a much better place. Out they went, the guest glancing at the receptionist through the glass door, his face livid, his small eyes lacking any expression.

3

The first time I went to Lisbon was 1987. It was early in January. I was writing a novel and part of it took place there. I did not realize just how young I was. I thought youth was behind me, my life more or less set on a path, my fate already decided: thirty years old, almost thirty-one, married, a father of two, a government job, a deed in my name and a mortgage that extended into the next century. Beneath the calm surface of my daily routine was a juxtaposition of fragmented lives without rhyme or reason, unfulfilled desires, scattered pieces that did not fit together. Much of what I did felt alien to me. Who I really was and what I really cared about remained hidden from most of those around me. Laziness and the sheer inertia of all my obligations had kept me living for years in conformity and frustration, inhabiting transient worlds that had little to do with each other, none truly my own. I was a government employee because I had found no other way to make a living, and I was also a writer, although I would have never used that word spontaneously when introducing myself, the way I had heard others do in Granada and Madrid. *Writer* was too serious of a word, too solemn, too definitive. To hear someone call him- or herself a writer seemed embarrassing, like hearing someone claim the title of poet. How could anyone claim that with certainty? I was a government employee but had no sense of belonging in the world of my colleagues. I was one of them only because most of my daily life took place in that office. They were affectionate toward me, but also saw me as the odd one out. I had written articles for newspapers, published a novel, and my job involved dealing with foreigners for the most part, the eccentric lot—artists, musicians, actors—intruders in the municipal offices where I received them. It was also clear that to those artists, who rarely knew about my dedication to literature, I was odd as well, a government employee sitting behind a metallic desk, a bureaucrat.

•

My life outside the office was just as fragmented. I was married but my wife worked in a different city. We only saw each other on weekends. A husband and a parent from Friday afternoon to Sunday night; the rest of the week, I was alone. On Fridays, I would take the bus to my other life. It took just over an hour. If, for a change, my wife drove to Granada with the boy, my two lives would overlap on Monday morning. My apartment was that of a solitary man. On Fridays, if it was her turn to come, I would spend one or two hours cleaning up the mess of the previous five days. Like a whirlwind from one world to the other, from solitude to company, from ghosts to real people. The same house became another. The boy in my arms, holding on to me like a tree trunk, his round face pressed against mine, his legs trapping me.

•

The city would also change during those two or three days: it became bright and serene, and night fell earlier; its topography no longer one of bars but of playgrounds, supermarkets, and bakeries. Mornings smelled like baby powder, sweat, and perfume, instead of alcohol and tobacco; kids' cartoons replaced Billie Holiday, John Coltrane, and Tete Montoliu. During those weekends, literature was almost nonexistent.

•

These two worlds remained segregated. Their respective inhabitants would hardly meet and in many cases were ignorant of each other's existence. I was able to immerse myself into any of those lives with ease, and the others would just disappear in the background, or pause, it seemed to me, waiting for my return, like a house that remains un-disturbed in its owner's absence. I rarely felt the internal tension of an impostor, but I also never felt like I belonged. The title of a novel by Patricia Highsmith summed up my life: *Tremors of Falsification*. Some-times while walking on the street with my wife and son, I would spot an inhabitant from my Monday-to-Friday world or my nightlife, and switch to the opposite sidewalk to avoid the encounter. I would often stay out until three or four in the morning, drinking and smoking with writers or musicians, then be punching my time card at five past eight, pretending to pay attention to my colleagues' chitchat before the office opened to the public. I was bored by the predictability of life in Granada, but whenever I was in Madrid, I felt fear, vertigo, and then unspeakable relief when I took the return train. When I was alone, I would go to bars almost every night. It was the eighties and it felt like something amazing and definitive could happen any night, an encounter, a revelation, an adventure that could change your life forever. But you had to hang in there and drink, take hashish, snort cocaine, smoke cigarettes until your lungs hurt. Even then, there was a part of me that stayed alert, distant, inhibiting me from fully aban-doning myself to those moments, to the stupefying bliss of cannabis and alcohol; like an edge of skepticism to everything I experienced, as if I was seeing myself from outside. Glancing at the clock, calculat-ing the number of hours before the morning alarm went off at seven; feeling the pounding in my head, the nausea, the taste of alcohol that will still be there hours later when you look at yourself in the bath-room mirror. I liked the dark glow of those flamenco nights when one doesn't know the time and everything seems reflected or submerged in a murky glass or the turbulent clarity of oil, when the stomping and clapping echoes in your temples and the voices of the singers seem to be on the verge of breaking; a claustrophobia of bars, brandy, and cognac.

But at a certain point I just wanted to go home, step out onto the dark street and breathe the air, fresh and cold, feel the silence. I re-member a night, one late September, still warm from summer, after a flamenco recital in Bibrrambla Square. I had started my weekly routine, once again living alone after a long vacation with my family. The singer had a serious face, aquiline, a mix of Roma and Sioux. We were friends. I had helped organize the concert and had brought him an envelope with his payment in cash, which he accepted without counting. Twenty-five thousand pesetas. He spent it all that night, inviting a band of friends, relatives, fellow musicians, acquaintances, and parasites, myself included, to bar after bar along the alleys and squares of Realejo and then Albaicín, secret dark taverns that required passwords to get in. An inexhaustible supply of hashish flowed from the expert hands of the flamenco musicians and their friends, who swiftly rolled the fragrant leaves with blond tobacco into cigarettes.

As I followed them into Albaicín, stumbling over the cobblestone, the thought that I might lose them and never find a way out of that labyrinth made me anxious. I was very attracted to one or two of the women in the group, but in the fog of intoxication, the blurry thought that there was something insufficient or shameful about me forbade me from acting on my desires. I let myself get carried away by the laughter and the music, but there was a part of me that remained removed from the scene, distant, disloyal. There was an art or antiques dealer in the group that night, who had one of those booming voices darkened by tobacco. The man ordered everyone around, calling new rounds of drinks and deciding what the next bar would be. He had the weathered skin of a sailor, blue eyes, and a mane of graying blond curls like an Irishman. He supported himself on a pair of crutches. Inside the bars, he placed the stiff leg on a stool and used his crutches to threaten anyone who contradicted him. The drunker he got, the more he stumbled down the alleyways, always on the verge of falling. In the thick of the revelry, his little blue eyes would fix on me with suspicion. In one of the last stops, he put his big hand on my shoulder as he was getting up. With his chin against his chest, he looked me in the eye and drawled:

—You are undercover all right, but I can't tell if you are infiltrating the underworld or City Hall.

•

I hid from each of my lives in a fragment from another. There was rarely a connection between my actions, desires, and dreams. I had accepted becoming a father the same way I had accepted becoming a husband, or taking an administrative position with the city government, without much thought, without a clear sense of consequences. Perhaps that is why I only found myself at home in literature and cinema, worlds where anything could happen and at the same time never have happened, worlds where the mind-numbing rules of the day-to-day did not apply, where shots did not kill, where misfortunes unleashed tears but not real pain, where stories had a clear beginning and end, leaving no residues, like cigarettes that leave no cancer, bad breath, or even ashes, just threads of smoke rising from the mouth of a beautiful fictional woman, preferably in black and white. I sought refuge in films and books, freedom from my mediocre reality, my self-delusion, my cowardice. Literature and film fed a solitude without introspection, like an adolescence. I only paid attention to myself and even so I could not see who I really was. Once, in an argument with my girlfriend, or maybe she was already my wife at that point, she said: "All that sensibility for characters in books and films, yet you're completely oblivious to those who are actually here with you."

•

I was a father and a husband, and also a foolish adolescent, an apprentice in the art of the novel, and a bureaucrat; I was undercover all right, but was I infiltrating the underworld or City Hall? If I liked a woman, I would look at her as if on a screen. My desires led to paralysis instead of courage. I was distressed by insecurities about my sexuality that were more appropriate for a fifteen- or sixteen-year-old, and the depressive mood of a child who was overweight and never got over the humiliations he experienced in gym class. I held on to that delirious belief, so characteristic of aspiring writers from small towns, that real life was elsewhere, that imagination is richer and more powerful than reality, and desire more important than its realization, that giants are more memorable than mills, fiction more perfect than the dull repetition of reality, that sickness and drunkenness are more romantic than health, sobriety, and calm, that the things that matter are always fleeting, because only the mediocre lasts, and forbidden and secret passions, and marriage-boredom, chaotic creativity, mind-numbing work, and delirium-lucidity, and reason, tasteless and cold, the night subversion and the morning submission.

•

It almost took me by surprise when it dawned on me that we were about to have another child. My wife had gone on maternity leave a month before the birth of our second child and had come to live with me in Granada. It was now more difficult to hide and abandon myself to the controlled mess that was my life without her. I worked and came home to a domestic life, as if it had always been that way: the child waiting for me, a clean house, dinner on the table. I would put my son to bed, read him a story, and wait for him to fall asleep. Then I would lock myself in my room and work on my novel. I became convinced that I had to travel to Lisbon if I had any hope of finishing the story the way I wanted.

•

I did not go to Lisbon to find the settings for a plot that was already in my head. I needed to find the drama there, fill certain gaps and key moments in the narrative. Or maybe I just wanted to escape for a few days and literature was my excuse. I remember the exact dates. I took a train from the Linares-Baeza station on the first day of the year. It was a cold, bright morning, and I was one of few travelers. The next day, my son Arturo, the newborn, would turn one month old. On the afternoon of December 2, 1986, I had been listening to a record of Gerry Mulligan and Chet Baker when my wife went into labor. I listened to music every evening until five or six, and then started to write. We lived in a small apartment provided by the city. It was on the outskirts of Granada, heading toward the Sierra, on the banks of the Genil River. That past returns to me in waves. In the mornings, I worked in a building in Los Campos Square, close to Mariana Pineda Square. It only took me twenty minutes to walk there. When the snow from the Sierra melted at the end of spring, or after a heavy rainfall, you could hear the river roar all night from my apartment. I was three months into writing the novel when my son was born. I had tried to start long before, again and again, but I would always get stuck or bored. Every page felt like punishment. Perhaps the story did not flow because it was trying too hard to trace or mask reality. Having emerged so literally from the familiar, it had nothing to do with Lisbon.

I had never been to Lisbon. The novel had been set in Granada because certain things I wanted to incorporate in the story had taken place or could have taken place there, and I did not know how or did not dare to tell them without the cover of a police plot. Literature is built with things that exist and things that do not. But I did not know how to create fiction from the world I saw around me, or invent characters with lives similar to mine. Back then, I thought fiction had to do with the imaginary, with the stuff of dreams and unattainable desires. Granada was a city without glory, but the characters of my novel transformed her into a different place. They were romantic projections of myself, of a woman I fell in love with the way sixteen- or seventeen-year-olds do, of the man, her husband, she was cheating on. To portray myself and her and him, as we really were, was as difficult as writing about the places where it all happened, about my everyday life, without the filter of literature.

Granada, as I closed my eyes and got ready to write, became a seaside town during winter; I was a jazz pianist, she was an actress, he was a villain. I imagined that my defunct love story, with its provincial sorrow and petty adultery, had the intensity and passion of a bolero, interrupted by police chases and revolvers in a city where the Alhambra and Albaicín faced the ocean instead of the Vega.

Then I realized something. Like in those dreams where two places merge seamlessly, in the sketch of my novel, Granada was also San Sebastián. I had lived in San Sebastián for a year in 1980 for military service. The imagination creates its own rules. The story did not yet possess an autonomous form, but it had begun to emancipate itself from my lived experiences and found its own stage and atmosphere. The narrow streets around the cathedral in Granada had become those of the old town in San Sebastián, emptied after the bars closed. A man and a woman agreed to meet under the arcades of Constitution Square on a rainy night. The shadows were borrowed from my memories but also from detective films in black and white, films with chases and mysteries, low lights and cigarette smoke, sensual women with guns, love affairs that were traps. At thirty, I thought youth was already behind me and I was suffering an intoxicating adolescence of literature.

•

Lisbon was in the title of the novel long before it was in the plot. A good title is not a tag that goes at the end but an open flame that sits far away illuminating an unknown material, a faint moonlight, a flashlight handled by something unknown indicating a possible path. Back then, I used a typewriter. At home, I had the same machine I had been using since I was fourteen or fifteen. At work, I had gotten used to an electronic Canon that accelerated the writing, as if awaking it with the padding of the keys. The Canon justified the margins automatically. The sheet came out clean, the type was sharp and neat, as if technology alone had refined the style.

•

But Lisbon had also been slow in coming to the title, which had been without a story for a while, like the cover of a book filled with blank pages. I remembered its origin when years later I found something written in an old notebook, one of those notes to self that are completely forgotten.

I had written: *The Winter in Florence.* There was nothing else in the notebook. Florence had been in my imagination before Lisbon and it had vanished like a vivid dream that disappears without trace upon waking. A sound technician who used to tour with jazz musicians came to my office one morning. I had not seen him in a long time. He was a friendly man but tormented by an internal struggle, pressure from work and nonstop traveling, the constant hustle to get paid on time and the stress of not having enough to cover the monthly payments on the expensive equipment he needed for his job. I liked listening to his anecdotes. Some years prior, he had mixed the sound for two consecutive performances by Bill Evans in a small club or theater in Barcelona. Evans was only scheduled to play one show, which was sold out. But the next day he missed his plane, even though his bassist and drummer managed to board. So the organizers improvised a solo concert for Evans that second night. With little time to promote the show, Evans played for an almost empty room. The sound technician said it was one of the most memorable concerts he had ever seen. Bill Evans—fatigued, sick, exhausted from touring, his old suit still elegant, with a sunken face and the mouth of a junkie—he played without pause for over an hour, barely breathing, absent, his head down, as if there was no one else in the room.

The sound technician also shared stories about the time he accompanied Chet Baker in Florence. After breaking down the equipment with a stagehand, he stepped out to the vestibule, and there was Baker in a short coat facing the glass entrance, waiting with his trumpet case in hand. Rain was pouring down. The technician had his van parked close to the theater. He offered Baker a ride to the hotel. The stagehand offered him the front seat, but Baker preferred the back. The technician told me that as he drove in the rain through the dark and unfamiliar streets, he would glance at Baker in the rearview mirror every now and then. His face was small, gaunt, and deeply wrinkled. His hair was dirty, the toupee like a relic, an air of decrepit youth. He sat motionless, upright, staring into space, oblivious to the city on the other side of the glass, gusts of monumental buildings beyond the curtain of rain. Depending on the streetlights, the face became visible or stayed with the shadows. The technician noticed how bright his eyes were. He swore he saw a tear. Chet Baker was dead a few months later. He had leaped or fallen from the window of a hotel in Amsterdam.

The plan was to go back to Spain the day after the Baker concert. But there was nothing really urgent for him to attend, or anything his assistants could not take care of, and he was tired after the long tour. Suddenly he did not feel like being back in Granada. It was winter and Florence was cold and rainy. There were barely any tourists in the streets or the museums. He realized with some amazement that it had been years since he had taken a break from work, always on the run from one city to the next, from one country to another, theaters and concert halls and hotels where he spent one or two nights

at most, assembling and disassembling equipment, suffering the whims
and eccentricities of the musicians, the hours in airports, the days and
nights on the road and at the wheel. Perhaps he was also tired from
raising a family and burdened by guilt from spending so much
time away.

He decided to stay a few days in Florence, taking advantage of the
cheap hotel rooms during the low season. He basically did nothing.
When it stopped raining he went for a walk with no destination in
mind, bundling up against the piercing cold that hit along the Arno
at dusk. The sun barely reached the halls of the Uffizi and the guards
rubbed their hands together over small electric heaters. On clear days
the sun tapped the ridges of the carved stones, and after a few hours of
walking outside not even gloves and coat pockets could keep one's
hands from freezing.

The time he had initially given himself ran out and he decided to
prolong it. He comforted his stomach with bean and pasta stews
served in the small taverns tucked in high-walled alleys that the sun
never reached. Architecture, frescoes—none of it did much for him.
In the Uffizi he went to a dark gallery where a newly restored *Birth of
Venus* hung under a light. At the museum, he mostly strolled on the
marble floors of the wide galleries lined with classical busts and looked
at the river that spanned beyond the big windows. He liked looking at
the green eyes of the goddess and the delicate lines of her hands
and feet, the wild, golden hair, ruffled by the same wind that rippled
the small waves. One day he discovered *The Sacrifice of Isaac* by Cara-
vaggio. The hint of brutality and fanaticism overwhelmed him in a
way that no other painting had. He would leave the gallery and then
be back shortly after, he said to me. He even became afraid of being alone
with the painting during those overcast mornings when the museum
was almost empty.

One afternoon he suddenly realized he could not remember how
many days he had been in Florence. Time references had vanished
from his mind. He could tell the time on his watch, but without a
calendar in the hotel room he simply could not remember what date
it was and thus had no idea how many days, or weeks, it had been since
the last date he remembered, the concert with Chet Baker. He also

could not remember his age. He knew the year he was born but not the current one and it filled him with terror to think just how old he could be. He feared that if he looked at himself in the bathroom mirror, he would find a stranger, maybe bald or with a head of white hair.

His only experience of temporality was winter, winter in its pure form, like a fog he could not exit, no matter how hard he tried. He inhabited that winter like Florence itself, like an island, like a spellbound kingdom floating above the past and future, in a present without succession or a beginning. Vertigo and a vast stillness combined into one. Acquaintances, loved ones, they all seemed so distant, as if he were remembering them from a time long past. He thought about calling the reception desk to ask the date, but felt too self-conscious. He thought about calling his wife, but the number blurred in his memory. He remembered the country code for Spain, the code for Granada, but as he tried to recall what came next the series disappeared and he had to start all over. He remembered Venus and Isaac, desire and fear, her naked body, the child's face contorted with terror, his jaw pressed against the sacrificial stone by the strong, merciless hand of the old man. After so many days of only interacting with strangers who spoke a different language, days of barely uttering a word except to the occasional waiter in a restaurant, the figures in the paintings felt more real than the actual people around him.

He realized he was having a panic attack. He took two sleeping pills and noticed how his thoughts began to gradually dissolve into sleep. There was no trace of temporary amnesia the next morning. He told me he was relieved but also disappointed. Once again, the day and the month and the year and the hour and his name and his job and his past—all occupied precise locations, like elements in the periodic table, within the compartments of time. He decided it was time to return to Granada; he had already spent plenty of money and could not continue neglecting his family. Now, many months later, he missed the winter in Florence, that winter without dates when he had lived in another country. "And now, back to this," he said, involuntarily throwing his hands in the air, looking at me across the table, where I probably had some pending invoice of his among the stacks

of documents, looking at the office with sorrow and pity, even a hint of
sarcasm, the office where I worked and relished any spare moment
to write using the swift electric Canon, and sometimes by hand, in
a notebook or on the back of some form, some piece of paper em-
bossed with an official letterhead and coat of arms, possible titles,
beautiful titles for short stories and novels that most of the time
never materialized.

•

I heard about Lisbon from a friend, the painter Juan Vida, who had
once traveled there for a few days. He told me about the grand square
with the statue of a king on horseback and elephants at the center,
and a public elevator like that of the Eiffel Tower connecting the lower
streets with a neighborhood on top of a hill. The elevator had a polished wooden cabin that creaked as it ascended and golden brass knobs
and handles. He told me that on clear days there was a white luminos-
ity dimmed by the mist of the river, and that entering the city was a
bit like traveling back in time because it reminded him of the Granada
of his childhood, the one of small storefronts with textiles or groceries,
and chattering crowds in the squares. As in Granada, there was a
Moorish castle atop a hill, and a neighborhood of balconies, winding
alleys, and stairways as labyrinthine as Albaicín. Lisbon had communal
squares like those of Bibrrambla, with grandparents soaking up the
sun, shoe shiners, and groups of people hanging out in the corners.
He drove out of the city and reached a resort town with houses painted
in pastel colors, wooded hills overlooking the sea, and a chasm called
Boca do Inferno, where it was terrifying to look down and see the
swells of the Atlantic break against the reefs, forming towering surges
of foam that could reach a bystander.

•

I had already written who knows how many pages but nothing had
really happened in the novel. It was tiring. Like climbing a dune, every
step sinking in the sand and never arriving. After pages and pages, the
two lovers whose affair threaded the story had not even met. Every
morning I came to the office and punched my time card, my arrival

time printed in tiny numbers that were red if I was late. Every afternoon I sat to work in my room, too small to call it an office, next to a window that looked onto the upper floors and rooftops of the housing complex, and farther up, in the distance, a line of arid hills leading to the Alhambra, the red, sun-dried bricks and the cypresses of the cemetery.

I thought I would see this same landscape for many years to come. At dusk, as the blue sky paled, the reds of the rammed earth walls became more intense. The truth is I lacked vision. I was incapable of imagining the breadth of the future. I could not imagine my three-year-old son as an adult, or the children who played around the buildings and bought candies at Juan's shop, at that time barely two years since it had opened in the new development that slowly filled up with people, young couples with small children, modest incomes, beneficiaries of government housing.

We were set to finish paying ours in a remote future, the beginning of a new century, the year 2001. I didn't think much about my second son, who was due in just a few months, except when I was assailed by an irrational fear that he could be born with some congenital disease. I would accompany my wife to the routine tests with the gynecologist and see the grainy shadow palpitating on the ultrasound monitor, slowly moving as if underwater. The doctor placed the transducer on the planetary curve of her belly and we could hear the resounding tapping, like a metallic drumroll, of my son's heartbeat, his minute stubbornness submerged in that aquatic refuge, warm and dark, where I could not project even my curiosity.

•

I bought the electric Canon in installments. Out of the box and the plastic wrap, it smelled so new, a combination of ink and well-oiled metal. I used to keep a stack of blank sheets of paper on my desk at all times. Paper gave materiality to the act of writing; the whiteness of the paper was evidence of the leap into the void that was required to create, the fact that something had to materialize out of nothing. Walking to the stationer to buy paper was the first step in a ritual that back then also included a pack of cigarettes, a lighter, and an ashtray. We lived in a fog of cigarette smoke and did not even notice it.

One afternoon in September, I sat in front of the new typewriter with the usual lack of confidence but suddenly found myself writing something unexpected, a first sentence completely improvised, long and full of twists, somehow containing, without tedious preambles, everything that I knew about the story up to that moment and a lot more than I had previously imagined. Until then, in all my drafts, the story had been told in the third person, but now the narrator, in the first person, was someone else, someone who saw himself from the outside, a witness who sometimes knew what was going on and sometimes had to imagine and speculate, someone who saw the story unfold and whose role was marginal at best, a stranger we know nothing about, a nobody.

I had been reading *The Great Gatsby* and was impressed by the narrative voice and gaze of Nick Carraway. Gatsby was not a hero whose exploits Nick happened to witness: he was a hero precisely because Nick was observing him. His legend was not in his person or his acts but in the perspective of another person; his ultimate ambiguity, that blank space at the center of his character and most of his biography, was the result of missing information. Being largely an invention of himself, Jay Gatsby exists only in the eyes of others. Everything that was unknown or left unsaid about Gatsby added to his persona and deepened his mystery like the negative space that on paper or canvas strengthens a composition. Painting is, in a way, also about not painting, just as writing requires that certain things are left unsaid, outlines that will be completed in the imagination of a reader or in the brain of a viewer examining a painting, instead of the canvas where figures emerge out of loose strokes and a few lines.

But I was not hiding anything: there were simply things that I did not know or that did not matter for the story, and my mistake, all that time, had been to try to fill every gap with unnecessary details, fill all the space in the story like a mediocre painter fills a whole canvas with paint or a pretentious musician leaves no space for silence. I was now sketching the characters mostly through the missing details, and the story was unfolding before me like a series of flashes or quick strokes in a vast, blank space. Like characters in a film, they existed for the most part in the present tense. They might come from a recent past but this would disappear without a trace in the immediate future. They would have no ties, no origins, no childhood memories, no fixed addresses, no jobs that grounded them in one place. They would be everything I was not. Inhabitants of a parallel universe in cities symmetric to the real Granada, where it would have been impossible for me to situate a story, cities consisting mostly of their luminous names, images from my own distant memories and what I had imagined while listening to others talk about their travels. The San Sebastián from my days as a soldier, the simple happiness of wandering the streets on my day off without uniform, hands in pockets, peeking into the Cantábrico at the mouth of the Urumea River, where at night the wind ruffled the furious foam of the waves under the luminous spheres of the Kursaal Bridge; the Florence of those solitary days of winter when a sound technician had been so close to Bill Evans and Chet Baker; the Lisbon of my friend Juan Vida, with its iron elevator and an Eiffel Tower and its square with a staircase that led into the waters of a river that seemed as wide as the sea; with the cliffs of Boca do Inferno, cliffs of shipwrecks and action films where men fight on the edge of an abyss, perhaps a cinematic montage of a face filled with vertigo and terror against a backdrop of breaking waves.

•

But in that intuited beginning, in that long first paragraph, another city, even less expected, had emerged: Madrid, real and imagined, reduced to a few scenes from a trip the prior winter, somewhat secret, an intimate failure, two or three days chasing ghosts of desire without success, moving through places that now returned as foci for the story, no longer gray and clouded by my experience: a large, somber hotel where I had stayed in the Gran Via, opposite the Telefonica building at the beginning of Fuencarral Street; Café Central, where I had listened to a jazz group; a small restaurant in Cava Alta, Viuda de Vacas; the moist light of Sunday morning in Santa Ana Square, a cold, golden clarity like that of the beer served at the German Brewery; the afternoon sun fading into the winter night, ascending through the wide and dark sidewalks of Alcalá Street in that sordid Madrid of the mid-eighties, when the mouths of Fuencarral and Hortaleza into the Gran Vía were tunnels of shadows for prostitutes and junkies and drug dealers standing under the neon signs of cheap hotels. Given my limited and somewhat frightened knowledge of the city, those places lacked any connection. Not tied to a continuous topography, they glowed in my mind like islands. They existed only to the extent of my novel, like those meticulous fragments of streets in New York City re-created in Hollywood studios. Literature was antithetical to reality and film was truer than life.

4

It was after midnight when he arrived in the empty city. He had seen it from above, leaning against the window, holding on to the armrests during the descent, when suddenly the wing tilted down and the sea horizon moved into the black sky. He saw the city below, a pale constellation of lights filtering through the fog. He saw the lit deck of a ship gliding on the vast sheet of water, bathed in moonlight. Cargo ships departed from Lisbon every day and headed to colonies in Africa, Brazil, Goa, India, Macao, an island at the mouth of the Pearl River. His flight was the last one that night. Less than half the seats were filled. He was one of the silent travelers, mostly men, sleeping or reading, businessmen or diplomats used to flying, opening and closing briefcases, reviewing documents, constantly checking their watches. They sat in the dark cabin enveloped by cones of reading light, smoking cigarettes, sipping whiskey, clinking ice cubes. No one could say he wasn't one of them. The coat, the suit, the tie, the white dress shirt, the glasses, any missing detail or imperfection would have been concealed by the dim light. He was only missing a briefcase and papers to spread on the tray table. James Bond carries his gun, ammunition, and silencer in a briefcase like that. But these men probably carried lots of money neatly folded in leather wallets, traveler's checks, and business cards. A reading light illuminated the open book and his manicured nails.

At Heathrow, his bag weighed twelve kilos. It was a British European Airlines flight, departure time 10:00 p.m., and scheduled to arrive at 1:15 a.m. Trivial yet exact details give a misleading sense of omniscience. He put the glasses on to make sure he would not forget them. He focused and tried to form the same hint of a smile he had in the passport photo. The owner of the boardinghouse in Memphis said he had a forced smile that made her uncomfortable. He would keep that same expression, reserved yet amiable, when he faced the immigration officer in the arrivals area at this late hour. The graying hair on the sides made him look even more distinguished.

He was reading *Psycho-Cybernetics* by Dr. Maxwell Maltz, the same book that now sits on my desk. He read it slowly, sometimes repeating certain sentences in a low voice, sometimes underlining them. *A human being always acts and feels and performs according to what he imagines to be true about himself and his surroundings.* He also carried a spy novel and an armful of newspapers and magazines. He had a few when he boarded the plane and also checked the ones the stewardesses passed around. Experienced travelers carried newspapers and magazines under their arms and weekend bags with airline logos. He paid attention to the front pages, scanning the photos and headlines, and focused on the side columns and the bottom corners now that the search for him, or the hunt rather, seemed to have been interrupted or maybe just displaced by other news. Three thousand one hundred FBI agents were involved in the investigation, the Royal Canadian Mounted Police, the Mexican police. His eyes shone with secret pride. Interpol agents were following a tip that placed him in some shady neighborhood in Sydney, Australia. He wanted to fold his newspaper neatly as he read it but the pages crumpled noisily with every turn. It was necessary to examine every page. Ads and odd news would sometimes distract him.

Newspapers had fascinated him since he was a kid. The photographs, the happy faces of men and women in ads for new cars, the smiles of housewives in their spotless kitchens. He paid attention to their gestures so he could replicate them: how to hold a glass of whiskey, how to make sure your cuff links show, how to light a woman's cigarette.

But the old name and the old photo, which looked nothing like the new him, were not the only things he was looking for. He also searched with apprehension for the name he was using now, the one he had filled out in forms and repeated out loud when asked. He knew that sooner or later it would appear. He imagined with a sense of impending doom the moment when they identified him. Doom and fear but also pride. According to psycho-cybernetics, imagining future possible scenarios, with as much detail as possible, allowed you to know the best exits ahead of time. A disciplined imagination was like a lab where you could synthesize different experiences.

He would approach the counter and wait behind the white line as the person in front of him was processed without fear or difficulty. When he provided the passport, issued just a week earlier in Toronto, he would notice a peculiar expression in the eyes of the immigration agent, a glance to the side and then toward him, toward his face, which he would turn slightly to the right, out of habit, out of shyness and seeming submission, his eyes fixed on the floor, chin close to the shoulder, the light eyes avoiding direct contact, blinking nervously like the wings of an insect.

He had lived that same moment the night before, or the morning before, he no longer remembered, in another airport, in Heathrow, after a much longer flight, one that lasted the entire night, a night that ended abruptly when the cabin lights came on and it was already seven o'clock, even though it had been no later than two when he closed his eyes and it was still dark outside, the runway shining under the rain. When the person ahead of him approached the desk he moved right behind the white line. They enforce their rules, only let you approach when they decide it's your turn. Unwittingly, he adopted the same posture he took when waiting in line in prison: shoulders back, legs apart, a vigilant glance left and right. Strict limits, white lines that can't be crossed without punishment. There was a British flag next to the desk of the immigration agent. There was a .32-caliber revolver in his back pocket. Liberty Chief, made in Japan. The past is full of exotic minutiae. In 1968, security checks at airports had no metal detectors and a fugitive with no documentation could obtain, via mail and without much difficulty, a birth certificate with someone else's name. That was enough to get a Canadian passport. The immigration agent spoke in such a weird way that it took him a while to realize the man was actually speaking English. On the wall behind him: a color portrait of the Queen of England—007 at the service of Her Majesty. The agent was freshly shaven and smelled of cologne. He was young, a novice, insecure but thorough—the worst combination. And his shift was just starting. He compared the passport and the entry form and noticed the only difference, a single letter spelled wrong. One letter, a split-second mistake, can change your life. The man's face matched the one in the photograph but the name on the form, written in capital letters, did not match the one printed beneath the smooth plastic surface of the passport. Sneyd, Sneya.

A typing error, he said, forcing a smile, pushing the glasses up his nose, the small nose, thinner after the surgery, beginning to sweat, the face so pale, whiter under the fluorescent lights, the gun in his pocket, successive blackouts lasting milliseconds, incessant blinking. The weapon's handle was wrapped in tape. The agent looked at the open passport and the entry form, then at his face, trying to make eye contact, glancing at the line of people behind him, extending across the room. Waves of rain were crashing against the windows. He reached into his coat pocket and pulled an envelope with an official letterhead, fumbling nervously with some papers until he found the birth certificate. This one had the correct full name, typed in capital letters, and stamped with an official seal, Sneyd, not Sneya, Ramon George Sneyd, Canadian citizen born in Toronto, October 8, 1932. He said he also had a certificate of vaccination and looked in several pockets until he found it. The hero in the novel he was reading was also Canadian, a veteran of the British secret service during the war. The novel was titled *Tangier Assignment*. On the cover: a woman with black hair, sitting on the sand, facing away, a tan line across her naked back.

The agent compared the immigration form with the birth certificate and the passport, following the letters with a sharp pencil, the tip suspended a few millimeters above the surface. He had sharpened it so much that it resembled a weapon. He circled the two names: Sneyd, Sneya. The small blade on the sharpener was probably as sharp as the razor the agent had used that morning, still dark, shaving in the mirror, his blue shirt freshly ironed and buttoned. "A typing error," he said, nodding, docile, guilty, almost grateful, his hands covered in sweat, the buttoned collar pressing against his skin; then walking, gliding away under the fluorescent lights, after the agent signaled him to go, already forgotten, erased from memory to make room for the next person in line.

●

He stayed in the Heathrow terminal from seven in the morning until the boarding time that night. A solitary man who spends an entire day at the airport, who just the evening before was boarding a plane for the first time. Everything must have been strange and confusing: the escalator, checking a bag, the myriad of signs. The announcements over the loudspeakers agitated him; flights about to depart, gate changes. He wouldn't have known what a gate was. He followed others and imitated their actions. Following the fat man eventually led him to the baggage claim.

●

He picked up his suitcase and stood there not knowing where to go. Behind the tall glass windows, London was a landscape of hangars and runways, a low and cloudy horizon where the light barely changed even as the day progressed. At the cafeteria, he pushed his tray to the cashier's counter and paid without making eye contact. He had to observe what others were doing so he knew what to do, where to pick up the tray, a fork, the napkins. He looked for a secluded table near an exit where he wouldn't stand out too much and where it was easy to survey the area. It was reassuring to blend in with the other travelers. If only an old acquaintance from prison, or a relative, his father, could see him now. His father now lived in a one-room cabin surrounded by junk, trash, and his German shepherds. He had spoken with journalists, probably in exchange for some money, but according to the papers he had refused to have his picture taken. "If the blacks find out I'm his father, they will burn this house down and kill my dogs." He also said his son wasn't smart enough to have acted on his own and that he was probably dead by now.

•

He recognized uniformed officers in the distance, guards or police. Plainclothes officers would be more of a concern, though he could recognize them at a glance. It was written all over their faces. On the frosted glass door of a police room, he saw the poster with the big white-on-black letters, WANTED, and the three photos, front, profile—both over eight years old—and a third one that was even less useful, the one where he was dressed in a waiter's uniform, his eyes like small buttons. It looked nothing like him. The rented tuxedo did not suit him and the bow tie was wrinkled and crooked.

He walked around the terminal kiosks, browsing pocket novels with colorful covers, magazines with nude women, magazines with glossy photos of yachts, sports cars, luxury suites, exotic destinations, blue skies, foamy waves washing over a beach at sunset, gold bracelets and watches on tanned skin, the dark honey color of glasses filled with rum, golden whiskey on the rocks, shimmering beads of condensation adorning the glass. Before taking a paper from the newsstand he reviewed every front page he could lay his eyes on. Perhaps he knew that the extradition treaty between the United States and Portugal excluded any crime that could lead to the death penalty. But it's also possible he did not plan to fly to Lisbon after arriving in London. He just saw the name of the city on the destinations board, the letters changing with the clicking sound of dominos, forming the name, Lisbon, awakening the memory of something he had heard or read somewhere, perhaps in a newspaper or a conversation with sailors at a bar in the port of Montreal, polished wood shining through the alcoholic half-light of the Neptune Tavern. Perhaps he had planned nothing at all and it was his survival instinct that kept him moving, trying to get as far away as fast as possible, or maybe he could not distinguish between a viable plan and fantasy. An entire day at the airport, looking for rows of seats where he could be the only one, facing the windows, a soft light filtering through the fog as it dissipated throughout the day, or sweeping across the gray and rainy sky, fading into the evening, shaping a block of time made solely out of boredom, while loudspeakers sounded final calls and departure gates for far-off destinations.

He exchanged the return flight to Toronto for a ticket to Lisbon and got fourteen dollars back. Later he said he had called the Portuguese embassy from the airport and they had assured him that once in Lisbon he would be able to apply for a visa to Angola or South Africa. A lone man facing away, suitcase between his legs, hair buzzed at the nape, protruding lopsided ears, a pile of newspapers on the seat next to him, a novel in his hands. Every now and then, his head would begin to nod, lowering slowly before a quick shake fended off sleep.

He went to the bathroom and splashed cold water on his face, took out the toiletry bag and shaved. Cold water and aftershave made him feel more alert. He put the glasses back on, his mask. There he was, a Canadian professor traveling in Europe, now on his way to Lisbon to represent the pharmaceutical company he worked for. Or maybe he was going as an officer or chef for a merchant ship set to travel to the Portuguese colonies in Africa. In the corner of a dark bar, he ordered a burger and a beer and was shocked by the prices after calculating the amount in dollars. He realized in a panic that he could run out of money before he ran out of time. He was the only one sitting alone. A radio was on but he could barely hear the news report over the laughter and conversations of other drinkers, their red faces glowing in the half-light. A split second of silence and he thought he heard his former name, pronounced with an accent that made it almost unrecognizable. A silent TV showed the mug shot, the face that was no longer his, scared, belonging to a past life, eight years ago. A headline ran across the photo: ON THE RUN OR DEAD? Cut to a street scene: bearded men, an angry crowd, flags and fists waving in the air. Then an ad: young people in swimsuits drinking orange sodas under palm trees.

Perhaps they would assume he was dead and stop the search; find a disfigured corpse and say it was his; save themselves the embarrassment of failing to catch him. He would become invisible, forgotten. A bearded stranger on a beach like Puerto Vallarta, living in a cabana with a view of the ocean, flanked by the jungle, trees rustling under the rain, birds singing.

•

But now he was in the Lisbon airport, birth certificate in the same envelope in the same coat pocket. He had not been as nervous during this flight, but it was still a relief to step down the stairway and touch solid ground. The night air brushed his face softly, an entirely new sensation that did not rise to the level of consciousness. The airport was small, dark, and mostly empty at that hour. Steps echoed through the corridors. If you see yourself as a fugitive, destined to be caught, sent to prison, perhaps the electric chair, you will act like one and draw suspicion. With autosuggestion you can mold yourself like clay and become another person, said the Reverend Xavier von Koss in his manual about hypnosis.

A faint smile formed on his face as he stepped to the window with his passport. If you say your chosen name with spontaneity, no one will doubt you. You must say it with conviction, like someone who has never changed his name and fabricated a new identity. He repeated the name in his head, trying to erase the previous ones, preempting the possibility that one might slip out. He repeated the name aloud, with different intonations, trying to get used to it. Ramon George Sneyd. He had read it in the birthdays column of a newspaper from 1932, sitting at a table in the Toronto public library, pencil in hand, muttering names line by line. He repeated the name in front of the mirror, paying attention to the way his lips moved, trying to fuse the sound and the image together. People who have never had to change their name don't know how hard it is to choose a new one. A name you've used your entire life becomes as yours as your face or hands. Adopting a new one is like getting used to those ridiculous names in novels that no one could possibly have. The ones in the James Bond novels are the best. Two thugs from New York: Sluggsy and Horror. "Sluggsy" Morant, Sol "Horror" Horowitz. When he finds a convincing name he commits it to memory, writes it down immediately if possible.

The last name Starvo could be in a James Bond novel, Stavro. The best names can be found in cemeteries and the death and birth notices of small-town newspapers. A good name is like the one of a city you forget the moment you drive past it at night, briefly lit by the car lights, then disappearing forever in the dark. A name picked at random in the phone book or a newspaper ad, after hours of lying in the hotel bed, the door locked, reading name after name in the columns, underlining the best ones. Names from the movie credits, when the lights are back on but you want to stay in your seat, in one of those cinemas that are open around the clock, hideouts for homeless people and alcoholics, people sleeping next to you with their mouths open, snoring, reeking. John Willard is a good name. Harvey Lowmeyer. John Larry Raynes. Paul Edward Bridgman. Galt, Eric S. Galt, Eric Starvo Galt.

•

He hides in the human waste of the slums but he is not one of them. At eight o'clock, he steps out of the roach-infested boardinghouse looking spotless. He wears his nice suit and tie, walks in his alligator shoes past the drunks sleeping on the sidewalk. He always did his best to be clean. When he had to sleep in his car, he used the bathrooms in gas stations to wash up. On a few occasions, he drove for three days, only stopping to buy food, use the bathroom, and nap one or two hours in the backseat. He missed the name Eric S. Galt as much as he missed his white '66 Mustang, which gave him almost fifteen thousand miles. The yellowed paint, the galloping horse badge in the grille, the silver spoke wheels, the red interior. He stepped on the accelerator and the Mustang surged like a colt.

In the bathroom of the hotel room, he left his only pair of underwear soaking overnight, then washed it and dried it in the morning. As you exit through the lobby, a receptionist might call the name you used to register. If you're not alert, you'll keep walking. Don't call yourself Smith, Brown, or Jones; you will draw a blank stare.

It's necessary to take a name that is unusual but not too eccentric. Mental discipline is necessary to truly embody a new name. You must also choose a simple signature. We only use 10 percent of our brains, says the Reverend von Koss in his book. He always scored above average on the IQ tests they gave him in prison. Not much, but enough. The elementary school teacher treated him like an idiot, but later, in his first year of secondary, a history teacher noticed his love of maps and newspapers and gave him a world atlas.

Once you choose a name you must repeat it over and over, like a rosary. And you must practice your signature often. The margins of a newspaper are good for notes but they must be ripped and destroyed once you're done. His mother sold the atlas and bought a jug of wine. You must stand still in front of a mirror, clean shaven, and repeat the name with different intonations, practicing different situations. Most important, you must be able to spell it without hesitation. In prison, his cellmate used to call him the Thinker, sarcastically, though not without some admiration, because he was always reading. Dictionaries, novels, magazines, books about yoga, hypnosis, photography, even gymnastics. Autohypnosis is the secret to success. Galt, *gee ei el tee*. Sneyd, *ess en ee wai dee*. And, if necessary, you must switch seamlessly from one name to another, from passport to passport, different lives, different dates of birth, different nationalities, different jobs, different parents. When asked about his parents, he said they were long dead.

He told the officer at the Lisbon airport that he was an executive with an international car rental company. The officer had a wrinkled shirt, stubble, and very dark eyes. António Rocha Fama was his name. It's a good name though it sounds made-up. He would focus his mental energy and send him hypnotic waves to distract him from the misspelling in the name, the one letter conspiring against his new life. The first rule in hypnosis training is to not blink. A single blink is enough to break the trance. A black woman with weary features was cleaning the floor, pushing a bucket with soapy water. How strange to see black people in Portugal. He thought Portugal would be like Mexico, with indigenous-looking people but not blacks. There were black people carrying bags and cleaning the airport bathrooms in London. He had seen a black man drinking at a bar next to two white people. The officer noticed the misspelling in the name, but he was tired and sleepy, his face was weary like that of the cleaning woman, who kept on pushing her bucket, leaning on the mop, a red rag on her head. It's like they never left Africa. He pulled out the envelope with the birth certificate, trying to expedite the process, a bit upset, a Canadian citizen with nothing to hide, an executive on a business trip. The officer ran a hand through his curly hair and returned the passport, placing it on the counter like a poker card. "Get this fixed at your embassy before your next flight," said the man, his eyes red from sleep deprivation.

•

Behind the taxi window, Lisbon looked as empty as the airport. The car tires bounced over the cobblestone. He saw villas, gardens, chipped walls illuminated by the taxi's headlights, buildings with balconies, scattered windows with a single light shining behind a curtain. Tunnels of light opened through the tree-lined road, revealing stairways to palaces, ruins with cranes and excavators, sheets of metal covering construction sites.

Arriving at a city when everything is closed and there is no one on the streets is like arriving in secret, protected by the night. He loved those moments in novels when the secret agent arrives at the foreign city where his mission is to take place.

In *The Ninth Directive*, one of the novels he had when they caught him, Secret Agent Quiller travels to Bangkok on the trail of an assassin who is planning an attack against a member of the royal family on a diplomatic visit to Thailand. Quiller is a loner and a cynic, but his superiors know there is no one better than him to navigate Bangkok's underworld. He saw his eyes reflected in the rearview mirror and awkwardly met an inquisitive look from the driver.

According to psycho-cybernetics, the human mind is a preprogrammed computer. Anything you do has to be projected in the imagination like on a screen where all details are within view. We can program ourselves for success just as we often do for failure.

The taxi stopped by a red light and he imagined himself planting his gun on the back of the head of the driver, who kept on talking in his incomprehensible language. He imagined the whole scene but dismissed it quickly. Where would he go after the robbery in this unfamiliar city? And what could this peasant driver possibly have? His knit cap, this old car. He had assured him in broken English that he would take him to a good, inexpensive hotel in a central yet quiet part of town. Typical taxi driver, the man looked like a thief, and even more so when he smiled with his big mouth to announce they had arrived.

•

It was a short street and it had two clear exits. A reporter for *Life* magazine wrote a few weeks later that it smelled of charcoal and rotisserie chicken. The only light at that hour, apart from the lampposts, came from the lobby of the hotel. Hotel Portugal, João das Regras Street, number four. He hesitated for a moment before going through the revolving door. It was obvious the building had seen better times, and that it was in a poor area, but maybe they would try to play him, a tourist easily tricked into giving away all his money. He went through the door, feeling somewhat light-headed, and fearing for a moment that he would get trapped with his suitcase. The lobby smelled like musty carpet and dust, and the low light made it look like some kind of aquarium. He pulled back automatically when the bellhop tried to take his suitcase. He had not seen him approach. No matter how alert you are, someone can always surprise you. With a lot of training it was possible to develop telepathic powers to anticipate an attack seconds before it happens. In secret government laboratories they were researching techniques to become invisible. Lee Harvey Oswald killed Kennedy while hypnotized by a special CIA team. The pale hand tightened around the handle of the suitcase, the skin tensing over the knuckles. Perhaps he reached for the gun, though it would have been hard to retrieve it fast enough from the back pocket with a coat on. He needed a holster. Before leaving for an evening of equal parts sex and danger, James Bond looked at himself in the mirror and made sure his gun was fully concealed under his fitted blazer. The coat Ramon George Sneyd wore had a tag from a Toronto shop. No one there remembered selling it to him. The best suits are made in London by the tailors on Savile Row. His had been purchased the previous summer in Montreal at a store called Andy's Men's Shop. It was the first suit he had ever owned. The receptionist at the Hotel Portugal watched him approach with tired eyes and a smile. His uniform, like the entire hotel, was from a different era. It was two in the morning. Lisbon at night was a city inhabited by just a few insomniacs.

•

Some things can be known; others never. The receptionist's name was Gentil Soares. He was a young man back then and could still be alive. At least he was in 2006, when a Portuguese journalist named Vladimiro Nunes interviewed him. Soares said the man stared at the floor as he spoke, and it was hard to understand his English because he spoke softly and barely opened his mouth. He said the man would sometimes spend the entire day in his room; other days he would leave very early and not come back until the wee hours.

The night he arrived he was wearing the glasses from the passport photo; after that he wore none or just sunglasses. He was very pale and had a look of combined exhaustion and alertness, anxiety and somnolence. When the receptionist asked him how many days he planned to stay in Lisbon, he said he had been hired as the chief engineer on a ship and didn't know when they would be departing. On his way to the elevator, he picked up a British newspaper someone had left open on a table. He did not tip the bellhop who carried his suitcase.

Room number 2 was on the first floor. He went out to the balcony, and although the street was quite narrow the smell of the ocean could still reach him, albeit combined with sewage. He could hear a conversation rising up from the street corner below. Whispers, a laugh. Standing by a doorway, a woman leaned toward a man who had offered to light her cigarette. In the still silence of 2:30 a.m., he heard a ship's foghorn. He collapsed in bed without taking his shoes off. He could not remember how many days he had been wearing them. It would be hard to remove them with his feet so swollen. But at least he had no sores and would not bleed when he finally took them off. He fell into a deep sleep, then jolted out convinced he had slept an entire night and day. It was dark again and something irreparable had happened. He was crouching in a cell, or hiding in a sewage pipe, gasping for air, when the vibrations of an underground train swaying the lamp chain awoke him. The clock confirmed he had only been asleep for one hour. He did not know transatlantic air travel disrupts the sleep cycle. He would not sleep well any of the ten nights he spent in Lisbon. He felt the ground move as the trains ran through the tunnels. He remembered the sounds of the eternal freight train that ran through his sleepless nights in prison.

5

I had never written in such a state, it was like a lucid somnambulism. No longer weighed down by the lived experiences that originally inspired it, the story took on a life of its own, separate from my will, the real and the imagined forming spontaneous configurations like in a dream.

To erase Granada, I wrote Madrid, I wrote San Sebastián, I wrote Lisbon. Those names radiated successive images and visual resonances. I was writing the names of characters and places and each carried the seed of its own story and the threads, seen and unseen, that connected them to each other. Only one name was missing and it did not matter. The name of the narrator. Not having a name was like not having a face. An observer who exists solely in the act of bearing witness. It was inspired by Scott Fitzgerald's Nick Carraway, but I did not know then that Nick Carraway took after Joseph Conrad's Marlow.

The one who tells the story has no place in it. He is a camera, an invisible man. That camera lens is the detective Philip Marlowe's point of view in the film with Robert Montgomery. It is the reader or moviegoer who forgets himself on the written page or in the darkness of the theater. One goes into a movie theater to cease to exist. It is because of that, not the size or quality of the image, that something crucial is lost when a film is experienced on a television set, in the domestic light of one's home, in the calcareous shell of one's identity.

If there are other people in the theater, your shadow becomes one with all the others, it dissolves in a collective stare. And if you have the luxury to be alone, the screen, the characters, the music—they are all yours, like a book. I either earned my education, or entirely missed out on it, in the two movie theaters of Granada. The Principe and Alhambra cinemas, very close to each other, one in the Campo del Principe square, the other on Molinos Street. I submerged myself in them like a diver in depths that are just a few meters from the shore but already a world stranger than the moon. That's how I've always sought to experience the things and places that I like, the cities I visit, the languages I want to learn, forgetting without effort all that is familiar, my life, my city, my country, my name.

•

Perhaps it is the same capacity for evasion that characterizes children's games, a withdrawal from the world but not from perception, reality temporarily suspended while the mind explores other possibilities, sometimes more promising, sometimes threatening. But I had not realized that my self-withdrawal, at the time, had a growing edge of exasperation, because I was no longer a child or an adolescent, and yet I was trying to hide in a similar way but with greater determination, since I carried a heavier weight of responsibility; the trap I had gotten myself into was tighter, because I could not see myself or what surrounded me, narcotized by fantasies, used to seeking refuge in daydreams like an opium addict who can no longer tolerate the jarring light of the open sky.

With meticulous patience, like a prisoner, I elaborated imaginary plans to change my life radically; meanwhile, in the real world, my wife's voice on the phone announced we would be having another child. In my mind, I was the pianist in my novel, endowed with all the things I would have liked to have, some beyond my reach, like musical talent, and others I had not dared to claim: unfettered freedom; the ability to experience different countries and languages; the full and solitary dedication to one vocation.

And yet, I also embodied, in a dark way, my narrator without a name, though not quite the neutral lens of my cinephilia, the one that observes but does not act, jealously following others' passions, which for some unbeknown reason exclude him. Nobody is just a camera or a gaze. Equally incompetent at marriage and fleeting affairs; as ill-equipped for an administrative job and family life as I was for the methodical chaos of bar life, I kept on retreating into an intimate paralysis fed almost entirely by fictions: the ones I created and the ones I found in films, songs, and literature.

•

Alcohol was becoming an insidious and frequent ally. Drinking seemed like a requirement for literary life, a path to relief and enlightenment. Great writers drank until they collapsed. Movie heroes drank and smoked. Jazz musicians were addicted to heroin or alcohol, or both, like Charlie Parker. At the end of her life, Billie Holiday could barely stand when singing and her voice had an alcoholic drawl. Edgar Allan Poe, Charles Baudelaire, Paul Verlaine embalmed alive in absinthe, William Faulkner embalmed in bourbon, Malcolm Lowry surrendering to gin and mescal, Carson McCullers's pale face and bloodshot eyes, Marguerite Duras swelling up from alcohol like a frog, Raymond Chandler, Ernest Hemingway, Dashiell Hammett, the best of the best, the aristocracy of literature and delirium tremens. In Granada, we had our own pantheon of legendary drunks, alcoholic oracles moving like shadows after midnight, known and unknown, distinguished professors, poets, wild bohemians from a previous era looking for old friends who could lend them some money or at least a cigarette. There was something sacred or frightening in those terminal drunks, an immolation, a radical renunciation of the status quo. In the bars, enclosed by a fog of smoke and voices, the literati held court and shook their glasses and cigarettes; as the night advanced, alcohol lavished them with a simulacra of friendship and extreme lucidity, aesthetic daring, and political vehemence. No one would achieve anything original or memorable without the willingness to pay the price, sacrifice one's health and sanity in exchange for the divine fruits that sprout on the edge of madness or even suicide.

After midnight, one had to become Lou Reed, Rimbaud, Jimi Hendrix, Antonin Artaud, Alejandra Pizarnik, Chet Baker, Scott

Fitzgerald. Poets from Barcelona or Madrid passed through the city, leaving behind legends of their alcoholic and sexual exploits. I was impressed by Humphrey Bogart's answer in *Casablanca* to a question about his nationality: "I'm a drunkard." Sitting in the dark, Rick Blaine works through a bottle of bourbon. The bar is already closed and he is alone. Beside him: a glass, the bottle, a pack of cigarettes, and an ashtray. Suddenly, a door opens and in the light Ingrid Bergman's tall silhouette appears like a mirage. Who wouldn't want to live in that world, that unchanged kingdom.

I had not tried bourbon, just as I had never been to Lisbon or lived in hotels, but that was the drink my characters could not get enough of. Up to that point, I drank sporadically and rather absently. But something changed. Gradually, I began to drink more, sometimes in the company of others, sometimes by myself as I got ready to write. Ingrid Bergman was a shadow on the silver screen, but cigarettes and liquor were within anyone's reach. I would start drinking and soon I felt liberated, excited, hopeful. The bar was welcoming, improved by low light and smoke, the sound of people, music, conversations with friends, the beginnings of inebriation, beautiful women, some of them strangers, eyes meeting across the bar. Stepping out on the street, en route to the next bar, the night unfolding before us like a promise, an abyss, an enigma.

In those days without cell phones, you could spend hours looking for someone and never find them, the more you looked the more you imagined seeing them from afar and the more your desire intensified; there were also unexpected encounters around a corner, sudden twists of fate.

The future of the night and your whole life could depend on a street turn; whether you stayed at a bar after a few hours of waiting; whether you left a few minutes before the one you desired appeared behind the glass. The next bar, the next glass, the next cigarette, so brief one must take another one, the imminence, a little longer, just one more hour, as if the night could be prolonged and dawn delayed, the shame and penance of daylight.

Sometimes I retired just in time, due to despair rather than good sense, convinced that I lacked the courage to truly let go and embrace the great madness of life, and that this would prevent me from ever knowing the secrets of love and writing. But other times I stayed and drank until I lost control of my steps and actions, as if a stranger that hides within came out to take over my will, dragging me from street to street, as I held on to whatever I could find to keep from falling.

I would search for my apartment in that revolving city, my footsteps echoing like a stranger's, someone whispering things in my ear. I would walk and walk and end up lost or sitting by a water fountain in some plaza, shivering in the piercing cold of night in Granada. Or I returned sunk in the backseat of a taxi, letting the cold air hit my face, watching the city go by, the city that only night owls get to see, the city of ghosts and the last drunks of the night, the one where the lights of early risers begin to dot the buildings, dark like blocks of shadow. And there were times when I woke up in bed or on the sofa, not knowing when or how I had arrived and whether someone had helped me. Alcohol corrodes entire memories. In the lost hours of the morning hangover, the remorse and fear, the shame at something I did not know, slowly thickened.

•

I recovered by taking refuge in my routine. The smell of alcohol made me nauseous, so strong in the urine of the morning after, in the sheets damp with perspiration. Writing had a healing power. I invented my story, or rather I watched it unfold in my imagination like images in a film. I did not elaborate an argument: images came in isolated flashes, like the posters that decorated movie theaters when I was a child, stills that made you want to watch the film or at least imagine it. I saw a man walking away in the wee hours of the morning. I saw a woman in sunglasses at a bar in San Sebastián's promenade, sitting by a window overlooking the Bay of Biscay. I saw long airmail envelopes with their red-blue borders and exotic stamps. I saw two lovers meeting after many years of separation and not recognizing each other, now they're only steps away, unaware that distance has already defeated them. I saw a coat pocket with a gun and a map of Lisbon marked with a cross. I saw a dear friend from those broke college years in Granada, now running a bar. The place was falling apart and he had no customers, but even in misfortune he still had that great smile of his, a glowing round face with an easy blush, more Irish or Nordic than Spanish, flashing blue eyes and curly blond hair.

When we lived together, he would sometimes wear a cassock from his days in seminary, instead of a bathrobe. I did not try to hide his identity when I transformed him into one of my characters: the character sprang from him like a joyful outburst made of his presence and kindness, just like his fictional name, Floro Bloom. The bar where my friend lost his health for some time and the little savings he had, was as hospitable as a garage, with a loose South American theme, in an area of ugly apartment blocks close to the Camino de Ronda trail and mostly inhabited by students.

Writing meant enveloping people and places in a cellophane of illusory beauty, exalting them in a fantastical geography. Granada was San Sebastián; a dark block of brutalist buildings became a promenade by the ocean; a depressing cafeteria was a jazz club with a neon sign, LADYBIRD. As soon as I started writing, names of characters and places would come to me, memories transmuted into movie scenes and song titles, some real, some made-up. I wanted the story to unfold like a film in the reader's imagination. I wanted it to sound like music, the same music that carried me and was in the flow and breathing of the words. Writing that is music and music that moves through a story like the soundtracks of those movies that for so many years had me spellbound at the Principe and Alhambra cinemas, a luminous alloy of images and words in foreign languages, Italian and Nino Rota's music in Fellini, English and Ennio Morricone's music in *Once Upon a Time in America*, French and English and Gato Barbieri's band in *Last Tango in Paris*, English and the incredible soundtracks of Stanley Kubrick, French and Miles Davis in Louis Malle's *Elevator to the Gallows*, Albéniz and the *pasodoble* "En er Mundo" in Víctor Erice's *El Sur*; music and cinema and foreign languages and also desire, because we had to wait for many of those movies until the end of the dictatorship, and in them we saw for the first time on-screen the supreme and breathtaking beauty of the naked female body, Dominique Sanda in *The Conformist* and *1900*, Eiko Matsuda in *In the Realm of the Senses*, the silver-haired woman walking under a blue light in *A Clockwork Orange* to an electronic

version of Henry Purcell's *Music for the Funeral of Queen Mary*, Marisa
Berenson, languid and nude, staring into the distance as if she could
hear the Handel suite or the Schubert piano trio that haunted *Barry
Lyndon*, Fanny Ardant in Truffaut's late films, Susan Sarandon massag-
ing her breasts with lemon halves in *Atlantic City* to remove the fish
smell, while Burt Lancaster spied on her through the window.

•

I wanted the writing to develop a sense of phrasing with the restless-
ness of jazz. Through a narrator that doesn't know anything about
music, I avoided all the technical details that would have been inevitable if the story had been told from the perspective of the pianist. To
write fiction is to see the world through the eyes of another person, to
hear it through somebody else's ears. It is the audacity to believe
you can know the secrets of another mind, no matter who it is—an
assassin, a fugitive, a man leaning on a balcony at dusk, one or two
minutes before a bullet shatters his jaw and pierces his spine, a musician who closes his eyes to play the piano.

I loved jazz but I think I loved jazz musicians even more. I loved
the music itself but also as an ethic and as an aesthetic model for
literature, the combination of discipline and abandon, hard technical
skill and absolute control but also improvisation and fits of passion,
lightness and depth, slowness and speed. That's how I wanted my writing
to sound, how I wanted to write, with a powerful impulse and without
knowing where it would take me, sometimes in a straight line and
sometimes letting myself get lost in detours that would take me to
unforeseen treasures.

The outlines of a scene, a metaphor, a name. I was going to write
the word *brume* and, without realizing it, typed *burma* instead. It suddenly hit me how beautiful a name Burma is. The word *brume* lingered
in it along with a suggestion of journeys in the Far East, a magical
sound. The strangest part of the story sprouted from that name, like an
open sesame to a cave of treasures. Burma was handwritten on a map of
Lisbon; it was a password for members of a secret organization; a name
that glowed in red or blue neon letters on the door of what could be
a brothel or the headquarters for a network of smugglers; the title of a

song in which, after a very long solo, a trumpeter puts his instrument down and hoarsely whispers into the microphone, Burma, Burma, Burma, just like John Coltrane in the mantra *A love supreme, a love supreme, a love supreme.* In a jazz composition the theme is announced in the first measures and then seems to lag far behind, as if the musicians proceed so deep into the detours of improvisation that they forget it completely. Perhaps a few loose notes strike like a quick reminder, an intuition of the past in the midst of the present, vanishing as quickly as they come. But then the flood subsides, the music runs back to its course, and the original theme returns but not quite as repetition; it has been transformed by everything that just happened, like one who returns from travel forever changed, and sees all that was left behind in a new light.

Jazz musicians interested me much more than writers or artists. They passed through my provincial eighties Granada like comets from another solar system. Thanks to my job back then, I was able to see many of the best and even meet a few. Writers, even second-rate ones, artists, aspiring local rock stars, tended to be arrogant and vain, wanted to be treated like geniuses. But jazz musicians simply did their job. They came from long tours looking tired but it only took a few minutes for the infallible power of music to take over. Once the concert ended, they put their instruments down and sighed with relief like someone completing a work shift.

Back then I could not have known that I was one of the last witnesses of a golden era. I saw Dexter Gordon, thin and long like a figure from Picasso's Blue Period; Chet Baker with the small, wrinkled face and slicked-back hair; Miles Davis in a yellow leather jacket, his face hidden behind the enormous sunglasses, arachnid fingers covered in rings moving up and down the golden valves of the trumpet; Art Blakey, his skin like old leather and tobacco, sweating profusely under the stage lights, a great reptilian tongue in his open mouth; Sonny Stitt, Carmen McRae, Phil Woods in an acoustic quintet, such relief after so many excessive amplifications; Johnny Griffin, small and daring; Tom Harrell in the depths of schizophrenia, quiet like a monk, head lowered, trumpet in hand waiting for his solo; I saw the drummer Billy Higgins playing effortlessly and with a wide, placid smile of happiness; I saw Woody Shaw, almost blind and barely able to move due to the diabetes that would soon kill him. Backstage, moments before the concert, his wife threaded his white curls tenderly with a plastic blue comb. I saw Paquito D'Rivera, who had recently fled Cuba, dressed in black leather and cowboy boots, entering the stage like a cyclone as he played "All the Things You Are." I saw Tete Montoliu, one of my heroes, many times, wearing green or rose-colored frames, his blind-man smile; face slightly cocked back as if to better hear something far away; his white, fleshy hands, and the shining wedding band; the formal suits, like a bureaucrat or cloth merchant; the impression that he felt lost on that stage and in the labyrinths behind the curtain; the stiffness with which he stood by the piano to accept the applause, the tips of his fingers resting on the edge of the keys.

Sometimes, after a concert, I went out to dinner with him and other musicians. He remained absent, often smiling the way he had onstage as he plunged through the twists and turns of improvisation. I noticed that his hands touched the world around him lightly, as if he were seeing through them, the silverware, the border of the plate, the edge of the glass. He smoothed the tablecloth, folded and flattened the napkins. The other musicians, relieved after so many hours of focus and exertion, enjoyed their beers and relaxed, leaning back on their chairs, sharing stories and laughing. Tete remained still in his gray suit and tie, hands on the table, a confused smile, submerged in the only world he knew, yet eccentric to it, separated by his blindness and Catalan seriousness, hiding the fury that would later be unleashed on a piano without hesitation, without any warning, all at once.

•

I saw Elvin Jones playing in a quartet with his wife, a Japanese woman whose petite figure accentuated his formidable size. The man was built like a tower or a tree. I will never forget it. Elvin Jones, thick-necked and head buzzed, entered the stage like a boxer enters a ring; he wore black trousers and a short silk robe with Japanese drawings of birds and bamboo stalks tied at the waist. Black high-tops, white socks. The robe opened at the chest. From the moment his hands fell on the skin of the drums and the metal brush touched the edge of the cymbals, silence gave way to the ancient and sacred sound of John Coltrane's music. It was a feat of musical virtuosity that bordered on spiritualism; if you closed your eyes it was as if the dead had joined the living onstage. You could hear the dead in the jazz instruments singing like human voices: Coltrane's saxophone, Eric Dolphy's bass clarinet, Jim Garrison's bass, all three taken from us too early, at the prime of their lives, each one unique and without equal, each one possessed by a different strain of that fever they shared, making music with an audacity jazz had never seen, the golden age, the early seventies, absolutely free yet deeply rooted in their origins—the blues, the spirituals, the work songs, the visionary sermons of Baptist preachers, aesthetic radicalism, political fury. The piano and the drums that night were like an opening into a world long gone, fragments of a time now preserved in records or in the memories of those who met them, in the New York clubs where John Coltrane and his band had played for hours without break, the Five Spot, the Village Gate, the Village Vanguard, remote, mythical spaces, cave-like basements at the end of a narrow staircase, catacombs.

Slowly, the other musicians stayed behind and gave way to Elvin Jones's solo. Under the blue and red lights, copious beads of sweat gathered on the shaved head. He smiled or grimaced with eyes closed as if in pain or exasperation, the large bright teeth shining in the dark. It put you in a state of heightened alert, dilated hearing, aware of every sound and melodic thread, every break in the rhythm, every harmonic connection. Elvin Jones continued his solo, guiding a powerful flow of music that transformed into unexpected rhythmic patterns, seismic trepidations that took over the drums for a few seconds, then gave way to subtle vibrations, like rain or rustling leaves, a polyphony of heartbeats, drumrolls, steps, train wheels, bongos palpitating around a fire. External time, the time of clocks and calendars, was canceled. The only time that existed was the one governed by the solemn religiosity and delirium of Elvin Jones's drums, beating against the feverish expectancy of the audience like a heart in the concave darkness of the body.

Surrounded by drums and cymbals, Elvin Jones kept descending into a whirlpool of his own making, seemingly lost for a few long minutes, then finding his way through a path insinuated just seconds before; eyes shut tight; the grin transformed into a great laugh; the vibrations of the metal, the stretched skin of the drums, the hollowed wood, the dried seeds in the maracas, bursting in a simultaneous deflagration; rain-whipped forests in which every leaf and every branch participate in a great collective percussion; euphoric calamities of crumbling glass walls and towers. Then, ever so slowly, as if emerging from under the earth, the austere pulse of the blues, which had never left, the impulse of the train, the primordial compass of the slap and pop. When he finished playing, Elvin Jones stood up to welcome the applause and stumbled across the stage, his robe like a second skin soaked in sweat.

•

I saw Dizzy Gillespie often for a period of ten years. I saw him at the height of his musical and physical powers and also in the decline of old age. Sometimes he wore a puffy hat that matched his prodigious cheeks. In his later years, he wore a kufi cap and a dashiki. I spoke enough English to tell him how much I admired him and to ask a few questions, but I always missed parts of the response. It peeved him that jazz was associated with alcohol and drugs, and the more worked up he got the harder it was for me to follow what he was saying. John Coltrane only came into his full powers when he stopped doing heroin. Heroin and alcohol did not make Charlie Parker a better musician, they just killed him at thirty-four. As for himself, he said, with his thumb pointing at his chest, and a huge smile, how could he tour all year around the world, at his age, if he did not care for his health like an athlete? One night, in the Isabel la Católica Theatre in Granada, I went to look for him backstage. I found him in his dressing room. He was sitting in front of the mirror, legs wide apart, the tunic rolled up to the waist. He was wearing black pants, big black shoes, and short red socks. As I entered, I caught a glimpse of Dizzy Gillespie's face when he was alone, without the great smile, without the swelling cheeks. The trumpet was on the floor beside him, and he had both hands on his knees. He looked exhausted, facing the mirror but looking somewhere far beyond, so absorbed in his thinking that he didn't hear me come in. He was seventy-three, and as of the beginning of that November he had already given three hundred concerts that year. We had had dinner together and he had talked the entire time, but as he smiled at me from the mirror it was clear he did not remember me. He had told me that most of the cities he visited were little more than names to him, webs of lights seen from an airplane, cityscapes that extended beyond the windows of a taxi or the hotel rooms where he usually arrived in the late hours and left before dawn. He asked me if Granada was by the sea.

6

He left the hotel one morning in May, walked down a dark, narrow street and out onto the sunny square with the statue of the king on horseback. The white light was reflected from all sides, from the limestone walls of the buildings, from the tiles on the ground. He had to close his eyes. It was the first time he had seen tiles like that. Before, he had only walked on the concrete sidewalks, which were no different from those in American cities. How did Lisbon appear to him as he walked out of the hotel for the first time? He had only seen it from the taxi window the night before—empty, poor, dark. He probably did not sleep well. He must have been exhausted from the transatlantic flight, and after so many nights on the run, nights when he could barely close his eyes, waiting for the last newscast of the day or reading every newspaper front to back, looking for the face and name that are no longer his.

Nothing remains of who he was, except that which cannot be erased—his fingerprints. But to check those, they must first arrest him, they must first suspect him. And that is very unlikely now and even more so in this European city, where he now finds himself, perhaps by chance, after seeing the name on the departures board in Heathrow Airport, the split-flap letters that changed so rapidly with those clicking sounds, making his head spin. Fast like everything else around him—the moving escalators, the slippery floor, the humming of the air conditioners, the signs, the storefronts with endless rows of newspapers and magazines and books, the voices on the loudspeakers echoing. It would be easier to reach Africa from Lisbon, to find one of those places with ongoing revolutions or civil wars; countries with powerful names, emphatic vowels—Angola, Biafra, Congo, Rhodesia—where white mercenaries fight colonial wars; brave soldiers of fortune in camouflage and berets who will welcome him as a hero when they realize who he is, what he has done. A geography book he read in prison had the names of all the Portuguese colonies. He repeated them at night to relieve his insomnia or during the long lineups and cell counts—the names of political and economic capitals, rivers, bays, harbors. He also memorized lists of techniques to seduce women, sailing terms, names of wines, the sites and dates of the World War, the islands in the Pacific, the names of the planets and their moons.

●

Outside the hotel it smelled like a port. Coal smoke and roast chicken. Nothing is more specific, more ephemeral, than a smell. It smelled and sounded like Africa in the corner of the square where João das Regras Street would lead him: black women wearing colorful tunics and head wraps; men chatting and smoking by a church, enjoying the sun in a state of calm he had never seen in black people in America. Music from an improvised drum and a thick smell of fried food permeated the air.

He had a map on which the hotel receptionist had marked how to get to the port, but he did not need it, he instinctually drifted toward places like that without searching for them—ports, cheap hotels, pawnshops, dive bars with prostitutes, secondhand book stands, pornography stores and cinemas, the corners and alleys frequented by drug dealers. Certain places can't be found by asking directions the way you would for a post office or pharmacy. I wonder how he saw the world, what he saw in the streets I see now. He must have been perceptive to cues that are invisible to me, like frequencies beyond my range of hearing, smells I don't heed—tar, cheap disinfectant, decomposing fish and fruit, stagnant water. What must it be like to live in a constant state of alert, for that to become your way of life, like a spy or a shadow. Calculating every step, every word; checking the peephole before opening the door, making sure it's bolted; sleeping with your clothes on, over the blankets, ready to go; memorizing each face in the hotel lobby; choosing the darkest corner of the bar from which to observe the entrance; noting emergency exits; checking the bathroom for windows to the backstreet; drinking a beer or two, a couple of shots of bourbon, feeling the warm beginnings of intoxication, but declining when the bartender suggests another round for this customer who looks nothing like the regulars, he who came one night and never returned or maybe he came back several days in a row, or several weeks; so quiet, so out of place; the only one that keeps glancing at the television—a show has just started, *FBI: The Ten Most Wanted Criminals*; it's on every Sunday. He fears his face will appear on the screen, but he is also proud, pride that often goes frustrated, except last time: number one of the Ten Most Wanted. Pride turned into arrogance, fear into terror and vertigo, the exaltation of impunity, a reckless challenge. As he sat at a bar in Toronto, his were the only eyes fixed on the television, staring at his unrecognizable face, barely able to hear the announcer through the noise of conversations and laughter, the voice that said his former name as a number appeared under the photo: one hundred thousand dollars.

•

How would someone who has spent more than half his life in prison react to the calm bustling of the average street in this city; someone who is used to always being on guard, always avoiding notice but also carrying himself in a way that thwarts antagonism. It had been a vast, gloomy prison with resounding domes and battlement towers with big searchlights.

Here in Lisbon, there seemed to be no threat. People muttered in an incomprehensible language. The hotel maid greeted him one morning with a smile and a brief nod as he walked out of his room. Her name was Maria Celeste. She had black hair and one of those serious yet friendly Portuguese faces. She was photographed in the room where he stayed. The photo shows her leaning on the marble edge of a dresser, wearing a black dress and a pleated white apron. She said he was well-dressed and kept his room tidy, but didn't seem to bathe. According to her, he left each morning at the same time.

The worn-out carpet muffled his steps. All the voices that spoke to him or that he heard in the street enveloped him in a suffocating and numbing gauze—he did not understand anything. He had observed the world his entire life as if from a window in an empty room. He passed by cafe windows and restaurants where big pots of food sat on display. He stared at the menus taped to the glass and the small, handwritten signs listing the daily specials. He was starving but the exotic smells also made him nauseous. He did not trust those small establishments with their paper tablecloths and everything so crammed; they were unlike anything he knew. The grocery stores had a unique blend of smells: freshly ground coffee, dried cod, spices, lard, herring, olive oil.

The smell of fried fat made him want to eat a hamburger. He liked to sit in those cafeterias that were open all day and order a medium-rare hamburger with lots of ketchup, mustard, and a Pepsi. He still had the habit—from prison—of eating quickly, leaning into the plate and glancing to the sides. It was odd to see the gentleman with the suit, tie, and glasses wolf down fries by the handful.

Some thought he was a plainclothes policeman or an informer. Now, as he walked through the square—wet morning light washing over the old king on horseback at the center—the pangs of hunger were making him lose focus. He could not see the newsstand the receptionist had mentioned. He entered another square, a bigger one with another king or whatever it was standing on a column. A former cellmate of his admired how he boasted of being an atheist and read a book by a philosopher named Nietzsche. The sidewalk was wider and crowded with street vendors and beggars, men without legs dragging their bodies between the tables of an outdoor cafe. Suddenly he recognized the pages of the *Herald Tribune* and the *Times* from afar. The newsstand was a small kiosk with vibrant colors and the newspapers and magazines hung from pins on a clothesline. In this new undecipherable world, those newspapers were the only things with words he could comprehend. He bought the *Times*, the *Tribune*, *Life*, *Newsweek*. The man who sold him the stuff found it strange that he made no eye contact and only extended his arm to offer a handful of coins.

Disoriented and hungry, he did something he had never done

before. He walked to one of the fancier cafes and sat down with some hesitation. The interior was lined with mirrors, dark wood, marble, and waiters in black jackets and bow ties, like in the movies. He was unsure about the etiquette and felt no one would be convinced by his suit, the shoes, the glasses. The secret agents in novels know how to fit in the most expensive cafes and restaurants. They only have to look at the wine list for a few seconds to know the best bottle in the house. A waiter approached him, silver tray in hand, and asked him something with a smile. He hunched his shoulders and pressed the newspapers against his chest. "Cafe," he said. The waiter responded with another sentence he could not understand. Later he would realize the waiter had been trying to speak English. "Coffee," he muttered, avoiding eye contact, then pointing at a glass case with small cakes stacked in a pyramid. He felt the urge to run away when the waiter left with the order.

But he did nothing. He stared at the people walking past the window. He looked at the cobblestone, the trees, the white-marble figures at the base of the column where the dark green bronze king stood against the blue sky. It was like being in a black-and-white photo, or one of those old movies they used to play in prison, where a man with slicked-back hair sits at a cafe smoking and looks up as a woman with a hat and a short veil appears. But he must be careful because the meeting could very well be a trap, the woman just bait, and as he gets ready to leave, a policeman or a traitor with a strange accent and a goatee suddenly appears.

The waiter finally came with the coffee in a porcelain cup, sugar, and a piece of cake on a plate with gilded edges and a monogram. He ate the cake in a few big bites, getting cream all over his newspapers. On one of the pages was his old name and the unrecognizable face. He looked heavier in the photo and was wearing sunglasses; a side shadow accentuated the cleft chin. It's important to change your weight often. Eat and drink as much as possible for a few months, then undergo a severe diet. As a result, some will remember you fat and some will remember you skinny. They will all have a hard time recognizing you later. Fatness and thinness are exaggerated in photographs. He looked up and saw his image in the mirror. His face was thin, more angular. He looked younger.

This time the newspaper said that someone had spotted him at an airport cafeteria in Caracas wearing a green trench coat and carrying a briefcase. They repeated the same things they always said, adding a few new details or witness accounts to make it seem like they were making progress. Some had seen him in Geneva, laughing and dining in an expensive restaurant with a blond woman who looked like a prostitute, ordering the most expensive wine and dishes. Others had seen him in a taxi, crossing the jungle between Mexico and Guatemala; or at the airport in San Juan, Puerto Rico, buying a ticket to Jamaica; or getting off a small plane in Cuba, where Fidel Castro was due to announce, any day now, that he had been granted asylum. Others said he had been beaten to death in Acapulco and was buried in some beach.

•

To feel, even if just for a moment, the relief of escape, the knowledge that your pursuers are far behind; to stare at this square and listen to all the conversations, the clinking of spoons and coffee cups, people's steps, the water fountain; to feel safe in a city where no one seems interested in recognizing you, a city on the other side of the world, far from all the anxiety of the previous months, the highways, the police car sirens, the motel rooms where you could only stay one night and had to leave in a hurry, ringing telephones, urgent door knocks, boarding calls in airports, the sound of steps behind you in a back alley. To see Rossio Square through the eyes of this man that first morning in Lisbon, the pale man in the dark suit and the sunglasses reading English newspapers in the Pastelaria Suiça, or pretending that he was reading, using the large pages as a screen, anonymous among all the tables although it would have taken little effort to notice how different he was, not because of any feature in particular, but something else about him, a strange aura of solitude like that of an animal or a statue, or one of the mannequins in the windows of those tailor shops he would later pass as he walked down the street with his armful of newspapers, a street that led to an arch of white stone or marble and into a misty glow where one could look up and see the silhouette of another bronze king on horseback atop a column; or perhaps, he found himself walking past the shops and bars of Cais do Sodré, not really knowing how he got there, turning onto the backstreets where it smelled of beer and urine and rotting fish, places barely reached by daylight.

The hotel and the food were very cheap, and when he had exchanged money at the airport they had given him a wad of cash so big that for a few moments he felt newly rich. But he would run out of money soon, he didn't know how to get more, and he still had to buy a ticket to Africa and get by until the departure date.

He took a taxi to Cais do Sodré on his first day in Lisbon, or maybe it was a streetcar. He walked down the narrow Arsenal Street or along the river. It was an intensely bright morning so he wore sunglasses. He began to recognize signs that confirmed he was on the right track: a certain thickness in the air, bars with foreign names, neon hotel signs, half-opened doors leading to darkly lit stairs. It was mid-morning and the streets were already lined with women and girls. Old women with thick makeup; women with low-cut dresses leaning out windows decorated with geraniums in tin cans; African women; Indian women; Arab women.

As he got deeper into the neighborhood, he began to see other men: sailors pushing their way along the sidewalks, marines in uniform; soldiers in their last days before departing to the colonies in Africa—a raw and alcoholic masculinity. He looked out of place in his suit and sunglasses, which gave him an air of distinction but also depravity. Almost instinctually, his eyes looked for the drunkest sailor, one who could fall behind the rest of the group so he could push him into an alley and steal his wallet and documentation. It felt like Montreal, Saint Louis, or New Orleans—a jungle of smells and human forms, the promise of decadence and adventure, docked boats that would soon be departing for cities that made all his favorite lies seem plausible. Head chef on a cargo boat on the Mississippi. First officer taking time off after a grueling voyage. A war correspondent trying to get to the colonies in Africa so he could report on the conflict. James Bond introduces himself as John Bryce, an ornithologist, when he arrives on the island of Dr. Julius No. He recognized a few drunk conversations in English and a faint familiar smell. John Bryce sounds like a real name. Ornithology is the scientific study of birds.

Neon signs lined a stretch of walls corroded by the salty humidity of the ocean. Pink, red, and blue incandescent letters hung below balconies and clotheslines. They announced the entrances to the Jakarta, the Oslo, the Copenhagen, the Burma, the Arizona Bar, the Niagara Bar, the California Bar, the Bolero Bar.

To smell, at last, something familiar—roasted beef fat and butter-fried potatoes, air freshener, the musty carpets of those bars with red and black curtains. His eyes set on the most tempting of them all. Inside a stone arch: a neon cactus with a Texan hat, a beer, and a name that still exists today, forty-five years later, TEXAS BAR.

7

I had been writing for over three months and the words were flowing like music played with eyes closed. I felt removed from my external reality like the musician who leans into his instrument, oblivious to the sounds of clinking glasses, cocktail shakers, and low conversations; immune to all distraction and attentive to every interior impulse and intuition, anything that could be fertile ground for my writing.

My son was born and by the time my wife returned from the hospital, exhausted and happy with the baby in her arms, a small cap and wool blanket protecting him from the December cold, I had already resumed my writing. I would go to the pharmacy to buy diapers and on the way back stop for paper and whatever cheap whiskey I could afford. Alcohol and nicotine seemed as necessary as ink and paper.

Any unexpected event or meeting could transport me right away to the world of my novel. A photograph of William Burroughs in the newspaper gave me the look of the old trumpeter who would play the role model and mentor: dissolute and severe, dignified, black tie and a coat, hat and glasses, the sunken face with a funereal air. One afternoon I stopped writing before the usual time because I had to go meet with an acquaintance who lived in Albaicín. I arrived, feeling ill-tempered and remorseful for abandoning my work, only to find more guests, a man and a woman. The man was tall, robust, black, very talkative. He wore a gold watch, thick rings, and had one of those French-

Caribbean accents. His booming voice reverberated in the air every time he broke into laughter. The woman was blond, white, almost colorless. She had light eyes, straight hair, and sat quietly with her back erect, drinking tea from a cup with pale blue motifs like the thin veins beneath her translucent skin. She seemed undaunted.

The man was an antiques dealer. The young woman was his secretary. As soon as I saw her, I thought of García Lorca's line from *Poet in New York*: "the blond women's chlorophyll." When we were introduced she spoke her name softly: Laurel. On the taxi ride home, I had already decided that in my novel her name would be Daphne, like the nymph who turns into a laurel trying to escape from Apollo, and that both of them would have a secondary but decisive role in the plot.

The first thing Adam does in Genesis is name the animals. In *Don Quixote*, a novel whose very thread is woven before the eyes of the reader, the nobleman Alonso Quijano invents a name for himself, his horse, and his loved one, Dulcinea del Toboso, a name he finds "musical and uncommon and significant." Names in literature sound so natural and inevitable, it's easy to forget someone had to come up with them. Proust's Madame Verdurin would not be as ridiculous if her name were not Madame Verdurin. The beauty of the Duchess of Guermantes would not have the same radiance if her name were not Orianne. Captain Ahab's name is a sign of his obsession, an attribute as defining as his prosthetic leg, carved from the tusk of a narwhal. The name contains the sound of the leg pounding the deck of the *Pequod* in those long nights of insomnia.

Fiction begins with the names of the characters. Philip Marlowe, Sansón Carrasco, Isidora Rufete, Frédéric Moreau, Clawdia Chauchat, Hans Castorp, Beatriz Viterbo, Moses Herzog, Teresa Panza. The wrong name can condemn a character to implausibility. A name is not a label or a symbol, but a sound that strikes a chord in the reader's imagination. Not knowing Lisbon, I tried to intuit its mood and feel from the syllables and vowels of the name. One never knows when interruption will lead to discovery, when a break from writing will be more productive for the work than its continuation.

•

It was at the end of a chapter, halfway through a page, when the words just stopped coming to me. The effortless flow of writing abruptly stopped, like a radio station whose frequency is suddenly lost, or the first part of *Don Quixote*, which ends unexpectedly as the duel between the nobleman and the Vizcaíno is about to start—their horses are ready, their swords are drawn, everyone around them is staring in silence. Cervantes says he can't continue the story because that's the end of the manuscript on which his account is based. Perhaps there is more truth to this joke than meets the eye: Cervantes dramatizes the creative act of writing, the emptiness of the page, the void that hangs from the last written word or the flashing cursor, the limit between what is and what is yet to be, that which is not even in the writer's conscience and doesn't seem to emerge from it but from the nerve endings at our fingertips, like ink flowing from a pen and transforming a sheet of paper.

Writing is like the exploration of new frontiers, much less laborious, but similar in nature to sailing in uncharted waters or pushing through an unknown forest in search of a clearing for cultivation. Writing is a journey from the known to the unknown. It is not the drawing of a map but the exploration of a new territory with the mere guidance of the cardinal points. Previous ideas are only a point of departure. The torch that illuminates the few steps ahead of you only lights up in the act of writing. Every pause is a brief relief and another point of departure. A period at the end of a paragraph can be the sudden discovery of the end of a chapter. Interruptions in the story stimulate a primal curiosity, the urge to know more, the insatiability of the "to be continued" on the last page of the comic books we devoured as children.

In other times, exterior pauses would also play an important role in modulating a story's rhythm: the moment when the pen ran dry and had to be dipped in more ink; or when you got to the edge of the paper on a typewriter and had to return the carriage or insert a new piece in the platen—the black-rubber fog of type marks, traces of every word typed.

A blank piece of paper goes in the typewriter and a finished one is added to the stacked manuscript. Progress was visible and tangible, from a few scattered pages at the beginning to the solid block of paper after a few months; each millimeter was the product of great effort, like the growth rings of a tree. And there was also the pause to light a new cigarette, and the way the smoke filled the room and thickened the air, the overflowing ashtray, the nicotine circulating through the blood and feeding and satisfying addictive reflexes in the neural connections. The thought of writing without tobacco was as absurd as typing without paper. It was the flame of the lighter that lit up the imagination, its reddish light coming alive with each puff. We believed, almost religiously, that liver cirrhosis, emphysema, and lung cancer were the side effects of the creative process, clear signs of talent.

Tobacco smoke was the very air of jazz clubs, bars, and the writer's studio, the translucent gauze that accentuated the glow of a woman's features and gestures in an old film. Quitting tobacco seemed like an existential capitulation, submission to the soft tyranny of health, marriage, parenthood, and office life. Being healthy was like being right-wing. Night was more poetic than day, torment and anguish more admirable than tranquility, drunkenness more visionary than sobriety. We did not suspect that intellectual brilliance could be as much of a mirage as the effervescence of cocaine.

•

I had finished a chapter with the word *Lisbon* and could not bring myself to start the next one. The daunting task of writing a novel set in a city that I had never visited could no longer be sustained. At the end of the chapter the protagonist is about to board a plane to Lisbon. Until then, he had been living in a Paris hotel, spending his days in bed reading detective novels. I had a general idea of what would happen when he arrived in Lisbon, but I did not know how to imagine it with the level of visual precision that is required to tell a made-up story as if one were simply recalling it. There would be night chases; a club with a neon sign that read BURMA; a sick man, pale like a skull, resting on a hospital bed; a small painting by Cézanne with one of those mountains he painted over and over throughout the years; a fight to the death on the edge of a cliff; a passionate encounter between two lovers, a reconciliation but also a farewell; a concert where master and student play together—the old master playing almost from the beyond, and the young student about to experience, in the course of two days, the vast yet fleeting power of love and music.

I was living vicariously through my writing. But everything was now on hold, like fragments of dreams that don't fit together; there were missing pieces, loose threads, isolated scenes. I had finished the chapter and added the page to the stack of paper that had been growing steadily since mid-September. I don't think I even got to put a new sheet of paper in the typewriter before realizing that if the novel was to continue I had no choice but to travel to Lisbon.

•

But that would not be easy. I had a newborn and a three-year-old. My wife was weak from labor, and to make matters worse, I was distant with her. She was depressed. It would have been difficult for her to take care of the children on her own. I also could not afford more than a day or two off from work. When I finally asked for permission at work and reserved train tickets and a cheap hotel room in Lisbon, I took even longer to decide when to tell my wife.

I took the train to Madrid in the early morning of the first day of January. I felt free but also filled with remorse, like a fugitive and a traitor. Years pass, memories fade, but regret for all the pain I've caused does not go away.

I arrived in Madrid mid-morning and the streets were empty. The roads looked wider without traffic. It was a strange stillness and silence. At the corner of the Bank of Spain there was a puddle of vomit and broken bottles, lasting residues of New Year's Eve. I didn't know anyone in Madrid. The train to Lisbon would not depart until eleven at night. It was one of those cold, bright winter days that by mid-afternoon have already given in to night and desolation, the dark tunnel that is the end of Sunday. I ate at a cheap restaurant on Atocha Street, one of those dull taverns frequented by travelers from the provinces who dare not leave the station's vicinity. Time seemed to stand still and the gloomy atmosphere was starting to get to me so I decided to go to a cinema. I watched *The Name of the Rose*. The young monk who learned everything from his mentor and years later finds himself remembering the old man made me think of the troubled pianist in my novel and his devotion for the teacher with whom he would share the stage in Lisbon. In novels and films, beneath the surface of events lie the skeletons of oral histories from time immemorial, the struggle and the search, the journey to enlightenment, wisdom, or regret.

It was already dark by the time I came out of the cinema and the streets were quickly filling up with people. I had left my bag in the lockers at the train station and was walking leisurely through Madrid with my hands in my coat pockets. Madrid overwhelmed me. I was used to Granada, where everything was at a smaller scale.

Back then, trains would leave from the old station, under the vaults of iron and glass. The platform was dimly lit and golden letters spread over the blue background of the Lusitania Express. It was like a scene from a novel, a promise of adventure. Lisbon was listed on the destination sign. It was all really happening: I was going to board this train, I was going to be one of the faces behind the window when the train departed at eleven o'clock that evening. The departure times, the track numbers, final destinations resounded over the noise of trains arriving and departing.

The fact that I would be spending the night in an uncomfortable bunk did not matter. By dawn the train would be running through the green and misty fields near Lisbon. Up until that point, I had only traveled a handful of times inside Spain. Now I was traveling alone to a foreign capital.

I only had three days, exactly three days and two nights in the hotel. I carried just the basics, a handbag, a notebook, a camera, a map of Lisbon; none of the burdens of family outings, the baby car seat, diapers, bottles, toys, pacifiers, thermometers, talcum powder, moisturizers, strollers, audiobooks, suitcases I could barely close, much less fit in the trunk, towels in case of car sickness.

I was alone, and this solitude combined with the imminence of departure made the commonplace shine under a new, mysterious light; a drunkenness that fed on itself.

The train rested on its track like a ship on a dock; all the windows were illuminated; an operator tapped the wheels and brakes with a hammer; crew members directed passengers; loudspeaker announcements echoed in the somber concavity of iron and glass; suspended against the vast glass wall, the clock struck closer to eleven as the minute hand gave a quick spasm; the arches of the great vault recalled the profile of a Gothic cathedral or a mosque, of aerial palaces reflected on the water. Some travelers leaned out the windows to wave goodbye, others stood by the train doors, one foot on the steps, one foot on the ground, as if not wanting to leave but also fearing the train would leave without them. It was an old express with tall cars painted military green-gray, long interior corridors, and individual compartments. In the sleeper cars, the golden signs stood out against a heraldic blue, like in the Orient Express. COMPAGNIE INTERNATIONALE DES WAGONS-LITS. Someone would be leaving Madrid on that train never to return; a beautiful woman would cross paths with me in the dimly lit corridor hours later when everybody else was asleep. The hour was finally here. The metallic doors began closing. A final announcement was made. Lisbon-bound, the Lusitania Express was about to depart.

The first few jolts of the train produced a physical and emphatic sense of travel; like that moment when musicians begin to play and their mighty stream of sound takes you with it; like immersing oneself in the first images of a film or the unmistakable first sentences of a book; as Gregor Samsa awoke one morning from uneasy dreams he found himself transformed in his bed into a gigantic insect; for a long time, I went to bed early; on the burning February morning Beatriz Viterbo died, after braving an agony that never for a single moment gave way to self-pity or fear; I wish I had seen nothing more than the man's hands; many years later, as he faced the firing squad, Colonel Aureliano Buendía was to remember that distant afternoon when his father took him to discover ice; I came to Comala because I had been told that my father, a man named Pedro Páramo, lived there. Every beginning is a once upon a time and the beginning of Genesis, the first verse of the *Iliad*, the first line of *Don Quixote* or *Lazarillo de Tormes* or *Moby-Dick*. Call me Ishmael. Well then, Your Worship should know first of all that they call me Lázaro de Tormes. If on a winter's night a traveler. The first time I laid eyes on Terry Lennox he was drunk in a Rolls-Royce Silver Wraith. Perhaps there is no better beginning than an impersonal statement of fact. Thus literature can claim or mimic the objectivity of the world. That is why my favorite first line is that of Flaubert's *Sentimental Education*; it marks the beginning of a trip and reads like an administrative record or logbook entry: *In front of the Quai St. Bernard, the Ville de Montereau, which was just about to start, was puffing great whirlwinds of smoke. It was six o'clock on the morning of the 15th of September, 1840.* At eleven o'clock on the night of January 1, 1987, the Lusitania Express left Madrid Atocha Station heading toward Lisbon. On May 8, 1968, at one-thirty in the morning, a traveler in his forties, wearing a dark suit and a raincoat, arrived at the Lisbon airport on a flight from London.

8

There is another, partially different, version of his arrival at the Texas Bar. It's morning, but perhaps earlier. He carries his suitcase, a raincoat, a travel bag. He has not stopped by the hotel. A young woman having a drink at the bar noticed the foreigner and his bag. He seemed lost, she said later. The bar was not too crowded yet, but it was quite lively even for that hour—Babelian, was how the old patrons and former waiters recalled it years later. Where could he have spent the rest of the night, from his arrival in Lisbon at one-thirty in the morning, carrying his bag, the city foreign and unfamiliar, the streets empty, balconies closed, ghost mannequins staring from behind the dark storefronts, the sound of water fountains doubling the silence of Rossio Square, its wet cobblestones shining like patent leather in the misty night.

Instead of taking him to the Hotel Portugal, perhaps the taxi drove directly to Cais do Sodré because he asked where he could find women and open bars. From the darkness and silence of the taxi, he emerged into the neon lights, loud music coming through the red curtains, the gregarious clamor of drunk, horny men. So unlike the others, so alone, so out of place. How many bars did he go to before settling for the Texas, all those hours with his suitcase and travel bag, exhausted, making his way through groups of rowdy sailors, couples dancing, women with low-cut dresses calling him from street corners or balcony windows adorned with red geraniums.

•

If he did not spend the first night in the Hotel Portugal, there is no way to account for those hours. He suddenly appeared in the Texas Bar with all the prestige of his patent foreignness, protected by the shadows in the wee hours of the morning, sitting before a beer, occasionally glancing at the woman who smiled at him from the other end of the bar. He signaled the bartender for another drink. In one of the many pasts he had improvised in conversations with strangers, he had run an exclusive cocktail bar in Acapulco for several years, nestled under a roof of palm leaves just steps from the water, waves washing over his feet and the golden sand, the sound of sea foam retreating. He did not smoke but had his lighter ready in case the woman down the bar needed a light; or maybe it was a matchbox; among his belongings they found one with the name and address of a restaurant in Toronto, the New Goravale. James Bond's Ronson lighter was silver and smooth like a cigarette case or a pistol. He examined his face in the mirror behind the bar. He was satisfied, albeit a bit nervous. *When you change a man's face you almost invariably change his future*, said Dr. Maxwell Maltz in his book. In the low light of the bar, he studied his reflection, the profile modified by cosmetic surgery, the nose less pointed, the chin less pronounced. He also glanced at the reflection of the young woman with short hair who kept looking at him. What a shame that he did not get a chance to correct his ears. *He was a solitary man*, he had read in a James Bond novel, *a man who walked alone and kept his heart to himself.*

From her corner at the bar, the woman raised her glass in a toast. They had noticed—almost recognized—each other the moment he walked through the red curtain and stood in silence letting his eyes adjust to the low light, taking in the unexpected breadth of the Texas Bar, a concavity of high stone arches and shadows, decorated with model boats, steering wheels, fishnets, paddles, portholes, identical to the Neptune Tavern in Montreal, which now seemed as though it were in a remote time, one that ceased to exist the moment he fired that shot. In the midst of all those people, the yelling, the loud music, the conversations, they instantly recognized their mutual oddity. She was by herself, sitting very straight, still new at this, barely smoking, barely drinking; alcohol and tobacco made her nauseous, made her lose sense of time, and even more so in this place where daylight could not reach her, this place where it was always the same endless night.

•

Imagination does not know how to predict anything. The woman's name was Maria, perhaps it still is. I have written first, middle, and last name and deleted them. When writing about real people it's easy to forget that they are vulnerable. Nor is she a stereotype: she stood out in that fog of faces and voices and smoke of the Texas Bar, precisely because she did not look like a prostitute. There's a photo of her in *Life* magazine, taken just a few weeks later. She's much younger than I had imagined. Her hair is short and dark, sixties-style. She wears no makeup, no tight dress, just a high-neck blouse, a sophisticated cut that highlights her slim figure. The blouse is rolled up above her wrists. Her hands are long, her nails oval. She is wearing a bracelet and a long pendant, perhaps a crucifix or religious medal. She is looking into the camera. Her smile is young, intelligent, pleasant. She seems to enjoy being photographed, but is also a bit nervous. When that issue of the magazine got to Lisbon at the end of June, newsstand vendors and waiters in Cais do Sodré would recognize her on the streets and tell her she looked like a movie star. She will keep a copy of the magazine well-hidden for many years.

Back then, she had just started sex work. She had to support her parents and her brothers; the parents are old, the brothers are lazy and sick. She pretends to work at a store; that is why she gets to the Texas Bar so early. She prefers that time of day, it's usually quiet, without the crowds and fights that come later. The men who come around in the morning are usually younger and educated, though often weird. She never stays at the bar or with a client past five in the afternoon. She must get back to her house in time, as if she had a regular workday. If no one in her family or her neighborhood finds out, if no one could even imagine what she does for a living, then sleeping with men for money will feel less shameful, a stain she can wash away before leaving the room with her money, before walking back onto the streets of Lisbon like a regular woman, her head slightly bowed, her steps quick and short on the mosaic tiles. The strangest things in life happen without much notice.

Almost forty years later, with her eyes the color of sour milk, her gaze fixed on a picture of Saint Anthony hanging on a wall that she can't see, Maria recalls the day she became a prostitute. It was a Sunday night. She had left the cinema and was walking home alone. She was feeling melancholic, thinking about the film, when she walked in front of a parked taxi. The taxi driver saw her coming. He was leaning on the car having a smoke. Out of the corner of her eye, she saw someone in the backseat, a lit cigarette, a bulky figure, male and dark. She had not ceased to be perplexed by the importance of tobacco in all those transactions. The driver observed her face, the outline of her lips, her chin and cheekbones, her eyes, the crooked heels, the wool coat, the simple skirt. He asked her something random just to make her stop. Did she live in the area? Was she coming from the movies?

He offered her a cigarette. It's American, he said. She shook her head. Inside the car, staring from behind the window as in a funeral urn, the fleshy face examined her. The driver moved closer to her and with a soft, affable voice, somehow disconnected from his beady eyes and facial expression, said that if she was interested in earning five hundred escudos, all she had to do was get in the taxi with the gentleman who was waiting for him, an acquaintance, someone he trusted. He would take them somewhere private and clean, not too far from there. The leather seat creaked as she got in the car. The ceiling light illuminated the man's hands but not his face. A thick band adorned his ring finger.

•

Time did not dilute the memories. As she descended into blindness, the near past blurred but those images of her youth only became more vivid. It was like being in the protective darkness of a movie theater while her past played on the screen in full color, the glossy ads of *Life* magazine, her photograph, smiling and calm, standing by the entrance of the Texas Bar. She kept a copy of that issue in her dresser, under an old pair of bedsheets that had belonged to her mother. But her daughter was getting older and Maria feared she would find the magazine and recognize her mother in the photo.

The imagination does not know how to simulate the unexpected, the abrupt, the changes that take place over a long period of time. In May 1968, Maria was twenty-five. In 2006, she is a blind woman who walks heavy and slow. A white frost covers her eyes. A journalist from Lisbon has found her. For the first time in many years, someone asks her about him. It brings her alarm, but also delight. She lives with her husband in a slum on the outskirts of the city. Her neighbors are mostly immigrants. The sidewalks are covered in trash and there's graffiti all over the peeling walls and metal shutters of defunct businesses. Young African men hang out on the street corners. Every now and then, a drug dealer's SUV roars by at full speed blasting hip-hop. Her apartment is on the third or fourth floor of a building with no elevator. Her house is clean and modest, with crochet decorations on the curtains and the furniture, framed images of Saint Anthony holding baby Jesus and the three pastors worshiping Our Lady of Fatima, the photograph of her dead daughter in a silver frame atop the television, family photos she cannot see but knows exactly where each one is and feels around them as she dusts the wall.

The broad, wrinkled face does not bear a trace of resemblance with the young woman who appeared in *Life* magazine. Her open eyes move in short, nervous spasms toward the voice that asks her questions, pausing at the light that comes through the window. Sometimes it takes her a while to answer, but not for lack of memory. Other sounds distract her, the animals: canaries on the balcony and in the kitchen, two dogs, one of them growling at her guest, two medium-size tortoises. The woman moves slowly through the narrow paths between the furniture, careful not to trip over the tortoises who are constantly walking around, making a peculiar sound with their nails on the linoleum. Music plays on the street, a reverberating bass, motorcycles. The woman speaks in a monotone, her voice as expressionless as her face, the sound barely rising above the chirping of the birds. One of the tortoises is stuck in the corner behind the television. It wants to move forward but its saurian, scaly snout keeps bumping against the wall.

•

She remembers the time when she frequented the Texas Bar and supported her family by sleeping with strangers. Her remorse has been
tempered by the passage of time and a growing sense of unreality.
That young woman was her but also someone else entirely. The day
she took the magazine out of the drawer and went outside to throw it
in the garbage, she was already starting to lose her vision. She had
difficulty distinguishing faces in photographs and reading the small
letters in English. She could barely see the pendant she wore that day
to pose for the foreign photographer, but she remembered it well, along
with the bracelet she wore on her left wrist, a gift from a client, gold;
the man was a jeweler.

She could not remember what had happened to the swimsuit the
American from the Texas Bar had gifted her. They were waiting for a
taxi. He was so pale, somewhat less attractive in the broad daylight,
thin lips, pointy nose, cleft chin. A green swimsuit, yes sir, she says
with a smile and her eyes closed. It was made with a synthetic fabric
that fit her body very well and dried quickly. She remembers touching it. They had walked into the store together after she saw it in the
display window. She liked the way she looked next to the tall American,
American or Canadian, she could not tell, with his dark sunglasses and
his hands in his pockets. He had left his coat and luggage at the Texas
Bar, saying he would pick them up later.

She remembered it vividly. She had walked toward him along the
bar, still unsure in her high heels, glass and cigarette in hand like the
actresses she had seen in movies. Once face-to-face, she saw his light
blue eyes and the graying hair on the sides. He looked distinguished.
He would whisper softly into her ear, burying his face in her hair,
speaking words that sounded all the more exciting and mysterious
because they were in a different language, an acoustic inebriation of
promises. Now and then, he would say something in Spanish, pronouncing his words very carefully. She smiled and nodded even when she
did not understand, throwing her head back, a trace of lipstick on her
cigarette as she removed it from her mouth, her hand on his elbow,
knees touching, both seated on the tall bar stools, their reflection behind

the bottles. She liked glancing at the mirror and seeing herself with a man so different from the regulars, so serious and shy, barely touching her; in fact, barely even looking her in the eye.

He said, or so she understood, that he had arrived that morning on a cruise ship. He did not mention where he came from, how long he would stay, or the purpose of his visit. He could be a businessman with lots of money. A blue-eyed man who speaks English and wears a suit and alligator shoes must surely be rich. There was also a certain ease in the way he handled money or offered to light a woman's cigarette, a reserved yet firm gesture. The lighter did not look expensive. The bar was filling up, the crowd was getting louder, but they remained in their own little world, very close to each other though barely touching. There were awkward silences when he would stare at the floor or at the bottom of his glass or simply close his eyes. Then he would begin to ask or propose something she could not understand: transactions of few, simple words in English or Spanish, aided by gestures, complicated by currency conversions, exhaustion, impatience, his voice growing darker in her ear.

•

Moments later he was walking clumsily next to her, a bit behind, not used to keeping up with the pace of another person, which was even more difficult on the uneven pavement and narrow sidewalks, the winding alleys and steep stairways. He saw her stop in front of a display window. Mannequins with frozen smiles stared from the other side. They stood in front of cardboard palm trees and under a paper sun that hung from a piece of string. He was the one who offered to buy the swimsuit, she emphasized, just as she had thirty-eight years earlier. *Like it?* he asked. She nodded. Now she repeated the words to show she had not forgotten them, *like, yes, beach.*

The salesman turned friendly after seeing her in the company of the foreigner, a man well-dressed and serious. He did not remove his sunglasses after he entered and had to lower his head a bit to get in through the door. He was tall in her memory. He took out a handful of bills from one of his pockets and left it on the counter for the salesman to figure out the change. That's also how he paid for the taxi and the room and the three hundred escudos he promised for her services. He watched with indifference as the money left his hands, money that did not quite feel real, and vanished, the way he had watched so many things happen in his life.

She fell silent for a moment, backlit against the light that poured in through the window, while the tortoises walked under the chairs, the table, and the narrow space under the sofa. She said she never felt anything with other men who paid her, but she had enjoyed being with him. She repeated the words she heard in her soap operas: that she had given herself to him, that they had made love. She folded her hands on her lap and turned toward her guest, who had long ago stopped asking questions. In a low voice and with unexpected cheekiness, she said: "He was a hunk of a man."

She watched him sleep after collapsing from exhaustion with a hoarse moan. His feet protruded from the bed. It was a small room, rather sordid, one she had used several times. The ceiling had water stains. The mattress was thin and the springs were loud. The dresser mirror reflected their bodies.

He passed out the second their bodies separated. There he lay next to her, his mouth open, breathing through his nose and making strange sounds, going into quick spasms, mumbling who knows what, a stranger with an improbable name for someone who only spoke English, Ramon, an American or Canadian with a small scar on his forehead and the chin of a Hollywood actor.

But she had to go. She had to get home soon after five. She washed her body in the small bathroom. Through the window she could see the clear sky, the sea of roofs, a few cats.

He was awake by the time she came out. He asked her if she had children. She still remembered the word he used: *Bambino?* But she did not speak to anyone about her daughter. The girl died young, she does not explain how but points to the photo atop the television, the girl's face smiling with the anachronism of the dead.

In the taxi back to the Texas Bar, she kept glancing at her watch. If it took much longer, she would be late. She waited in the car while he collected his luggage. Seeing him come out with bags and coat under his arm, so pale, his sunglasses still on, she had an intuition of how odd he was, of everything she did not know and would never find out about him. She later remembered it was she who recommended the Hotel Portugal.

He kept looking out the rear window and occasionally looked at himself in the rearview mirror. Sometimes he stopped to look at her, sitting very straight beside him, her knees together, the bag with the swimsuit on her lap, in her mind becoming the woman she was for her neighbors and her parents. She would ask the taxi driver to drop her off a few blocks from her house so she could approach as if coming from the tram.

He said that he would like to see her in the swimsuit, that they should go to the beach early the next day, *beach*. The taxi stopped at the corner of João das Regras Street. She pointed at the sign, HOTEL PORTUGAL. Before saying goodbye they agreed on the next day: nine, hotel door, swimsuit, *beach*.

At exactly that time, she showed up at the hotel, unsure about her appearance, fearing she would make the receptionist suspicious. The receptionist looked at the register and with a tone of pity and mockery said that Mr. Ramon had left the hotel just an hour earlier; in fact, he had left Lisbon as well. Apparently, he had received an urgent telegram and had booked a plane ticket by phone.

•

In the course of several days and nights, he was also seen in other bars. Witnesses remembered him being alone most of the time, sitting in a corner, drinking his beer slowly to prolong his stay. The neon names of the bars glow in a distant time like in the night fog of Lisbon, exotic names flashing intermittently like a secret code: Arizona Bar, Niagara Bar, California Bar, Europa Bar, Bolero Bar, Tagide Nightclub, Maxime's.

At Maxime's, he met Gloria. He spent at least a night with her. She was blond, slender, and had short, curly hair. Perhaps she was the one who walked into the lobby of the Hotel Portugal with him and was not allowed to continue to the room. He offered her a dress and a pair of stockings and she thought it was a gift, a present from her foreign customer who was so formal and shy. But it wasn't a gift. He was trying to pay her in kind. She remembered he had a nervous habit of pinching the tip of his right ear and was always looking for American and British newspapers. When asked how they communicated given the language barrier, she laughed and said they spoke the international language of love.

Who knows what lies in the memories of others, how many successive pasts they hide. They spoke softly in the room of the boardinghouse where she took him after they were turned away from the Hotel Portugal. Neither one understood the other and he told her what he had done. It was a relief to be able to say aloud why he had been on the run for over a month, to hear himself reveal his true identity and his crime without consequences. He was not inventing anything. To speak the truth and remain invisible and unpunished. To speak words that correspond to actual events, real names, real places, the hunting rifle he leaned on the windowsill of that disgusting bathroom, the focused scope, the tip of the index finger curling around the trigger as the man in the blue suit rested his hands on the railing of the balcony.

The image from the binoculars acquired an absolute precision in the lens of the scope. He could see the man's mouth moving, the broad black lips, the slanted eyes. He stared at the freshly shaved skin, the neatly trimmed mustache, the blue silk of his suit, the expensive cuffs, the great pretender, the holy preacher and lustful ape, laughing silently in the lens, right in the crosshairs.

He said it all in his usual mumble while the naked woman followed the instructions he delivered with his hands and the few Spanish words he remembered from his days in Mexico, arching her spine, her blond hair tousled over his groin, the dyed mane that covered half her face when she finally looked up, a sweaty lock on her forehead, wiping her lips with the back of her hand while he continued talking and talking in that squalid room where no one could find him, at the end of a narrow street and an even narrower stairway. The open window let in the voices of drunks on the street, the smells of the port, the sirens of the boats moving through the fog.

A red lightbulb hung from the ceiling. The bed and the two bodies were reflected in the closet mirror, a piece from a bourgeois room thirty years earlier. She smoked and looked at him talk, observing the thin, colorless lips pronouncing words she did not understand, the shifty eyes that did not look at hers, the protruding ears, the hair that remained perfectly combed. Several weeks later, when foreign agents and plainclothes policemen started asking her questions, she learned to wait for the moment when they would pull out his photo and make a flirtatious yet shy gesture before nodding nervously, flattered, feeling pity and perhaps a retrospective disgust for the man who was now in a London prison cell, paler than ever, awaiting deportation and, in all likelihood, the electric chair.

9

I left the Santa Apolónia station and started walking, not really knowing where I was going. I was in no hurry to get in a taxi and arrive at the hotel. It was eight in the morning, the sky was clear, and the air was warm and slightly humid. The light was so soft you could almost touch it, a welcoming caress. I was coming from winter and the hard, icy light of Granada and Madrid. My eyes have never seen light like the one that washes over Lisbon; its colors have an attenuated quality: the blue of the sky and the red of the roof tiles, the blues and greens and yellows and ochers of walls punished by the maritime weather; the brightness of the azulejo tiles; the red, open flowers on the tops of tropical trees with trunks like the backs of elephants.

With my bag in hand I passed the line of taxis without stopping. The sun was climbing over the buildings, stretching over the motionless blade of the river, the azulejo tiles of the facades, windows, clotheslines, the stepped terraces along the hillside. Warm smells of breakfast emanated from the cafes and bakeries. I was walking alongside rows of abandoned businesses; streets named after old trade goods, Terreiro do Trigo, Jardim do Tabaco. The feeling of remoteness was even more pronounced than in Paris or Italy, the only places outside Spain that I had been to. Everyone has clear images of Paris, Florence, Rome. No image can capture Lisbon. As I walked, I could hear bits of conversations coming from kiosks, cafes, grocery stores; the language had an acoustic equivalence to the city's light: the volume was much lower than in Spain, a muttered tone, familiar yet indecipherable, vowels that evaporated at the end of words.

To my left was the river, the docks, the buildings of the harbor, and the high prows of the ships; to my right, at the foot of a hill that ascended toward the white bell towers of the churches and a roofline with Chinese curvatures, were small businesses, arches like tunnels leading into uphill alleys, narrow like the ones in Albaicín and with a similar smell too, humidity, sewers, garbage.

The thought that no one here knew who I was gave me a feeling of lightness, an impudent happiness that was self-sufficient and unconcerned with consequences. I had freed myself from all ties, obligations, routines, loyalties, like Jules Verne's aeronauts ridding themselves of all the heavy and unnecessary things that kept their balloon from ascending. I was discovering a capacity I had rarely exercised in my life: the ability to radically change my circumstances and immerse myself in the unexpected; to forget entirely what I had left behind; to lose myself, like in a jungle or a submarine, in the things that really interested me, a novel, a film, a song, an emotion; to disappear entirely, without a trace, not even a thread that could guide me back, no remorse, no nostalgia, no memory.

I did not miss anyone and no memories could distract me from that present. I was not thinking about my wife, who was overwhelmed taking care of the two children. I was not thinking about the three-year-old boy nor the baby who that very same day was turning one month old. I was not thinking about my job in Granada that awaited me in just three days.

In an effort to resist all thoughts, I even stopped thinking about the book that brought me to Lisbon. I was my gaze, my ears, an objective camera, the strength of my legs, the joy of breathing that humid air and the smells of the harbor, the sounds of the seagulls and boat sirens; I was the hand that tightened around the bag handle; I was the simple, impersonal happiness of sitting at a cafe, watching strangers, hearing voices nearby, drinking a coffee with milk that soothed my stomach after the night of poor sleep on the train, eating a fresh roll, soft and warm to the touch, and learning its name, *pão de Deus*.

The three days ahead were a blank canvas as full of promise as the blank notebook in my pocket. The arrival by train, the cool morning, the sunlight shining on the river, the rooftops, and the streets were the clean and definitive beginning of something, the first page of a novel, the fullness of a world that has just begun.

●

I walked tirelessly and without a destination. I was hypnotized by the city and disoriented by the lack of sleep. The name and address of the hotel were written in my notebook, but I did not know how far it was and I had no map. I was following the river in the direction of a boat that was sailing west. The silhouette of the 25th of April Bridge could be seen in the distance. Those of us from the interior are quite affected by the sight of the sea and the beauty of bridges extending high across rivers wider than one could have imagined.

I turned a corner and found myself in the emptiest square I had ever seen. One of the sides was open to the great expanse of the Tagus River, boundless and blinding in those mornings when the sun infuses the water with a mercurial brightness, the shimmer of polished metal. I recognized the sight that the painter Juan Vida had described for me one day at the office while doing a quick sketch on a piece of paper: the triumphal arch supported by its six columns, and in the distance, in the exact center of the square, surrounded by an iron gate, a pedestal with an elephant and a horse, and high above, much higher, a bronze king on his grand horse, mid-stride toward the south, crushing the bronze snakes in his path, while the king looks west toward the mouth of the river, feathers shooting from his helmet like a geyser, and the usual seagull looking out from the top. The dimensions of the square exhibited an Austro-Hungarian excess. People were leaving the docked ferries in waves and quickly disappeared through the arcades and into the shaded corners and streets. Remembering Juan's sketch of Commerce Square, I identified the two columns flanking the stairway that leads to the water. On top of each column there is a stone ball, and on top of each ball a seagull. The square enters the river like a ship's prow with the entire city at its back.

The tide has subsided but the slippery algae makes it difficult to go down the grooved ramp. The wind has a moist freshness and smells of the sea. A figure, just a few meters away standing still before the water, appears to be much farther away, dwarfed by the vast oceanic backdrop, isolated, dazed, anonymous in her silhouette of a traveler on a riverbank, like a Friedrich figure, placed there by the painter or the photographer that captures her image to emphasize the vastness of the space.

Some faces are prophetic, says Balzac. There are also places that shake you as soon as you arrive with a feeling or premonition of stories about to become visible in your imagination like a flashback, invented memories that are more persuasive and vivid than real ones, fantastic lucid dreams that a rude awakening saves from oblivion.

What I was experiencing was already translating into the future pages of my interrupted novel. I began taking photos and notes. I did not want to forget anything. Standing at the center of the square, I took a photograph of Cais das Colunas that mirrored Juan's sketch, and right in the middle there was a figure facing away, a figure that could have been me staring at the river or a character in my story. I wish I could tell a story the way a photographer can: stripped down to basics; or the way Edward Hopper can tell without telling, suppressing all kinds of plot details and leaving the core, the essence, the pure schema of oral histories, which exist and are passed on without anyone having to write them, invariable in their basic form but never told with the same words, like a jazz composition that remains the same but never sounds the same, as impersonal as words and turns of phrase can be, yet capable of conveying in each instance the most intimate things, songs that are simultaneously public, shared, secret.

I am the one remembering that January morning almost twenty-seven years ago, and I both am and am not that young man who has just arrived in Lisbon, the young man standing on the edge of Commerce Square a few steps from the soft waves that wash over the ramp and recede as if slipping on the polished stone and the green algae. I am the one who takes that photograph where a figure will appear in the distance facing away, and I am also that silhouette, which could belong to an anonymous traveler or a fictional character. In a painting or a photo, there is no need for a figure to have a name or a face that turns around or, even less, a personal history beyond the immediate and visible. There is an exact equivalence between lack of information and mystery. There is no before or after. A drawing is mostly empty space. The square and the pier and the river and the figure say without words everything that needs to be said. Poetry is going no further than a story needs to breathe and weigh with everything that is left unsaid.

•

My hotel was cheap and far from the center, on a dull street I have forgotten, beyond Eduardo VII Park. I remember the narrow bed with a worn blue comforter, facing a window overlooking a horizon of roofs. I did not tire of looking at that light without edges, the soft red of the tiles and the pale blue of the sky made up of glazes instead of a continuous glare.

My early arrival meant the morning kept dilating. Time in Lisbon seemed to have slower flow, it was soothing, like the light. I left my bag on the bed, unopened, and washed my face. I looked different in the mirror, in my newcomer's solitude, free of biographical burdens, a guest who fills out a form and shows an identification document, a photograph, a name that might as well be fictional, an address, a place and date of birth, nothing more, a signature at the bottom of a page.

I left with my camera and notebook. The receptionist gave me a map of the city. I had the entire day ahead, and the next one, and the last one, until ten at night. I would get the most out of every hour until the train departed for Madrid. It was January 2. My youngest had turned one month. Maybe he had had a bad night and had turned red crying, extending his tiny hand into the darkness, looking for his mother. He was so small, he barely filled out his pajamas. His nails were transparent and fragile like the wings of an insect. His hair was blond and soft, his forehead broad, his eyes light and astonished. It's possible I barely thought about him.

I wasn't thinking about anything or anyone who wasn't in my small island of time and fiction, in my three days of refuge in Lisbon. I was going on thirty-one years old and had never breathed such complete freedom, the ability to give myself entirely to my vocation and whim, to wander alone and explore the promising and foreign city, hospitable to my purpose from the moment I stepped foot on it and allowed myself to get lost in its winding and slippery sidewalks, its cobblestone alleys and stairways; as leisurely as one rides the tram, looking out the window, sedentary yet in motion, passing and watching things pass, witnessing the city unfold like a handheld fan, ascending and descending before its eyes, sometimes on the crest and sometimes on the trough of a slow swell, sometimes so close to a wall you can almost touch it, then, suddenly, facing the great maritime expanse, like being on the top of a bridge or the edge of a waterfall.

I understood from the beginning that this was the city I needed. I came to her guided by the momentum of my novel; now I just had to keep my eyes and ears and imagination open to new discoveries. The map of Lisbon in my pocket was also the paper on which I would draw the routes of the characters, the meetings, the chases, the escapes that were becoming more tangible as I explored the city, gradually taking shape around the plot of its streets like words that become visible under a flame or images that come to life in a darkroom.

•

Perhaps the last time I had indulged so carelessly in daydreams was as a child playing by myself the whole morning or afternoon, imagining entire worlds in the bedrooms and the attic.

Time and money. Everything was cheaper in Lisbon. For the first time in my life I did not feel broke. I could take a taxi back to the hotel and eat in good restaurants without feeling remorse. In places like that I was almost a fictional character, a foreigner traveling by himself, studying the menu and the wine list, secretly amazed that I could afford to eat there, pretending that it was nothing new to me.

I discovered that I enjoyed eating alone and observing people. It was my private feast. For my first lunch, after a long morning walk, I ate my first seafood casserole, my first *vinho verde*, a half bottle served very cold, my first *aguardente velha*. The sweet drowsiness dissipated after I started walking again. Now the shadows were more humid, and the sun shone golden over the facades and balconies facing west.

Lisbon was the crisp light seen from the shade, the exotic next to the provincial, the faces and the colors and the smells of Africa next to the cafes and the stalls selling roasted chestnuts, their warm smell dissolving in the cool air of the evening. In Rossio Square, from the sunny sidewalk of the Pastelaria Suiça, I spotted the strange metal lattice of the Santa Justa Lift tower. Riding the elevator was like being in a futuristic device from the nineteenth century, one of Jules Verne's flying machines, a cabin in Captain Nemo's submarine. On the highest point of the lookout, leaning over the railing, I contemplated the Alfama hill, the square towers of San Jorge Castle rising over the woods, the dark cypresses, the high garden walls, the river in the distance, the copper brightness of the setting sun. For a moment I thought I was seeing the Alhambra from Saint Nicholas Square. The tower of Graça Convent reminded me of Santa Maria Church. The horizon of the Tagus River was smooth and hazy like the Vega. I was seeing what I had imagined when writing the first drafts of the novel, my mirage city, a Granada by the sea.

10

His mother was nineteen years old when he was born. She gave birth eight more times in the next twenty years. Sometimes she got drunk by herself, other times with her husband, who was also an alcoholic. They lived in a cabin without water or electricity. Their second daughter, Marjorie, was burned alive at six years old while playing with matches. The police stopped his mother often for public drunkenness, disorderly conduct, theft, and prostitution. She stole when she didn't have money to buy cheap wine, and when she didn't steal she prostituted herself. She even forced her twelve-year-old daughter into sex work so she could buy alcohol. The Department of Children and Family Services took away her small children. A social worker who came to the house opened one of the closets and a stack of empty bottles fell on her. The children were covered in lice and spent their days playing and fighting in the trash.

•

His father bought and sold scraps and drove an old pickup truck that was always on the verge of breaking. He got tired of the scrap metal business because it made no money and he felt that others were taking advantage of him. He sold what little he had and bought a farm, but the farm turned out to be a wasteland with a dilapidated cabin, which he soon turned into a garbage dump.

His father was constantly changing his occupation and address, dragging the growing family along. He also changed his last name several times, coming up with different variations so it was harder for creditors and law enforcement to find him. A man is in a better position when he can leave as few traces as possible. Change a letter in your last name and you are already ahead. Sometimes he went by Raynes and other times by Ryan, Roy, Rayn. None of his children had exactly the same last name. Despair would overcome him and he would spend entire days in bed. The children had to remain quiet or leave the house, even if it was winter. Hard, honest work is useless when the game is rigged by swindlers and the powerful, the leeches, the parasites that feed on the efforts of others, communists, blacks, Catholics, Jews, bankers, tax collectors, preachers. Blacks spent their days doing nothing and reproducing like animals.

The only job worth his respect was thief. The thief steals from those leeches in the banks without any help. He gambles everything on his revolver, his sawed-off shotgun, his machine gun unloading on the tables and the stacks of deceitful forms and the frosted glass windows of the banks.

A sudden burst of energy would come over him some mornings and he would wake up his eldest son and tell him he could not go to school because he needed help with the business. There was no better school than the school of life. The teachers were accomplices of the preachers and the communists and the Jews and the blacks; they were parasites, just like them, enjoying long vacations at the expense of hardworking folks for whom there were no Saturdays or Sundays, no Fourth of July holiday, no Thanksgiving. Dressed in his father's old clothes, which were too big for him, the boy sat on the pickup truck, shivering, hungry, dozing off to the old man's angry rants. It was a point of pride for the townspeople that no black person had ever dared to spend a night there. His father slammed on the brakes as they approached the neon sign of the pool hall, still shining even though the sun was already out. Work cannot be the only thing in a man's life. His father would buy him a soda, or nothing at all, and leave him to spend the rest of the day sitting on a stool, forgotten, starving, watching his father play pool in a fog of smoke and drunken conversations, spellbound by the artificial light that illuminated the green baize, the trajectories and the clinking sounds of the ivory balls.

•

At age sixteen, in 1944, he found his first job as a tanner in a shoe factory. He stayed there for two years. During that time in his life he was organized and hardworking. They said he was a stingy adolescent. In two years, earning a meager salary, he managed to save a thousand dollars. He did not smoke. He was withdrawn and very shy with women. His boss was fond of him. He went to live with his grandmother, his great-aunt, and his uncle, who described him as a good boy, clean, responsible, and trustworthy. He saved almost every penny that fell into his hands. He wanted to get somewhere, be someone. He seemed strange because he lived such a solitary life. He was only close to his boss, a German man who treated him like a son and took it upon himself to teach him the craft of tannery. Rumor had it he was a Nazi. Even during the war, he spoke of Hitler with admiration, and condemned Roosevelt for making alliances with Stalin's hordes of communists to attack Germany. The factory supplied footwear for the army. At the end of the war, the military orders stopped and the plant had to close. He said his life would have turned out quite different had the factory remained open.

•

He joined the army six weeks after he was laid off. During basic training, he was noted for his marksmanship skills. He was stationed in Bremerhaven, Germany, with the military police. Bremerhaven was still a city in ruins. The black market and prostitution were as visible as the destruction brought by the war. Groups of veteran Nazis ambushed American soldiers who ventured alone at night through the dark streets, the piles of rubble where a dim light would sometimes glow from a basement, the red sign of a cabaret. In the cabarets, black soldiers mingled with whites and German women who had no qualms about taking them to bed. It was in Germany that he started drinking and getting into fights. Charged with drunkenness and insubordination, he spent three months in a military jail. In December 1948, he was discharged early from the army "for ineptness and lack of adaptability to military service."

•

In 1949, he spent eight months in prison for stealing a cash register from a Chinese restaurant where he broke in through a ventilation duct. His military ID fell out as he was getting away. In 1950, he was sentenced to two years in a state prison in Illinois for assaulting a taxi driver. He put a gun to his neck, but the man jumped out of the car and took off running. He got in the front seat to drive off but the man had taken the key. Between 1955 and 1958, he served a sentence for mail fraud in the federal prison in Leavenworth. In Leavenworth, he took courses in Spanish, writing, typing, and sanitary hygiene. In 1957, citing good behavior, prison officials authorized him to finish his sentence in a penitentiary farm with a more lenient regime. He refused to be transferred because the farm did not segregate blacks and whites.

•

In 1959, police arrested him twenty minutes after he robbed a supermarket for $190. He and his accomplice had a good plan, but had gotten so drunk while working out the details that when they got to the supermarket everything went wrong. In the struggle to immobilize him, one of the police officers hit him in the head with the butt of his gun. The wound is visible in the side mug shot, like a saddle sore in the dirty and disheveled hair. In a full-body photo, he's wearing a plaid shirt and frayed pants, a pair of big old shoes and no socks. The judge sentenced him to twenty years in the state prison in Missouri. When they took him out of the courtroom in handcuffs, he pushed the guards and took off running. They chased him for fifteen minutes before finally catching him.

•

In prison his behavior was irreproachable. Perhaps it was there that he discovered and perfected his talent for going unnoticed. He got along with other prisoners, but those who were closest to him saw him as a loner. He never spoke about his family or his past. The most he ever said was that his father and mother were dead. At the prison library, he read law books, geographical encyclopedias, self-help books, and spy novels. He had a special liking for maps and travel magazines and the James Bond books.

He did exercises to stay fit, calisthenic routines, push-ups. He could walk on his hands. He did yoga in his cell and maintained the poses for hours. He was extremely thrifty. He did not smoke or play cards. He took amphetamines and trafficked in them. Someone once saw him injecting himself. His veins were very thin and he had trouble hitting them with the needle. He earned small sums of money renting out old detective novels and erotic magazines.

In his quiet and furtive way, he was always examining different escape options. He told another inmate that his goal was to dig a tunnel all the way to Virginia and hide there forever in a cave, in a forest. He kept putting finishing touches on different life plans, working out details so small they acquired an illusory reality: once out of prison, he would plan one final stunt that earned him twenty or thirty thousand dollars; with that money he could live the rest of his life, spending very little, hiding on a beach in some fishing village in Mexico.

•

In December 1966, at his request, he underwent a psychiatric examination at the prison hospital. He complained of pain in the solar plexus, tachycardia, and something he called "intracranial tension." He told the psychiatrist that he had learned all those words in a medical encyclopedia in the library. He read very close to the page, mumbling words, writing down the most difficult ones in a notebook so he could look them up in the dictionary. At various times, he claimed to have symptoms of cancer and heart disease. He would consult medical books and recognize every one of his symptoms as he read the description for some condition. He remembered waking up one night when he was ten years old and thinking he had gone blind. The psychiatrist diagnosed him with obsessive-compulsive personality and sociopathy. "The subject belongs to the anti-social type with anxiety and depressive features." His IQ was 108, slightly above average.

On April 23, he escaped from the prison hiding in a bread cart that other prisoners loaded into a delivery truck. The order for his arrest took nearly two weeks to be made public. In the poster with his mug shot and fingerprints the latter are wrong. The reward for any information leading to his capture was fifty dollars. He was offended by the amount when he found out. He had assumed, with unfounded optimism, that his escape would somehow land him on the FBI's Ten Most Wanted.

•

After jumping from the truck, he started walking along the bank of a river following the railway line. He hid in a tunnel under the tracks until it got dark, listening to the radio, waiting for a news bulletin to alert people about his escape. He walked the entire night, occasionally eating half-melted chocolate bars. He went into hiding at dawn and took off after nightfall. When he saw a nearby house with lighted windows, he took a detour before the dogs started barking.

He ran out of chocolate bars on the third day. His feet were very swollen but he would not take his shoes off. Had he done so it would have been impossible to put them back on. The third night he came to an abandoned trailer close to the river. He found half a bottle of wine, some food, and a blanket. He went into the woods and slept with the blanket under a tree. A downpour woke him and he started walking again, holding the dripping blanket over his head and shoulders. At daybreak, he sat shivering under the sun to dry. On the fourth night, his legs could barely hold him. On the fifth day it rained again. Using matches he had found in the trailer, he made a fire under a railway bridge. He tried to put it out when he heard people approaching. They were railroad workers and they asked him what he was doing there. He told them he was out hunting and would put out the fire as soon as it stopped raining. He arrived at a small town the morning of the sixth day. He waited on the outskirts until it was dark, then he went into a store and bought two beers and several sandwiches.

•

On May 3, 1967, he started working as a dishwasher in a restaurant in a Chicago suburb, the Indian Trail. He used the name John Larry Raynes. The owner, Mrs. Klingman, remembered him fondly and had been sad to see him leave so soon. "He was a very nice man," she recalled, a year later when strangers began coming around to ask questions about him. "He was here two or three months. What a shame he had to go. He started as a dishwasher, but we promoted him right away and gave him a raise. I could not believe the state he was in. He had been hunting for a while and his feet were injured. My sister brought him one of those long bands from the hospital and taught him how to put it on. He was very grateful. I hope he's okay now. Soon after he left, we wrote to him at the address he left us to tell him how much we appreciated him and to assure him we would always have a job for him."

He worked at the Indian Trail for eight weeks and earned $117. "He was very shy," said a female coworker. "He was never the one to start a conversation. He was quite solitary. He said he had to leave this job because he had to go back to sea or he would lose his merchant mariner license."

•

Every evening, after leaving the restaurant, he took a bus back to a rented room. Every night he drank one or two beers before going to sleep. He read the paper, the *Chicago Tribune*, in its entirety, especially the classified ads. He listened to his transistor radio. Sometimes he read cheap mysteries or spy novels set in Canada and Latin America, magazines with gaudy illustrations on the covers: half-naked women with red lips and open mouths, their eyes dilated by fear, being attacked by wild animals, natives, and alien monsters, while men in safari clothes came to their defense. He bought the books from street vendors. He wrote down every expense. A few nights a week he treated himself to a bar where he would sit and drink vodka and orange juice. He did not like the taste of whiskey.

•

In July 1967, he was in Montreal. This was the first time he started going by the name Eric Starvo Galt, borrowed from one of the evil megalomaniacs of the James Bond novels, Ernst Stavro Blofeld. He rented a room in a boardinghouse near the docks by the Saint Lawrence

River. His street was lined with bars, nightclubs, and cheap hotels. In the first floor of the building was the Acapulco club, sporting a neon sign that promised SHOWS FROM ACAPULCO, SOMBREROS, SERAPES. At the time, some six thousand ships came to the port of Montreal every year. That's where the heroin from Marseille came in. Whenever he struck up a conversation with someone at a bar or restaurant, he told them he was a sailor on leave and that soon he had to get back on a ship. He frequented the Neptune Tavern. The lamps there hung from old helms attached to the ceiling. The furniture was dark oak and had gilded copper fittings like the storage chests in boats.

•

On the morning of July 19, he robbed a supermarket at gunpoint and escaped with 1,700 Canadian dollars. That afternoon he bought a brown suit, wool pants, a white shirt, a yellow shirt, a yellow swimsuit, red pajamas, socks, underwear, and ties. At the exclusive hair salon of the Queen Elizabeth Hotel, he got a haircut and, for the first time in his life, a manicure, done by a young woman in uniform. On July 21, he commissioned a brown wool suit made to measure.

•

Until then, he had never owned a suit or worn a tie. He had never slept with a woman who was not a prostitute. With a knowing grimace, based mostly on his fictional experience, he would say to one of the other inmates at the prison that women were only for using and throwing away, that a man on the run should never trust them.

On July 31 he was staying at the Grey Rock Inn, a hotel next to Lake Ouimet in an area with forests and mountain tourist enclaves. That night, in one of the hotel lounges where a dance orchestra was playing, he met an attractive woman in her mid-thirties who had noticed him because he was the only person sitting alone at a table, not dancing. She had two small children and was going through a bitter and complicated divorce. She had come to the hotel with a friend looking for a few days of respite. "He was clean, elegant, shy. It was his shyness that attracted me to him. He was an educated man who listened attentively and did not talk much. There was so little aggression in him. All the other men there just kept hounding you, trying to touch you, they just wanted to take you to their rooms or cars as soon as possible. Eric was different. He wasn't loud or presumptuous. He was generous with his money, but without waste and without making a big deal when he invited me. I managed to get him on the dance floor. I don't really like dancing. But how clumsy he was. He had no ear for music. I tried to teach him, and he played along. He told me he was from Chicago, and worked for his brother's business. I think I felt very comfortable with Eric. He seemed so lonely and lost. Not that I pitied him, I just wanted to help him have some fun and not be so alone. As the night went on he became more comfortable with me and also more protective. When other men approached me in jest, Eric drove them away, calm but very firm. A woman likes that. Especially a woman who feels rejected. We drank a lot, but neither one of us got drunk. We knew exactly what we were doing. Later we went to his room. I stayed there till morning. My experience with men is pretty limited, but it would be a lie to say Eric did not behave normally. As for his impression of me, I felt very flattered."

She was surprised that a man so well-dressed would drive such an old car. He explained, with obvious embarrassment, that the car actually belonged to his brother's wife. They met again some time later, in Montreal. He was more nervous, more absent. The conversation turned to racial issues and suddenly he seemed like a different person, violent, tense with anger, though he never raised his voice. He told her she defended blacks only because she did not know how they were and had never had to live near them.

•

On August 25, he came to Birmingham, Alabama, on a train from Chicago. He spent the night in a hotel across from the station. In the hotel register he signed John L. Raynes. The next day he rented a room in a boardinghouse that had no name or sign. It was in a seedy area, frequented by prostitutes, drug dealers, and drunks. He used the name Eric S. Galt and said he was a naval engineer who worked designing boats at a shipyard in Pascagoula, Mississippi. The owner of the boardinghouse thought he was an exemplary guest, well-dressed, decent, out of place in the neighborhood. "He left every morning after breakfast and did not come back until dinnertime." At night, he sat quietly to watch television in the living room. He never received visits or phone calls.

•

On August 30, he bought a used white '66 Ford Mustang. It was a sleek sports car, low roof, sharp hood, red leather interior, and a radio with plastic imitation-ivory buttons. James Bond drove a red Mustang in one of the films from that period. He had seen the ad in the local newspaper. The seller was surprised to see him take the wad of hundred-dollar bills from his pocket, in broad daylight, right on the sidewalk, and start counting. He told him he worked as a sailor on a cargo ship in the Mississippi, between New Orleans, Memphis, and Saint Louis. The car had 14,291 miles. He loved the work, he explained, but the shifts, twenty-one days at a time, were exhausting. The seller thought it odd how pale he was for someone who worked on boats, and also that his hands were thin and soft. He noted the lack of a wedding band.

•

The owner of the boardinghouse was delighted with him. "I can't imagine a nicer person than Eric S. Galt. Quiet, polite, clean. He paid on time and in advance at the beginning of every week. If we made small talk, he talked mostly about the weather. He seemed like a nice guy who was temporarily out of work."

•

A driver's license application in Alabama states that he was born on July 20, 1931, weighed 175 pounds, stood at five feet eleven inches, had blue eyes and brown hair, and was a merchant sailor unemployed at the time. He passed the practical exam with a high score. According to the medical certificate, he had perfect vision in both eyes.

•

He purchased a secondhand portable typewriter. On September 1, he used it to write a letter to a company in Chicago that sold photography supplies. He ordered a Kodak projector, a Kodak Super 8, and a control with a six-meter cable. On October 5, in a photography store in Birmingham, he bought a Polaroid camera. He would carry it with him everywhere until the day he was arrested, eight months later. He liked buying things by mail and filling out the order forms that came in the magazines using his typewriter. He sent a money order for one dollar to a company in Hollywood, requesting a product, E. Z. Formula, that could turn a glass surface into a one-way mirror. The product had been advertised in a pulp magazine. He read and clipped offers for correspondence courses, hair-loss treatments, manuals to learn karate or hypnosis or stenography. He wrote to the Modern Photo Bookstore in New York and ordered the *Focal Encyclopedia of Photography* from an ad he clipped from *Modern Photography* magazine. He left a very clear imprint of his left thumb on the coupon.

•

Every Sunday at 9:00 p.m., he would find a bar where he could watch *FBI: The Ten Most Wanted Criminals* and the countdown of the Ten Most Wanted criminals in the United States. Every Sunday, he expected to see his name and mug shot on the list.

•

He did not have a passport, or a birth certificate, or a social security number, or any documentary evidence of previous employment. He had a driver's license, a car registration under the name Eric Starvo Galt, a safe-deposit box at a bank, and the address at the boarding-house. He felt more confident using a real address in conjunction with the fake name: 2608 Highland Avenue, Birmingham, Alabama. He carefully filled out all the order forms in uppercase and typed the addresses on the envelopes. Whenever he left the house, he took the stamped envelopes with him. He took some small satisfaction in sliding them into the blue mailbox.

•

As soon as he was settled in Birmingham, he enrolled in dance classes. He was mostly interested in Latin dance, cha-cha, bolero, mambo. The instructor said he was "a clumsy loner who came once or twice and could not have learned how to dance even if he had come every day for the rest of his life." He was quiet and evasive. He had a straight, sharp nose, a strong southern accent, and he talked like someone from a rural area despite his city clothes. He wore a gold ring with a dark stone.

•

He came back to the boardinghouse every evening with *The Birmingham News* under his arm and some weekly magazine. He read them carefully in his room, word by word, from the headlines on the first page to the classifieds, news about agricultural competitions, calendars of religious services at different churches, lists of births, and obituaries. On October 1 he saw a classified ad for a used gun, a .38-caliber snub nose revolver, Liberty Chief model, made in Japan. He called the number and went to the seller's house, who later could not recall his face. He paid sixty-five dollars. The seller's son did remember him: he said the man was probably in his early to mid-forties, around 170 pounds, five feet eight or nine inches tall, had dark hair, graying on the sides, a southern accent, and was wearing a sports shirt and jeans.

•

He was suffering from insomnia, a sore throat, and a dry cough. He feared it was pneumonia, or lung cancer. A doctor prescribed him antibiotics. He visited a psychiatrist, who sat there nodding, paying more attention to the clock than the patient, and who finally prescribed him an antidepressant.

•

On October 6, early in the morning, he packed the car with his suitcase, typewriter, and cameras, and said goodbye to the owner of the boardinghouse. He told him that he had finally found work on a merchant ship that was leaving from Mobile the next day. He drove through Alabama, Mississippi, Louisiana, and Texas almost without stopping.

He covered almost 1,250 miles in thirty hours. He took amphetamines to stay awake. He saw the highway, straight and unchanging,
open before the headlights, the neon signs of the gas stations, the
clusters of old cabins where black people lived, motels, twenty-four-
hour fast-food restaurants, a horizon of monotonous forests, cotton
plantations, and increasingly arid red plains. On the afternoon of
October 7 he crossed the border into Nuevo Laredo, Mexico. They
put a sticker on his window identifying him as a tourist and marking
the date of entry. While in prison, he had read an article about Puerto
Vallarta, in *True* magazine: white-sand beaches, palm trees, bunga-
lows by the ocean. You had to take a dirt road from Acapulco, which
was more of a mud river by the end of the rainy season.

He arrived in Puerto Vallarta in his white Mustang. No one in the
town had seen a car like that. First he stayed in the Rio Hotel, then in
the Tropicana, which overlooked the beach, Banderas Bay. He could
see the ocean from his room and, in the distance, the water shooting
from the mountainous humps of the whales. The typewriter was on
the backseat of the car. He was now a writer; an American author who
probably came to Puerto Vallarta seeking tranquility, determined to
finish his novel, perhaps a screenplay. He wore his hair slicked back,
and gold-rimmed sunglasses. The Polaroid camera was always on his
shoulder. He also carried the Super 8. The clicking sounds of the typewriter could be heard through the open windows and thin walls of the
hotel. John Huston had directed *The Night of the Iguana* a few months
prior in Puerto Vallarta. In the film, if you pay close attention, you can
see for a few seconds the facade of the Rio Hotel and its sign.

•

He began to frequent two brothels in Puerto Vallarta: Casa Susana
and Casa Azul. Casa Susana had a lounge with dirt floors, a bar, and
a jukebox that played American hits from different decades. The vinyl
would start skipping sometimes and you had to hit the machine on
the side. Women fanned their faces while waiting for clients, glisten-
ing in the heat, their lips and eyes with heavy makeup, their legs
open. Naked children and animals ran around the tables, pigs, hens,
dogs. In Casa Susana he met a young woman who went by Irma, after

the movie *Irma la Douce*. Her skin was dark, her hair was dyed blond. Her real name was Manuela Medrano Lopez. Irma later said that the American with the white sports car, Eric, would take her in the Mustang to secluded beaches and take photos of her, dressed or naked, sometimes in erotic positions. He had her sit on the passenger seat with her legs open and her skirt pulled up. He made vague promises about hiring her to star in the films he would be making for a pornography company he was starting in Los Angeles. Eric, the American, was quiet and never laughed. Sometimes he treated her to things, other times he haggled over payment for her services. He took his Polaroid camera everywhere, along with a small Spanish phrase book, though he could barely say a few words and could understand even less. He was very interested in learning Latin dancing. Occasionally he got in his car and disappeared. Manuela Medrano figured he was probably going to one of the plantations in the jungle to buy marijuana. One day he was very drunk at one of the tables in Casa Susana and asked her to marry him. She laughed and said no. How could she trust him, she said, if he was always walking away with other women. She said it in Spanish and a bit of English, with single words, and many gestures, pointing to one of the other prostitutes he had been with, perhaps to make her jealous, a girl with darker skin, younger and very petite, whom they called Chilindrina. He got very serious, pulled out his revolver, and pointed it between her eyes.

•

Women in Casa Azul waited for clients in narrow, horizontal cubicles positioned at different heights, like cells in a honeycomb. Hand ladders led to them. Cries, moans, and sighs filled the space and could be heard from outside, acting as an invitation, an aphrodisiac made of sound. They saw him go up and down the ladders many times: sunglasses, Hawaiian shirts, the skin so pale it did not even get red from the sun, refractory like lime or pumice stone.

•

The most secluded beach was in Mismaloya, fifteen kilometers from Puerto Vallarta. It had one bar in front of the beach. Few tourists ventured that far. The waiter from the bar recognized him months later when they showed him the photos, although he said he never knew his name. He recalled that the man would come in a dazzling white car and with a blond woman, that he would order a few drinks and go sit with her under the shade of the palm trees by the water. In *The Night of the Iguana*, Ava Gardner bathes in the beach of Mismaloya at night, drunk and carefree, in the company of two young men who later surround her playing maracas.

•

He left Puerto Vallarta on November 14, 1967. The night before, he had gotten very drunk at Casa Susana, talking to Irma or Manuela in a mumbled voice she would not have understood even if the music from the jukebox had not been so loud. He got in a fight with a black sailor, who was just as drunk, after the man bumped into him accidentally. The other man was taller and stronger, but froze after seeing the pistol. Looking for the right words in his Spanish phrase book, he told Manuela that he would come back for her after he resolved some unfinished business in the United States. With a stash of marijuana hidden in the spare tire of the Mustang, he drove along the highways on the edge of the Pacific all the way to Los Angeles.

He took his time. He enjoyed driving while drinking a cold beer and listening to country music. He liked the songs of Johnny Cash most of all. Sunglasses, shirt open at the chest, elbow resting on the open window, the moist ocean breeze blowing on his face—he saw himself as if from outside, in disbelief and admiration, like watching a movie or reading a novel where he was the protagonist, hitting the road, the Mustang roaring, the music turned all the way up.

•

On November 19, he rented an apartment in the St. Francis Hotel on Hollywood Boulevard. It was an area with cheap hotels, liquor stores, and strip clubs. The St. Francis was mostly filled with retirees who received modest pensions, lonely old men, alcoholics, many of them with some kind of disability. There were also strippers and belly dancers who worked in the nightclubs nearby, places with names like the

Fez, Seventh Veil, and Arabian Nights. On the first floor of the St. Francis, there was a dimly lit bar called the Sultan Room. The place was mostly frequented by residents, who sat at the bar for hours, sipping their drinks slowly. Across the street, on the corner, was the Rabbit's Foot, which opened earlier—at six-thirty in the morning it was already serving alcohol. The neon signs of the Sultan Room and the Rabbit's Foot glowed opposite each other, intermittently, with some of the letters missing. A waiter from the Rabbit's Foot remembered him: the southern accent, the dark suit, a bow tie, the big ears, the furtive expression.

•

While living at the St. Francis, he bought a portable television set. It was a Zenith with plastic casing, a handle, and two directional antennas. In the Sultan Room he met Maria Bonino, one of the waitresses. She had been an exotic dancer and stripper under different stage names: Marie Martin, Marie Dennino, Mary Martinello, mostly in a nearby club called the Mousetrap. She introduced him to Charles Stein, an occasional songwriter who trafficked LSD and also consumed it. Stein was a bald hippie with a beard, beaded necklaces, sandals, and dirty feet. He said that after receiving the Christian faith, he was able to feel the vibrations of the universe. Next to Stein, Eric Starvo Galt stood out even more: dark suits, ironed white shirts, ties, shiny shoes. Stein always carried binoculars and a camera in the glove compartment in case he spotted a UFO. They traveled to New Orleans and back in the Mustang, more than three thousand miles in just a few days, to pick up Stein's nieces. Sometimes Stein would brake abruptly as they drove through the desert at night because he was sure he had seen a UFO. Later he said that throughout the trip, Galt had made two or three calls from pay phones along the highway. Stein had woken up in the passenger seat, where he had been sleeping for a few hours, and noticed he was alone in the car, which was parked on the shoulder of a road near a gas station. It was four or five in the morning and he was shivering. In the distance, a phone booth glowed in the dark, and inside, Galt stood still, listening attentively. After hanging up, he returned to the car and drove off without speaking a word. Stein said he was certain the name was fake: his face did not look like a Galt, let alone an Eric; he was more like a Bill, or Bob, or Jim.

•

Christmas Eve, 1967, was the first one he had spent out of prison in eight years. Christmas, he later explained with some contempt, is a holiday for people who are close to their families. It meant nothing for a solitary man like him. "A night like any other to sit at a bar, then go to your room and drink a few beers while watching television." He had forgotten what he did that night, though he did remember that on December 31 he drove through the desert to Las Vegas. He wandered around the city for a while, and watched people play slot machines. He slept in the backseat of his car on a parking lot. At dawn, he woke up shivering and drove back to Los Angeles. The highway was wide and deserted. It was the first morning of 1968.

On January 4, he went to see the Reverend Xavier von Koss, master hypnotist, president of the International Society of Hypnotism, and, according to his business card, "a world-renowned authority on hypnosis, autohypnosis, and self-improvement." The Reverend von Koss explained that in order to strengthen his self-esteem he had to set clear goals in his life. Von Koss said he tried to hypnotize him, but as soon as he asked him to close his eyes and focus on the ticking of the metronome, he noticed a very strong subconscious resistance.

At von Koss's suggestion, he bought a few books: *How to Cash In on Your Hidden Memory Power*, by William D. Hersey; *Self-Hypnosis: The Technique and Its Use in Daily Living*, by Leslie M. LeCron; and *Psycho-Cybernetics*, by Dr. Maxwell Maltz. A copy of the last one, quite worn and underlined in many places, was in his luggage when he was arrested at Heathrow Airport. Around that time, he also bought, by mail, several books about sex, perhaps in preparation for his project of producing pornographic films: *Female Sexual Response, Sexual Anatomy, Unusual Female Sex Practices, Sexual Sensibility in Men and Women.*

On February 26, he placed an order with a sex shop for a pair of Japanese steel handcuffs with velvet and lace. He also placed personal ads in the sex magazines that came to him in brown envelopes with no markings. The text was always the same: "Single man, white,

36 years old, looking for discreet encounter with married, passionate woman."

•

He would stare at himself in the mirror for a long time, studying the features that would make him easier to identify, easier to remember. He took Polaroid photographs of his face from multiple angles and under different lights, and compared them. Almost everything about his face was unremarkable. Dark straight hair, blue eyes, a slightly cleft chin. He had a small scar on his forehead but it was barely visible. The real problem was the nose and ears. The tip of the nose protruded too much. The left ear was larger than the right one, it stuck out more and the earlobe was longer. He sent some of the test Polaroids to women he corresponded with through pen pal clubs.

•

In his book *Psycho-Cybernetics*, Dr. Maxwell Maltz, a plastic surgeon and professor of plastic surgery at the University of Managua and the University of El Salvador, explains that the human mind works like an electric brain: it programs itself to achieve certain objectives. An electronic brain determines the time of launch, the trajectory, and the target of a nuclear missile; similarly, the electronic brain of the human mind determines the life trajectory one must take to achieve a certain objective, which is equal to success: the success of a car salesman who gets ahead of the competition, an athlete who gets to the finish line first or earns the highest score, a worldly man who wants a good job, the skill to be a great dancer and seduce the most attractive woman at a party. The information an electronic brain needs to function adequately is provided by the programmer. A human being moves, feels, and acts according to information he assumes to be true about himself and his surroundings. If that information is wrong, the result can be disastrous.

•

On January 15 he began a bartending course at the Lau International School of Bartending, which lasted until March 2. According to the director of the school, "He was a nice person, with a slight Southern accent, very intelligent, with skills to thrive in this line of work." By the end of the course he had learned to mix 122 cocktails. Another student recalled that it would take him a while to understand directions and even longer to learn them because he was always nervous. He heard him say that he had been a head chef on a merchant ship. Others remember him being left-handed: this student was certain he was right-handed. He was not a smoker, though another student was sure he had seen him with a cigarette between his nervous fingers and well-groomed nails. On the last day of the course, he showed up with a waiter jacket and bow tie he had rented. Every student got a photo with the director of the school handing them the diploma with a big smile and shaking their hand. He closed his eyes right when the photographer snapped his portrait. He said he was leaving Los Angeles because he had been hired to open a cocktail bar in New Orleans.

The human brain programs itself based on a specific self-image. Autosuggestion and hypnosis can be powerful aids. In support of his thesis, Dr. Maxwell Maltz cites research by Dr. J. B. Rhine, director of the Parapsychology Laboratory at Duke University, where it had been experimentally shown that humans have access to knowledge, ideas, and events that do not come to them through the channels of rational intelligence. Man creates a mistaken self-image and condemns himself to failure. He sees himself as ugly or awkward or not attractive to women, and that image is transmitted extrasensorially to them, thus making them see him the way he sees himself. But thanks to autohypnosis, the brain can be reprogrammed to counteract those negative images. It is in this way that the true power of the mind can be revealed, says Dr. Maltz. Dr. Theodore Xenophon Barber had conducted extensive and rigorous research on hypnotic phenomena at Harvard's Laboratory of Social Relations.

A man programs his brain so he can see himself as a winner and a seducer and the miracle happens, provided the mind has visualized the objective down to the smallest detail, over and over, preferably in a dark room, with eyes closed. Golf champions have confessed that the most fundamental part of their training is the meticulous visualization of every play, including the final trajectory of the ball toward the hole, the friction from the grass, the light dew, the exact amount of pressure one must exert on the golf club. Salespeople who would end up surpassing their company's goals saw themselves approaching a client with a big smile, their hands ready to shake with just the right amount of force. It's not enough for dancers to rehearse the same steps again and again, they must also program their minds, psycho-cybernetically, to see their bodies sliding across the dance floor, effort-lessly hovering over it.

●

In December, he signed up for a rumba class at a place called the National Dance Studios. It was a sad, cavernous place, hard hit by the decline in popularity of ballroom dancing, frequented mostly by lonely people. The class was intensive: twenty-five hours of group lessons, then another twenty-five of individual tutoring. "He looked like a southern gentleman," said one of the female instructors.

●

On March 5, he had the tip of his nose shortened in a surgical proce-dure performed by Dr. Russell Hadley, on Hollywood Boulevard. Two days after the surgery he returned to have the doctor remove the bandages and evaluate the healing. At his third visit, on March 11, Dr. Hadley removed the stitches. Months later, when plainclothes officers started coming to his office to ask questions and show him photos, Dr. Hadley was shocked he could not remember this patient's face. In his book about psycho-cybernetics, Dr. Maltz claims that after undergoing cosmetic surgery in prison to correct their most unpleasant traits, hardened criminals had changed their behavior en-tirely, working for early release for good conduct, and later becoming good and useful members of society.

●

On Monday, March 18, he left Los Angeles. Now he was crossing the country from west to east, taking the long way through Arizona, New Mexico, Texas, Louisiana, Mississippi, Alabama, Georgia, and finally Memphis, Tennessee. He stopped an entire day in New Orleans on March 21. From there he drove to Selma, Alabama, where Martin Luther King was participating in various public events. Shortly before,

King had been in Los Angeles. He drove to Atlanta from Selma, and stayed there five days. He always looked for the worst neighborhoods, places on the outskirts of the city, with bars and liquor stores that stayed open twenty-four hours, drug addicts and hippies, cheap dinners, pawn shops. The boardinghouse he found in Atlanta did not have a front desk. A man ran the place from a small room on the ground floor. He was so drunk he could not find the registration book or tell him if any of the rooms were available. He had been drunk for fourteen days. Even so, he was surprised to see this well-groomed man wanting to get a room in his building. Perhaps he was an undercover police officer. On the passenger seat of the car sat a folded map of Atlanta with red circles around the places where King could usually be found: his home, his parents' house, and Ebenezer, the church where he was pastor.

•

On Friday, March 29, he traveled from Atlanta to Birmingham, Alabama, where he had not been since October of the previous year. He checked into a motel using the name Eric S. Galt. A few hours later, he went to a gun shop to buy a hunting rifle and a scope. He said his name was Harvey Lowmeyr, or Lowmeyer. He did not have to present any identification. He told the clerks he was planning a deer-hunting trip in Idaho with his brother. They got the impression the thin, pale man did not know much about hunting, the outdoors, or firearms in general. He held the rifle awkwardly with both hands, while reading the instruction manual. He wore a pair of thick reading glasses and his nails were well-groomed. His suit seemed well-cut but was wrinkled, as if he had slept in it. The tie was lopsided. His breath had a faint smell of alcohol. He returned the next day, a Saturday, first thing in the morning, wearing the same suit, the same glasses, and said he needed a more powerful rifle. The one he ended up choosing had a firing velocity of nine hundred meters per second. This was a weapon that could kill a charging rhinoceros. He asked the clerks to install a scope on the rifle. They watched him leave the store and walk to his car, shoulders hunched, rifle case in hand, like a suitcase, feet turned out, one ear bigger than the other.

•

On Monday, April 1, he took a bag of clothes to a dry cleaner in Atlanta: four shirts, three pairs of underwear, one pair of socks, a towel, a blazer, dress pants, one tie. The woman behind the counter thought it was strange to see a man so well-dressed in such a poor neighborhood.

•

On April 3, on his way from Atlanta to Memphis, he got off the highway and followed a dirt road to a secluded spot: a meadow with a fallen white picket fence and an abandoned shed. He took out the rifle and mounted the scope. During military service he had excelled as a sharpshooter. He loaded a magazine, felt the pull pressure on the trigger, and the fit of the stock on his shoulder. In the scope everything looked as if it were within arm's reach: a rusty can, the trunk of a tree, a bird feeder hanging from a branch. It only took a little pressure and boom. Behind the crosshairs, objects exploded into shards of glass and dust, and after every shot, a great silence fell over the field.

•

The drive from Atlanta to Memphis was seven hours. He made two more stops on the road. First he stopped at a drugstore to buy a Gillette shaving kit. The cashier would later remember him due to his suit and tie, not the most common attire in the area, and not very appropriate for the heat and humidity. A hundred kilometers later, he stopped at a barbershop and got a haircut. The sky began to turn gray as he approached Memphis. The wind was whipping the trees. Lightning bolts flashed across the dark horizon.

•

At about a quarter past seven in the evening, Eric S. Galt rented a room at the New Rebel Motel, just outside Memphis. Raging waves of rain hit the windowpanes. Thunder rumbled as if the earth's crust were opening. The night watchman saw the white Mustang parked in front of his room, where the light was still on at five in the morning.

•

On the morning of April 4, he bought a newspaper that had a photo of Martin Luther King on the front page with a caption that mentioned the hotel where he was staying, the Lorraine, the one he always stayed at when in Memphis. A hostile editorial asserted that King was back in Memphis to encourage new riots and unrest among blacks and stoke the dangerous extremism of the sanitation workers who had gone on strike.

At three in the afternoon, he rented a room in a boardinghouse not too far from the Lorraine Motel, in a dilapidated neighborhood on the fringes of the city with the usual scenery of pawnshops, liquor stores, and drunks. He said his name was John Edward Willard. In a place like that there was no need for identification.

The woman in charge of the boardinghouse thought he looked as out of place as the car parked by the entrance. Someone knocked on the door of the room she used as an office. She opened without removing the chain, and there he was, a pale man with a triangular face, squinting with a forced smile, a smirk that lacked connection to his other facial features.

She took him down a hallway to one of the vacant rooms. It had a padlock. A wire hanger stuck out of the hole where the doorknob had been. There was a gutted green sofa and a dirty lightbulb that hung from the ceiling, a boarded-up fireplace, and a misshapen mattress on a bed frame. A garland with Christmas ornaments and dusty plastic leaves hung over the mantelpiece. The woman, Bessie Brewer, who was heavyset and wore a man's shirt, apologized for the strong smell of disinfectant: the previous resident, an old drunkard, had died in the room the previous week.

With a smirk, he asked the woman for the bathroom. It was right next to the room. A sign taped to the door read TOILET & BATH. The toilet had no lid and there was a puddle of dirty water in the tub. Through the window, across a lot littered in trash: the rows of balconies in the Lorraine Motel, the sliding glass door of a room open, a translucent curtain billowing up like a boat's sail. It was April 4, 1968, a Thursday.

11

I was looking for a hospital with long corridors, cold tiles, echoes, high ceilings with white globular lamps; a nightclub with a sign that was just one word, BURMA, leading into a labyrinth of metal stairways, slow freight elevators, musty, redbrick basements or storage rooms that smelled of tropical goods; a secluded house where a woman lived alone, and where a fugitive man, probably wounded, would come at midnight; a jazz club or a theater where an old musician, who is very ill, would play his last concert.

I wanted a train as the setting for a chase and a cliff where two men fight and one of them falls, his silhouette becoming smaller and smaller against a backdrop of foaming waves crashing on a reef, a sea of cinematographic transparency, a dark aqua-blue sky like a day-for-night shot and a bad dream.

I was looking for settings for my novel but, above all, a visual impulse that could lead me to the encounters between my characters and their discoveries. I was not transferring to the real Lisbon the threads of the plot I had developed in my imaginary city. The plot was taking shape as I explored, as I meandered through a quest that resembled a tireless search for one face in a sea of people; a face you love so much you don't even know how to remember it, and it vanishes from memory the moment you cannot see it anymore; a face you could search for, day in and day out in vain; a face that is always unexpected when you finally see it, in one of those places where the possibility of imminence acts like a magnetic field: corners you can't turn without a twinge in your stomach; stairways, doorways, hallways, streets that prove favorable because they once had a sudden presence, a shadow.

•

Lisbon was a real city and a scale model of Lisbon. The strict order of the streets in Baixa had the neatness of a model city made to scale, the lines of identical windows, the simplified shapes of the houses. Rossio Square teemed with pedestrians and business activity, and it was also an abstract square, a model with an axis of symmetry extending south in the perspective of a triumphal arch and a king on horseback, with its neoclassical theater on the north side, its column crowned with the statue of a king in the center, its calligraphic signs, its pinks and blues, which lit up at night over the rooftops. Out of breath, climbing up the Calçada do Carmo, I saw a large hospital with faded pink walls and high windows facing east. Perhaps this is where the student would find his teacher, ill and disheartened, lying on a white iron bed, in a cold room at the end of the hall, his face yellow against the whiteness of the pillow, his body barely creating volume under the blanket. The sounds of Lisbon would reach the room like a maritime murmur.

Behind Rossio Square, the mouth of an alley led to a flashing red sign and the velvet curtain of a peep show, so thick it muffled the heavy bass beat that would throb in your temples and chest the moment you entered. Right away, that place, which I had just discovered by chance, became part of my novel. I felt the impunity of doing something exciting and shameful in a city where no one knew me. A woman behind a ticket window provided change. I was one among many strangers moving like shadows under the pink and green lights; dark, lone figures in winter coats and with lit cigarettes wandering around some kind of basement with concrete floors, black curtains on the walls, a potent smell of air freshener and humidity, low ceilings, blasting music.

Narrow doors were numbered along a corridor, each one with a red lightbulb that turned on when someone went inside. A light would go off and a man would walk out avoiding eye contact. I opened a door and found myself in a small room that was almost pitch-black. I had never been in a place like that. I remember the faint light filtering through the small window, the roll of toilet paper on a shelf next to the machine where the coins where deposited, and the music, which was all the more deafening in such a narrow space.

As the coins went in the slot, the glass became transparent, as if a layer of frost had dissipated. On the other side, a naked woman lay on a circular bed with pillows that was a rotating platform. She was surrounded by one-way mirrors and saw her body reflected from all sides, knowing that behind each one was a man watching, hiding.

She was slim, attractive, flexible. She writhed and wriggled, lifting her hips or leaning on her hands and knees with slow, rhythmic movements, an expression of disciplined boredom on her face, indifferent to her effect. Eyes surrounded her but she could not see them. Rotating slowly, she could not tell which rooms were in use and which were empty. On her back, her bare feet waved in the air like fish, her toenails painted red, her heels pink.

•

Years later, in Madrid, a new acquaintance told me a story. We were having a drink in the restaurant of a hotel. He was one of those people who must confide in someone, as if a newfound joy could only be complete if shared, if witnessed, if no longer just a secret between two lovers. It was mid-morning, in January. I still could not orient myself well in Madrid. The restaurant window faced Goya Street. No one knew that you had come to meet me here and that at that moment you were waiting for me in a room.

It was pouring. There was a lot of traffic, a lot of people on the sidewalk in front of the hotel. The lamps were turned low and there were pockets of shadow around the bar. My interlocutor would pause sometimes to take a sip from his coffee, which was already cold. He was very thin, somewhat younger than me, prominent cheekbones, bony hands. He spoke and stared like a convert, like someone who has been enlightened. He spoke without looking at me, so possessed by the intensity of his story that he forgot everything else, the coffee, the gray morning light of winter, the fact that we barely knew each other.

He was still in disbelief about what was happening to him. If he

turned to look at me, it was only to see the effect of what he was saying, unsure that I was able to understand, approve; ready to challenge
me if necessary.

He told me he was living the great love of his life. He had never
liked a woman so much, never had he experienced such sexual inti-
macy and surrender. But he couldn't tell anyone how they had met. It
was the secret that brought them together and also a punishment.
They had to agree on a new story. The truth is that he had met her at a
peep show where she danced for several hours every evening or night,
depending on her shift. He was working on an article about the world
of sex shops, strip clubs, XXX cinemas; the sex business was just
starting to proliferate openly in Madrid. He fell in love the moment
he saw her behind the glass. He filled his pockets with coins and in-
serted them one by one so he could continue seeing her. He was possessed by a combination of sexual arousal and tenderness that rendered
him helpless, like a powerful narcotic. He pressed his face against the
glass to study her every feature, her face, her body, simultaneously
offered and forbidden, so close, yet beyond reach.

He became a regular at the bar next door so he could see her
leaving. He knew that he could not be going to the peep show every day
or the employees would find him suspicious. The first time he saw her
outside, he almost did not recognize her. He felt even more attracted to
her now, seeing her dressed for winter, wearing a dark coat and a wool
hat. She looked younger without makeup and the chiaroscuro lights.

One night he found the courage to approach her. He showed her
his newspaper ID and his camera. She hesitated but finally agreed to hear
him out. They went to the bar where he had waited so many times, pale
and anxious under the fluorescent lights, oblivious to the people around
him, the noisy television, the soccer game. Neither one paid attention to
their surroundings. They became lovers that very night.

Now they had been living together for a week in a rented flat. He
did not have a contract with the newspaper and they only paid him
per article. She danced at the peep show and modeled for art students
some mornings. This was the only way she could afford dance school.
Some nights, without telling her, he returned to the peep show and sat
in the room where he had seen her for the first time. Seeing her again
behind the window consumed him with jealousy and desire.

I listened to him divulge his secret while I held on to mine, anticipating the moment when I would finally be able to cross the lobby, take the elevator, and walk toward the room where you were waiting for me.

•

There was no time to lose. The rolls of film and the pages of my notebook were quickly filling up. Intoxicated by so many images and exhausted from all the walking, I could not fall asleep that first night. I still had a full day, one more night, and the last day. The moment I turned off the light, I felt even more awake. My memories from that first day in Lisbon were already contaminated by fiction. Insomnia was a silver screen in the concavity of my closed eyes. I had phoned home and could hear my son crying in the background. It was strange to feel so far away after less than two days of travel. It was even stranger to think that in three or four days I would be back in Granada.

I had to get the most out of every hour, every minute. The next morning I ran up the steps of the Rossio station and took a train to Cascais. I was in search of a specific place, though in particular, the resonance of its name, Boca do Inferno. Juan Vida had told me that peering over that cliff felt like being on the edge of the world. There was a lighthouse, not cylindrical, but in the shape of a prism, surrounded by palms, painted white and blue. There was a restaurant called Mar do Inferno. I left the station and took off walking. The morning was bright and blue. The wind and the blinding breadth of the sea gave me vertigo before even reaching the cliff. I had stared down such a deep abyss. It was all the same, to have come here in search of something or as an escape: it was impossible to go any further. It was the overwhelming and primitive intuition of *finis terrae*, the final frontier between the known and the unknown. Large cargo ships moved across the horizon, blurred against the brightness of the sea, rippled by the wind. I peered anxiously over the edge and took some photos. I could feel the ocean's mist on my face. I imagined the place at night, the roaring sea, the white waves crashing against a deep blackness, the intermittent glow of the lighthouse. It was not clear how it would happen, but I knew one of my characters would fall from that cliff at night.

Later, I wrote notes eagerly, alone and happy, sitting by a window in Mar do Inferno, hungry after the long walk, starting to feel the effects of the *vinho verde* I was drinking as I waited for the food, letting myself be carried away by the soft, simultaneous intoxication of wine and imagination, by the sheer intensity of the real world, this simple and clear moment in my life, the taste of the food and the friendliness of the waiters, with my little Portuguese dictionary at the side, my notebook, my pencil, the camera, the novel that was taking on a life I had not anticipated.

•

I felt even more immersed in my imaginary world when that evening, or the next day, I left the Sintra station and started walking through a path along some house gardens, seeing in the distance the scattered city, a slope of dark pines, two strange, conical chimneys jutting out like towers or geological excrescences from the roof of a palace. I walked to the sound of gravel crunching under my feet. Memory imposes a golden sun in the late afternoon, the smell of moist and rich soil, woodsmoke in the cool air, lights turning on in the ocher and pink walls of the houses, the tall and secluded buildings, reminiscent of sanatoriums, at the end of the narrow roads on the slopes of the mountain. There were houses deep in abandoned gardens and others that suggested a serene and final retirement, a long and sumptuous convalescence as in *The Magic Mountain*.

In Sintra, not in Lisbon, was the sanatorium I was looking for. I took photos of towers, outlooks, gardens, fences, the names of houses written on azulejo tiles. I jumped over a wall and ventured into a tunnel of jungle greenery in an abandoned garden and then onto a porch with a door half-open, stepping on broken glass; I did not dare to go in.

There was a house name that I liked more than all the others: Quinta dos Lobos. I could almost hear the gate opening at night, in a cold and humid air that smelled like a forest.

I have not been back to Sintra. I don't know if I remember what I saw then or what I wrote in one of the final chapters of the novel. On the ride back to Lisbon, I noticed that the train cars were quite old and connected by platforms with handrails, instead of covered passageways.

As the train picked up speed it was more difficult to balance on those mobile, metal plates.

I imagined two men who are in love with the same woman and come across each other by chance in Lisbon. Their mutual hate stretches back a long time. They would no longer fight on the edge of the cliff in Cascais, but on that platform between the train cars. I did not have to will any images, they just came to me in waves, effortlessly, like the countryside that flashed past the train window. The train stopped at a station along the way. I saw the illuminated interior of the train coming in the opposite direction and the faces of its passengers, our eyes meeting in the brief and exact instant when the two trains intersected. Right at that moment, the hero of my novel would see, in the other train, like a mirage, the face of the woman he has not seen in years.

I had to be on that train to imagine that moment of mutual recognition, that exchange of glances. No matter what I did I could not escape the dreaming of the novel. To walk around the city was to walk through that imaginary world. I got off the train in Cais do Sodré in a daze of solitude and fiction. On the sidewalk, a man leaned over to kiss a woman in a wheelchair. As I walked around at dusk, the neon signs of the bars and nightclubs began to light up, the red lights from their interiors spilling into the sidewalk, the names of port cities, Oslo, Copenhagen, Jakarta, or states or places in America, names with an exotic musicality mysteriously associated with sexual innuendos, Arizona Bar, California Bar, Niagara Bar, Texas Bar. Sometimes fiction wants to supplant reality, sometimes it settles for adding certain secondary details. In that vocabulary of glowing names of the Lisbon night, in the street corners, the low passageways and arches, the end of back alleys, it would not have been too much to add just one more name, invented or anticipated or drawn by me, blinking in the distance like an invitation, several months after having appeared as a typing error on a blank sheet of paper, *burma*.

12

He would return to the Hotel Portugal around dawn, lock himself in his room—number 2 on the first floor—draw the curtains, and sometimes not come out again until nightfall. It was always the same scene: disheveled and reeking of alcohol, the greasy hair tightly slicked back, sunglasses, no eye contact, the daily newspapers bunched under his arm.

He would bring food in a paper bag, stuff he bought in the shops nearby: crackers, cans, condensed milk. The hotel maid, Maria Celeste, would find bits of food on the bed quilt, which often looked as if it hadn't even been removed, as though he slept on it, fully clothed, even with his shoes still on, leaving crusted mud at the bottom of the bed. He made no phone calls and received none. The cans of food left rings on the newspapers.

He soaked his underwear in the sink. He washed his shirts by hand. On the nightstand or next to the bed on the floor were his books, the old paperbacks he carried with him to the end, a poorly printed hypnosis manual by Dr. Adolf F. Louk; the psycho-cybernetics book by Dr. Maxwell Maltz; Quiller and Robert Belcourt spy novels; and a booklet from the locksmith course he had taken. In the drawer he kept pornography magazines, and also *True* magazine and *Man's Life*.

The margins of his newspapers often had calculations, small additions and subtractions, lists of expenses. He tore them out and ripped them into very small pieces, which would end up in the toilet or in his pockets, along with ad clippings, American coins, and other bits of paper. Caution had become a nervous habit. He tore bits from the corners of paper tablecloths, receipts, and coasters and rolled them into tiny balls.

He checked the daily section of a Portuguese newspaper that listed every arriving and departing ship by name. He drew circles on his map of Lisbon: the Canadian embassy on Liberty Avenue; one for that of the Republic of South Africa, which was farther to the north, beyond the statue of the king; and one around the statesman with the lion and the park where he had fallen asleep one morning, under the humid shade of a tree, after a night of drinking.

He had woken up abruptly, fearing that he had been robbed. It was a hot day and the tight shirt collar chafed his neck. He felt his pockets for the passport, the gun, and the money—the wad of twenty-dollar bills and Portuguese notes that kept getting lighter. The fact that he was quickly running out of money was as overwhelming as the feeling that he was running out of time. They both seemed to trickle through his fingers, through the empty days, the delays, the waiting, while all those people kept tirelessly looking for him, the thousands in America, in Europe, in Mexico, in Canada, police officers, detectives, federal agents, scientists in lab coats, analyzing every-thing from fingerprints, hair, and handwriting to the saliva he left on postage stamps. Or at least, that's what they say in the papers. Snitches, prison guards, men in gray suits knocking on doors and showing their government IDs, waiters, the people who owned those boarding-houses and Laundromats, prostitutes, everyone remembering, or act-ing like they did, giving out information in the hopes that they will be the ones to get the hundred-thousand-dollar reward, or not even that, maybe just for the pleasure of ratting on him, making up details, nodding at the photos, everyone after him like a pack of dogs, everyone adding a thread to the web of persecution, perhaps knowing much more than what's in the papers, hoping that this will make him over-confident, that he will continue using his latest alias, the one on the Canadian passport and the plane ticket to Lisbon, lists of passengers and passport applications with thousands of names, verified one by one, until they find the odd one out and notice the similarity between the photo of the fugitive and the applicant, Sneyd, Ramon George Sneyd. According to J. Edgar Hoover, there are 3,075 FBI agents assigned exclusively to finding him; so far they have spent $781,407 and the agents have covered 332,849 miles; the Department of Justice is reviewing 2,153,000 passport applications in the United States; the Canadian government has to review 200,000; 53,000 fingerprints have been checked. He never imagined all of this would happen over the death of a black man; it baffled him until the end of his life.

•

The lethargic mood among the people of this city was slowly taking a hold of him. It was like a spell, an invincible exhaustion he could not shake. He was spending entire days in bed or walking aimlessly until he lost a sense of time.

He avoided wide streets and unshaded areas. It was instinctual by now. He walked past small jewelry shops assessing the possibility of a robbery. But he didn't know the four or five indispensable words or where he would sell the loot. It terrified him to think he could get arrested in this country and sent to a prison where he would not understand what anyone was saying. And what could he possibly steal from the other stores? They were filled with worthless stuff. It was hard to escape through those narrow, winding streets, and where would he go, he didn't even have a car.

Loud, heavyset women would stop to stare at him as he walked by. The foreigner with the thick, dark suit—completely inappropriate for the heat of May—stared at his map, wiping the beads of sweat from his face with a handkerchief. He turned a corner and there it was: the great river and its mist enveloping the red pillars and cables of the bridge. He saw the tall port cranes and yacht sails beyond the redbrick terminals, massive ships anchored in the center of the river, ferries in mid-crossing, leaving behind big arcs of foam.

The sound of the boat sirens combined with that of the trains, trams, and seagulls. He could not get used to walking on the cobblestone of those narrow streets with their crooked steps and angles. He descended toward the docks, trying his best not to trip. Fresh laundry fluttered on the clotheslines over his head. The smells of the port grew stronger with each step: tar and algae, fish, machine oil, paint and rust, coffee and cod.

He liked to buy sailing magazines and study each photo in detail: the shiny navigation tools, the wood decks where blond women in bikinis sunbathed, their dark lenses, the tall cocktail glasses, the long menthol cigarettes. With his diploma from the International School of Bartending, it would not be difficult to get a job as a waiter or even a butler on one of those yachts—white jacket, cap, his expert hands mixing cocktails for the wives of millionaires looking for a good time. They would look at him over their sunglasses as he approached with their drinks, perfectly balancing the tray despite the swells.

The pale face and demeanor gave him away, but he still liked to tell strangers, particularly women he met at bars, that he was in the merchant navy. Sometimes he was an officer, sometimes a bartender or cook; it all depended on his whim and the gullibility of the listener. He would spend weeks at a time on the Mississippi as the ship slowly made its way from New Orleans to Saint Louis. Sometimes it was the Gulf of Mexico, the islands of the Caribbean, the ship anchored in Havana.

In the cool shade of the bar, drinking daiquiris and mojitos under large ceiling fans, he would correct the waiters on their mixology. A sailor on shore leave, dressed in a white linen suit. Mulatto women in short, tight dresses would approach him and give him inviting looks, just like in the rum ads. He would follow them to rooms upstairs where curtains blew in the sea breeze.

Everything had the gloss of a double-page ad in *Life* magazine. He crossed the railroad tracks and walked to one of the docks where a cargo ship was being loaded. On the prow, in white letters, read the name *Minerva Zoe*. An officer with a buzz cut, hair so blond it was almost white, told him that the ship would be sailing for Angola in three days. The officer stared at him for a moment as if trying to remember something or simply annoyed by the presence of a man who looked so out of place on the dock. The *Minerva Zoe* was a merchant ship but it had room for a few travelers. The ticket cost around three hundred dollars. For a Canadian citizen, the only formality was a visa, which was easily issued by the Ministry of the Overseas. But Angola was not the best place to go on vacation, said the officer, a half smile forming on his red face. He was probably Dutch or Nordic. There was a war, even if the Portuguese newspapers rarely talked about it or covered only the victories, a cruel war, *a most vicious bloody war.*

•

He dreamed of seeing everything he had imagined in his countless hours in prison cells, motel rooms, staring at the ceiling or the wall, rigid, completely dressed, sometimes with the revolver under his pillow, or a sharpened shank with a duct-tape handle, always alert, listening to every sound. He imagined the shore fading in the distance, his elbows on the railing, or even better, looking out the porthole in the safety of his cabin, feeling the vibration of the engines, the incredible relief of leaving once and for all, even more final than stepping on the gas of a car or taking off in a plane.

He would no longer be the one staring at the boats from the dock, watching the hull separate from the stone edge, watching the passengers and their waving hands get smaller and smaller. The cabin would be smaller than even the worst rooms he had stayed in, but it would not feel like a cell or a trap because, even when he lay in bed, he would still be moving, farther and farther away.

The city would begin to withdraw into the horizon, its white glow fading in the mist, taking with it the red rooftops and bell towers, the hints of blue tile, the webs of clotheslines. The ship would glide under the red bridge and cross its long shadow; the sun shining on the water with an intensity that hurt his eyes. He had studied the mouth of the river on a map. Escape would only be a reality when the cliffs and the lighthouse were behind, when all that stretched before him was the open sea like he had never seen it.

•

At night, from his room in the Tropicana hotel, he could see the foamy waves washing over the sand and the glow of bonfires where fish was grilled. But that memory, from just a few months prior, no longer seemed his. It belonged to somebody else's life in a distant time, or not even that, an invented life, a movie or a novel, a rum ad, a fabricated past that makes for a good story at a bar, improvising details on the fly, the white Ford Mustang convertible, one hand on the wheel, driving full speed, kicking up dust on the dirt road, his shirt open to the chest, sunglasses, the camera and the typewriter on the backseat, and next to him, disheveled and dark, the woman who said her name was Irma just like he said his name was Eric, neither one believing the other. They had probably found her already, faster than he had anticipated, just like they had found the shy brunette from the Texas Bar and the fake blond from Maxime's, who had also used a made-up name, Wendy or Patty. He had just arrived in Lisbon when he learned that they had followed his tracks to Puerto Vallarta and found Irma. They had published a cropped photo of him in the newspaper and he instantly recognized it from an occasion when he posed for a photo with Irma, something he should have never allowed. He had been drinking mojitos and smoking pot on the hotel terrace. He remembered watching the still silhouettes of the oil tankers in the distance while Irma laughed and spoke in Spanish, then her friend snapped a photo. It shows Irma next to him wearing a floral dress with cleavage, her face is too dark, he looks uncomfortable, very tan, red rather, with sunglasses, his hair is slicked back and it looks black in the photo. He looks unrecognizable, which is a great relief; every photo they find and print is so different from the previous ones that it can only make their search more difficult. Meanwhile, he is perfecting his ability to leave no strong impressions on others, so they can only remember him in the most general ways.

•

Hiding in his hotel room during the day and walking through the streets of Cais do Sodré at night—he could not tell if he had managed to become truly invisible, to vanish like a fading shadow, like a gangster from a movie who can just get plastic surgery and all of a sudden look like Humphrey Bogart, or Ernst Stavro Blofeld, the supreme villain from James Bond, who can be fat, pale, and bald in one novel, and slender, tan, with white hair in another.

He was one figure among the many reflected in the mirrors of Maxime's or the Texas Bar; a figure appearing and disappearing outside window displays.

He was invisible in Lisbon and at the same time it seemed he could be anywhere. He had vanished on April 5 at dawn. It was the day after the shooting. He had driven all night from Memphis to Atlanta, perhaps stopping somewhere secluded to sleep for an hour or two in the car. Someone saw the white car from a window high above. It was entering the parking lot between the two towers of the housing projects. The sky was already blue, but the streets were still in shadows. The car arrived with the headlights on. It seemed out of place in that working-class neighborhood. The engine ceased. The headlights turned off. In the dark and monotonous brick buildings, a few scattered window lights were starting to turn on. Even more odd than the Mustang is the presence of the white man inside. He gets out and takes a plastic bag from the trunk. The sound of the car door resonates in the stillness of dawn.

He looks around but not up, not toward the window where someone watches him, someone who will remember him days later when the Mustang is still parked in the same spot, arousing the curiosity of the residents and the children who like to get close and peek inside, noticing the exotic sticker from the Mexican border. Someone will remember seeing the white man in the suit and tie at daybreak, taking his bag from the car and disappearing around a corner.

An hour later, a similar man is seen picking up clothes from a Laundromat in Atlanta. The shopkeeper, Miss Peters, said he was serious, well-dressed, shy, very clean. She saw him leave on foot instead of in the white Mustang he usually parked outside.

•

People had seen him in the airport in San Juan, Puerto Rico, trying to buy a ticket to Jamaica or Aruba. A wiry man with auburn hair and blue eyes. He seemed nervous. His lips, thin and dry, moving in silence, showing a slight overbite. He was wearing a brown suit with a blue shirt and black shoes. One hand pulled on an earlobe, the other was tightly clasped around the handle of a dark suitcase.

A Mexican taxi driver recalled taking him from Tapachula to Ciudad Hidalgo, all the way to the edge of a river that marked the border between Mexico and Guatemala. He said the man had a beard and a scar over his right eye, and carried a gun and a green backpack.

On April 21, he arrived at a gas station in Pennsylvania in a blue Mustang. He asked the employees if he could sleep in the car for a few hours. He said he had to be in Chicago the next day and was trying to save time by not stopping at a motel.

On May 5, a woman saw him praying in a church in Tucson.

On May 8, he was at the bar of the International Inn in Tampa. Two days later he was on a cruise from Jacksonville to Key West, but also having breakfast in the Chicago airport. A woman was certain she had seen him in the lobby of the Miami International Airport Hotel. He was wearing dark pants and a shirt open at the neck. He seemed restless and tired. Eventually he fell asleep in an armchair. He left the hotel at 1:45 p.m.

On May 9, he was in a restaurant called Lido in Curaçao. An American tourist heard the southern accent as he ordered some food. She noticed his shirt was open and very wrinkled. In her memory his hair is light brown and longer than in the photos; his face is red from the sun and he has a cleft chin.

On May 11, he was driving a red Mercury somewhere in Arkansas. The driver who saw him said he had a pointy nose and one ear bigger than the other. Some people saw him in a village in the Sonoran Desert. They said he was living with a very young woman and a child around seven years old. But he was also on the front page of *The New York Times* in a photo sent anonymously to the FBI: the mayor of New York City welcomes his counterpart from Toronto, a crowd is gathered around them and there you can see the face with the aquiline nose, the sunglasses, the slicked-back hair, undoubtedly his, says the person who mailed the photo with a red circle around the face.

People saw him in a hotel in Columbus, Ohio, wearing a hat that darkened his face. He had two bags and paid for the night in advance. He was waiting for a flight in the international terminal at the Los Angeles airport. He was the ghost of airports and Greyhound stations, diners and hotel bars.

In the Denver airport at 10:30 p.m. one night in May, he was sitting in front of a television, absorbed in an issue of *Life* magazine. He tore one of the pages, folded it, and put it in his pocket. It was an article about the assassination of President Kennedy. He left the magazine behind.

Someone also spotted him on a night bus from Houston to Mexico City, in a drugstore on the outskirts of Alliance, Ohio, in a barbershop in Stanford, Florida.

He had been staying in a small house outside Kansas City close to an airport. A small plane had taken him to Belle Glade, Florida, and then to Cuba.

According to an anonymous letter sent from Canada, his corpse was buried outside Mexico City. The letter included a diagram and a cross marking the location of the body.

On May 17, he arrived at a gas station in Oklahoma City in a white Chevrolet truck with New Mexico plates. He was wearing casual clothes, light pants, tennis shoes. He was working at a gay bar in Los Angeles. He spent a night in the Woodland Motor Court in Thomasville, Georgia. He arrived in a '66 white Mustang and his only luggage was a small toiletry bag.

He was in Argentina and Switzerland, in the Hotel Clark in Los Angeles, the Carolina Hotel in Columbia, South Carolina, the Holiday Inn in Tucson, where he had a bad cough, in an RV park in a wooded area in Arkansas, working as a bellboy at the Sun Castle Club in Pompano Beach, Florida, hitchhiking somewhere in Georgia. At 2:45 p.m. on April 29, he was having lunch at Glenn's Bakery and Coffee Shop in Crescent City, California. He seemed nervous. Someone saw him in the last row of a flight from New Orleans to Frankfurt. He had grown a thick mustache and was frequently seen at a fishing supply store in Portland, Oregon. He was on a bus from Palo Alto to San Francisco.

He was watching television while waiting at a gate in the Portland airport. He was in the last seat on a Greyhound leaving Tulsa, Oklahoma. He was whispering to the person next to him: "I killed a man. They are looking for me in forty-eight states. I can tell you everything about that nigger, King. There's twenty of us involved in this, but we are all cops so no one suspects us."

In a Dallas suburb, they saw him in the white Mustang with a revolver and a machine gun. There was a panting Doberman in the backseat. He got violent when drunk and started yelling about blacks, Jews, and Catholics.

Around 3:00 a.m., in the cafeteria of the Greyhound station in Jackson, Florida, he was wearing a black shirt and gray pants, and drinking an orange soda. He was a bartender in a hotel in Monterrey. He worked as a cook at a beach restaurant in Isla Mujeres. He was walking along a highway close to Phoenix, Arizona. He was the man drinking alone at the Aztec Bar in El Paso. He drove a '67 Plymouth Fury convertible.

He was in Oaxaca and a mall in Cleveland the same day. Before going to Isla Mujeres, he had stayed at Hotel Isabella in Mexico City. He had dyed his hair blond and carried an automatic pistol. He was in Merida, Yucatán, and left from there for New Orleans. In New York City, at the Oasis Bar on the corner of Seventh Avenue and Twenty-Third Street, he was wearing a blue blazer and jeans. A waiter asked him what he did for a living; he said he was a sailor.

Early one morning, he was walking out of a bank in Geneva with a leather briefcase under his arm. An informant for the Australian police recognized him at a bar by the port in Sydney. He was at airports in Seoul and Hong Kong; also in a park in Taipei, sitting in the shade, feeding the ducks. He looked tan and was wearing sunglasses. In the Sheraton Hotel in Washington, someone spotted him in the audience of a conference on tropical diseases. He did not talk to anyone and seemed distracted. Everyone was dressed rather formally, and he was wearing a beige or white shirt open at the neck and somewhat dirty. He was wearing no socks.

•

He would buy the usual newspapers and magazines at the kiosk in Rossio Square and rush back to the hotel, ignoring everything around him—the mosaic sidewalks, the white houses, the rose-colored walls and gardens leading up the hill to San Jorge Castle. He could no longer afford to sit on the terrace of the Pastelaria Suiça. He walked through a shaded side street connecting Rossio and Figueira Squares, no longer staring at the bronze king on horseback, or the street vendors, or the beggars, or the groups of black people enjoying the sun, or the small restaurants that had once surprised him with those exotic smells. He no longer stopped to look inside the window of the locksmith shop across from the Hotel Portugal. He would go straight to the hotel and ask for his keys without looking at the receptionist.

Once in this room, he would lock the door and lie in bed with his shoes on. He rarely took them off even though his feet were always in pain. They had not stopped hurting since the prison escape, when he had to walk six days and six nights. He examined every page of the newspapers while eating cream pastries, potato chips, roasted peanuts. Sometimes the most valuable information is in some easy-to-miss corner.

He also went through the Portuguese newspaper, but looking for the movie listings and information on arrivals and departures from the port. On a few occasions he went to the movie theater just to feel the darkness and listen to the voices in English. He watched *Planet of the Apes*, and also a movie about some white mercenaries in Africa called *Dark of the Sun*. He liked to pronounce the names of ships, destinations, ports. Mozambique, India, Beira, Sofala, Angola, Luanda, Patria, Infante Dom Henrique, Veracruz. Later he would look for them in the white letters painted on the sides of the ships at the port. He would suddenly catch his name in an article and feel a knot in the pit of his stomach that would unravel into curiosity and then vanity. It amused him to see stories in these serious papers so full of errors, fantasies really, plots straight out of spy novels. A group of experts in chemical and subliminal manipulations had programmed and trained him to carry out the assassination and leave a false trail of clues. An organization called the International Revolutionary Council, which counted King as a member, had planned his murder to unleash a revolution among black people.

He read the newspapers for hours at a time. Door locked, curtains drawn, the sounds of Lisbon in the background, the periodic rumbling of the underground train. Every now and then he would look up and see his reflection in the mirror, a stranger, his only confidant and interlocutor in the world, just as Charlton Heston on a future planet Earth, surrounded by apes who were in control, at least for now. He read that the person who fired the shot that afternoon was actually a woman dressed as a man; or that it was him but in a state of trance induced by FBI psychologists; or under orders by the Chinese secret service with the objective of creating social chaos in the United States and accelerating the international triumph of communism; or he had done it for a bounty of fifty thousand dollars. Some papers had him outmaneuvering the FBI and being now well beyond their reach; others had him dead, killed so the truth about who the murderer really was would never come out.

•

Sometimes, in moments of extreme isolation, fatigue, and insomnia, he feared being dead, a ghost, and not knowing about it. How different could it be, death versus this eternal wait in Lisbon. He had been living as Eric Starvo Galt for a full year when, suddenly, in Toronto, that identity had ceased to exist. For several days, he used two different names and was registered in two different boardinghouses; one belonged to a Polish woman, the other to a woman from China. Neither one spoke or understood English. One knew him as Paul Edward Bridgman, for the other one he was Ramon George Sneyd. He could be the decomposing body found in the trunk of a Chevrolet Malibu parked in the Atlanta airport—facedown, pants pulled to the knees, pockets inside out, shot in the head. Or maybe he was the body mentioned in the anonymous letter, the one buried in the ruins of Cuicuilco, next to a 1,400-year-old pyramid.

Any unidentified cadaver could be his. They found his body close to a mine in Pennsylvania with three bullet holes in the chest. At some point they felt certain they had found him in an Acapulco beach, buried under the sand, beaten and beheaded. The crabs had already eaten his eyes and the tips of his fingers so it was impossible to confirm his identity. A plastic bag with sand soaked in blood and other fluids was sent to the FBI.

He was the mystery protagonist, the straw man, the scapegoat, the gun for hire, a single thread in a web that extended all the way to the assassination in Dallas of John F. Kennedy, *a sophisticated killing machine*, according to a man with a high-pitched voice on the television. There is an organization that trains assassins and brainwashes them to kill public figures, said this supposed crime expert. It was all like the machinations of Dr. Julius No in his underground lair at Crab Key; or the SPECTRE network led by Ernst Stavro Blofeld from his impregnable fortress in the Swiss Alps.

•

He read until his head began to spin, the printed words becoming blurrier and blurrier as the room got darker. He never bothered to turn the lamp on, reading with whatever little light still came from the window, leaning uncomfortably against the headboard, his neck awkwardly propped up on a folded pillow. The pages would fall to the floor as he began to doze off. Suddenly, he was in his prison cell in Missouri, the sounds of the people in the nearby square were echoes from other cells, and the bell from the tram was the sound of a door locking. Other times, he was in the Rebel Motel on the outskirts of Memphis on the night of April 3. Wind from a tornado tossed the trees. Thunder rattled the windowpanes. Hail descended like a rain of gunshots. The room was always the same but it was never clear which motel or city. The alarm of not knowing where he was jolted him out of sleep like a ringing phone. He was lying on that dirty bed in Memphis in the heat of the afternoon. He had fallen asleep just when it was most important that he be watching the second floor of the Lorraine Motel and preparing the rifle.

Sometimes he dreamed that he was in room 5B and had sat down on the bed or sofa for a moment and ended up falling asleep. He tried to wake up but it was impossible. Meanwhile, in the motel across the parking lot, the man was finally walking out onto the balcony and leaning on the rail. He was in an undershirt. He would stay for a few moments, then turn around and go back into his room, disappearing through the turquoise doors of room 306. In the dream, he knew what would happen in just a few minutes. It would be a brief moment but just enough time if he managed to wake up and act quickly.

The opportunity appears again. The man, his skin black and shining with aftershave or perfume, walks out a second time. Now he is fully dressed in a dark blue suit, white shirt, and gold cuff links reflecting the red-tinted sun of 6:00 p.m. The man's shadow fans out across the door. He must wake up right away, get up quickly, wrap the rifle in the blanket, run to the bathroom without being seen, lock the door, rest the barrel on the windowsill, adjust the scope, ignore the drunkard who will come banging on the bathroom door, wipe the sweat of his hands on his pant leg, focus, get his balance right. But most importantly, he must wake up once and for all and confirm where he is, what room, what hotel, what city, what day, what month, what year, what hour, facing what window or balcony, in Memphis, in Birmingham, in Puerto Vallarta, in Atlanta, in Acapulco, in Los Angeles, in Selma, in Montreal, in Toronto.

•

His eyes finally opened and he jumped out of bed. The room was pitch-black. A long, screeching sound was for a second the gate of a cell before it was the metal shutters of the hardware store across João das Regras Street. It was closing time. He was in Lisbon. He began to notice the other sounds—the tram, the street vendors, the clinking sounds from a restaurant, a distant television, a news bulletin, the faint moaning of a woman in a nearby room.

Without turning the light on, he walked to the bathroom and washed his face. The newspapers rustled under his feet. He stared at the dark and blurry reflection in the mirror and combed his hair back. He stared intently while tightening the knot of his tie, which he hadn't undone in a long time. The face he saw was the one from the old police photos, the one that belonged to the names that were now printed in the newspapers and the WANTED signs, the names that flashed on the television screen on Sunday nights during the FBI program, where he continued to be number one on the list of the Ten Most Wanted.

He looked into his eyes for a full minute without blinking. To change a man's face is to change his destiny. He contracted the muscles in the corners of his mouth until he achieved the exact same smile he had in the Canadian passport. He put his glasses on and there he was, once again: Ramon George Sneyd. It was nighttime when he left the hotel. The revolver was in his jacket pocket. He caught glimpses of himself in the moving windows of the tram, a gaze stripped of substance like his own reflection, like his shadow, invisible and unpunished, lured away by the neon signs that were already lurking around the corner, the dark and narrow streets of Cais do Sodré.

13

Seen and unseen. I had just arrived in Lisbon and it was already time to leave. The trip was over in the blink of an eye. You wake up in a moving train and see a light of daybreak unlike any other. You close your eyes for an instant, and before you know it, it's three days later, and you're sitting at the Santa Apolónia station at nighttime. The immediate past has the temporal elasticity and amplitude that are usually confined to dreams; fantastic journeys unfold in a moment of somnolence, entire stages of one's life vividly invoked a minute before waking.

The Lusitania Express was ready to depart. The row of windows illuminated the platform. As soon as the train began to move, Lisbon would be nothing but a memory: scribbled words in a notebook; receipts and matchboxes from restaurants; a roll of film; a worn map of the city covered with pencil markings, routes, annotations, circled destinations; a small Portuguese dictionary; an anthology of poems by Fernando Pessoa, which I had purchased the first morning along with the dictionary and the map, with a page folded at the beginning of "*Opiário* de Álvaro de Campos," where I had found a verse that somehow would have to make it into my novel, *Um Oriente ao Oriente do Oriente*, the music of a litany or spell, like John Coltrane's invocation *A love supreme, a love supreme, a love supreme, a love supreme, a love supreme.*

The sadness of leaving so soon and seeing the cliffs and walls of all my obligations rise again before me was tempered with the knowledge that I had used my time wisely, that all the visual cues I needed for the novel were now impressed in the zones between my memory and imagination: the faces of two lovers who see each other for a split second across moving trains; the hospital with rose-colored walls in the wooded hillside at sunset, just as the lights are starting to turn on; the wall of that abandoned garden and the name on the azulejo tiles, QUINTA DOS LOBOS; the young woman behind the one-way glass who takes her clothes off to the rhythm of slow music, rotating inside a prism of pink lights and mirrors. Her skin is pearl white against the red satin of the bed, and her eyes, provocative and contemptuous, refuse to look into the circular mirrors that surround her with the gaze of those who watch from the anonymity of the private rooms as coins clink into the metal slots next to the toilet paper.

•

I was leaving like a spy who has accomplished his mission, the photos on the reel of my camera containing valuable, secret evidence. The night before I had been in the Hot Clube de Portugal in Alegria Square, a dark and empty square, one of the places I had circled on my map. In that same square, perhaps still there in 1987, was the neon sign of Maxime's Club, where Ramon George Sneyd met several times with Gloria Sousa, a prostitute with platinum blond hair and a loud laugh, who had probably accompanied him the short distance between Alegria Square and João das Regras Street.

I had arrived at number four, a closed metal door on a street lined with deserted buildings, chipped walls, and broken windows, barely illuminated by the weak lights that hung from one end of the square to the other. I thought I was probably mistaken. There was no indication that this was a club or had ever been one. The wind swung the streetlights above, enlarging and disturbing shadows. It reminded me of being a child and feeling my father's strong grip around my hand as we walked back home at night, our footsteps resounding on the cobblestone streets.

With a determination that back then was out of character for me,

I dared to knock on the door. Perhaps there was actually an illuminated sign above the door, which I have forgotten, and its absence adds a certain fictitious satisfaction to the memory. I had come to the Hot Clube to hear some jazz, have a drink, and, most important, see the space where the musicians in my novel would perhaps play. I knocked on the door again and this time it opened as if I had accidentally used the right password.

A young black woman with a mane of curls, an Ethiopian princess in a turtleneck, said the club would open in an hour. I could have fallen in love with her instantly. I don't remember much about the interior of the club or the concert that night. But memory is cunning, it completes its sleepless marvelous task in secret, breaking the substance of lived experience into fertile soil for fiction; here, it offers me images of jazz clubs that only came much later, low brick vaults with posters on the walls, narrow stairways and basements in New York, the neutral facade of the Village Vanguard.

In the end, my imaginary musicians played in a club that was partially of my own making. The entrance belonged to the facade of an old movie theater with Art Nouveau tiles. I saw the place on my way from Rossio Square to Sapateiros Street. It had a splendid name, Animatógrafo do Rossio, and had endured, like so many other things in Lisbon, in a state of decay that was a testament to time but did not signal its end, a postponement—half mercy, half neglect—which resulted in the anachronism that attracted me so much, as it stood in contrast to the barbaric impulse in Spanish cities to demolish the old and build the new. I did not go past the entrance. I imagined its interior like those of the theaters in my hometown, with gilded moldings, red curtains, and narrow corridors—old-fashioned luxury that began as artificial but acted as a cocoon for our cinematic daydreams—worn red velvet, squeaky chairs, hollow columns. In a place like that, my jazz apprentice would accompany his master at the piano. The master was a trumpeter, somewhere between Clifford Brown and Chet Baker, and his skin color would never be revealed in the book, just as the word *jazz* would never appear, and certain details about the female protagonist would be missing. She would take a long time to appear but then she would disappear right away; she would arrive without warning, like an apparition, and the moment she started to become more tangible she would vanish, like a ghost, because she was not a real woman but a projection of desire, fed by films and novels and, above all, by the male difficulty of seeing women as they are, to look at them as individuals and not from a place of cowardice or rapture, adolescent fascination and paralysis.

•

But that's what I was. I was about to turn thirty-one and I was still an overgrown adolescent, a spy trapped in my public identity as a bureaucrat, a married man, and married by the church, father of two children; undercover, but was I infiltrating the underworld or City Hall . . . docile to each obligation, weighed down by the thick net of family ties that I had managed to escape for three days in Lisbon, but where I was now returning on that train in the middle of the night. Like an adolescent, I fed a melodramatic self-pity and inhabited the real world with resentment, feeling like a stranger but also superior and barely paying attention to what surrounded me. I did not want to see the effect of my attitude on those closest to me, those in my home and in my life; the life that felt like a sentence, a routine as uninspiring of emotional and intellectual stimulus as administrative work.

I do not doubt there were moments of happiness that I took for granted and never thanked, moments I failed to notice and have forgotten, or would be ashamed of remembering now, so many years later. Lodged in those blank spaces is remorse as intense as the memory of the pain I caused. Remorse has an extraordinary resistance to the passage of time. It feeds on memory and when there is none, it latches on to amnesia like an organism capable of adapting even to the most extreme conditions.

A January, twenty-seven years later, finds me thinking about how my then wife must have felt when I was in Lisbon. She was still recovering from the birth of our second child. It had been the days of Christmas vacation, which we usually spent in Úbeda with her family and mine, the familial skein in which she felt so warmly protected but that for me was suffocating; parents and grandparents and uncles and cousins, everything multiplied by two, endless trips and visits, and us, arm in arm, pushing the stroller with the baby, the other child holding on to her hand or mine, or holding on to both of us at the same time, asserting his place between us now that his brother was here, perhaps intuitively trying to keep us together, because he sensed, with that primal instinct kids have, the inverse magnetism of the two adults, the seed of everything he would see and hear in just a few years, too young to understand but old enough to experience the pain, to smell the toxic air of dispute and bitterness.

I wonder what she was thinking during those three days in which I called no more than once or twice to ask about the baby. I wonder what she imagined I was doing. She had every reason not to believe what I said. I had lied to her several times, and she always saw right through it. An adolescent about to turn thirty-one, still seeking refuge in literature and music from his mediocre life.

•

A group of Spaniards drank and laughed loudly in the train cafeteria. The volume of life was being dialed up again. I had gotten used to the Portuguese manner, the polite and muffled tone of the voices. I had lived those three days in a frontier state of mind, a no-man's-land between imagination and the real world, with a clearly set beginning and end.

Now I had to go back and sit before the typewriter, create words out of lived experience, resume the thread of the novel. There was nothing beyond the final period of a sentence. The blank page did not signal a particular direction. The train advanced in the darkness and I could feel the proximity of the task ahead, the moment of truth when I sat to write again; a stack of blank paper on one side, the current manuscript on the other, and in the middle, the typewriter and the keyboard, so familiar to my touch. This time I would also have detailed notes to guide me and the photographs I would get developed as soon as I got back.

The train was fairly empty and I was the only person in my compartment. I sat quietly next to the window, waiting for sleep as I watched the passing bursts of shadows, the reflection of the moon on the river, the scattered lights of small villages in the distance. When I woke, the sun was rising over the barren plains near Madrid. I remembered the entire trip as if I had dreamed it. In Atocha I took another train and by noon I was already with my family. I have not preserved a single image from that reunion.

It was January 5 and the Three Kings Day Parade would take place in the afternoon. My wife and I had agreed to take our elder son to see it. On my way there, I bumped into an old childhood friend whom I hadn't seen in years. He hugged me and we decided to go for a beer. It was still a while before the parade. At the bar we came across more old friends. The beer soothed the anxiety of being late, but I still felt remorseful, and also angry at my obligations. I allowed myself to feel like the victim of oppressive circumstances beyond my control, trapped by responsibilities that my friends, who were less cowardly or less complacent, did not have to endure. Just the day before in Lisbon, I had been living the imaginary life of a novelist, almost like a character in a book; now, in the city of my adolescence, as I became more intoxicated with beer and hashish and the effusive displays of friendship that drunkenness encourages, I was once again acting like a seventeen-year-old, indulging myself in sentimentality and nostalgia.

We kept hopping from bar to bar and it was getting late. The parade and the fireworks had ended long ago. By this point, leaving my wife and my son waiting was not nearly as bad as the fact that I hadn't even called to tell them I was okay, to make up some excuse, to justify my tardiness, to say I had changed my plans. I thought the harm was done and so it did not matter if I went with my friends to yet another bar and had another drink. The feeling of guilt was a preview of the hangover to come. We laughed, shared stories, and compared memories from our days at the institute. It was three or four in the morning and we were drunk and fumbling through the streets. Didn't I have the right to go out for a night with my best friends, the people I had known since I was a little kid playing on the streets? I feel so ashamed now. I imagined that after the parade my wife had probably taken the kids to sleep at her parents' house. At five in the morning, I did the same and went to the old house where I grew up.

I struggled to open the door and somehow made it to my old room. I lay on my bed feeling nauseous as the whole room spun in the darkness. For a moment I was back in the train returning from Lisbon, but with no trace of the dignity I had experienced there. I was wrecked and full of anger.

14

He liked sedentary people, the kind who wait and watch others go by, people who guard lobbies or sit at reception desks, those who check passports at the airport all day or sit behind store counters just watching the streets.

He found public officials fascinating, but they also intimidated him, asking for paperwork, setting deadlines, pausing or accelerating the time of others; they sat behind their desks wearing dark suits or uniforms, and interrogated the prisoner, taking notes, mumbling and deciding months and years, his entire life contingent on those scribbled notes, those whispered words.

Now he lowered his head instinctively whenever he entered an office, and stood quietly, staring at the ground, until his presence was acknowledged and he was explicitly asked to sit down. In some stores a little bell would ring when the door opened.

He would gulp and clear his throat as he entered, adjusting the knot of his tie and feeling his hair; if possible he liked to check his reflection somewhere beforehand, or in the little mirror he still carried from his days in prison, and give his hair a quick comb. The man who sold him the rifle in Birmingham said he seemed very humble.

He approached a counter or desk and spoke so softly he was often asked to repeat himself, and cleared his throat each time to get the words out. Bureaucrats live sheltered lives in their offices like mollusks in their shells, allowing only the slightest opening; surrounded by small objects, the tools of their trade, rubber stamps, ink pads, staplers, plastic bottles with white fluid to correct typing errors, calendars filled with notes, a little toy next to the typewriter; so many things at their fingertips, pencils, sharpeners, ink, instruments for the tasks they repeat day after day for the same number of hours, nine to five, Monday to Friday, the same trajectory to work every day, the same routine at the end of business hours when they pack their things, put files away, cover their typewriters, and get on with their lives, oblivious to their power over the fate of others.

The woman at the travel agency in Toronto, Kennedy Travel, smiled as she handed him the passport, along with the round-trip ticket to London. "Safe travels, Mr. Sneyd," she said. He was stunned by how easy it had been to get a passport, his first, and the ticket to another country.

The phone rang and the woman quickly forgot about him, unaware that she had just changed his fortunes. She greeted the caller and began asking questions, explaining travel options and itineraries, spinning a pen between her long, painted fingernails. He stood there watching her, so comfortable in her cubicle, surrounded by color posters of beaches and blue skies, castles nestled in forests, river cruises. He felt tired, temporarily acquitted, incredulous that his escape was going according to plan.

He stood there in his horn-rimmed glasses, making the same face he had in the passport photo, the photo that looked nothing like the one in the WANTED signs, the face that now belonged to a different name, a name that no one could associate with that of the fugitive, or any of his previous identities, John Larry Rayns, John Willard, Paul Edward Bridgman, Harvey Lowmeyer, Eric Starvo Galt. A few minutes later, the woman hung up the phone and saw the glass doors close behind the silhouette of the pale man. To her surprise, she had already forgotten his face.

•

Now he waited in another office, this time in Lisbon, and his life was once again in the hands of a bureaucrat. One of the officers at the

Ministry of the Overseas saw him come into the office, opening the glass door slowly, timidly, one hand on the doorknob and the other holding a coat, an odd thing to carry during a hot month like May, much like the dark suit, the crocodile shoes, and the tie pressed tightly around his neck.

But if his gestures showed an excessive politeness, his eyes expressed something else. In the brief instant when he looked up from the floor, and the official caught the look in the light blue eyes, the expression betrayed was one of fear but also malice, obstinacy, and exhaustion—and something else, a hint of mockery, a silent sarcasm. He was signaled to sit on a bench and wait, and so he did, with his back straight and the coat neatly folded on his lap. He sat quietly, as if inside an urn, or behind a glass wall, isolated in his foreignness and inability to speak Portuguese.

•

The senior officer who would later give him information about visas for the colonies noticed the crocodile shoes as he made his way down the hall with a folder under his arm. He seemed very pleased with himself. A man strolling into the office after a mid-morning coffee, puffing his cigarette, proud of his place in the world, a veteran with his name and title inscribed on a frosted glass door and a plaque on a desk, a name he signed on all sorts of important documents with the golden fountain pen that protruded from his breast pocket above the honorary badge that reminded everyone of his many years of service.

He examined the world around him as methodically as he read every document that came for his signature. He scrutinized everything, from the cleanliness of the stone steps leading to the office, down to the smallest details in the uniforms of his subordinates. He expected every wall clock in the office to match the time on his watch. He was fluent in English and French and took it upon himself to personally attend to special cases like applications from foreigners.

Some of the most important letters he preferred to type himself instead of dictating to his secretary, and he used a stand-up typewriter, some said, because he did not like to wrinkle his pants. He enjoyed his reputation as a legendary seducer of married women and wealthy widows.

The typewriter sat on a lectern in front of a window overlooking a corner of the square, the river, and the stairway that descended into the water. Sometimes he stopped typing mid-sentence to watch a boat gliding over the river or a woman walking by the shore. He typed with his index fingers—nails well-groomed and nicotine yellow—and his glasses resting on the tip of his nose.

He had noticed with distaste the shoes of the man in the waiting area, the foreigner his assistant later mentioned as he opened the door for his superior and lowered his head. "He is Canadian," said the assistant as he stood by the large desk, much bigger than his, solid wood instead of metal, decorated with a crucifix and a framed photo of the head of state with a personal dedication. "He wants to go to Angola for business, or to look for his brother who lives in Luanda. It's hard to understand him. He doesn't speak Portuguese."

•

Foreigners are always in a hurry. But they must wait. A few minutes' wait is a reminder of who is in control. They think their passports give them rights to whatever they want. They call and ask to speak to superiors, as if standard processing times did not apply to them. They think they can come, raise their voices, speak in their language, and others are supposed to understand and obey.

So he let a few minutes pass before pressing the bell that signaled his assistant to let the visitor come in. Phones ringing, typewriters clattering, the constant rustle of voices and hard steps on the wood floors combined with the squawking of the seagulls and the sounds of the church bells coming through the open windows. Every few minutes a siren marked the arrival or departure of a ferry.

Alone in his office, content in the knowledge that retirement was just around the corner, and in a good mood after the morning stroll, a coffee, and a cigarette, he leaned back in the chair, rubbed his hands, and waited for the foreigner to walk in. The assistant opened the door for the man and asked his senior officer if he was needed for anything else. After receiving a response in the negative, he mumbled "*obrigado*" and left as quietly as he had come, making sure the door barely made a sound.

Now that the foreigner was in front of him, the face seemed vaguely familiar. Like many foreigners, he had made the mistake of coming to Lisbon with a winter wardrobe. Dark-wool suit, coat, that tie so tight, and, worst of all, those absurd summer shoes.

He approached the desk with some hesitation. His voice was barely audible. Something about a brother or an in-law, who lived in Angola and had not written back to the family in many months, making them very worried. The accent made his English hard to understand. He was looking for something in his pockets and mumbling about how he had enlisted as a mercenary in the war or that his import/export business had something to do with mercenaries, when the senior officer leaned forward with a very serious expression. "Portugal does not have colonies. It has overseas provinces. And in the overseas provinces there is no war, much less mercenaries," he said in English.

But the man did not hear him or, perhaps, he did not understand; he kept looking for something in his pant pockets and in his coat. He seemed nervous, his brow glistened with perspiration. The senior officer noticed a strong smell of sweat and deodorant. He was pulling things out of his pockets and placing them on the edge of the desk or in a different pocket. A folded map of Lisbon, a matchbox, a disposable razor, a coaster from a bar.

Finally, something fell to the floor. He picked it up and handed it to the senior officer with a sigh of relief. The passport, he said, and then he took out two more documents. The senior officer adjusted the glasses on the tip of his nose and looked at the documents for a few seconds before dismissing them with a quick gesture. Why would he need the holder of a Canadian passport to also produce a birth certificate and whatever that other card was, a vaccination certificate, perhaps. It was always one or the other, they either lacked the necessary document or brought extraneous ones that made the process more confusing. He felt the paper on the passport to check its authenticity. He had a slight suspicion; after all, the foreigner seemed too nervous and was offering things no one had asked for.

But his tactile expertise did not lie. This was a real passport. And the man in the photo was clearly the same one in his office, though the photo looked much older than the passport's origination date, just one week ago, in Toronto.

The man in the photo, Ramon George Sneya, looked calm and confident, like someone leading a successful life; he sported a good haircut, glasses, and the hint of a smile, which tempered the dull suit; a university professor, perhaps, or whatever he was now saying he was— a businessman responsible for expanding a luxury yacht company, looking for new markets in Africa.

But the man in his office was not clean-shaven like the one in the picture, and he seemed dirty despite the smell of deodorant. He also looked older, though that could be lack of sleep, an illness, or perhaps some kind of tragedy. That could explain the nervous tics, the incessant blinking, the scratching of the neck, and the constant pinching of the right earlobe, which also seemed larger than the other one.

It was then that the senior officer realized why the man looked familiar. It was the pale face, the winter suit in May, the look of distrust and fear but also the imploring eyes, the contrast between the passport photo and the person in the flesh, the way he searched for documents in pockets that were filled with all sorts of things, the impatience, the cheek chewing, the blank stare at the passing ships and the steps of the pier. This foreigner reminded him of the refugees he had seen in that same office when he was much younger, almost at the beginning of his long and honorable administrative career—the year was 1940 and it was the beginning of summer. They were people who had fled the cold countries, some dressed in rags but also with a dignified expression, others with the latest fashion, men and women, worldly and haggard, women with long cigarettes and red lipstick, imperious men who were obviously used to giving orders wherever they came from, but here, in the waiting room, felt desperate and powerless. They kept producing useless documents, some authentic, some falsified, and kept talking about departure dates for flights and ships. They all wanted the same thing this man was asking for: a visa. They filled the waiting rooms and hallways. Some could be seen walking in circles on the square below, in the searing heat and humidity of May, while others waited outside the building for the postal service, eager to get the documents that would allow them to get as far away from Europe as possible.

At first glance, their expressions seemed identical despite the minor differences in origin and social class, and they continued coming day after day to wait, in the lobby, in the hallways, outside, under the arches, by the stairway to the water. And then, one day, suddenly, they would not be back, they would be gone forever and someone else would come to take their place, another face, another silhouette in the multitudes of that city which never changed, the city where he, now a senior officer, was just a young man then, at the beginning of his career, advancing on his own merits, his excellent handwriting, his impeccable typing; studying English at night while he listened to the BBC so he could practice his pronunciation; sticking to the same routine every day, industrious and sedentary, critical of everything in his path, ready to explain to whoever came for a visa that there were rules and processing times that had to be respected.

It brought him great pleasure to call his secretary and order him to help Mr. Sneyd fill out a visa application. He spoke slowly, not entirely sure the man could understand what he was saying in English, because he kept looking at the floor and nodding, but that could also be just one of his nervous tics. "When is that freighter leaving for Angola, is that what our visitor asked?" "In three days?" He raised three fingers to the man's face and repeated "three." He opened his hands in the air, feigning frustration at the slow pace of the colonial administration, the destination. No matter how hard he or his subordinates tried, the visa to Angola would take at least seven days. "Seven days," he repeated. The man kept his head down, and then glanced at the sides as if trying to find an exit that was not the door.

15

A novel is a state of mind, a warm interior where you seek refuge as you write, a cocoon that is woven from the inside, locking you within it, showing you the world outside through its translucent concavity. A novel is a confession and a hideout. The novel and the particular state of mind in which you must submerge yourself to write it feed each other; a unique wavelength, a song that you hear in the distance and try to identify through the act of writing.

The state of mind is born with the novel and ends with it. It is a house that feels like your own but where you will never live again, a music that will cease to exist when you stop playing. The book will remain, of course, the printed word, like a recording, but the product will begin to feel alien, and a painful emptiness will weigh over you for some time, as if you had been conned.

Every day of work is sustained by the anticipation of the end, its promising proximity. You sit to write, hoping to rekindle the fire of creation, see your soul at the white heat, as Emily Dickinson says. You fear the trance is not going to happen that day; distractions, chores, laziness, depression, the venom of insecurity—any of it can prevent you from sustaining the requisite state of mind. Because a novel is like an ember that must continue glowing beneath the cool ashes after the flames have died, an ember that you must carry in secret, while you get through everything else that occupies your life besides writing—the seven hours at the office, the time preparing dinner and putting dishes away, taking the children to school, preparing their lunch, giving them a bath, driving to see family or run errands.

The more days you let pass before returning to the novel, the deeper the fear becomes. You fear that when you finally get to sit down and write, the ember has extinguished, the state of mind that fuels the novel has been dissolved. There will be regret for all the pages left unwritten, a negative and impossible accounting of all the words that would now exist on paper if only you had kept working instead of taking the child to the pediatrician or giving in to some social event.

I returned to Granada with my wife and children after the Christmas vacation, and the manuscript was exactly where I had left it before going to Lisbon and Úbeda, next to the covered typewriter.

The images I had visualized so vividly while in Lisbon now seemed to lack all color and sense of reality. I had to punch my card in the office every morning and stay there until three. We were not sleeping well because the baby woke up constantly. For one reason after another I kept postponing the day when I would resume my writing. On my desk, in front of the window, I now had not only my typewriter, the two stacks of paper, and a pack of cigarettes, but also the notebook with all my notes and photos from Lisbon.

I have yet to experience the day when the task of writing does not feel impossible and overwhelming. That's how it was twenty-seven years ago in that apartment in Granada, and that is how it is at this very instant, an evening at the beginning of February 2014, as I write in front of a window facing a snowy street in New York.

The fifty-eight-year-old man and the troubled young father I was back then have only that in common: the uncertainty that never goes away, the despair that must be overcome with equal effort, but also, quite often, the gradual flow that begins to wash over the depression, the return of that state of mind in which a story can grow on its own like an organism, sometimes in small spurts, and other times in spasms, flash floods that make you forget time and even yourself, like a runner who achieves such a level of focus he forgets he is even running.

Once I dove back into the novel, I could no longer get out. I recovered my discipline and rhythm, and the transition from depression to euphoria, from the blank stare to the rapid-rain drumroll on the keyboard, became easier and faster each day. I remember evenings and nights of domestic calm, a familial and conjugal sweetness; Sunday mornings strolling along the Paseo del Salón and the Paseo de la Bomba with our elder son in one hand and the little one in the stroller. Writing without interruption was soothing. Work has always been my most powerful remedy against angst. The birth of our second child had awakened in our elder son, the three-year-old, a certain self-sufficiency and protectiveness. After a partial, yet firm, attachment to his baby bottle—a friend once noted that he handled it with the panache of an adult drinking a gin and tonic—he abandoned it overnight. Seeing his baby brother drink from the bottle must have made him think it was no longer appropriate for a boy his age.

Every night, I read him a story before tucking him in. The light from the room where I worked filtered into his, and he asked that I leave both doors open until he fell asleep. I read him old Spanish stories, which we knew by heart. But repetition did not dull their spell. The knowledge of what was about to happen intensified the suspense instead of weakening it. Any variation, caused by my oversight or boredom, was unacceptable. In the room next door, I was spending hours every day developing a plot that could hold a reader's attention and curiosity with a compelling tale of the unexpected. My son was overwhelmed by the anticipation of what he already knew.

He preferred tales I made up to the storybooks, and he asked me to tell them again and again, always attentive that I did not change any details. The characters were part fantasy, taken from his favorite movies and cartoons, and part reality: a boy with a different name, but clearly him, with parents like us, who occasionally had superpowers, a friend who was identical to the neighbors' daughter, and a little brother who, for some mysterious reason, did not speak yet.

With little more than three years, my son could already calibrate the connections and differences between reality and fantasy, and distinguish fixed elements and random variations in a narrative system. He expressed his wishes about possible arguments, but also intuited

that a story would lose all its value if it adapted entirely to his whims
and demands. A narrative is not convincing if it doesn't give you the
impression that it could exist on its own, unfolding with the chance and
spontaneity of life, even if at the same time there is a clear set of rules
at work under the surface.

Fiction had a visible, physical effect on him. It was addictive. A
story stoked his desire for more, instead of satiating it. Halfway through
a tale, the boy would fall asleep with the calmest of expressions on his
face, just like his little brother after breast-feeding. I would tiptoe out
of the room and start writing.

•

The closer I got to the end, the faster the rhythm of the novel became.
The speed of the writing corresponded to the urgency of the characters'
missions. The slow, ballad pace of the first few chapters accelerated
toward a bebop-vertigo; toward that moment when the hands of a musician begin to move so fast, it is no longer possible to follow them or
imagine that there is any control in what they are doing, when they
throw their heads back and squint and smile as if inside a dream.

The Lisbon that belonged to the real world was being distilled
into an abstract city, a model made to the dimensions of the plot unfolding within it, like the sets of Rimini or Rome built by Fellini in
Cinecittà, or the gloomy New York of black-and-white thrillers filmed
in Hollywood. The anonymous narrator had never been to Lisbon, so
this was an imaginary city. Parallel to the worlds of real cities are those
that belong to their counterparts in literature and cinema or music or
photography or painting. I wanted my readers to imagine Lisbon as
vividly as I imagined Brussels when listening to Paquito D'Rivera's
"Brussels in the Rain"; I wanted this imaginary city to reveal itself
like the spectral Vienna of *The Third Man*: a hallway, a cemetery, a
road, a nightclub, a sewer, a crumbling stairway on the hillside of a ruin.

I have not opened that novel in many years. I think I would feel
embarrassed and puzzled reading it, much like I would if I could observe the young man who wrote it: in the flesh, not through the filter
of a distant past, with the adjustments and forbearance of memory. I
remember flashes, images, takes of a camera in motion: the last one of

them all, a sidewalk on Madrid's Gran Vía seen from above, perhaps from a window two or three stories up, the Telefónica Building is lit and rain glistens on the open umbrellas, a woman in a white coat is seen ‚from behind, disappearing in the midst of a crowd by the metro entrance, vanishing suddenly, definitively, like only fictional characters can.

•

I typed the final period and pulled the sheet from the machine. I placed it facedown on the stack of paper that had been growing, one millimeter at a time, over the past five months. It is not guaranteed that you will reach the end of a book with an unambiguous sense of relief at having completed a stubborn and lonely task that has taken years, or a few months at the very least. The moment you have anticipated for so long arrives and nothing happens, you feel almost nothing, except fatigue. The room is the same, the window, the desk, the noise coming from the street. Suddenly, an inkling of futility and error dawns on you, and exhaustion turns into distress at the thought that you will have to review the manuscript from the beginning, and will probably find all sorts of unacceptable weaknesses in the plot, inconsistencies and gaps, words repeated too many times.

But that time I felt a great lightness, a quiet happiness. I left the room and my wife was feeding our elder boy dinner. The little one was sound asleep in the crib. I took out a beer from the fridge and sat down to drink it at the table with them and have some dinner, even though I wasn't hungry. She saw my face and with a smile asked if I had finished. It seemed unbelievable, but yes. It always seems unbelievable.

16

He would not do anything else if they gave him up for dead and stopped looking for him. He would not care if they thought he was that corpse in the Atlanta airport or the one in that beach in Mexico who could not be identified because the crabs had eaten its fingertips. He would stop but first he needed money, he needed to rob a bank or jewelry shop and get just enough money—say twenty or thirty thousand dollars—to live the rest of his life in complete anonymity somewhere far away. That would be more than enough because he was used to getting by with very little. From the moment he started making money, he had learned to keep track of every expense, and he never spent more than what he could afford. He had a strict budget for basic necessities and small treats here and there; his rooms were always in cheap boardinghouses and he only bought simple food. The rest were small expenses: radio batteries, the occasional book or pornographic magazine from a secondhand shop, a newspaper or two every day, a few beers to drink at night in his room, and women, of course, mostly prostitutes, but always the least expensive, as he had told a cellmate once, the ones who were ready to do business even if there was a language barrier, after all, only a few words are necessary, words that are similar in any language, universal gestures, the universal language of love, like the blond woman at Maxime's had said while laughing. She was different from the other one, the first one, the one he had met at the Texas Bar and gifted a bathing suit. He had promised her that they would go to the beach together, but he ended up deciding against it. He liked her but he could not afford to take any risks, and it was always safer to meet a person only once, man or woman, it did not matter, you could not give anyone the opportunity to form a memory of you, to become so familiar with your face that they will recognize it right away if they see it in a newspaper or on the TV.

He asked her to come to the hotel at nine in the morning, the day after his arrival in Lisbon, May 9. Sometime before that, however, after returning from breakfast, he asked the receptionist to tell the lady he had to leave town in a hurry for an urgent business matter. He sat close to the balcony, behind the curtains, and waited for her to appear. A few minutes before nine, he saw her walking from the direction of the square with the king statue. It was a bright morning. She was wearing a light summer dress, a cardigan and a shoulder bag, flat shoes. No makeup.

She glanced at the balconies of the hotel but did not see him. He remained still on the chair, dressed in the dark suit and black tie, with his eyes fixed on the street below, until he saw her again, this time from behind, walking away slowly. He would continue going to the Texas Bar for the remainder of his time in Lisbon, but he would never see her again.

•

He would stay in Lisbon, if only he had a way of getting money. Lisbon was better than Puerto Vallarta. It was safer. Puerto Vallarta was too close to the United States, and although it was quite secluded, it was also very small and an American did not go unnoticed. Also, American tourists came to Puerto Vallarta often and they would recognize him; they would surely hear about him in the bars and in the brothels. Lisbon was better. All one had to do to disappear was go up one of those narrow stairways to nowhere, or get a room in one of the big, gloomy buildings that lined the side streets, or get a room in one of those boardinghouses tucked in the small, quiet squares, like the one he had seen by the Texas Bar as he got in the taxi with her, feeling more fatigued than aroused, nodding off as they sped through those narrow and winding streets, harsh sunlight followed by shade, women yelling in the background, clothes hanging on lines from the balconies above, yellow trolleys appearing and disappearing around the corners.

The taxi came to a stop in a small square under the imposing shadow of a tree. He paid the driver while she waited outside. She was standing by the entrance to a house. He could hear her speak in her incomprehensible language, aided by gestures and a few English words here and there, *room, cheap, clean, bath, money*.

The stairway was illuminated by a skylight. He followed her up the steps. They were painted blue like the railing. He watched her hand slide on the wooden surface. No nail polish. He was trying to keep up with her, but the steps were steep and he was running out of breath. He was also starting to feel anxious, impatient to get what he wanted, always the same, the woman on her knees, her head moving faster and faster between his hands.

•

He could stay in a room like that, with an open window overlooking the tiled roofs and a big tree filled with birds whose song would drown out the noise of the city, making it feel so remote, a bay or a lake of silence at the end of the world. It would be like reaching the end of a tunnel that stretches all the way back to the prison cell, after a long journey that required crawling through sewers, squeezing through the narrowest passages, digging into the ground with one's bare hands, like a mole.

•

He would not do anything else if he was safe, if he wasn't running out of money so quickly. He would be content just to watch others, without fear, without being seen. Every day he felt more and more confident in his ability to dissolve in the fog of the crowds and never stand out. He would be able to watch others with curiosity instead of envy or contempt, passing along all the places where people remained bound by their schedules, their obligations, their kids, their women, the tasks they would have to repeat until the day they died.

He would stay in the room of the boardinghouse and enjoy the view from the window, or lie in bed reading novels, scanning newspaper articles, searching for possible clues about the hunt, or, even better, he would sit at a cafe, a table in the back and facing the entrance or maybe close to the back door, or perhaps on the terrace of the Pastelaria Suiça, under the shade of the awning, sipping a coffee all morning, enjoying the breeze and the sound of the water fountain.

There were still some evenings and nights when he managed to relax in the bars of Cais do Sodré. He would choose a quiet corner and drink one beer very slowly. Sitting by himself, he felt like a diver at the bottom of the sea, watching all the reds and blues that propagated through the mirrors and liquefied in the cigarette smoke; a diver who is protected behind the glass of his helmet, and is free to watch all the animals and aquatic plants, plants that are actually animals and fish that swim with their mouths open, silently, leaving a trail of air bubbles.

He watched faces and lipsticked mouths floating in the smoke, in the aquatic darkness of the bar, the glow of lit cigarettes, the hum of laughter and words in foreign languages. He watched others get drunk with alcohol and lust, men and women, courting each other like exotic animals. The rumor was out that he was stingy with money, so women left him alone.

As far back as he could remember, he had observed the world and the lives of others like a three-dimensional film that plays around him but of which he has no part, like the full-color ads in magazines that he liked so much, the ones with happy, fictional lives, unashamedly laden with promises, because behind the cars, alcohol, menthol cigarettes, air conditioners, color TVs with remote control, tanning lotions, there was something else all these people seemed to believe in: unabashed happiness, adventure, the immediate gratification of desire, sexual fantasies.

•

It all fascinated him. On the full-page spreads of *Life* magazine everything was bright: a shiny sports car, photographed from an angle that accentuated the shape of its nose, like a shark, and a background of palm trees under a blue sky, a helicopter, and a name in bold letters,

Pontiac Firebird; a spray to stop feet from sweating; a businessman or insurance salesman who smiles with all the confidence of someone who will never let you down, *Always with you when you need us*; a young, attractive couple drinking J&B whiskey; a happy family around a breakfast table raising their big glasses of orange juice; a double page featuring the new Chrysler models, including not only cars but also rockets, tanks, trailers, excavators, school buses; an overabundance that multiplies the pages of the magazine, almost overflowing from them; tall glasses of blond, foamy beer, with beads of condensation on the glass; a Volvo with a metallic shine; an air conditioner from Frigidaire offering a cold breeze in the middle of a hot summer for all the happy people who gather around it; Redwood aftershave, which is all man to make a woman feel all woman; the twenty-six flavors of Crest toothpaste; tobacco and alcohol, the distinguishing qualities of masculinity; the smoke from Marlboro cigarettes, which expands the lungs and invigorates the rugged cowboys in the pictures; *a frosty Four Roses whiskey sour in a tall glass is the new summer cooler. It cools you off from the inside out*; a man in a blue blazer stepping down off a plane with a bag of golf clubs, welcomed by a stewardess who offers him a flask with Old Crow whiskey; cars have names that allude to fire and thunder: there's the Pontiac Firebird and, a few pages later, the Ford Thunderbird.

He read with the door locked. Room number 2. Lying in bed without taking his shoes off, dropping the magazines and newspapers on the floor as he dozed off. As soon as he entered the room he secured the latch. He remained alert to every noise that came from outside. Even when relatively safe in a hideout, it was important to remain vigilant, like a mouse or a cockroach, he thought. He had read that mice and cockroaches were extremely sensitive to danger; their hearing and sense of smell, the antennas of the cockroach, the sensors in their legs and stomachs capable of perceiving every floor vibration, the creaking of the bed when you got up—they were alert and ready to disappear before the bathroom light came on.

He perceived the world in an indirect manner, with a degree of distortion that was consistent, but he did not know how to calculate, as if he were still in prison and any piece of valuable information came in fragments, transmitted through unreliable channels, word of mouth, two or three steps removed from the source, in incomplete newspapers that were so old they barely had any value. In prison, the exterior world filtered in like the murmur of voices and metallic echoes that came from other cells. Prison was similar to a military camp; in both, the exterior world felt erased and muted, and you got used to living as if it did not really exist. But you also lived every hour of the day obsessed with the idea of returning to an outside world, which felt increasingly distant and unreliable as you adapted to isolation and mental confinement, and also because people on the outside, even those closest to you, would slowly become estranged, even if they still sent letters and packages, and visited on occasion when it was obvious how uncomfortable they felt, how impatient they were to get away from the contagious smells and sounds of prison.

•

He could not trust anything. There was no way to confirm what was true. The government declared top secret the discovery of an alien spacecraft that had crashed in New Mexico. Much of what the newspapers publish is propaganda and lies. President Roosevelt allowed the Japanese to attack Pearl Harbor so he could push the United States into war with Hitler. The black preachers decrying racial segregation in the South were, in fact, secret Soviet agents, and the FBI did nothing about it because they were infested with communist double agents.

As a boy, he would find newspapers on the street and get absorbed reading them. If his father caught him, he would knock the paper out of his hand and ridicule him. Newspapers are only good for wiping your ass. The news is lies to deceive idiots. The people who write the newspapers are in someone's pocket, they are thieves, just like doctors, lawyers, Catholic priests, and the Jews.

Sitting alone in his cell, or on a bench at the library, or in one of the motel rooms where he lived after escaping, he imagined there had to be a method, a code he could use to understand all those things, to distinguish truth from lies, like those machines that could decipher enemy messages, a sure way to get reliable information, and perhaps intercept messages between the powerful, the people who own the world, the Jews, the ones who control everything from a distance, the communists.

As a young man, during one of his first long stints in prison, he had followed with great interest the efforts of Senator Joe McCarthy, the only politician with the courage to tell the truth and point his finger at the traitors. While other prisoners played cards or demanded that he change the station so they could listen to stupid dance songs, he pressed his ear to the old radio so he could hear the impassioned voice of Senator McCarthy speaking live, calling out his enemies, who were much more powerful. He had only seen a blurry photo of the senator in the newspaper, but he imagined him as a heroic prosecutor from a movie who unmasks the real culprits, the ones no one had suspected. It was inevitable that they would target him, spreading lies, repaying his sacrifice with ingratitude and revenge. And the majority of the people, brainwashed, now applauding his fall like they had applauded his rise not long before, cheering on the streets, spitting on the corpse and legacy of a man they had admired and feared.

•

At night, the outside world filtered into his dark cell through the small transistor radio he had purchased in the commissary. He pressed his ear against the plastic casing so he could hear the faint voices of the newscasters, the ads, the songs of Johnny Cash, which he loved. You could hear police sirens in the background of live news reports, also gunshots, the cries of angry people in the streets, the sermons of the preachers. Among them, that firm and solemn voice, the name that was becoming more and more familiar, the biggest liar of them all, the black man with the slanted eyes, the one who elevated his voice with each biblical reference, electrifying the dark-skinned multitudes who followed his orders, commanding them, like barbarian armies, to take over the cities of the South. He was the false prophet with the tailored suits and the gold cuff links, the one who launched the assault on the schools and the buses and the lunch counters, the wolf in sheep's clothing, the covert communist who quoted the Bible from memory, the licentious preacher who slept with white women who had no dignity.

•

The small radio was the most valuable thing he took with him the day he escaped. He kept making sure it was in his pocket as he crouched inside the bread cart. The radio would help him stay awake during the long nights of walking that followed. Later on, in the motel rooms, it was the sound of the radio that lulled him to sleep. The headlines and quotes he read in the newspaper were easier to understand if he attributed voices to them, if he read them out loud, pronouncing the difficult words slowly, *extemporaneous, neurophysiology, realpolitik, extrasensory, telepathic.*

All those nights, driving through the deserts in Arizona, New Mexico, and Texas, it was the human voices from the small radio that kept him company. His eyes never strayed from the tunnel of light created by the Mustang's headlights on the highway, but his hand moved automatically to the radio dial as soon as a station began to fade. He listened to women who called the midnight shows to announce they were going to commit suicide or to demand that a real man show up to their lonely rooms. He listened to preachers go on and on about the impending Apocalypse or the coming of Jesus Christ in an alien spaceship. He listened to live reports about black people rioting and he could hear the cries, the explosions, the breaking glass, the police sirens.

He continued listening to his radio even after he bought the portable TV in Los Angeles. The TV lost its image or sound constantly and you had to keep moving the antenna. He would leave it on and stare at the screen while listening to the voices on the radio. That face seemed to always be there when he turned on the TV at night, just like in the magazines and newspapers. The prophet, the Moses of his people, the Nobel laureate, the shameless communist who was now blatant about his decision to betray his country, taking the same side as the yellow hordes of North Vietnam, the Vietcong; the champion of the poor who traveled in first class and stayed in luxury hotels, the one who bit the hand that had fed him, now announcing another march in Washington, hundreds of thousands or millions of black people invading the capital, descending like a plague.

•

It was much easier to study the man's face on the TV screen. The camera acted like a set of binoculars. Before that, he had been just a photo in a newspaper, the name in the big headlines, the menacing and unctuous voice on the radio. He placed the TV on a shelf in his room in the St. Francis Hotel in Los Angeles, and when the static finally cleared it was that face again, the dark skin shining with sweat under the camera lights or the midday sun. The headline announced that he was giving a speech in Los Angeles at the moment, so close, he could have driven there in less than ten minutes. On the back of the TV, with the tip of a nail clipper, he carved the words: *Martin Luther Coon.*

•

He turned on the car radio as he was leaving Memphis on April 4. The sun was setting, and as he crossed into Mississippi the sounds of police sirens began to die down. He was listening to the news when it suddenly hit him: the little transistor radio was in the bag he had left behind with the rifle. It was like losing a talisman. Losing it was making him as anxious as the fact that he had left his fingerprints. He drove straight to Atlanta that night, taking only secondary roads and stopping once for gas. He struggled to stay awake but could still hear the voices from the radio; confused, anguished, vengeful voices describing a person who was yet to be identified but was clearly him— a man in his forties wearing a dark suit. And yet, somehow, it felt as if they were talking about someone else, someone far away who had nothing to do with him. An exalting and dangerous mirage of impunity. Standing between him and the man hunted by the police and the FBI was a blank and infinite space like the expanding time that separated him from the moment of that single shot, the face in the crosshairs, the pain in the eardrums, the recoiling of the rifle. In the confusion of voices, at least there was one that would never speak again. He was half-asleep at the wheel when a voice on the radio said something that put him on alert, though he never quite felt in danger, because with every minute that passed, the farther away he was from Memphis and the more remote it all seemed. The voice had said that the murder suspect had fled toward Mississippi in a white Mustang with Alabama plates.

•

But the opacity of the external world would not dissipate, not even now, under the clear light of Lisbon, so far away from Memphis, so close to his final escape. The murky consistency of all those words and images—the glass wall that separated him from others—remained. Invisible metal bars, walls of air that confined him; he felt them press against his chest, like a sharp headache, which could be the sign of a brain tumor. No matter how hard he tried, there was no crack in that wall, no escape. He counted the coins and old bills on the bedside table and tried to calculate how many more days he could afford to stay. He leaned on the railing of an elevated park, watching as a ship left the dock. To the west, he could see the red arches of the bridge surrounded by fog. In the full-page ads of *Life* magazine, men with golden tans sail to the islands in the Caribbean or the South Seas, invigorated by the smoke of their long cigarettes and their Canadian Club whiskey or Bacardi rum, served in tall glasses with ice. The English and American newspapers that he bought at the kiosk by Rossio Square came several days late. He had purchased a portable radio in Toronto, but it was of no use here because all the stations were in Portuguese. Sometimes he listened and could discern his name, not understanding what else they were saying about him, the name that was now linked to the other one forever, the Big Nigger, he liked to repeat, the unexpected martyr, the hero, the victim, the saint who was worthy of an exorbitant reward of a hundred thousand dollars for whoever could lead them to his murderer.

He could have disappeared forever with much less than a hundred thousand dollars, erased from the face of the earth, secluded in the room in that small square with the big tree, at the end of the stairway with the blue railing. But he was locked in another room, in the Hotel Portugal, a room he would not be able to afford in a few days' time. He was locked there, waiting in silence with his magazines and newspapers, listening to every sound that came from outside the room. He heard steps in the hotel corridor around midnight. They stopped by his door, then continued after a few moments. He heard voices coming from the adjacent rooms, muffled laughter, the hoarse groan of a man having an orgasm, faint music from a balcony across the street, the clinking of silverware and a family talking over dinner. And two or three nights, around the same time in the wee hours of the morning, he heard a woman moaning, almost howling, on the other side of the wall, so close, he could also hear the rhythmic sound of the headboard hitting against the wall.

Everything in his life happened behind a wall, visible or invisible; everything was always at a distance, like looking inside the other cars as he passed them in the Mustang, or staring at the reflection of the couples in the Texas Bar or Maxime's or the Niagara Bar or the California Bar or the Arizona, now that he had no money to pay for company, or even a second beer, so he sat in a corner for hours sipping the one slowly, avoiding eye contact so no woman would approach him. He stole furtive glances at them, and felt like he was watching from the other side of one of those special mirrors he once imagined he would use to shoot pornographic films, in another life that wasn't past or future, a life that never came to exist. Perhaps that is how he would think of those days in Lisbon many years later: days that had never existed, days when he did nothing and was almost nobody, Ramon George Sneyd, or not even, Sneya.

17

I leave the apartment early on a Sunday morning. I haven't slept well. I fell asleep after 1:00 a.m. and woke up from a nightmare within the hour. At 3:00 a.m. I was reading Mário Cesariny and Fernando Pessoa in Portuguese with the help of a dictionary. In Pessoa, I underlined *Tudo começo é involuntário.*

At 4:00 a.m. I was standing by the window observing a man in a large and somber studio in the old building across the street. I could not see his face. He was deep in concentration, in silence, typing on a computer, which emitted the only light in the room. I would have liked to be able to see what he was typing.

At 5:00 a.m. I was the one in front of a computer screen with the window to my back. I was reading an FBI memo that was largely a translation of a report in Portuguese signed on June 24, 1968, by Chief Inspector José Manuel da Cunha Passos. The report had the official letterhead and seal of PIDE, the state police under the Salazar dictatorship, and it provided a full account of their investigation into the activities of the suspect, Ramon George Sneyd, during the time he spent in Lisbon between May 8 and 17. The report lists the nightclubs he frequented and it includes transcripts of interviews with people he came in contact with, as well as the fruitless investigation into the main bank offices of the city, in order to ascertain whether the suspect had carried out any financial transactions there.

In the FBI's Internet archives, there are old photocopies and scanned pages, copies of copies of copies. Sometimes the type is quite blurry and entire names or sentences or pages are redacted. The light from the laptop illuminates my hands and the notebook where I take notes.

The chief inspector's report is hard to read. It looks like a worn carbon copy. My eyes begin to hurt. On May 15, the suspect was in the offices of South African Airlines inquiring about flights to Cape Town and Salisbury, the capital of Rhodesia. On the morning of May 16, he visited the Canadian embassy, located at 198 Liberty Avenue, and then he proceeded to Foto Lusitania close by, where he ordered six passport photos. By this time the light in the studio across the street has long turned off, and that entire building is in the dark. In a column, with capital letters, Chief Inspector Cunha Passos has typed the names of all the seedy establishments where they confirmed the suspect's presence: Texas Bar, Arizona Bar, Niagara Bar, California Bar, Europa Bar, Atlantico Bar, Bolero Bar, Maxime's Night Club, Garbo Bar & Night Club, Fontoria Night Club, Tagide Night Club, Nina's Night Club.

At 6:00 a.m. a blue light has begun to rise over the rooftops and the cables of the tram. A few minutes later, the first trolley appears; it is lit and empty like a ghost ship. Chief Inspector Cunha Passos is pleased to report that his men are investigating all the crimes committed in Lisbon between May 8 and 16 to confirm whether the suspect participated in any of them. My eyes burn from staring at the computer screen. At 7:00 a.m. I take a break and stare at the gray-blue light that enters the room, the blue on the rooftops is much lighter now, and the clouds over Magdalena Church have a pink hue. Through the American embassy in Lisbon, FBI director J. Edgar Hoover sent a personal thank-you letter to the chief inspector, Mr. José Manuel da Cunha Passos.

•

I force myself to go out, mostly so I can stop looking at the screen. The sleepless night produced in me a strange feeling of lightness, a distance from myself that has been heightened by the novelty of being in Lisbon. The small bars and cafes that were open until midnight are now closed.

I go down Fanqueiros Street, turn on Arsenal, and reach Commerce Square. Today, it is almost deserted. No multitudes descending from the ferries to start the workday. I preferred the urban and nomadic feel of Mário Cesariny's poetry, much more worldly than Pessoa's, inhabited by real human presences and not just projections of himself. *Em todas as ruas te encontro,* says Cesariny, *em todas as ruas te perco.*

I see a small solitary figure against the backdrop of the river. Even at this early hour, there is usually someone sketching, reading, writing, or just staring at the horizon from the edge of Cais das Colunas. Perhaps it is someone staring at a cell phone, oblivious to this breathtaking view—the red bridge, this blue horizon, the river meeting the salty ocean breezes.

I approach the marble flight of steps. The tide is low, exposing a white beach, rocks, and algae. Seagulls and storks peck in between the rocks and pull small crabs. I reach the last step and my shoes sink into the wet sand. Little crabs flee sideways in all directions. Small air bubbles tell the storks where their prey is hiding.

I see a large tire with a rusty rim. It is covered in seaweed and rocky clusters of mussels. Fish larvae shine in the small pockets of water. Old wood planks and blue tiles come and go with the tide. I step around the translucent body of a dead jellyfish. What an inexplicable anatomy, like an alien castaway.

On these steps and this beach is the frontier, the realm of a primordial life that makes the leap from the ocean to the ground, slithering on the sand, rocking back and forth with the soft waves at the mercy of the tide and the movements of the passing ships. Primordial life and human garbage, a trail of trash that marks the high contours of the tide on the sand: cigarette butts, plastic bags, lighters, condoms, clothespins, bottle caps, a mustard packet from McDonald's, a credit card. On the wet sand, the birds have imprinted their cuneiform steps. I tread carefully around them. My long shadow follows. I pick up a few smooth fragments of blue tile and feel the rounded edges with my fingers. I put them in my pocket. There is nothing that is not memorable one way or another.

•

Someone watching the river from the center of the square will see me as a solitary figure, quite abstract, a hieroglyph of human presence, a shadow. It suddenly occurs to me that he could have been that same silhouette one early morning in May, forty-five years ago, in this unchanging scene. The great expanse of the river, the empty square, the white-stone arches, the bronze horse on the pedestal and the king with his plumed helmet. He has stopped on his way back to the hotel after a night of drinking or being with a woman. He stands on the edge of the steps, his sunglasses blocking the clarity of morning, his anxiety temporarily numbed by all the alcohol.

He liked to come here to clear his mind, and if the tide was low, like it is now, he would also descend to the beach. There he would stand motionless, his back to the city, watching the river and breathing in the smell of the water, remembering the Mississippi, spellbound by the similarity, the wide and green horizon on the other side, the bridge in the distance to his right, like in Memphis, the same violet mist, the slow ships passing him by.

•

Standing on this beach and breathing the air of the Atlantic soothes the mind of the insomniac but does not alleviate the intoxication, the fever. I imagine his footprints on this sand, the steps of Ramon George Sneyd. Who can ever know what really happened inside somebody else's mind, the way a place must have seemed and felt. He secretly carries the monstrous distinction of being the most wanted criminal in the world, number one, Sunday after Sunday, on the FBI's list of infamous celebrity. Vanity and terror. What he did just a few weeks prior probably fades in the banality of his immediate situation, the routine of the helpless wait, the fatigue of being on the run, his shock that they are going to such great lengths to find him.

On my way back to the apartment I will follow the route that would have taken him back to the Hotel Portugal. I will sit at my desk and when I turn on the laptop the same page from the FBI's website will be staring back at me. If I fall asleep after breakfast, the thought of him will filter back into my dreams, ruining the sweetness of our bedroom with the curtains drawn and the warmth of your body still present.

•

Back then, before I met you, I believed the task of literature was to create perfect forms, symmetries and resonances that imbued the world with an order and significance it otherwise lacked. I loved to concoct arguments, police mysteries, surprising twists, unexpected outcomes, stories that opened emphatically and ended like a drumroll, like a stab or flash of lightning that suddenly illuminates the plot. I loved Chesterton's detective stories. I was convinced that some of his best had actually been written by Borges. I studied Bioy Casares's arguments the way an architect would have analyzed the blueprints for a building designed by Le Corbusier or Mies van der Rohe. I wanted to create endings that did justice to the mysteries they resolved.

•

But gradually, in another future life, I began to realize that beauty, harmony, symmetry, are properties or spontaneous consequences of natural processes that exist without the need for an organizing intelligence, just as natural selection operates without an ultimate purpose, and certainly without a Supreme Being determining its laws in advance. The symmetry of a leaf or a tree or a body is self-organizing, a virtue of the instructions encoded in its DNA. The sinuous curves of a river or the ramifications of a delta draw themselves on a plane like the veins on a hand or a wave retreating from the sand. The highest aspiration of literature is not to improve an amorphous matter of real events through fiction, but to imitate the unpremeditated, yet rigorous, order of reality, to create a scale model of its forms and processes. Emily Dickinson once wrote, "Nature is a haunted house—but Art—a house that tries to be haunted."

•

Over the course of a month in Lisbon, I have come daily to the small beach next to Cais das Colunas. This trip is the first time I noticed it. Every day, the highest point of the tide is recorded by a dotted line of small objects, beads on a necklace threaded by water: tiny shells, bits of plastic in different colors, fragments of blue tile, wood chips. There are successive lines, fossil impressions of every stage of the tide, roughly parallel to one another, a dendrite geometry. The lines intertwine to form the contours of a mountain landscape reminiscent of Chinese painting; lines of uncertain appearance but the precision of ink flowing from a brush on a sheet of rice paper; they are the work of the water washing over the sand, returning small objects it once took and has been pounding, shredding, abandoning for years, for centuries.

•

I come to Commerce Square and the small beach first thing in the morning, at mid-afternoon, and sometimes even late at night. I follow the same path each time, as if repeating a musical motif while exploring different variations marked by the character of the light, the time of day, the smell of the air, the people, the tram. Early in the morning, there are homeless people or old hippies huddled under blankets or sleeping bags. Every few days, a quiet young man comes to the beach and works tirelessly for hours on sand sculptures: a siren, the god Neptune with a crown and trident, a whale, a giant turtle, a family of frogs sitting on a sofa with their legs crossed. The sculptor comes barefoot and with his pants rolled up. His hair is long and he wears a full beard. His skin is the color of copper. I think of him as a castaway who has gotten used to solitude and silence after years on a desert island. Eventually the tide will rise and slowly chip away at the sculptures, and the wind will soften their features almost to the point of erasure, like sphinxes in the sands of Egypt.

•

There are always people hanging out around the steps of Cais das Colunas, like on the edge of a stage that is the river and its maritime amplitude. There will be someone taking photos. There will be couples, some in each other's arms, some keeping a safe distance. People sit by the lower walls or the stone benches along the parapets. Two women are having a conversation on one of the lower steps. Between them is a bottle of white wine and a bag of chips. The tide is rising and will soon force them to move back. They pour wine in plastic cups and look each other in the eyes as they talk. The river wind tousles their long gray hair.

This is a powerful place. In it, presences that stood ages apart suddenly become simultaneous. In the tower on the west side of Commerce Square, we went to see an exhibit about the tens of thousands of European refugees that came through Lisbon during the summer and fall of 1940, a great wave that rose after the fall of Paris and the German occupation of France. *Lisboa en tempo de guerra, A última fronteira.* Seaplanes departed to England or America from the waters of the Tagus River, while those from Casablanca and Tangier arrived. From the beach of Cais das Colunas, I see the sun shine on the windows of the exhibit hall. The silhouettes that now stand by the edge of the water could have belonged to Erich Maria Remarque or Arthur Koestler, or any of the nameless refugees who did not manage to leave Lisbon and are now lost to history. One of those figures facing away could have been me in January 1987, or Ramon George Sneyd in 1968.

18

You see the mistake when it is already irreparable, a second or a tenth of a second after the fact; or even right before, just as it is happening, but you continue like some kind of impotent witness to your own actions. Later on, you replay that moment in your head, over and over again. You examine every detail and every second like an insect under a magnifying glass, in the silence of a room locked from the inside. Memory was unforgiving about the details of past mistakes.

•

He could pinpoint the exact moment when he had missed his chance to change course. The exact take in the imagined sequence of events. Photographic memory. He was ever-vigilant, his eyes like a camera moving on a rail, scanning every detail of his surroundings as he turned corners and advanced toward closed doors. But it wasn't just photographic. This was an olfactory and tactile memory.

He remembered the feel of the bag handle, the plastic seam digging into his left palm seconds before he unclenched his fist and dropped it on the sidewalk of South Main Street. He had seen a group of police officers running toward him. They were heading toward the epicenter of the shot. The sun was beginning to set.

He remembered the rifle's rearward motion and the ache it left in his shoulder. He remembered standing outside the bathroom after the shot and staring at the weak glow of the red EXIT sign at the end of the hallway. Only the last three letters were on, forming a strange word, XIT.

He had placed the binoculars inside the bag and wrapped the rifle in the same blanket he brought it in. He remembered the sharp pain in his eardrums, the scent of gunpowder, the nauseating smell of the bathroom. XIT, like an incantation, conjuring the way out. He walked down the narrow hallway in a straight line. He remembered feeling like he was floating or walking on the moon. It had been a perfect shot, like a transoceanic missile guided by an electronic brain. A perfectly executed mission from a spy novel. Not a single mistake so far.

He blinked and a shadow suddenly appeared in the distance close to the exit. He lowered his head and tightened the sweaty grip around the bag and the rolled-up blanket. He walked toward the figure, staring at the ground, his chin almost touching his chest. The ringing in his ear was subsiding. The world was slowly filling up with other sounds again. He shot a quick side glance as he passed the man. A set of bulging eyes stared back from behind thick glasses. He remembered the teeth, the thick, wet tongue, the moving lips forming words he couldn't quite hear. The man had been standing by the entrance to his room with the door wide open. Inside, a television was on and another person lay in bed. The man had said something, a question or an affirmation with the word "shot." "It was a gunshot, no doubt," he replied as he exited.

•

He remembered the small door window at the end of the dark stairway. On the other side was South Main and the corner where the street sloped down toward the end of the city and the train station and the open road to Mississippi. He only had to get to the Mustang. He had to stay on the sidewalk and not look toward the Lorraine Motel and the balcony where the man lay bleeding. He had to ignore the screams and perhaps the ambulance sirens. He had to focus for the twenty or thirty steps between the door and the Mustang. He had imagined it many times: walk straight to the car, open the trunk, place the bag and the blanket inside, drive away.

•

He anticipated what was about to happen or what he would do a few seconds later. Imagining things and situations in detail willed them into existence. There were no police sirens yet, which was surprising. The sun was setting but light still permeated the evening sky. He had passed Jim's Grill and its blinking pink sign with the neon green Irish shamrocks. Now he was approaching the corner next to a music store, Canipe Amusement Company.

That's when he saw the police officers walk in his direction, though not exactly toward him. They were surveying the windows above the street and the terraces. They were old and slightly overweight. One of them was having difficulty removing his gun from the holster. Suddenly, the white, shining Mustang, which was already within view, seemed miles away. The bag and the blanket felt heavier than ever. The plastic seams on the handle were digging into his left palm. Any second now, the police would notice him and point their guns at him, yelling that he drop the bag and put his hands where they could see them. Everything would be over.

The danger of imaging even the worst-case scenarios with such intensity is that you inadvertently cause them to happen. You're about to make a mistake, you know that you'll regret it as it is happening, and a second later there is no turning back. The moment that is passing is already part of the irreparable past. You replay it in slow motion, under the magnifying glass of insomnia. Break each movement into second-by-second sequences like those photos of bullets in mid-shot or the flapping wings of a bird in *Modern Photography* magazine. Identify the exact fraction of time, the threshold that makes the difference between ruin and salvation, captivity and escape, the exorbitant price, twenty years in prison for a split-second error in a robbery, the electric chair for a gun fired by mistake.

He loosened the grip on the bag but still held on to it. One of the police officers walked right next to the Mustang with his gun out. He reached for the keys inside his pocket and it took him a second to recognize their contour. The recessed entrance to the music store created a shaded triangle, a corner where he could wait for the police to pass, hide the bundle. He knew, as he seamlessly dropped the bag and continued walking toward the Mustang and the officers, that he was making a mistake. His precaution had been pointless. The officers had not even looked at him as they passed. A few seconds later he was already by the car and they were busting into the boardinghouse.

He could have walked back to the music store and collected the bag and the blanket. It would have taken less than a minute to retrieve the bundle and place it in the trunk of the car.

But doing so seemed as impossible as turning back time. His fingers were numb but he could still feel the plastic seam of the bag handle. He flexed them as he reached for the door of the car. The car keys could have fallen and now he would be lost. Police and ambulance sirens sounded in the distance.

He felt an urge to turn around and see it one more time, the sign for the Lorraine Motel and the crowd on the balcony scrambling to help a man who was already dead. But he had to resist the temptation. Staring at the scene would only make him suspicious and aggravate his previous mistake. He felt intoxicated, frightened, elated, overwhelmed by the irrefutable fact of what he had accomplished, incredulous that it had actually happened. He could still take a few steps back and retrieve the bag, the rifle, the blanket, put it all in the car and escape. It would buy him time. It would make it much harder for them to piece together all the clues they would eventually find.

The sirens were getting closer. Why didn't he use latex gloves or put tape on his fingertips. He was standing next to the car and could not manage to get the key in the door. The handle was a soft yellow, almost white, and it radiated the accumulated heat of the day. His hands were shaking when the car door finally opened. He sat at the wheel and watched as the red and blue lights of the police cars got closer. He started the engine and the accelerator vibrated powerfully under his foot.

Within a few minutes, a quiet street with low buildings would take him south past the train station and onto a country road that led to the state border. A thick jungle darkened on both sides of the road, interrupted by cotton fields, rustic houses, and industrial buildings with broken windows reflecting the last of the sun from the west. The city lights were quickly disappearing in the rearview mirror. How effortlessly speed multiplied the distance to the crime scene. On the radio there were bursts of music, commercials, and sermons. He turned it off and all he could hear was the soft breeze of nightfall in the fields. Perhaps the bundled blanket with the bag and the rifle remained unnoticed by the doorway to the music store.

Once you make a mistake it continues its irreparable course, like the ticking of a time bomb. You replay it in your head so often it seems incredible that you cannot correct it. You want to remember every single thing that you've left behind and could be used to identify you. The mental effort is so intense you end up confusing your memory and even blocking it. Distance from the site of the error is no remedy, only a mirage. It doesn't matter how fast you're going, the bundled blanket is going nowhere, it's just waiting to be found.

It was six twenty-five and he was already in Mississippi. White gas-station lights began to appear. Tall motel signs radiated neon pinks, blues, and greens against the dark forest. Since the beginning of his escape, he had spent countless nights, in Toronto, in Lisbon, trying to remember every little thing he had inadvertently left behind, as if a full inventory would earn him some kind of advantage, some kind of absolution.

•

A pillowcase; a pair of bedsheets; a pair of underwear; a cotton shirt; a rubber sandal; a light jacket with a black-and-white square pattern; a short-sleeved Arturo Rosetti shirt; Diplomat Hong Kong sport shorts; a knife with a rusty blade; an old quilt; pliers; a box with first-aid tape; maps of Georgia and Alabama from the Standard Oil gas station; a copy of the *Memphis Commercial Appeal* with a front-page column about Martin Luther King's visit to the city, and a photo on the inside where King could be seen leaning against a railing in the Lorraine Motel with Room 306 clearly marked behind him; a roll of toilet paper; a Gillette travel kit, which included a razor blade, shaving cream, aftershave, deodorant, hair pomade, and a replacement blade; a white and yellow towel; a handkerchief; a tube of Colgate toothpaste; a pair of black socks; one spray can of Right Guard deodorant; a Channel

Master pocket radio with the serial number scratched off; a bottle of Bufferin headache medicine; a tube of Brylcreem hair cream; a bar of Cashmere Bouquet soap; a red toothbrush, brand Pepsodent; a hairbrush; a small bottle of Head & Shoulders shampoo; Kiwi black shoe polish; Palmolive's Rapid Shave shaving cream; a loose brown button; two pins; two cans of Schlitz beer; two plastic hangers; a few strands of hair on the brush; a chewed toothpick; a pair of binoculars; a Remington 760 Gamemaster .30-06 caliber, a Redfield variable scope with a fingerprint that was identical to the one found on a can of Schlitz beer, a fingerprint so clearly pressed it would have been almost too easy to find in the FBI database. You make a big mistake and you see it as it is happening and there is no turning back. But the small blunders, the ones you don't realize until much later, can be just as lethal—like that time you pulled a beer from a six-pack and noticed how good the ice-cold metal felt on your fingertips.

19

The sun stung his eyes as he came out of the arcades of Commerce Square. The humid heat seemed to emanate from the misty river, the still water of the high tide, which flooded the base of the two columns flanking the marble stairway at Cais das Colunas. Some of the steps were covered in dark algae, others glistened with oil slicks. The smell was unmistakable: rotten fruit and dead animals, like the Mississippi in New Orleans. Submerged in a hot fog, the view of the other side reminded him of Memphis. He left the shade and walked toward the water, holding the unnecessary trench coat under one arm, feeling the weight of the gun in his back pocket.

The weapon was useless if you did not know how to say anything in Portuguese. Hands up, this is robbery, don't move, give me all the money. He didn't know how to say any of it. He imagined pressing the gun into the forehead of one of those old jewelers in the tiny shops. Panic would flash in their eyes. But the spaces were so small he wouldn't even be able to fully extend his arm. He would fill his pockets with jewelry and then what? Where would he go without a car in this city of narrow streets and dead ends? And who would he sell the stuff to?

He felt for his wallet, now filled with coins and a few crumpled bills. Time and money were trickling through his fingers like sand and there was nothing he could do about it. He could not think of another exit, not even a daydream.

He walked along the water feeling the sun and tasting the humidity. Cargo ships with exotic names painted on the prow, white passenger liners, sailboats with burnished wood and gilded rails. The time of staring at them and imagining grand escapes had passed. So much time under the spell of a life at sea, always stuck in a port city, anchored to the firm ground, watching those special others, that race of blond men with golden skin, strong arms, and expert hands, climbing the rope ladders, raising the sails, and gliding away.

Time had run out. He walked back to the shade, away from the blistering sun and the still, oily water, the blue haze that exaggerated the distances and blurred the outlines of the bridge, that red gate to the Atlantic Ocean and all those places he had seen in the atlas in school and at the prison library, the islands, the southern coasts of Africa and America, the routes by way of Cape Horn and the Cape of Good Hope, the coasts of Biafra and Angola, the mouth of the Congo River, the vastness of South Africa, where a man could disappear without a trace and become an explorer of deserts and jungles, perhaps a foreman in a diamond mine, or a hunter of elephants, rhinos, and lions, or a mercenary with a green beret and a camouflage uniform.

The rifle weighed around eight pounds and could have taken down a charging rhino two hundred meters away. He said his name was Harvey Lowmeyer when he bought it. He liked that name and he liked the fact that he only used it on that occasion. The shop owner and his assistant did not ask for identification, though they had observed him from head to toe with suspicion and ridicule. Both were heavyset and red, like oxen, and chewed on something as they spoke. They were expert hunters and assumed the pale man with the soft hands and the suit and tie did not know what he was doing. When the FBI agents interrogated them, they said they did not believe for a second the story that he was going hunting with his brother in Canada.

They said it was obvious he did not know how to handle a rifle. They described him as out of shape, thin but with a belly, which he kept touching nervously. He did not try to negotiate the price. He paid in cash and turned his attention to the instruction manual. The glasses kept sliding down his nose as he read. His eyes were bloodshot. A few hours later, he called the store and asked if he could exchange the rifle for a larger model. He said his brother or brother-in-law had told him that they were going to a region in Canada where the deer were huge. The shop owner and his assistant had a good laugh after hanging up the phone. He was back the following morning to exchange the rifle. This time they installed a scope and sold him soft-point bullets, which expand on impact and tear through tissue and bones more effectively.

•

He did not remember the sound of the shot. He remembered the rearward motion of the rifle, the sharp pain in his shoulder, the ringing in his ears after the explosion, the sudden silence that surrounded him as he escaped. It was like being inside a bubble that sound could not pierce.

Now, as he replayed every second on this hot Lisbon morning, he felt a similar silence creep in. He instinctively turned away from the main axis of the square and looked for one of the shaded, narrow streets to exit. Sapateiros Street. He walked at a quick, steady pace, not really knowing where he was going. Lisbon was a city of dead ends. After a few days, the routes he had traced in the pocket map had begun to resemble the outline of a prison. Potential escape routes, like narrow passages or stairways, led to basements or walls or reinforced doors. The arch at the end of the street could suddenly drop a metal grating as he approached. If he got inside the strange public elevator that went up to the church, he would basically be stepping into a cell.

But the most impenetrable wall was the river itself. There was no sound, only the feeling of blood pulsing in his temples and a sharp pain rushing through his head. These could be the symptoms of a brain tumor. He had read about it in a medical encyclopedia. He took a few loose aspirins from his pockets and swallowed them.

When he returned to the hotel room, he would have to go through every pocket and count the money he had left. American dollars, Canadian dollars, grimy Portuguese bills, coins from four different countries buried in every crevice of his pockets; lint, sand, water on his fingers; the imminence of destitution, like the vertigo of a stumble in a dream; scribbled calculations on the margins of newspapers, on the back of the weekly invoice from the Hotel Portugal, which he had to pay as soon as he returned before the receptionist reminded him again. He had to limit himself to just one beer when he went to the bar. When he got his change he put every single cent back in his pocket, avoiding eye contact with the server. In the last few days he had not returned to the Texas Bar. He was avoiding the blond woman with the loud laugh. This primitive city had no hot dog stands, or cheap places to get a burger, or strip clubs, or pawnshops where he could easily sell stolen merchandise, or boats that could take him around the world, or offices that were recruiting mercenaries. There was nothing. He had no way to stay and no way to leave. This place was on the ass of the world, a dead-end alley that reeked of garbage and urine, with lines of wet laundry hanging overhead, and poor, dark people who ate disgusting food and only knew how to mumble or yell in their incomprehensible tongue.

None of the addresses listed in the phone book of the hotel, which were almost impossible to find on the map, had been useful. There were no places left to visit. No place where others would not be looking at him with suspicion. He had traced the route between the hotel and the South African embassy and gotten lost for hours in some neighborhood trying to find it. Luís Bívar Avenue, number ten. It looked like the waiting room at a medical office. Posters with city skylines at night or desert landscapes with elephants. Blond children with school uniforms and big smiles playing in a park. One of the receptionists asked him what he was there for and then said he would be right back. He was very thirsty and could not stop gulping. Perhaps the man had recognized his face and went to call the police.

But the man returned with a folder and took out the forms. He would have to fill out every one and also provide his birth certificate, proof of vaccination, school diploma, and reference letters. They would take everything into consideration and get back to him with an answer in a few months. He cleared his throat and asked vaguely about the possibility of getting political asylum. He hadn't stopped pinching his right earlobe.

The receptionist did not catch what he was saying, or perhaps he just smiled and acted like he did not understand. He said he wasn't

sure if there was a Rhodesian delegation in Lisbon, obviously there was
no embassy, but perhaps there was an informal representative.

He went outside, a narrow square with trees and a corner cafe or
grocery store. He wasn't sure where he was even after looking at the
map. He bought a packet of biscuits and a Coca-Cola. He was surviv-
ing on cookies, salty chips, canned food, and powdered soups he mixed
with water from his room and warmed with a submersible heating
element. Later on, they would find crumbs of food in every pocket and
oil rings on his maps.

He ate the biscuits and took a long gulp of Coca-Cola, sitting on
a bench, with the coat folded next to him and the map of the city
opened on top. In every place he had visited in the course of a year,
he had left a trail of road and city maps with annotations, itineraries,
dates, and circled addresses. On the map of Lisbon he had circled the
Overseas Ministry, the Canadian and South African embassies, and
Belém Tower Avenue. The authorities would also find, among his pos-
sessions, a brochure with flight schedules from South African Airlines
in which he had highlighted all the flights to Salisbury, the capital of
Rhodesia.

He stiffened when he sensed someone approach. The employee
from the South African embassy sat next to him and, without making
eye contact, handed him a folded piece of paper and left. The note read:
Delegation of Biafra, Avda Torre de Belém 16.

•

This was not uncommon in spy novels. Strange characters like this man
from the embassy were usually the ones who relayed secret messages.
They would ask the secret agent to meet them in some unsuspecting
place so they could deliver instructions for the mission, maps, passwords, and keys to secret places. The man squeezed his hand for a
second as he handed him the piece of paper. The hand was softer and
warmer than his. He watched him walk away out of the corner of his
eye. The smell of his cologne stayed behind. What if this was all a
trap. He looked for the address on his map and saw that it was quite
far. He would have to return to Commerce Square and take one of the
trolleys. He walked while eating the biscuits. His stomach was full

but he still felt hungry. He felt light-headed as he continued chewing on the mouthful of sugary flour.

The trolley ran along the port, passing warehouses, cranes, and boats, then slowly made its way through the fog and up the red bridge. Why did it all have to be so slow. Every stop took an eternity as elderly people got in and out. No one seemed to care. The smell of the water and the cries of the seagulls reminded him of Saint Louis. He imagined a city by a river or an ocean where he would live anonymously and safely, where no one would be able to find him, a city where the air was similar to here but thicker, the air of a bay in Africa, a tropical island, or perhaps somewhere in the Amazon rain forest or the South Sea.

He had shown the conductor the address and now the man was gesturing that his stop was next. He got out on a corner and stood for a while staring at the map. It was the same odd silhouette that kept appearing throughout Lisbon between the eighth and the seventeenth of May, a presence or a ghost, as improbable in this city as it was in any of the others where people had allegedly seen him.

He was now on the outskirts of Lisbon on a quiet street with low houses and gardens. Belém Tower Avenue. He stared at the number on the building. Number sixteen. There was no flag, no official plaque, nothing. It was a one-story building surrounded by a white wall and overgrown plants with violet flowers. He could hear a dog barking inside and a lawn mower. The Biafran regime was not internationally recognized. Being pariahs among the countries of the world, perhaps they would be willing to offer political asylum to a fugitive. They were at war and paid mercenaries in diamonds and oil. They needed excellent shooters, men who could take down rhinos and elephants without trouble and handle machine guns in crowds.

He folded the map and put it inside his pocket. He cleared his throat, straightened his back, and checked the gun in his jacket pocket. According to the book on psycho-cybernetics, you had to visualize the way you wanted others to see you. You had to sculpt it, outline it, fully embody it into your physical presence. The most important thing was to show no sign of hesitation. He rang the bell and waited, stiff, his head held so high he could feel the shirt collar on his nape. The lawn mower was close and he caught a faint whiff of gasoline. The dog was still barking.

He rang the bell again. This time the iron gate opened automatically. He took a few steps and then heard it close behind him. If necessary, he could get out by climbing the vines. A straight path led to the house through the garden. The dog barked furiously somewhere he could not see.

A black woman in a white uniform opened the door while taking a drag of her cigarette. It felt as if they had been waiting for him. A black man with muscular arms sat behind a metal table in the vestibule. He was wearing a safari jacket. There was nothing on the table except a phone, and a flag was pinned to the wall behind. It bothered him that it had to be a black man who was sitting at that table. He stared at the solid gold watch, the gold bracelet, and the green stone on his finger. He started to say something and immediately hated the tone of his own voice. He mentioned travel plans, business interests, charitable projects. The man waved him to go down the hall behind him. "All the way to the end, the last office."

The linoleum floor reminded him of the boardinghouse in Memphis, a distant past, so far away. He remembered the hot air and the smell of fermented urine in the bathroom as he got ready to fire the shot. There was always the possibility of another world behind a closed door that would open at the lightest push. "Come in, please," said a deep voice with a British accent.

The office was smaller than he had imagined and looked more like a storage room. It had no windows and all the furniture was mismatched. There was a bookcase with law books. A black man sat behind a desk and a white man stood next to him. They were both large and their bulk made the room feel even smaller. The white man was smoking a pipe and wore a light suit and thick glasses. White smoke rose slowly from his mouth. The black man was in military uniform but the attire seemed too elaborate to be real. He had combat boots, a beret attached to the shoulder of his camouflage jacket, military badges and pins, and a pair of gold-rimmed Ray-Bans.

The white man pulled up a chair for their visitor, who proceeded to sit on the very edge of the seat. The black man began to talk. The

British accent was his. He spoke for a while about a variety of topics. His white colleague stood next to him, opening his mouth only to let the long threads of smoke rise through his yellow teeth.

Different gestures accompanied every sentence that came out of the man's mouth, as if hinting at hidden meanings. He spoke about the tragic state of the world; the collapse of morality; wars and unrest everywhere; riots and looting in black neighborhoods in the United States; the rebellious students in Paris, mama's boys hanging red flags all over the Sorbonne.

In moments of crisis, it was essential that the real men came together in armed struggle to save society. And you should expect nothing in return for your sacrifice, for sometimes they will even stab you in the back. In that perfect pronunciation, he said the name Oswald Spengler: "a few soldiers always end up saving Civilization." He mentioned with reverence the French legionnaires who fought at Dien Bien Phu, and the paratroopers who lost their lives in vain in Algeria.

There was a moment of silence. A small fan hummed from one of the shelves. The visitor cleared his throat, said his name was Ramon George Sneyd, and placed a passport on the desk. The white man leaned over to see the nationality. They left it unopened. The black man remarked on his accent, saying that it did not sound very Canadian. They listened to what he had to say, exchanging glances every now and then.

He could tell they were not buying his story, just like the two shopkeepers who had sold him the rifle in Birmingham. The glasses, the pale face, the soft hands. Someone knocked on the door. A chill ran up his spine. It would take him no time to pull out his gun and then they would look at him differently.

The man who came in was also white—as white as these Portuguese people could get, anyway—and went up to the one with the pipe and said something in his ear. He could not tell what language it was but knew it was not Portuguese. The room felt hotter and his shirt was soaked in sweat. The black man waved goodbye with his sunglasses as the other one left, then leaned on the desk and stared at him intently, almost with pity, while rubbing his hands together.

He suddenly realized that the language they had spoken was French.

He remembered it from his days in Montreal. One word had jumped out: *journaliste*. So these two thought he was a journalist trying to pass for a mercenary or political refugee, a journalist who was perhaps also a spy.

The black man got up abruptly and puffed his chest. He was bigger and more muscular than he seemed while sitting. There were dark patches of sweat in the armpits of his shirt. He thought about how the smell of someone's sweat was enough to identify their race.

The black man walked around the desk and extended a handshake. His grip was strong, almost painful, and the expression on his face was a combination of pity and a warning. In his aristocratic British accent he told him softly to leave and never show his face there again.

The white man with the pipe took a few steps forward as if to get a better look at his face. He felt the stare behind the thick lenses fixing on the tip of his nose and chin, perhaps identifying the signs of plastic surgery.

•

He struggled to assign specific dates to his most recent memories; they lacked a clear sequence. The night he had arrived in Lisbon, the young brunette at the Texas Bar, the office with the balcony facing the river and all the maps of the colonies on the wall, the blond woman from Maxime's, who laughed so loud and faked her moaning, the military man with the Ray-Bans, the South African embassy, the freshly painted black prow of a ship soon headed to Angola. The newspapers he bought at the kiosk by Commerce Square were the only way he had of confirming the date and day of the week. But that wasn't always the case; sometimes the newspapers would not arrive for days to this godforsaken city where time seemed to belong to a different world, a much slower and lethargic world, like that of the prison. Everything was slow here, the trolleys, the way people walked, the government offices where employees looked at a file for an eternity while taking long drags from their cigarettes.

He was now the fastest person on the sidewalk of the narrow street, passing others, almost pushing people out of his way, as if he were late for something. But there was nothing and no one waiting for him, he just forged ahead with his head low like in those circular walks at the prison yard, with the coat under his arm and an invisible abyss or blank space in front of him, in the white stone of the sidewalks, with their drawings of arches or waves, his secret time pulsating faster and faster, every minute and every hour fading away as he advanced, vanishing into thin air just like the money that would soon run out and leave him with nowhere to go, no next stop on the map, no destination in a travel brochure that could make for his next hideout. Beads of sweat were running down his forehead as he arrived at the kiosk with the newspaper stand. He quickly surveyed the front pages of the newspapers and confirmed that his name and photo were not in them. But he would have to read each paper carefully, slowly, from beginning to end, to make sure he didn't miss a story with his picture. He was alarmed to realize that the man at the kiosk now recognized him as a regular and greeted him, even though he had never made eye contact or said anything, he simply pointed to the papers he wanted—*The Times* of London, *The Daily Telegraph*, the *International Herald Tribune*, the *Financial Times*—and placed some money on the counter. Sometimes he extended his hand with the coins and waited for the man to count the amount. The kiosk attendant would later recall that he looked nervous, as if he were late and had to get somewhere fast with all those newspapers, which he could start reading compulsively the moment he stepped away. It took less than ten minutes to get back to the hotel from there. Just a quick walk through the square, down a street, and through the lobby and he would be in his room with the newspapers laid out on the bed.

But this time something caught his attention before he walked away from the kiosk: the familiar red rectangle with the white type of *Life*. May 3, 1968, this issue had taken a while to get to Lisbon. The cover had an old black-and-white photo of schoolchildren posing for a class portrait. The little faces looked serious, some had uneasy smiles. The girl in the corner had a dress, the rest were boys in old overalls. He stared at each one of them. The faces looked familiar. He stopped on the last one on the right in the second row, but he would not have known it was his except for the red arrow that pointed to it.

He remembered the photographer who came to their class that

day. He never got a copy because his parents did not pay the five cents. You can only see his hair, forehead, and the two little eyes. He paid for the magazine and placed it between the newspapers as if protecting it or hiding it. As he walked, he thought about the red arrow and could almost feel it now pointing at his head. Marked since he was a child, they would say, self-satisfied at having found this old photo. Who knows how much they had paid for it. He could imagine the dirty finger of the traitor who pulled it out of an old shoebox and pointed at the head of the small child. Now he could really feel them getting closer.

20

Every end has a prelude. But it takes a while to know when you've reached it. Endings and preludes happen in an insidious manner and later you see their traces in all those moments that seemed ordinary. I returned to Lisbon one November, almost four years after my first visit and the completion of the novel that took me there. In that time the novel had changed my life, not as much as it was about to in the next few months, but much more than I had ever imagined.

Slowly and unexpectedly, the book had become a bestseller. It received awards and a movie was in the works. Dizzy Gillespie was composing the soundtrack and also playing the part of the ailing jazz trumpeter. The boy who was born when I was still writing was about to turn four. We'd also had a daughter who just turned one in September. I had quit my job as a public employee and we no longer lived in the government housing by the river but in a house with a garden in a quiet neighborhood with trees, still in the city but more secluded, with spacious rooms and big windows and a room I could use exclusively for writing and listening to music. Now I was writing on a computer. I still had days when I got up and could not believe that I had the entire morning to myself, instead of having to drag my body to the office. Morning was now the gift of time, a gift that can disappear in the blink of an eye if you don't learn to administer it wisely. The children now see me every day of the week, my wife works close to Granada, and we all live together.

•

This time I took a flight to Madrid and then the 11:00 p.m. Lusitania Express to Lisbon. In the last two or three years, I've lived in a daze of commitments and traveling. Success came unexpectedly and probably undeservedly or at least arbitrarily, like most things, and I had not learned to be more protective of my time. What keeps me grounded, to some extent, besides my love for writing, especially the habit of writing, is life with my family, my wife and my children.

Every trip is a hassle but sometimes also a needed break, a nice treat. You visit a city and someone comes to pick you up, they take you to a nice hotel, and then to an auditorium where people want to hear what you have to say. You were unknown not too long ago and now people come up to you after a talk and ask you to sign their copy of your book. People take your photo and interview you for the newspaper and the local radio. Younger people who like your work address you with deference and timidly present you with a book of poems or stories they have self-published.

A few years ago that was me. The organizers take you to late dinners after these events, and the dinners last an eternity followed by a round of drinks at a bar. The dreamlike quality of every night, in every city, was fueled and heightened by alcohol. I would go for late-night strolls after my hosts had dropped me off at the hotel. I was still looking for something but I did not know what, anything but returning alone and drunk to my hotel room. *Your solitude, shy in hotels*, says García Lorca. Smoking in bed in the dark, unable to fall asleep, I would be overcome with remorse for all the things alcohol made me do or say. I always returned home with a Tintin book for my children.

•

I had stopped drinking a few months before that return to Lisbon. It happened on a regular weekday. I had had a few beers around noon with a group of friends. Then we went to one of our favorite restaurants, the San Remo, had some food and wine and continued talking. But then we got a bottle of whiskey, and probably one of those poisonous herb liqueurs that were so fashionable at the time. I don't think anyone left the place feeling drunk.

That night my wife and I were going to a housewarming dinner at our friends' new place, a couple with small children, like us, with similar likes and literary interests. From the balcony off their dining room, I could see the Vega, the lights glimmering faintly in the distance. We drank beer, then wine with dinner, followed by whiskeys and gin and tonics as we talked and smoked cigarettes.

It was quite late when we returned home. We were both tired but in a good mood. I felt a pleasant dizziness and did not think much of it. I figured some fresh air on the balcony before going to sleep would make it go away.

I fell asleep quickly. Moments later, I woke up feeling like I was going to die. Somehow I made it to the bathroom. I barely closed the door before violently throwing up. The floor was revolving under my bare feet and the spasms sent me against the walls. I could not stop retching. There was vomit everywhere. I could not recognize myself in the mirror. I feared that my wife and children would wake up and see me like this. My body was drenched in sweat and I could smell the alcohol on my skin and breath. Later I found myself sitting on the toilet with my head on my knees, sweating profusely and struggling to breathe.

Somehow I managed to clean that mess. I took a long, hot shower and put on a clean pair of pajamas. I went to the children's room to check I had not awoken them. Then I slid back into bed next to my wife. She seemed to be asleep, though it's possible she heard it all and was just pretending to save me the embarrassment. Before finally closing my eyes, I caught a glimpse of the alarm clock. I was surprised to realize the whole incident had been much shorter than I imagined.

•

I would not taste a drop of alcohol for many months afterward. I immediately began to lose weight. My face looked younger in the mirror. It was a marvelous thing to wake up with a clear head each morning. I also started smoking less. Suddenly, I was in a state of lightness and physical well-being that was entirely new to me. I started writing every day and listening to Bach. Billie Holiday and some of my other favorites were now associated with alcohol and I could not take them.

I discovered how the mind, free of alcohol, instead of growing atrophied for lack of chemical stimulus, can generate its own euphoria, self-sustaining flashes of neural excitement. A rather sickly disciple of Borges, I had loved in excess, like he says, the sunsets, the slums and misery. Now I was learning to love the mornings, the downtown and serenity.

It was, of course, a somewhat sad serenity, the fragile calm of convalescence. The months leading to that night of agony and shame in the bathroom had been a time of growing confusion, a delirium sustained by alcohol, lies, guilt, the simulacra of double lives that were quickly becoming more suffocating than the life I was trying to escape. That is why I was so attracted, then, to stories about spies, traitors, and impostors, novels about fugitives who fake their own death, acquire new identities, and are free at last of those who are after them. I lied like a coward when I was at home but I also lied whenever I left. I returned after every trip slightly hungover, ashamed, afraid that something was going to give me away. Always with a new Tintin book.

•

Staying calm did not take any effort. Some of the temptations that had been irresistible under the influence of alcohol now seemed trivial. Previously fascinating people now seemed boring and repetitive as I listened to them at the bar, drinking water or a Coca-Cola. The warmth and excitement of certain friendships ended up having more to do with the shared habit of drinking than old affinities and loyalties. Years before, when I was still in university, a friend who had to stop drinking by doctor's orders said something I would later put in the mouth of the old trumpeter in my novel: without alcohol, life loses its brilliance, everything seems black and white. But for me it was the opposite. Now colors looked more vivid. Deep inside, however, I was afraid that without alcohol I would not experience the world with the same intensity and this would affect my writing. I was certain that I had saved myself from a great danger, something dark and perhaps irreparable, and, in any case, I needed a break, less traveling, more time with my children and my wife, acceptance of who I was and what I had, a new house, a life in Granada, a new novel in the works, which seemed to promise and require a new kind of writing, one that was less mediated by literature and more faithful to my personal experience and the people who had raised me.

Perhaps it was possible to live contently with what I had, within the limits I had created with my acts and indecisions, a calm without drama, with literature as the space where I could unleash my passions in a way that I could not do with my life. Do not lie and do not harm and do not suffer. I drank tea while I wrote, or water, or nothing. The brain produced amazing stimulants. And without alcohol the excitement of writing lasted much longer, the words flowed from my fingers and materialized on the computer monitor, acquiring a life of their own.

•

This was my frame of mind when I traveled to Lisbon a second time. I had a few hours in Madrid, before the train departed. A journalist who had interviewed me in Granada a few days before had given me her number, but I decided not to call her. We had dinner after the interview. She was younger, red-haired, attractive, with a beautiful Madrid accent, and a quick and sharp sense of humor.

I wandered around the downtown, the streets brought bittersweet memories. Every time I passed a telephone booth, I thought about the phone number in my pocket but could not bring myself to dial. I ended up heading to the train station much earlier than necessary.

This time I was traveling in one of the sleeper cars. One of the attendants approached me with a copy of the Lisbon novel and asked for an autograph. I could not sleep that night. I felt alone and restless, and I wanted to enjoy every minute in this comfortable little cabin, with the warm reading light over the bed, the rhythm of the train, the night scenery outside the window.

I don't remember my first impression upon arriving, nor the location of the hotel. I remember, almost like a flashback, the clear sensation of walking under the November sun, down Liberty Avenue, and seeing once again the cobblestone sidewalks of Lisbon, the small polished stones, white and smooth like bone.

That is all I remember from that trip, a benevolent flood of light, the sudden memory of the city, recovered after almost four years. I don't remember what I did or who I spent time with or who invited me. Sleep escaped me that night as well, as I found myself enveloped in that claustrophobic insomnia that is unique to hotel rooms on the last day before you have to leave.

•

I took a flight back to Madrid. I was scheduled to participate in a public homage to Adolfo Bioy Casares. I bought a bottle of scotch in the duty-free shop. With great caution, I was beginning to drink again, in moderation, one glass of wine with dinner, a beer, a pour of scotch on special occasions, sipped very slowly, rediscovering the aroma of smoke, wood, and peat without the numbness of habit.

The feeling that I lacked solid ground, that I was floating from side to side, was accentuated when I returned to Madrid. I was not familiar with the area around the hotel and could not place it in my mental map of the city. Hotel Mindanao. It was enormous, exemplary of a vulgar modernism, one more cement block on a wide and nondescript avenue of tall buildings from the seventies, practically indistinguishable from so many others in Madrid or any other city.

By mid-morning I was checked in; the room was very similar to the one I had just left in Lisbon. I had nothing to do until seven. I thought about calling the journalist, but I found an excuse—I told myself she would probably come to the event that night. I probably ate lunch alone at the hotel restaurant. I went to the room and called the house to say hi to the children. Then I lay in bed feeling exhausted but unable to sleep. I was nervous and somewhat daunted by the prospect of meeting Bioy. Some of his novels and stories had a decisive influence on me, much like Borges or Onetti: the lean and rigorous plots, the presence of mystery and the magical in the everyday, irony, the way of invoking sexual desire and love. I still had to prepare my remarks for the evening.

•

Also in attendance would be Enrique Vila-Matas and the poet Juan Luis Panero, a big, cordial man, with a voice and laughter to match his size, and a rotund eloquence that immediately brings to mind good conversation in a Spanish cafe. He was comfortable around Bioy. When I arrived at the event, I found Bioy polite, warm, thin, and beginning to bend under old age, which seemed to have recently arrived. He was an elegant man, not only in his dress—English wool suit, flexible leather shoes—but in his manners, the way he leaned in to listen, the way he said thank you. His hair was gray-blond; his eyes were light and framed by heavy eyebrows. Borges and Bioy were responsible for my love of detective stories and fantastic tales, which have in common the discipline of poetry. But in Bioy, there was also the love of women, the implicit vindication of a male subjectivity in awe of women and bound by respect, hopelessly seduced by the combination of intelligence and beauty, vulnerability and sensuality, the concealed, the forbidden.

•

I saw the journalist in the audience, but she wasn't *you* yet, she could have easily been somebody else. She was in the back, near the exit, standing. She had either just arrived or was about to leave. It was the third time I had seen her and the first time her presence affected me and made me wish she would stay. I only knew her name and occupation. She could have left at the end of the event as people began gathering around Bioy. But she remained there, standing in the same spot, even after the room began to empty. Everything was happening with uncertainty, a constellation of improbable events. Just two days before, I was in Granada, yesterday in Lisbon, and this evening in Madrid, standing next to Bioy Casares, watching her out of the corner of my eye as people came to say things to me, to thank me, to give me books or envelopes, to ask for autographs.

•

I was finally free and I was getting ready to approach her when another woman came up to me. She was older, foreign, blond, blue-eyed. One of those round faces that even in old age preserve an air of youthfulness, a childlike form. She extended her hand and introduced herself. Her name was Dolly and she had a Buenos Aires accent. I thought the journalist would end up leaving if I could not excuse myself from this conversation.

Dolly, Dolly Onetti, she repeated. She said she had a message from Juan. Dolly always called Onetti Juan, instead of Juan Carlos. There was no writer alive that I admired more than Juan Carlos Onetti. Dolly was wearing a big coat and a small English hat. She said Juan had read my novel and wanted to talk to me. She gave me a paper with an address and a phone number. I was supposed to call in the morning to confirm, but they would expect me around noon.

•

I continue making my way toward her as in a dream where you walk and walk but don't seem to advance. As I got closer I saw her smile, her eyes, almond-shaped and slightly downturned, her reddish hair, her lips painted red. She said she had only waited to say hi and bye. No doubt I had to stay and have dinner with Bioy and the other writers. I asked her to come with us. The restaurant was in the same hotel. I asked her to at least stay for a beer.

She glanced at her watch and looked around searching for something, a phone. I lost sight of her for a few moments and thought she had left. She reappeared, still shy, but a bit more calmed, putting a few coins back into her purse.

I did not know about her personal life and, for some reason, did not even wonder who she had to call to say she would be late. It was unclear how long she would stay. Would it be a few minutes, just a beer at the bar. Or would she stay a bit longer and drink a glass of wine with me while we waited for a table. She sat next to me because I was the only person she knew at the table, but we were still strangers to each other.

Bioy was attentive toward her, intuiting her discomfort and wanting to make her feel welcome. It was the amorous and melancholic courtesy of a seventy-six-year-old man toward a twenty-eight-year-old woman.

Dinner went on and on, with that exhausting persistence of Spanish dinners and despite the obvious fatigue in Bioy, who had arrived that morning from Buenos Aires. The poet Panero dominated the conversation. The journalist observed everything and listened attentively to the writers' long-winded anecdotes but not without a sense of irony. She had barely touched her food or drink. She told me that she liked the effect of alcohol but not its taste or smell, so she rarely drank. Every time she signaled it was time for her to go, I would ask her to stay a bit longer. She would go to the bathroom, or to the pay phone, again. If she took longer than I expected, I feared she had decided to leave and skip the long round of goodbyes. To my delight, she always returned.

•

I could not overcome the impatience and the exhaustion. I had lost count of how many days I had gone without sleep. There must be a purgatory where the punishment is a never-ending cycle of Spanish dinners that start late, go on for hours and hours, and continue past the end into rounds and rounds of goodbyes.

We finally got up from the table after many hours. Standing by the elevator, pale and exhausted, Bioy shook everyone's hand. Panero gave him a big hug with a few pats on the back. And then the journalist and I were left alone and there was no longer an excuse for her not to go. We walked out of the hotel. It was two or three in the morning. The avenue looked even more abstract at that late hour. There were no taxis. The avenue was a slope: in the distance, high above, there was a line of green taxi lights.

A few minutes ago time seemed to be standing still, frozen in that never-ending dinner. Now time was running out and all we had were the few steps to the taxi line, the moment when she got in a car and was finally on her way home, to whom and where I did not know. She would then disappear from my life as abruptly as she had materialized in the auditorium, in the background, beyond the crowd, where her beauty and the wry smile stood out, just like at the restaurant table, following the conversations like a stealthy cat, examining everything without making a sound.

She was quick and precise in her judgment, critical without cruelty, effortlessly sophisticated, and at ease in what she said and what she liked, films or songs or books, but with no use for solemnity or reverence.

She moved with the wondering grace of someone who is fully in the world, like a child at a fair, possessed of the hard-earned dignity that comes with managing to live and work in a city like Madrid. She was in her own time, indifferent to the latest fashions. Her mane of red hair, her face like a silent film actress from the 1920s, bare nails, a pair of Walkman headphones, short boots, fitted trousers, Mickey Mouse socks. I was surprised by how strongly I desired her. At the last possible second, as we stood by the taxi, I took a deep breath and said, almost in a whisper: "I would like you to stay with me."

•

I remember a soft light forming large shadows in the room and outlining the contours of your naked body. Hours went by, but it was still night outside our window and across all those roofs and balconies, that abstract city that somehow was the same Madrid of just a few hours ago. It all felt so new under that light—the city, my confusion, my gratitude at having met you. It was a night without tomorrow or yesterday, in a room beyond the reach of the world, a moment of sweetness and vulnerability, our eyes staring into the other's, and our faces so close, so unknown, so amazing, so secret, the face that no one else will see.

•

Between dreams I saw you get up and walk naked across the darkened room. I heard the shower and then I saw you come out in silence, gather your clothes from the floor, and quickly dress. You whispered something in my ear and kissed me. Then you turned off the night lamp. I slept so deeply that night and had the most vivid dreams, the white and blue walls of Lisbon, the burning red of bougainvilleas, the morning light of Madrid.

I woke up to your voice but when I opened my eyes you were not there. It was your voice on the radio and you had left it tuned to that station. It was one of those clear and articulate radio voices that can make you fall in love without even seeing the person behind it. The woman with this voice had spent the night with me. I did not know if I would see her again.

•

So many things were happening at once, I struggled to organize them in my mind and memory. At 11:30 a.m. I was crossing Madrid in a taxi without the slightest idea of where I was. This was still a city of fragments for me, memories and impressions from one- or two-day trips. I was en route to the address Dolly Onetti had given me. America Avenue. From there I would go to the airport and take a flight back to Granada.

The flurry of meetings and events, the afterglow of our night together, mitigated the anxiety of meeting Onetti. I could feel my heart racing as I rode the elevator to the last floor. Behind that door at the end of the hall was the writer to whom I owed one of the key impulses of my craft.

I took a deep breath and rang the bell. Dolly opened the door and let me in. I remember a dark room and the open backlit windows with views of Madrid. "Juan is not feeling well," Dolly said in a low voice. "He has a bad cold and wasn't able to get any sleep last night."

It was an apartment with modest furniture; aged things, worn by use; photos and posters on the walls; and shelves upon shelves with the all-too-familiar paperbacks, those unforgettable editions of *The Seventh Circle* and Bruguera. "Juan never stops reading detective novels. Finishes one and starts another. A few days ago, he took all the ones he had read to a used bookseller and came back with more. Since he doesn't sleep, he finishes them right away."

•

Onetti was in a small room that was kept bare like in a hospital. He was on his side, propped on an elbow, and with a cigarette in hand. He wore light blue pajamas and slippers. His legs were visibly thin. His ankles were purple. I could see his stomach through the half-buttoned shirt. He had large bulging eyes and a sparse beard, and wore no glasses. His face had the bloated look that is caused by alcohol. His hands were long and crooked, only capable of holding cigarettes, glasses, books, and lighters. Dolly told me that at least he was now drinking only wine, mixed with water.

There was a glass with wine on the bedside table, along with a few books, newspapers, clippings, an ashtray, two packs of cigarettes, a bottle of wine, a glass with water, and some medicine bottles. A long and narrow window opened onto a balcony with potted plants and a view of the Madrid sky over that redbrick tower on America Avenue where the Iberia sign turned on at night.

I regret to this day not having written right away every word and every detail from that conversation. The memory seems worn from all the times I have invoked it. Above his bed, there were a few photos pinned or taped to the wall: a female fox terrier who had died recently, la Biche, friends and grandchildren, and his daughter, with Nordic features, and a beautiful young woman with tan skin and brunette hair. She had come to visit Juan not too long ago, said Dolly with a tone of indulgence. They had talked for hours. "Juan always needs his Lolita." We talked about Humbert Humbert and Lolita: Onetti said that the novel should have ended with the night he rapes her, everything after was an unnecessary addition. Why couldn't Nabokov be content with a short novel, he said, with that signature expression of tragic error in his big eyes.

He told me about his love for Faulkner, whom I had discovered thanks to him. He showed me a letter he had written to the newspaper, mocking the obsession that bishops and church clergy have with regulating or prohibiting sex, even though they have no experience of it. He recalled the joy of walking out of a bookstore with a new Faulkner novel, reading it as he walked and bumping into people.

The long yellowed fingers extracted cigarette after cigarette and lit them with a plastic lighter. Propped on his elbow, Onetti took long puffs, letting the column of ash form slowly and fall on his shirt, which he then shook without fuss. It was amazing that there were no cigarette burns on the bed or his pajamas. Dolly told me that the thought of him falling asleep with a lit cigarette kept her up at night.

I wish I had dared to tell him about you. I had always tried to learn from him how to write about desire and love, the wonder and gratitude of reaching what had never been imagined, what one did not even know existed. I quoted from memory a passage from *The Face of Disgrace* while secretly thinking about you: "And I suddenly had what

I had never deserved, her face, overcome with weeping, and happiness under the moonlight." That was Onetti for me: the ecstasy of beauty or unexpected abundance, as Larsen declares in *The Shipyard*: "Now at last I can breathe again: I can look at you, say whatever I like. I don't know what life still holds in store for me; but meeting you is reward enough. I can see you, look at you."

•

He was generous about my Lisbon novel. He told me that it had been right there on his nightstand, next to the medicines, the cigarettes, and the detective novels. It was then that I saw my meeting with him in the light of that story I had finished more than three years ago and was already leaving behind. Without that novel I would have never met him, I would not have been there that morning, I would not have returned to Lisbon, I would not have met you.

Graham Greene says that some novels are written with memories of the past and others with anticipated memories of the future. The image I had created of the young musician visiting his teacher was not that different from what I was doing now.

Dolly said that Onetti insisted on drinking bad wines and cheap whiskeys and that this was bad for him. I asked if I could give him the bottle of scotch I had purchased at the duty-free shop in the Lisbon airport. She said yes, with a gesture of resignation without drama. "At least he will drink something good."

She brought two glasses and I poured the scotch. I had yet to eat any breakfast and I also wasn't used to drinking anymore. The scotch had an immediate effect on me. He told me the three things he liked the most: "Writing, a sweet and gradual binge, making love." Dolly recalled a story of their early years together, when she was just an adolescent, and he remained quiet and then said: "Ruben says there are only two things, regret and oblivion."

Sometimes he got very quiet and terribly serious, with a big eye fixed on me or the wall or just looking into space. I glanced at my watch and felt disloyal. Soon I would have to leave for the airport. He asked Dolly to give me one of his most treasured books, the first volume of Joseph Blotner's *Faulkner: A Biography*. Dolly asked why he did not give me the second volume as well. "That way he will come back for the second when he is done with the first one." But time passed and I never went back. Dolly gave me the second volume as a gift after he died. When we said goodbye, Onetti squeezed my hand and said: "It's beautiful to feel like a friend."

21

A story demands an ending. Narrative consists of an unstoppable progress toward a conclusion. You must feel that momentum, let it take you along, still and in motion, guided by an impersonal force that is bigger than you but not overwhelming, the velocity of a train or a car, its movement forward as powerful as the retreat from everything you leave behind.

A final period is a line in time. The gesture can be decisive and yet as pointless as drawing a line in the water or sand. It is difficult to find the beginning but it's even harder to find the end. There will be nothing beyond that. The child begrudgingly accepts that a story has come to an end, even though the anticipation of the ending was the magnet that kept his or her attention. And they lived happily ever after. But the child sees no reason why the story can't continue. How did they live ever after? The story comes to an end but the child wants to hear it one more time. You go back to the beginning and they see it with new eyes.

•

Here's a possible ending if we look at this story under the austere clarity of facts. On May 17, 1968, Ramon George Sneyd, a Canadian citizen, paid his bill at the Hotel Portugal and took a taxi to the airport. Only the dates and the sights of Lisbon imbue his stay with a measure of consistency, a temporal arch, a spatial continuity, the bare minimum of symmetry. He had arrived nine days prior on an overnight flight from London. He would be returning to London on a flight that departed at eleven in the morning. His luggage weighed twelve kilos at Heathrow Airport. It was now two kilos heavier.

The immigration officer at the Lisbon airport noted that his passport did not have the entry stamp for Portugal. Thankfully, the man could speak English. Sneyd, nervous, polite, somewhat distracted, searched his pant and coat pockets for the other passport. He opened it to the page with the entry stamp and pointed to the misspelling in the name that had forced him to go to the Canadian embassy in Lisbon to get a new passport. He placed the two passports on the counter next to each other. He kept adjusting his glasses and refolding the coat under his arm. The two photos were nearly identical even though they had been taken a month apart. The same uncomfortable hint of a smile, the same subdued disposition, the same tie, the glasses. Perhaps the officer had already identified him and was just creating a distraction while the police arrived.

The officer studied one of the passports, then the other, then his face, spelling the name. The two versions were almost identical, Sneyd, Sneya, the smallest difference but enough to trap him, to delay him.

The tension made him aware of the weight of the revolver in his pocket, the crazy possibility of reaching for it and taking off running and shooting anyone who got in his way.

The officer returned the old passport and stamped the other with one of those metal devices that had dates and an official seal and that were used in customs, courts, police stations, prison offices where bureaucrats gathered like parasites to push papers, them on one side and the prisoner on the other, their desks always elevated so they can look down. The officer returned the new passport and made that gesture that guards always make, the one they train for their entire lives: the extended hand that authorizes you to pass, to cross the limit, a tired gesture full of contempt, like the one the prison guard had probably made after inspecting the truck with the bread cart, while he waited and tried not to sneeze from the flour falling on his face. It had been one year and fourteen days since the escape.

•

The plane takes off from Lisbon one bright morning in May. That could be a possible ending. The relief of avoiding capture combines with vertigo as the plane begins to tilt upward. He holds on to the armrests and watches the horizon out the window slant down. Commerce Square is a white spot gradually disappearing next to the wide metallic river. This is the last time he will see Lisbon.

When the plane stabilizes, he takes off his glasses and wipes his forehead with a handkerchief. Relief will be short-lived. In just two hours, he will have to wait in the immigration line again, show his passport, explain himself.

A plane taking off or a departing train is an excellent sign for an ending. The story is a game that remains within the strict limits of the board where pieces move in discontinuous paths. It is a powerful focal point marking a circular contour of light against the dark. The characters enter a limbo of nonexistence and we're not allowed to rescue them. Unlike real people, they have the power to vanish without a trace. There will be no detectives investigating the last hotel room where they stayed, searching for fingerprints, hairs, any useful piece of paper. The only thing that Ramon George Sneyd or Sneya left in his room on the first floor of the Hotel Portugal, where he had spent nine days, was a mess of newspapers and an issue of *Life* magazine. The receptionist, Gentil Soares, saw him leave without saying goodbye, clumsily pushing the revolving door after his suitcase got stuck. He was relieved to think he would never see him again.

•

An ending is a place to rest. It has an element of absolution. The fugitive does not have to keep running. But Ramon George Sneyd is still on the run. He is falling apart; too much indecision, too many mistakes, missteps, and dead ends. When he traveled from Toronto to London and from London to Lisbon, he had felt propelled in a definite direction, the peak of his grand escape: Africa, ultimate freedom. At his most deluded, he had even imagined the glory of a hero's welcome. In South Africa or Rhodesia they would surely embrace the man who had put an end to the great enemy of the white race. A few soldiers always end up saving civilization, the man with the British accent and the fake uniform at the Delegation of Biafra had said. But now he was retracing his steps and flying back to London with the gut feeling that he was heading straight into the lion's mouth, the final dead end. It was like being an incompetent thief, once again, and sprinting for the corner that the cops are about to turn.

After the end in Lisbon, Ramon George Sneyd goes back to London and rents a room in a shady neighborhood. The only end he sees in sight is misery. The money is quickly disappearing, the English coins and bills he does not understand. He believes that taxi drivers, waiters, and newspaper vendors are probably stealing from him. He speaks to no one. He can barely sleep. He buys several newspapers and locks himself in his room to read them. The sole window faces a dark brick wall covered in rain. During the day the sound of traffic and loud music does not cease. At night, he listens to the planes leaving the airport for Africa or Asia, the Far East, the Pacific.

•

He reads the books that he brought from America and a few others he has purchased at street stalls. He keeps rereading the same chapters of *Psycho-Cybernetics* but is not able to concentrate. He reads a worn, stapled pamphlet with the title "How to Hypnotize," written by Dr. Adolf F. Louk of the Louk International Hypnosis Institute. He tries to breathe deeply, like the pamphlet says, closes his eyes, and follows the first steps of autohypnosis, but his mind is already elsewhere. He has pounding headaches. The migraines, the heart palpitations, the sharp pain in his stomach, or perhaps in the intestine—you can also get cancer there.

He lies in bed reading newspapers, his shoes and coat still on, eating chocolate bars and potato chips. He dozes off and his own racing heartbeat wakes him up. The headaches are unbearable. He imagines sharp knives or drill bits piercing through his skull. He is sure he has the symptoms of a brain tumor. He keeps swallowing aspirins with water from the tap.

When he gets tired of the newspaper or when he is suddenly convinced that the books about psycho-cybernetics and hypnosis are a scam, he looks for one of the novels. Risking your life to rob a bank or traffic drugs is a game of idiots. It takes no effort and no risk to write books that lie to ignorant, gullible people and make millions. He reads novels about spies involved in risky international missions. He reads *Tangier Assignment*, where Robert Belcourt, secret agent of Her Majesty, uses the cover of a film producer who flies all over the world first class and stays at luxury hotels. Robert Belcourt is an extraordinary name, masculine and distinguished. Belcourt produces films and also writes them. On white beaches, surrounded by palms, and beside hotel pools, he meets beautiful women who sunbathe in bikinis and drink cocktails and want to be with him.

Reading this makes him think of his days in Puerto Vallarta. Memories blend with the images from the novel. The head of the British secret service sends Belcourt to every corner of the world on the most dangerous and top-secret missions, those that must leave no evidence of government involvement. Belcourt speaks French, Spanish, Italian, German. It's his mastery of Italian that allows him to infiltrate the Mafia that controls drug trafficking in Tangier, although his real mission is to execute the head of the Soviet secret service in North Africa.

•

He is falling asleep, his eyes hurt, but he forces himself to continue reading. He knows that as soon as he puts the book down and turns off the light, sleep will leave him.

He counts the coins and the British bills and stacks them on the nightstand. Then he leaves his room and checks phone booths for change. He walks staring at the floor in case he finds stray coins. There are not a lot of white people on the sidewalks and inside the shops and at the newspaper stand. He sees black people, Pakistanis, women from India wearing saris, men with beards and turbans. The smell of spicy food turns his stomach and the shops are blasting Caribbean or Asian music. He walks past a newspaper stand and something makes him turn abruptly. He thought he had seen his name on a big headline, his face in the mug shot of a thief or killer the police are after. But it's someone else.

It seems they're not looking for him anymore. He's still spending money every day on newspapers, but getting them at different stands, so it doesn't call too much attention. He starts reading them on the street and bumps into people. Even when it's raining he can't help but take a quick first look at the sections.

He looks to the right and is about to cross the street when a black car or a red bus almost runs him over from the left. He can't get used to the change in traffic direction. He still confuses the different values of the coins and makes mistakes when converting to dollars. The Indian or Pakistani men at the newsstand are surely giving him the wrong change. He hasn't talked to anyone since the night with the blond woman at the Texas Bar, just a few words here and there with waiters and the hotel receptionist. He lives inside his assumed identity like a castaway on a desert island, an ape in a cage, he thinks, as he stares at himself in the small mirror by the sink in front of the bed. The mirror is the cell's only window, the bulletproof glass that separates him from his only visitor, himself. He looks at himself and no longer has patience for another attempt at autohypnosis. He looks for bars that might be showing the TV program with the FBI's Most Wanted. It's possible that he is no longer in the top ten.

Not seeing even the smallest news report about the search makes him nervous. It accentuates that rare sensation he has of not existing. He will end up being erased or just vanishing like the money he counts every night.

But he knows they are still working on it, obstinately, like termites, adding every little detail he left behind, the fingerprints he forgot to wipe, perhaps the passport application, or the testimony of one of the receptionists or the person who took his passport photo. They said they had found a fingerprint on the rifle, a receipt for dry-cleaning, and later the prisoner number he thought he had scratched entirely from his transistor radio. They must be so close they don't want to give him even the slightest clue that might put him on alert. Three thousand seventy-five FBI officers, said the person on the radio. That's how many people were on the case. Three thousand seventy-five agents against one man and they haven't been able to catch him—he prides himself though the feeling of exaltation doesn't last long. Even with their laboratories and their microscopes, their networks of informers, their fancy weapons and their golden badges. How many more would be looking for him in Canada, Mexico, or even here, in London. If they've discovered the new name on the passport, all the checkpoints at the airports have been alerted. He doesn't have the means of acquiring a new identity; this is a skin he can't shed. He has no choice but to remain Ramon George Sneyd. He dislikes the name more and more, every time he says it or writes it in the logbook of the hotel.

Despite the familiar language, London feels even more alien than Lisbon. The city of Memphis and the leading newspaper of the city are offering one hundred thousand dollars for anyone who can provide information that will lead to an arrest. That was a real headline, a front-page announcement, unlike the rumor of a secret fifty-thousand-dollar bounty for whoever did what so many boasted of wanting to do, but only he had the guts to execute. The head in the crosshairs of the scope, the single shot that had left the ringing sound in his ears and pushed him back, almost making him fall inside the bathtub. His brother had told him: "There ain't no money in killing a nigger."

He remembered the times when he had wads of hundred-, fifty-, and twenty-dollar bills in his pockets. He peeled money from the deck, counting very fast. One part of his brain counted and the other remained vigilant. He paid the hick who sold him the '66 Mustang two thousand dollars in one hundred twenty-dollar bills, counting them in broad daylight, in front of the bank, with a level of confidence that intimidated the other. Both were looking at the money, the hick and his son, a slob just like the father, also with glasses and looking almost as old. Both had big stomachs and sparse hair, both had that churchgoer face, both were itching with impatience, dying to get their dirty hands on his money, even though later they would say that he seemed suspicious, that he had to beg them to sell him the car. Posing together for the newspaper photos, father and son.

•

The receptionist would always greet him with a smile when she saw him enter with all his newspapers. She was very young. Her name was Janet Nassau. She didn't get discouraged from all the failed attempts at starting a conversation with him. About the weather, the traffic, Canada, a modern country, with its vast open spaces. Every time he came in or left was like the first time. There was no air of familiarity even after a few days of being there. He always seemed puzzled, like someone who has entered a dark room after being under a bright sun. In ten days he did not receive a single letter or phone call. He always said his room number when asking for his key, as if he expected the receptionist to have forgotten.

She felt pity for him. She felt the urge to protect him, to defend him against whatever was tormenting him, whatever misfortune had brought him to this hotel, to England. He never made eye contact, but sometimes she caught a glimpse of the light blue eyes behind the glasses. He always left before nine in the morning like someone going to an office. He came downstairs and left the keys on her desk, which she took in an almost affectionate way. If it was raining, she reminded him to take an umbrella. He listened for a moment with his head slightly cocked, as if not understanding what she was saying. She wanted to fold his coat collar down, recommend that he use less deodorant, brush the dandruff from his shoulders. If he was going through a financial hardship and was trying to get a job, he needed to look his best.

As soon as he left, she asked the bellhop to keep an eye on the reception for a moment. She went up to his room. She knew it was risky, but she could not help it, she wanted to know more about him. Sometimes he would not return for hours, other times he was back in less than half an hour with a few newspapers under his arm, like a professor carrying books from the library. He could be a professor. A scholar at a secluded and respectable Canadian university. A professor of theology or Semitic languages, something detached from the vanities of the world.

She opened the door carefully, and closed it behind her right away. She looked around the tiny room. There was very little natural light. She was moved by the fact that he had made his bed. He had smoothed the blue quilt so there were no wrinkles and folded it perfectly below the pillow. A hand-washed shirt hung by the window. There was a small hand radio and a paperback novel on the bedside table. On the cover of the book there was a woman in a bikini seen from behind; she was looking over her shoulder, her mouth was half-open and her lips were red, she wore black eyeliner and had a wild mane of hair. She took a step toward the table and stepped on one of the newspapers. She should leave now. She could hear a vacuum cleaner somewhere in the building. She opened the drawer carefully. It was dark and she could barely see what was inside. She turned on the table lamp, making sure not to move the novel or the radio. There was a pornographic magazine inside. It looked worn and did not have a cover. There was a full-color close-up. It took Janet Nassau a few seconds to realize what she was seeing. She closed the drawer right away and felt dirty. In the closet there was a jacket and a pair of sport pants, also the small suitcase he had brought with him. The spray can of Right Guard deodorant was on a shelf by the sink, next to a plastic glass with a toothbrush and a tube of toothpaste with an airline logo.

She opened the latch quietly to leave the room, feeling remorseful, afraid that he would show up right that second. She returned to her desk. It took a while to calm down. When he returned a few hours later, she tensed up and almost could not smile. She gave him the key along with an envelope from the hotel manager. The guest looked at the envelope with some confusion, perhaps thinking that it was a letter. "I have to go to the bank," he said, not looking at her, as if talking to himself. "I will go today and get some money."

•

He sat on the bed without taking his coat off and stared at the wall and the closet. He took off his glasses and rubbed his eyes. It was 2:00 p.m. on a Monday at the beginning of June, but the rain and the cold made it feel like an evening in December. The room was not much different from a prison cell. It was only missing the toilet without a lid next to the sink. In one coat pocket he had approximately twenty-five British pounds in bills and coins. In the other one, next to the bill from the hotel manager, he had his gun, the handle wrapped with tape. He had swallowed two aspirins without water. If he closed his eyes and remained still the medicine would act faster. He had to concentrate so he could get on the right frequency for psycho-cybernetic autosuggestion. Perhaps it did not work because he had missed some crucial step in the book, he had not had enough faith, he had not made a real effort to project the right image of himself, the one he wanted others to see. The blond ditz at the reception desk, for instance. If he had looked her in the eye with the necessary intensity and sent telepathic orders to put the envelope away, now he would have extra time to find the money. He could have just gone to his room and stayed there for a day or two reading his novels, looking for another article from that reporter who wrote about the wars in Africa and the mercenary armies. Then he could have left without paying by hypnotizing the bellhop and the maid and the receptionist and anyone else who crossed his path.

•

He seemed absentminded when he left and forgot to leave the key on the desk. The receptionist was going to call him, but stopped herself, her mouth half-open, the name on the tip of her tongue, a hint of a smile. He was probably in a hurry to get to the bank before it closed. It had stopped raining and the streets were filling up again.

He was looking for a shop he had passed several times. It was a narrow jewelry shop, tucked between an electronics store and a textiles store. It reminded him of the old shops in Lisbon, where he would see old people behind the counters, hunched over, examining jewels or watches.

He found the place. There was a pale man with gray hair discussing something with a customer. He was holding a little black box with a shiny object inside. A bell rang when he went inside. There was a glass door in the back and he could see the profile of a woman with gray hair, glasses, and a dark dress working at a small table. He walked around, looking at the display windows while the old man finished with the customer. The woman had looked up when the bell rang. A black ribbon hung from the legs of her glasses. She looked sick, like someone who has aged prematurely. He reached inside his pocket and squeezed the gun. He could feel the sweat on his palm against the tape. He should have taped his fingertips as well.

When he saw the client get ready to leave he turned around so the person could not see his face. The bell rang again as the person exited and the sound of traffic entered for a few seconds. The old man asked how he could help. His nose was covered with small purple veins and he had a pale complexion.

He looked at the scrawny arms under the short-sleeved shirt, then grabbed the man by the collar and jabbed the gun barrel in his neck. The small eyes stared at him from under the white wiry eyebrows, showing more incredulity than fear. He twisted the old man's arm and pushed him against the wall.

The woman was suddenly gone from her post. A bit more force and the frail arm would break. He pushed the old man toward the cash register and demanded the money. A shadow and her breath alerted him but it was too late. He caught a glimpse of some heavy object and instinctively recoiled toward the exit. The blow almost knocked him to the ground but he caught himself on the counter. He could hear their heavy breathing behind him and then he felt the old man's fingers in his eyes. The alarm went off and he felt his head was about to explode.

He pushed the old couple back as hard as he could and ran for the door. In a flash of panic he noticed that the coat had gotten caught on something and one of the pockets had torn. But he didn't stop running. The alarm blared in the distance. He saw the entrance to the metro and pushed his way in through the rush-hour crowd. Seconds later, he was locked in a toilet stall trying to catch his breath. He fixed his clothes and checked all the pockets: the revolver, a few coins and crumpled bills, the hotel bill, a comb, the passport. How stupid of him to have taken his government ID to the robbery.

He went over to the sink, splashed water on his face, and combed his hair, parting it carefully to one side. The receptionist noticed the tear in the coat when he returned to the hotel, even though he was holding the pocket to hide it. She knew there was no way he would have made it to the bank before closing.

The next morning, she was happy to see the pocket was already sewn. It's great to see a man who can make his own bed, wash his shirts, and use a needle and thread when necessary. He put the key on the desk and, without looking at her, said he would pay his bill when he came back. He was going to his bank, he said, not just any bank.

This is a man who is going through a hard time but you know he is trustworthy, the hotel employees recognize him and say hi, they imagine what he's going through, the death of his wife, perhaps a bad divorce that has forced him to live in a hotel.

•

She saw him return three hours later. Police and ambulance sirens had been sounding for a while. According to the bellhop, there had been an armed robbery at the bank nearby. He had heard that the bank teller had resisted and the burglar had shot him or hit him in the head with the gun. She had worried that it was the same bank where the guest had gone to withdraw his money. She asked him as she handed the key with a smile. He heard the question but could not understand it at first due to her accent. He seemed confused, his head cocked to one side. Finally, he shrugged his shoulders and said he hadn't heard anything. Up close, the stitching in the coat pocket looked very rough. His forehead was covered in sweat. Something fell as he pulled the money out of his pocket, and the glasses slid down his nose as he bent to pick it up. She could see the bulk of a heavy object in the stitched-up pocket.

It was the passport that had fallen out. He paid with brand-new bills, five- and ten-pound notes, and said he was checking out, he had a flight to catch that afternoon. She said she hoped it wasn't an emergency. Once again, he stared at her lips as if he didn't understand what she was saying.

The bellhop had been leaning on the counter but did not offer to help bring down the man's bag. The guest had not tipped him even once in ten days. The police sirens faded and rain began to pour. There was thunder and hail. Janet Nassau felt bad for him. What if he didn't find a taxi that could take him to the airport. He would get drenched. She saw him come down with his suitcase, a plastic bag, several newspapers under his arm, and a camera around the neck. She gave the bellhop a dirty look. The guest was feeling through his pockets, probably trying to find the keys. Janet Nassau prepared a smile for him, she was ready to ask him if he needed anything, she could call him a taxi, or perhaps it was best if he waited until the rain ceased. It thundered and she lost her train of thought. The guest put the keys on the desk and a moment later he was gone, just like that, without a word.

•

The rain fogged up his glasses. The street was barely visible. He could only see the moving headlights and the traffic lights. Water ran down his face, getting in his eyes. He turned a random corner and found himself on a quiet street with low houses, identical facades and red or black doors with golden doorbells. There was no way he would find a hotel on this street. But he couldn't have stayed in the other after the robbery. As soon as he had taken off running from the bank he realized just how close the hotel was. The confusing topography of London's streets had made him think it was actually farther.

He had walked around looking for a bank that was far enough but he had almost gone in a circle. Everything had been done so hastily. He hadn't even taped his fingertips. He had approached the counter and discreetly pointed the gun at the bank teller under a handkerchief. The old man leaned in because he was hard of hearing and obviously hadn't seen the gun. He pulled the handkerchief back. It seemed the old man couldn't see well either. When he finally understood what was happening his hands began to shake and he dropped the money he had been counting. He pushed the gun through the metal bars and pressed it against the old man's forehead. With the other hand he took the money from the counter and put it in his pocket. He demanded the money that was in the metal box. The bank teller could not stop shaking and dropped the box with all the coins and bills on the marble floor, making a loud noise.

Every set of eyes suddenly turned toward the man in the trench coat who was now running for the exit. The alarm had yet to go off. He saw his hand reach for the door almost in slow motion, and before he knew it, he was already in the street running as fast as he could. It was like running away from the jewelry shop again. Almost an exact replay of the prior day, or was it the same day just a few hours earlier, the same gray light of early morning or the rainy afternoon, now with lightning flashes anticipating a storm. He ran holding on to the revolver in one pocket and the cash in the other. Once in the hotel room, he counted the money on the bed and tried to convert it to dollars. The immediate relief would not last past the weekend, but at least he had bought himself two or three days. Tomorrow was a repetition of yesterday just like every hotel room he found was identical to the previous one.

•

Five o'clock on Wednesday, July 5. The stormy sky was so dark it felt like nightfall. He walked close to the walls, searching for a temporary refuge from the rain, which had soaked his shoes, his hair, and the coat. A small pink sign flashed from a nondescript building. ROOMS. He rang the bell and heard it echo toward the back of the house. It was still raining and no one was coming to the door. The neon sign was the only indication that the place was inhabited. A tall blond woman finally opened the door. No one is a mere passing silhouette, an extra, an auxiliary figure in the stories of others. Her name was Anna Thomas and she had been born in Sweden. Hotel Pax was the name of the inn. She saw the man on the sidewalk under the weak light of the vestibule. He was completely drenched and holding a suitcase, a bag, and a bunch of newspapers and books under his arm.

She invited him in, quickly, she said, out of the rain. At first the man was hesitant to come in, he seemed worried about dripping water on the carpet. She could hear the water sloshing in his shoes. They were an odd choice for this kind of weather, crocodile skin or something similar, something a tourist would wear in the Caribbean.

He asked her if she had any aspirin. He was shivering and his eyes were glossy with fever. He had a hard time articulating words. His lips moved but the sounds barely came out.

The next morning Anna Thomas brought his breakfast to the room, along with warm orange juice with honey and a tube of aspirin. She pressed her ear to the door but could not hear anything. She knocked softly. There was no answer, so she left the tray on the floor. She had not taken more than a few steps down the hall when the door opened. The guest picked up the tray quickly and closed the door. She noticed that he was still wearing the suit and the trench coat.

He stayed three days in Hotel Pax. The wallpaper in his room featured blue peacocks. He would leave around 9:00 a.m. and return half an hour later with a few newspapers and magazines under his arm. He would not leave again for the rest of the day. The second morning Anna Thomas pointed at the front page of one of his papers with a big photo of Robert Kennedy. How terrible, she said, hard to believe he too had been killed. The guest nodded and kept walking. He had paid for one week in advance. The following Saturday, Anna Thomas found the room empty.

There is a possible ending, a definite line drawn in time. The morning of June 8, Ramon George Sneyd, or Sneya, was detained at Heathrow Airport as he was boarding a plane to Brussels at 11:50 a.m. He had heard that in Brussels there was a recruitment center for mercenaries who wanted to go fight in the Congo. The police officers were friendly and they escorted him to an office to review his documents. They were almost apologetic and said it was a simple routine check. One of the officers showed a pained expression when they found the revolver in one of his back pockets.

•

A Liberty Chief .38 revolver. A Polaroid camera. A hi-fi deluxe transistor radio. A Noveline trench coat. A brown wool suit. A blue hat. A blue shirt. A jacket and a pair of sport pants. Two pairs of sunglasses. A Collins pocket dictionary. A plastic comb. A plastic wallet. A Portuguese coin. Twenty-one airmail envelopes. A roll of tape. A pamphlet titled "How to Hypnotize," by Dr. Adolf F. Louk, director of the Louk International Hypnosis Institute. A bottle opener. A blank notebook. A matchbox from the New Gonevale restaurant in Toronto. A nail clipper. A map of Portugal. A spray can of Right Guard deodorant. A small shampoo bottle. A map of London. A birth certificate with the name Ramon George Sneyd. Two bars of soap. Sixty British pounds in five-pound notes. Hair pomade. A paperback novel titled *The Ninth Directive*. Shaving cream. Another paperback novel, quite worn, titled *Tangier Assignment*. A toothbrush. A book titled *Psycho-Cybernetics*. An inhaler. A hand mirror. Black shoe polish.

•

They gave him the list and asked him to read it and sign it. He searched for his glasses, first in the coat, then in the jacket, and read the document slowly, mumbling some of the words in the list under his breath. A police officer handed him a pen to sign and he thanked him profusely. He hesitated before writing "R. G. Sneyd." One of the undercover police officers came back into the small, windowless office. He got close to him and, in a polite tone, as if suggesting a mere hypothesis, said that perhaps his name was not Ramon George Sneyd; perhaps his name was James Earl Ray. He did not respond. Leaning back in the chair, feet apart, head against the wall, he stared at the pen in his right hand, the trench coat on his lap, the mended pocket. Perhaps he thought, half in disbelief, half with an odd feeling of gratitude: I no longer have to run.

22

I like the title of Louis Althusser's memoir, *L'avenir dure longtemps*. The future lasts forever. The future lasts much longer than literature is usually able to convey. A final period strikes at the end like a final drumbeat, a final note by Thelonious Monk, jarring or round, perhaps doubtful, an unexpected conclusion that doesn't culminate as much as interrupt. But time continues flowing, even though we're not allowed to see what happens to the characters after the end.

Almost nobody has possessed Flaubert's unique talent or wisdom to include in a novel the future it does not tell, because it comes after the anticipated ending, and it seems so superfluous to the reader that, after a while, it will be forgotten. Memory, or the lack thereof, can correct a novel retrospectively, distill it, make it even better sometimes. The reader of *Madame Bovary* will remember a novel that ends with Emma's agonizing death, almost unbearable to read in all its graphic detail, which Flaubert re-creates even more intensely than an erotic scene. We forget, but the novel continues after Emma's death, just as it began long before she appeared.

Charles Bovary goes on living, isolated in his disgrace, shame, and ruin. He keeps a tormented reverence for his dead wife, but soon begins to discover unexpected and cruel things about her, letters that confirm and detail the infamy and prolong her presence after death, infecting those who remain with an illness that lacks that infallible cure for all ills in literature, the final period.

Only after the successive deaths of Emma and Charles does the novel reveal its only innocent character, the victim of so many, the one the reader had probably forgotten or barely even noticed. She is the daughter Emma brought into this world unwanted, a burden that pestered her existence.

The girl's story is just as long and painful as any, but she does not have the right to a novel, not even a substantive role in a novel about those closest to her. When her father dies, she ends up in the custody of relatives who mistreat her. The last thing we know about her is that she is working in a cotton mill. Now I don't even remember whether she had a name. A novel is truly great when there are many possible novels within it: the most tragic, in this case, would be titled *Mademoiselle Bovary*.

But in real life, the future lasts forever and real-life stories end by disintegrating into others, dispersing, unraveling loose threads without a clear plot that intertwines with other stories and ends up traveling far from their starting point. They resemble African or Asian musical compositions in their open form, the way they're prolonged without fatigue and significant variation for hours, days, nights, flowing like rivers, without a sequence or beginning or end.

But fiction, like European music, is an art of limits. What begins must end. "In my beginning is my end," says T. S. Eliot. A departing plane or train provides a clear and convenient ending to any story. Arrivals and departures determine the temporal boundaries of a story, as the two columns in Commerce Square frame for the viewer the expanse of the sky and the Tagus River, the hint of ocean that begins beyond the other limit, the red silhouette of the 25th of April Bridge. The train starts, the plane lifts in the last frame or in the last lines and after that the passenger aboard is beyond our reach. The plane is en route to Lisbon but for us, the audience, it might as well float over the Atlantic forever.

How to begin the story of something whose origin is unknown to you. On May 8, 1968, at 1:30 a.m., Ramon George Sneyd arrives in Lisbon. On April 6, a man named Eric Starvo Galt, who has just arrived in Toronto, rents a room in a boardinghouse owned by a Polish woman who can barely speak English. On Saturday, March 29, a man, who said his name was Harvey Lowmeyr, bought a hunting rifle at a weapons store on the outskirts of Birmingham, Alabama, on the highway to the airport. On April 4, around 3:30 p.m., someone named John Willard rented a room in a run-down boardinghouse in Memphis and paid for a week in advance. On April 5, around 9:00 a.m., Eric S. Galt picked up his laundry from a dry cleaner in Atlanta. The more precise the topographical and temporal details, the more emphatic the beginning or end of the story will seem, the more powerful the appearance without warning or the abrupt departure of the character. At 9:00 a.m. on May 17, 1968, the receptionist at the Hotel Portugal in Lisbon sees the guest from room 2 disappear through the revolving door, his shoulders more slouched than when he arrived a week earlier. At 11:00 p.m. on January 4, 1987, I left Lisbon from the Santa Apolónia station on a train called the Lusitania Express.

•

The future continues: a few days later, at 8:00 a.m., I was once again a civil servant in Granada. I was also a father with a three-year-old son and a one-month-old baby, who still moved in the crib with the helplessness of newborn mammals, with his red skin, his hairless little head, his eyes with swollen lids and no eyelashes, his hands and his feet so small, holding on to anything with the obstinacy of biological survival, his mother's chest, his open mouth, his smell of baby and mother's milk.

•

The ability to see far is more limited in time than in space. On December 2, 2012, in another future life that has already lasted many years and I could have never imagined in that first trip to Lisbon, I am walking in Rossio Square at night, feeling a little light-headed from the day of travel and the undulating patterns of mosaics on the sidewalks of Lisbon. We have come because my son, who was only one month old the first time I walked these streets, now lives here and is turning twenty-six today. We hadn't noticed how much time had passed since we last visited. But now it feels like time sped up and we remember what took place ten or fifteen years ago as if it had happened yesterday.

From the moment we arrive, as we look at the colors of the city from the taxi window, the pinks and blues, the ochers and worn yellows on the facades, the sun of the early afternoon, in a December with a more merciful weather than the one we left just a few hours ago in Madrid, we're overcome with remorse for having taken so long to return, the strangeness that this has even been possible. How can there be so much distance in such a short span of time, barely an hour-long flight.

You have drawn the curtains in the room where we will stay for two or three days. It's a tall house on a hill, and the entire city opens up before us like a fantastic diorama. The Tagus River, the 25th of April Bridge peter out in the distance toward the southeast, and next to us, almost in front of us, a wooded hill is crowned by a white church shining under the afternoon sun, and just beyond: the walls and towers of San Jorge Castle adorned with flags flapping against the blue sky. It reminds me of the Alhambra seen from a garden in Albaicín. And the house itself reminds me of those in Albaicín. Narrow stairways, low roofs, hermetic facades that hide an interior with amazing views, shaded rooms and hallways that open without warning onto a vast world. There is a balcony with an iron railing and planted geraniums and cacti. The staircase leads to a small enclosed garden with a pomegranate tree and a lemon tree. There is space for a vegetable patch. The plants would get good light and be protected from wind or heavy rains. In the church tower, a bell strikes the hours with diaphanous sonority.

•

Close the shutters, draw the curtain, don't turn on the light. From inside this room, Lisbon is just a distant murmur. I knew nothing about life or desire or the passage of time the first time I was here. I wrote by ear. Shedding their clothes while their eyes remain fixed on each other, two lovers become strangers again, as if they went back in time to the first time they found themselves alone in a room. They undress each other and everything that has accumulated since they met simply falls away. The two bodies emerge from the clothes on the floor under the light of a vulnerable innocence, a water that washes away their familiarity and fatigue, and returns them to each other young and mature and even more beautiful after all this time, uplifted by wonder and the gratitude of mutual desire, anonymous in a foreign city and in a room where they have never been.

They give themselves to each other as desperately as they did back when they fought for every chance meeting, never knowing when the next opportunity would come. Now they have lost track of how many rooms and cities they have shared together; how many hours protected by the soft light of a bedside lamp, in the mid-morning or midday or in the afternoons that slowly drift toward nighttime; rooms with windows that open into urban canyons of concrete and steel, bays, forests, low winter skies, internal courtyards, the hill of the Alhambra, a street in Madrid where evenings are illuminated by the blue sign of Bar Santander, a square with cafes and trams in Amsterdam, the perpetual and silent rain of Oslo, a backyard in New York occupied by an immense maple tree that radiates its red glow into the room every November, a dark forest with moss and trunks covered with lichen on the outskirts of Breda, the pine trees and blue still waters of Formentor Bay, the white balconies of Cádiz, a street in New York submerged in a white whirlwind of snow, the church and outlook of Graça and San Jorge Castle, which are glowing in the night by the time we open the curtains and the window shutters, having just awoken from a short sleep, naked and holding each other, in this strange room that we have made ours, secret like a refuge.

I remember a particular line in a letter that Jorge Guillén wrote to his wife: *To live in many cities and love the same woman in all of them.* I could not imagine that the intensity of what seems so ephemeral in film and literature could actually be preserved for so many years, and even grow deeper, with a side that is sweeter and more serene and another that has seen madness, in those instants when mutual pleasure approximates pain and loss of consciousness. We both have a face that only exists then and that no one else has seen. I watch you put on lipstick at the bathroom mirror. Your back is facing me and a soft light washes over your shoulders. You are laughing about something, and I desire you even more than the day I met you.

•

Every beginning is involuntary. I walked down the slopes of Mouraria; it was nighttime, the streets were barely illuminated, and there was trash in every corner. Paint was peeling off from all the walls, like some kind of epidemic. Blind balconies, boarded-up windows in huge houses where no one had lived for a long time. It brought relief and sadness to see any sign of human presence: clothes hanging on balconies, bright lights coming from open windows along with the sounds of a family dinner.

Lisbon was dirtier than I remembered. In a small square I saw a group of men, some with beards and robes, congregating around the light of what appeared to be a storefront with the metal shutters partly raised. There was a sign in Arabic painted on a wall. Perhaps the store was now a mosque. At the bottom of the hill I went down some cobbled steps and entered a narrow street with more people and lots of stores selling electronics, phones, fruits.

I saw women in saris, women covered with veils and long gowns, groups of kids playing in the street at night like I hadn't seen in a city in a very long time. The stores were small, messy, and deep as caves. It did not feel like I was in Lisbon. I did not remember ever passing through this neighborhood. I did not have a map and did not know how to orient myself. Somehow, an alleyway led me to Figueira Square. Now I realize that I probably walked on João das Regras Street and passed the entrance to the old Hotel Portugal, which was about to close, and probably still looked the way it had in the seventies, with that slow descent into ruin that characterizes buildings in Lisbon. But I did not see the sign and did not look into the vestibule where the receptionist Gentil Soares had worked forty years ago.

At night Figueira Square is a strange inverse of Rossio Square, desolate and dark, with its statue of the king on horseback off-center, creating an impression of emptiness. Now I was beginning to recognize the city, not because I knew where I was, but because I was feeling all those familiar sensations. Lisbon in December was cold fog, like a very light gauze, and the humid brightness of the white cobblestone, smooth as bone, and the smell of charcoal and smoke rising from the stalls that sold roasted chestnuts.

Walking alone I was returning to my mental state during that first trip. I turned onto Douradores Street as soon as I saw its name on a street corner. Among the wandering ghosts of literature and cities, Bernardo Soares is as ever-present in Lisbon as Leopold Bloom is in Dublin, Max Estrella in Madrid, and James Joyce in Trieste, which is so similar to Lisbon. But Joyce, thin and alcoholic, hat pushed back, bow tie, a short mustache and thick glasses, also looks like Lisbon's Fernando Pessoa. The two were contemporaries and walked in sister cities.

•

The trip, the return, my son's birthday, the hotel room, the view from the window, the walk down through Mouraria, aroused a peculiar state of alert from deep inside of me, an expectation of something, an interior resonance to every stimulus, a willingness to let myself go that was accentuated by the lassitude of love. Images and sensations from what had secretly happened to us in that room just an hour before came to me in waves. *Moments of their secret life together burst like stars upon his memory*, says Joyce in "The Dead." One of the most beautiful stories about the passage of time was written by a man of twenty-five.

I wanted to see you again and fast-forward to the time of our meeting with my son. I was thinking about how fatherhood and motherhood modify the perception of time: 1986 was not an abstract date in the past but the year that my son was born; my son, the man whom we were now visiting in Lisbon. He was born around this time, 8:00 p.m., this very day in a distant December in Granada. It was a cold night with a light, damp fog, particularly around the two rivers. We were living next to one when he was born. It feels strange to write the word *living* in the first-person plural when it does not include you. To live in pronouns, says Pedro Salinas.

Douradores Street ends on a road where the tram passes and now I can see that it is Conceicao Street. It's that time of day when businesses are about to close, like in provincial cities, notions stores, stationers like the ones I frequented in my hometown, in October, after school, illuminated at dusk, welcoming you with the warmth of a human breath, one that smells of ink, paper, and wood.

I still have some time before our meeting so I go into one of the shops. There is an instinct that guides you to the things you will like the most. I find some notebooks with solid cardboard covers, good stitching, and thick paper, nice to the touch, but not too soft. As I open it, the notebook suddenly acquires the consistency of a future book, a promise of words to be written from the first to the last page.

•

Later I open the notebook to the first page as I wait for you at a cafe. I also bought a pencil at the stationer's, for no other reason or purpose than to feel the comfort of this simple and perfect tool in my hand right away. I write *December 2, 2012, Lisbon*, out of habit, just for the desired sensation of pencil on paper.

I have chosen a table in the back where I can easily see the entrance to the cafe. You will appear any moment now. I like to see you arrive, those few seconds before you see me, when you're lost in thought and more purely yourself because you're alone and unaware of my proximity; to see you as if I did not exist in your life.

That's how I saw you one of the first times. You were crossing the street on your way to the cafe where we were about to meet. I could see you more clearly because I had not imagined that I would fall in love with you. I like seeing you without the filter of habit and familiarity; the way a stranger would notice you on the street without knowing who you are. That way I can see you anew again, with my eyes truly open, behold each of your features, every angle of your face. There is a split second before the moment of recognition when you are just an unknown and beautiful woman. A second later that woman who has awakened my desire is you.

To love the face is to love the soul, says Thomas Mann. I saw you once among a group of people around a large table on a terrace in El Escorial. I was distracted and barely noticed you. I saw you again a few months later and could not remember where I had seen your face. I saw you then in Madrid, in the back of an auditorium. You were standing close to the door, as if you were about to leave. You were smiling. It was an expression of irony and patience. Every time I looked away I feared you would leave. And then, as in a dream, I was trying to make my way through the crowd so I could meet you, but I kept getting stuck in introductions and goodbyes, and all I could see in the distance was your patient smile and your red hair.

I saw that great smile welcoming me at the airport gate, in the lobbies of stations and in the hotels of Madrid. Once I was on a train on my way to see you, I was about to arrive, but I could not remember if we had agreed to meet in Atocha Station or Chamartín. It was a time before cell phones when people could lose each other, and no matter how much they walked, never find each other. I got off in Atocha and regretted it the moment I stepped out of the train. I was so worried. I went to the lobby, halfheartedly hoping that I would find you, but there were hundreds of faces.

It dawned on me that if I did not find you I would not know how to get to your house. I had only been there once and did not remember the name of the street. It was 10:00 p.m. when I stepped out onto Charles V Square and looked for a taxi that could take me to Chamartín. With some luck I would get to the station at the same time as the train, or just a few minutes later. But no taxi would stop. I kept walking from corner to corner looking for one. In my distress, it didn't occur to me to simply go to the taxi line by the arrivals exit. I could no longer tell how long I had been waiting. I imagined the train had long ago arrived at Chamartín and you had already left. What if I got to a phone booth and called your house? But I would lose more time.

A taxi stopped and I was so flustered I almost did not get it. The drive to Chamartín Station felt like an eternity, a dream where you advance and advance but get nowhere. I went through the automatic doors and at first I did not see anyone. It was late and the station was mostly empty. But then I saw you before you noticed me. You were staring at the arrivals board. You looked younger and seemed more vulnerable than I remembered.

I have just looked up from my notebook and there you are. You're entering the cafe and you're looking around searching for me. You glow, your hair is tousled, your lips are painted red.

My son and his girlfriend are with you. He and I hug for a long time. He is a young man, strong, my height, with a thick beard and straight brown hair. His eyes are big and clear, like his mother's. He appears quiet and shy, at least when he's with me. But nobody is fully him- or herself in the presence of parents. There is a familiarity between him and his girlfriend. They've been together since they were fifteen. I was seventeen and his mother eighteen when we met. Young people don't know just how young they are, how close they still are to that infancy they imagine so far away, while their parents still see it in them or wish they could. I was his age when his mother and I married. When we divorced he was five years old.

The four of us sit at a table. The cafe has iron columns and plaster moldings. The waiters look like old-timers. There's a pleasant hum of conversation in the background and the warm smell of pastries and roasted Portuguese coffee fills the space. I am happy just to look at him and the tender feeling reminds me of those words from the Gospel, which embody fatherhood so differently from the anger and vengefulness of the Old Testament: "This is my beloved son, in whom I am well pleased." That's what you think the first day you pick up your kid from school and see him with the other children, confused and almost anonymous among them, just another child but also your son, your beloved, in whom you are well pleased.

Now it is they who know and talk and we are the ones who ask questions and listen, and are thankful that they speak Portuguese and can translate the menu for us and place our order. When we remember ourselves in our youth what we remember is the image we had of ourselves then. That is why, when we see a young person, they seem more childlike than we were at their age—that and perhaps also the temptation of condescension. At the same time, the young person sees the parent far removed from their youth, almost settled in old age. Each one has a hard time seeing the other the way they are, but it is even more difficult to intuit how the other sees him- or herself. And thus it is very likely that they don't know just how similar they are.

The only thing that separates them, what the adult knows and the youth can barely imagine, is how long the future is, all the unexpected paths life can take: life is not a single one, not only because of everything that can change, but also because how we ourselves can change, becoming not just another, but various possible and successive others. Perhaps the baby I held in my arms twenty-six years ago and the young man who now sits with me at a cafe in Lisbon have as much in common as the troubled and inept father that I was then and the man I am now.

The biggest difference between parents and their children is that the parents belong to a world their children don't know how to imagine because it is the world that existed before they were born. In 1986, my son's mother and I had modest but stable lives: she was a tenured teacher and I was an administrative assistant; we had a family and lived in a government-subsidized apartment. Sometimes we struggled, but we always made ends meet. At twenty-six you had a three-year-old son. You were twenty-eight when we met.

At an age when we had barely traveled anywhere, my son and his girlfriend have already lived in several countries. They are fluent in several languages and move from one country to another with an ease that would have been unimaginable for us at their age. But unlike us back then, they live in the air. They do freelance projects and rent an apartment for a few months at most. After dinner, they take us to the apartment they share. We walk through the alleys and stairways of the Alfama district. It is the first proper home my son has had since he left the family house. There are maps and posters on the walls, and books everywhere. It is a frugal and provisional life, emancipated from mine, largely oblivious to it, the way it was with me and my father when I was my son's age. I escaped for three days to Lisbon. My son lives and works in the city and studies the language. I came as a fugitive, running away from the life in which he had just arrived so I could lose myself in my fantasies and literary aspirations. He lives here peacefully with his girlfriend. Even if they wanted, they could not bring a child into this world, not without knowing how they'll make a living or where they're going to live a few months from now.

•

Walking with them we soon lose track of where we are. They take us through narrow streets we don't recognize. From time to time we see a light coming from a diner or small pub. We walk through squares with white churches and I'm reminded of the Mudéjar-style churches in Albaicín, with their geometric forms, limestone walls, and latticed windows. You walk ahead, chatting with his girlfriend. He and I walk a few steps behind. Sometimes we don't see you but your voice and the sound of your steps on the cobblestones guide us.

Now that I am finally with him, on his birthday, after months of not seeing each other, I'm overcome with a strange shyness that is probably familiar to him. If only I had your self-confidence, your talent for casual conversation. I would like to tell my son things about myself that I have never shared with him. I could not tell him when he was a child and now that he's an adult I don't know how to start. I remember a conversation I had with his older brother a few years ago, one night in Brussels. We walked and talked for hours through a city that he knew well and I did not. I told him about my life and he told me about his. The bars and restaurants were closing and the streets were slowly emptying. We ended at the bar of the hotel and continued until the waiters cleared the tables and started to turn off the lights. We were reconciled and hurt, each conscious of the place the other one had in our life, the pain that can only be caused by those we love.

But perhaps it is also good to walk and let the conversation unfold spontaneously like these streets. We can enjoy the cool night and the simple fact of having each other's company. My son tells me about his job. He translates subtitles for documentaries and fiction films. Sometimes he gets a lot of projects and has to work twelve- or fourteen-hour days; other times he has nothing to do. There are agencies that take a long time to pay him and others that try to haggle with him. Occasionally he has to work on subtitles for gore films and ends up nauseated by so much blood, horrified by the kind of public that would feed its imagination with these sorts of things. He likes to discover independent films from unexpected countries. He particularly likes documentaries.

I ask him what he would like to get from his work, if there's anything he feels he lacks, if he needs money. I think about the incurable discontent I felt at his age, the feeling of being trapped in a life and a city and job that I did not like, the desire to write, but also the suspicion, the fear that I was writing for nobody. With an ease that surprises me, he says he is happy. He would like to have a bit more stability but can't complain. He works on things he likes and it's usually enough to pay the bills. He plays guitar with a pop band and has started to write songs. They would like to stay in Lisbon, but if his girlfriend can't find a job they'll have to return to Granada. Perhaps he's better equipped to enjoy a quiet life than I was at his age. He most enjoys translating documentaries about travel, the lives of musicians, the history of the twentieth century, diseases, scientific discoveries, animals, jungles, polar expeditions, underwater investigations. He lives within them for days at a time as he translates and it feels like he is traveling to all those places right from his room in Alfama, hour after hour as he sits by the laptop.

I note what he already knows, that there's a risk in those jobs where you spend a lot of time by yourself and isolated from external reality, jobs where the only structure is whatever schedule you can create for yourself, short of the anguished discipline that comes with an impending deadline when you have left everything for the last minute. As a child he was intrigued by my work. If I was writing in a notebook, he sat across from me at the table and started writing in his school workbook. The appearance of white or green letters on the black background of the old computers made him really curious. After the electric Canon, on which I wrote the novel about Lisbon, I bought a computer. It was crude and large, a Jurassic Amstrad that was becoming obsolete when I finally learned how to use it. I left it printing a long text one day, on one of those printers that was as loud as the old telex machines. My son came into the dining room with some amazing information: "There's an invisible father writing in your room."

Sometime later, the invisible father became even more invisible because he stopped writing in that room and living in the house. He became a visitor who sometimes arrived without notice from other cities, in a taxi, with a travel bag, and a very heavy laptop.

We have arrived at a big square that overlooks the Tagus River. A statue of a saint on a pedestal, like a huge golem, stands out from the shadows with that lunar glow that white stone has in Lisbon.

For a time, when my children were still kids, I lived with the certainty that I was about to die. But it wasn't death that scared me, after the first strike of terror at the doctor's office. I was dying of sadness thinking that I would have to stop seeing you and that I would never see my kids become adults. A child barely resembles the man or woman he or she will become. I thought I was going to die and never see their adult lives and faces. A future ten or fifteen or twenty years later was a forbidden country for me, hermetic like North Korea or

Outer Mongolia, where it was prohibited to travel with one of the old Spanish passports.

This moment, this night, are the future that I never thought I would see. I never want to forget the exceptional gift of being alive. The Tagus River has an oily glow in the moonless night. The silhouette of the 25th of April Bridge reminds me of the George Washington Bridge at night, extending over the dark expanse of the Hudson. In the middle of the river there's a large cargo ship floating, with a tower several stories high, cranes, and lights that illuminate the foggy surface like an empty football field.

The flow of ordinary life weaves and unravels its arguments, its symmetries, its resonances, without anyone having to invent anything, just as the waves of the river draw themselves or the arms of a delta or the nerves of a leaf without the intervention of a hand or a higher intelligence. In a way, a novel also writes itself.

With a curiosity that is just as sharp but somewhat more reserved than when he was a child, my son asks me if I'm working on something: he remembers the notebook I had open on the table when they came into the cafe. Sometimes it's better not to talk about it, or you might jinx it. Other times saying it to whoever is interested is a way of bringing it into existence. I tell my son that this afternoon during my walk, as I watched the shadows of people in Figueira Square and then on a long and narrow street in Baixa, I remembered something that I read in a book about the assassination of Martin Luther King, a small detail that made a strong impression on me and had suddenly given me the urge to write: the man who murdered King, James Earl Ray, had spent ten days in Lisbon while on the run.

23

In prison he began to write. The cell was illuminated day and night, and the windows were covered with steel plates. It was a holding cell in the Memphis courthouse. The plane had left London in secret at midnight and arrived at a U.S. military airport before dawn.

The aircraft landed on a runway far from the terminal and several policemen and a doctor came on board. They removed the handcuffs and ordered him to undress completely. He stood naked, surrounded by them, wearing nothing but his glasses, obedient and in shock. They put the handcuffs back on while the doctor examined him. His flesh was pale and he had gained weight in the past two months at the London prison while the extradition process was completed. After the medical exam they gave him a different set of clothes: a plaid shirt, overalls, and rubber sandals. They strapped him with a bulletproof vest. He posed no resistance, letting them do whatever they had to do, keeping his head low and slightly cocked, his eyes staring at the floor.

A convoy of armored vehicles and police cars took him from the airport to the courthouse in Memphis through a street where they had blocked all traffic. He could not see anything out the window or the cell where he ended up. Soon he began losing his sense of time. He started writing on yellow notepads from the first day, with the marks of the handcuffs still fresh on his wrist. He told the guard who stood next to his cell in London that he would become rich writing and selling his story to Hollywood.

In a cell that was specially built for him, he wrote for hours under incandescent ceiling lights, leaning on the metal table, his face very close to the paper and his left arm covering what he was writing from the eyes of the security cameras. He missed his portable typewriter, the clinking sound of the keys on the balcony of the hotel room in Puerto Vallarta, the cool night, the ocean breeze, the smell of beach fires and grilled fish.

His handwriting was slanted and spaced. He wrote fluidly, with misspellings, never crossing anything out, filling sheet after sheet, without margins, front and back. He wrote with sweat dripping from his face, despite the fans, which were always on, huge and roaring like airplane propellers. There was a big clock on one of the walls but this did not help, he had no way of knowing whether the hands were marking an hour in the morning or the afternoon. The incandescent lights on the ceiling created a perpetual artificial day.

He was allowed to have maps, pencils, pens, and ink refills with different colors. He also had an appointment diary from the previous year and one of the current, in which he could fill the day boxes with everything he remembered, all the places he had been, the names of the cities, giving that period of time—the fourteen months since his escape from prison—the clarity of an order it otherwise lacked.

He drew diagrams to remember the layout of a bar or a bedroom or the bathroom at the end of the hallway in one of the boarding-houses where he had stayed. He tried to hypnotize himself to block the voices of the guards who played cards or watched sports, yelling as if they were in a bar. He closed his eyes and tried to sleep, but the light was so bright it filtered through his eyelids, pressing to the back of his skull. He would wake up with nosebleeds, and sometimes drops of blood fell from his nose onto the sheet where he was writing. They gave him permission to keep a roll of toilet paper next to him. He swallowed blood and felt nauseous. There was not a single angle in the cell that was not visible to the security cameras, including the toilet in the corner. One of the police officers watched him with the un-blinking objectivity of a camera lens. At first, they collected his urine and feces and took them to a lab. Latex gloves, masks, plastic containers with hermetic seals. His food and water were tested for poison before he ate or drank. They unrolled the toilet paper entirely and rolled it up again before giving it to him. They examined the pencils, the notebooks, the eraser, the pencil sharpener. One of them brought a small screwdriver and removed the small blade from the sharpener.

•

He liked to feel the pen on the paper, the pressure of the tip on the soft thickness of his notebook. He wrote, remembering places with graphic precision and aiding himself with maps and the diagrams he had drawn; the layout of the room where he had stayed only one night, the orientation of the boardinghouse in Memphis in relation to the Lorraine Motel, the location of the balcony with the glass door slid open and the white curtain flapping in the wind. He wrote, letting himself be carried away by the free association of ideas and images, and had to adjust the chronology of events afterward. He intentionally left some gaps, blank spaces in his narrative, and omitted certain names. Those were secrets he would take to the grave. There were scenes that he described over and over again in successive drafts, hoping to stay as close as possible to the facts or at least attain a bare minimum of internal cohesion. There were others that changed from paragraph to paragraph. He reread what he had written and, upon noticing the contradictions, would tear the sheets violently and rip them into tiny pieces.

•

The act of writing allowed him to see himself from outside, often facing his own back. He saw himself like a character in a film or one of the novels he had read and reread while on the run. His writing began to slide into fiction. He organized meticulous sequences that could be corroborated and began to introduce in them fictitious events or figures. The new characters were constructed from different people he'd met, combined into an arbitrary portrait of part memory, part fabrication, part things he had read in books.

Perhaps he had started profiling the figure he would call Raoul long before he was taken to the windowless cell in Memphis. He would continue writing and talking about this character for many years, until the end of his life, like someone who keeps revising the drafts of a story that never ends and never seems to click into a final form. Raoul appears and disappears. Sometimes his name is Raoul. Sometimes he is Roual. He has a Hispanic accent and his hair is dark and wavy. Other times his hair is black but also a bit reddish, as if Raoul came from a mixed background, Hispanic and Irish perhaps, French-Canadian. It is also possible that Raoul dyed his hair. The hair color and the name could both be false. But what does it matter if his hair was dyed and if Raoul was not his real name? His real name was not Eric Starvo Galt and yet that was the only name he gave Raoul. Years later, in another memory, Raoul's hair is blond or light brown, the color of sand.

Beyond those changing details, the descriptions remain extraordinarily vague. Raoul is neither tall nor short, neither thin nor fat. He once said he recognized him in a photograph: a big man with thick black hair and fleshy features. It turns out to be a photo taken by three passersby in Dallas, November 1963, close to the place where President Kennedy was assassinated. Raoul always wore dark suits and shirts, but never ties. We don't know his eye color. He was close to Raoul many times and they talked and traveled together in the car for many hours and met in bars and cafeterias and hotel rooms, but he never provides any information that can help identify this person. He is a featureless face, a backlit silhouette sitting at the bar of the Neptune Tavern in Montreal, one summer day in 1967.

•

He sits alone at a secluded table. He's already going by the name Eric Starvo Galt. He's wearing a new suit, his first one ever, and his hands feel soft after a manicure. He has robbed a supermarket or a brothel and is trying to get a passport or identification that allows him to stay on the move. After a few years, he will have perfected the story and will be able to narrate it in the style of a detective novel. Raoul is observing him from a distance and after a few minutes comes to his table and sits across from him. He waves to the waiter and orders a drink.

Raoul seems to wrap himself in mystery, he writes and speaks in a long-winded manner, probing, exploring. *His words drifted like a cold fog*, he writes, many years later, from another cell, old and sick, still combing his hair in a seventies style, stiff with pomade. He writes that he suspected Raoul of being a junkie, because he was always wearing long shirts and jackets, as if trying to hide his arms.

Raoul's innuendos seem to amount to some kind of proposal, offering something in return, something he needs more than anything else, money to find a good place to hide, a passport. He has an old car. Raoul suggests that he drive to the nearby city of Windsor and wait for him on a certain street close to the bus station. Raoul asks questions but does not answer any. He parks his car in the specified location. A few minutes later, Raoul appears on the sidewalk carrying a gift-wrapped package in his hand. He lowers the window and Raoul gives him the package and asks him to put it under the seat.

He must now drive across the border and meet Raoul on the other side on American soil. He notices a taxi in the rearview mirror, and sees Raoul in the backseat of the car. He prefers not to know what's inside the package. The taxi does not follow him past the border. He waits at the cafeteria by the railway station, just as Raoul asked him to.

He sits in the back, close to the kitchen and the emergency exit, but with a clear view of the entrance. The package is on his lap under the table. He gets distracted for a few seconds and when he looks up Raoul is standing in front of him. Raoul has a gift for sudden entrances and exits. He sits across from him and demands the package. He covers it with a light coat he had under his arm, takes out his wallet and counts one thousand dollars in fifties and twenties. The bills look and smell new. Raoul tells him to drive to Birmingham, Alabama, and wait for instructions there. He doesn't tell him how long he'll have to wait. He just assures him that after that job, he will receive twelve thousand dollars and a passport, and he will be able to go "anywhere in the world."

•

He is like a secret agent on a mission so important not even he can know about it. He travels by train from Detroit to Birmingham. He arrives early in the morning and rents a room in an inn close to the station. Later he remembers the name of the hotel and marks its location on the map of Birmingham. He has also marked the boarding-house where he will later rent a room and the post office where a few days after arriving he went to ask if there was a letter for Eric S. Galt.

The letter came many weeks later. The name on the envelope is typed and there is no return address. Inside, there's a sheet of paper with a date, a time, and the name of a cafe, Starlight, which was located across the street from the post office. He showed up a bit earlier to check out the place, to note possible exits, and to see if he could catch Raoul arriving; he wants to know if he will come in a car, in a taxi, or by foot. Night is falling and the street is mostly empty of people and traffic. The red neon sign of the cafeteria illuminates the sidewalk.

He takes a table in the back, by the bathroom, and orders a coffee. The waitress is in a bad mood. She seems tired, ready for her shift to be over. He describes the coffee, sugar, and the open newspaper on his table. He hears the toilet flush and out comes Raoul.

Raoul takes the newspaper and the coffee and tells him to follow him to one of the booths. This time he counts three thousand dollars. It is always in twenties and fifties, and Raoul counts with the speed of a bank teller, glancing once to the side to make sure the waitress is not watching them. Along with the money, he gives him a new set of instructions. These are quite enigmatic. He's to buy a used car in good shape, and pay no more than two thousand dollars for it. He also needs to get a Super 8 camera and some basic equipment according to the specifications typed on the sheet of paper. Raoul writes a phone number on one of the napkins with the name of the cafeteria. He tells him it's in New Orleans and asks him to destroy the napkin as soon as he has committed it to memory. He will receive new instructions by mail in a few weeks, but if there's an emergency, he should call that number. He implies that the next step will probably be a trip to New Orleans. He leaves the cafeteria abruptly, without saying goodbye or shaking his hand, and with a rolled-up newspaper under his arm. In October, he gets a letter with an appointment date and time at a motel in Nuevo Laredo, Mexico.

•

After a few years, in the monotonous eternity of the prison, the details of this story only get more precise. They are purified and sharpened, like the prose he uses to tell them, so different from the confused legalese he churns out obsessively, claiming his innocence, suggesting conspiracies where he is always the victim, the scapegoat, a cog in a machine controlled by the government and intelligence agencies.

He was only following instructions and waiting, he writes. He presented his driver's license with the name Eric S. Galt at the window of the post office and smiled briefly and thanked the clerk, who kept telling him there was nothing for him. When the new instructions finally came, at the beginning of October, he loaded the typewriter and the camera in the Mustang and drove almost without rest to New Orleans, where he had to call a number to find out the place and time for his next meeting with Raoul. He dialed the number from a phone booth and there was no answer. It was unwise to call twice from the same phone booth. The third or fourth time, someone picked up. Raoul had had to leave earlier than planned. He would meet him in Nuevo Laredo. The voice said the name of a motel and the address and hung up.

At the border post they told him how to get to the motel. He had just put his head down, exhausted after four days of driving, when someone knocked on the door. It was Raoul. Once again, it was obvious that he had been spying on him. Raoul started talking as if they had already been chatting for hours. He did not explain anything and did not ask about the drive or his life during the months of waiting. Raoul never loses his shadow-like elusiveness. A taxi was waiting outside the motel. Raoul got in and ordered the driver to follow the Mustang. They crossed the border back into Texas. Once they were past customs, Raoul got out of the taxi and climbed into the Mustang.

They drove to an isolated house at the end of a dusty shantytown. There was another car parked in front of the house. The driver had a Native American profile and remained still as Raoul opened the trunk of his car and took out a spare tire, which he then switched with the one in the trunk of the Mustang. They drove back to the border. Raoul got out and walked the pedestrian bridge. He obeyed and drove through customs. He stopped the Mustang and saw Raoul approaching in the rearview mirror, a hat over his face and long sleeves despite the heat. Raoul got in and asked him to drive to the motel. They arrived and to his surprise the car from the house was parked there and the same driver awaited inside.

Raoul switched the spare tires again. The next morning, he came to his room and handed him two thousand dollars. The bills were new and smelled of ink. Their texture was slippery. He asked Raoul when he would get the promised passport and Raoul stared back at him as if he had not understood the question. Another man came into the room silently. It was the Native American driver. He knew right away that the man had a gun on him, but he also had his in his back pocket and could have reached for it in the blink of an eye if necessary. Raoul told him to be patient; that perhaps it was better if he stayed in Mexico for some time and checked in with him every now and then by calling the New Orleans number.

•

The story then takes a new direction, still blurry; the idle days in Mexico feel like preparation for something, a point of no return. How naive of him to imagine that he could stay in Puerto Vallarta forever, spending his days in the cool shade of a hut by the ocean, watching the whales spout their geysers in the distance. By the middle of November, he was driving north in the Mustang with the Alabama plates. The yellow paint had turned almost white from the sun. He rented a room in a hotel for retirees in the squalid periphery of Hollywood Boulevard.

After a few weeks he began to run out of money: he had to pay the hotel, the bartender school, the dance classes, the locksmith correspondence course. He calls the number Raoul wrote on the napkin from the Starlight Cafe. Someone who is not Raoul, perhaps the Native American driver, answers and tells him to be patient, to continue checking at the post office every two or three days, where the next set of instructions will arrive. Beneath the visible life where he appears to be just some impostor, meekly dedicated to memorizing cocktail recipes and rumba steps, is the waiting, the calls, the typed letters with no signature that order him to travel to different cities for secret appointments.

That point of no return begins to close in as he drives to New Orleans in December, under the pretext of going to pick up the daughters of an acquaintance who is a dancer at a strip club, in the company of a lunatic who smokes dope and invokes Mother Earth and sees UFOs in the desert skies. In a deep and dark pub, the Bunny Lounge, on the corner of Canal Street and Charles Avenue, Raoul waits for him, sitting in the back, drinking a beer. He probably imagined these scenes like in a movie or a James Bond novel where the brand of everything the characters carry or use is detailed.

This time Raoul has a clearer and more tempting proposal: if he helps him in a gun-smuggling operation with Mexico, he will receive twelve thousand dollars and the passport he desires so much. When he asks him if he still needs the film equipment, Raoul just shrugs his shoulders. He gives him money, not much for now, five hundred dollars. In early April, perhaps sooner, he will receive a message to return to New Orleans to the same bar and the same table. Raoul's beer has lost its foam and he has yet to take a sip. The waiter has not come to bother them even once.

•

He is not a conspirator, much less a murderer. If he is a spy, he doesn't know what he is spying on or on whose orders. The narrative that is perfected throughout the years is one where he is basically a sleep-walker following orders, a fugitive who was on the run though no one was looking for him; it's as if he had been hypnotized from far away, an innocent who little by little gets closer to a trap that others have created specially for him, while distracting himself with occupations and interests that lead nowhere: he never makes the pornographic films, he never finishes the locksmith course, and he quits the dance school; he receives his bartender diploma, but he does not look for a job, and when he is offered one he turns it down, saying that he has been hired to work on a cargo ship on the Mississippi.

Halfway through March, he interrupts his life in Los Angeles. He does not go to the last appointment with the plastic surgeon who operated on his nose. The signal has arrived, the call. He shows his driver's license at the post office and the clerk does not even look up to confirm the resemblance. It now feels as if that has always been his name. He's able to say it naturally, without a second of hesitation, and he can sign it just as well. He has put the letter in his jacket pocket and only opens it after exiting the building and putting on his sunglasses.

•

The time has come, for what he does not know. He pays the hotel bill and loads the Mustang with his few pieces of luggage. The typewriter, the Polaroid, the Super 8 camera, the clothes he's just picked up from the dry cleaner, a small radio, a portable television. He drives to New Orleans, taking the same route he took in December. This time he's alone for several days. He sleeps in the car. He listens to music or the voices on the radio to stay awake; sometimes he talks to himself aloud, his voice hoarse and strange from hardly speaking.

In New Orleans, the Bunny Lounge is as empty as the previous time but Raoul is not there. He waits two hours and then calls from a pay phone on the street. A voice he has not heard before says there has been a change of plans. Now Raoul is waiting for him in Birmingham, in the same place as the previous year, the Starlight or Starlite Cafe, across the street from the post office. The point of no return is at the end of the full circle.

Raoul's presence is increasingly lacking in details and explanations. He meets him in Birmingham on the morning of March 23. Raoul asks him to drive him to Alabama, a three-hour trip in a straight line east. He does not explain why they couldn't just meet in Atlanta. We don't know what they discuss during the trip. He drives and Raoul is next to him, Raoul who does not answer any questions, a figure almost featureless, with no history, not even a full name, just Raoul, or Roual, in different versions.

●

In Atlanta Raoul tells him to find a place to stay for one or two weeks. The arms-smuggling operation must be planned slowly, cautiously. He finds a room at a boardinghouse where the owner has been drunk for ten days and forgets to actually register him. The only thing the man will remember later is that the guest was very well-dressed and seemed out of place in that neighborhood of junkies, drugs, and beggars. But he will not remember the other man who was apparently with him. He always saw him alone, dressed in dark colors, with a suitcase in hand, white shirt and a tie.

No one will remember seeing Raoul in any of the places where they supposedly met. No waiter at the Starlight Cafe or the Bunny

Lounge, no receptionist, no other guest. If anything, they remember him, alone. There was no trace of Raoul anywhere. But that doesn't mean there is no proof of Raoul's existence: on the contrary, the very lack of any tracks is evidence of Raoul's cunning and his flawless plan.

Raoul reveals the next step of this plan in a cafeteria in Atlanta. That's where he gives him the order that will send him directly to his ruin, the trapdoor. It involves another trip and another purchase. He must return to Birmingham. He must buy a hunting rifle with a scope. Once the purchase is complete, he must continue the journey north to Memphis. In Memphis, he will have to find the New Rebel Motel and rent a room. Then, he must wait.

•

It's Wednesday night, April 3, and there's a heavy rainstorm. The radio says there's a tornado approaching. He is registered at the New Rebel Motel and is waiting for the next order. The suitcase remains unopened on the floor because he doesn't know when he will have to leave. Next to the suitcase, there's a long cardboard box, also unopened. It's the rifle. Before they parted ways, Raoul mentioned he was going to New Orleans for a few days to work out the last few details.

He waits, listening to the radio, reading a novel, leafing through the newspaper. (He bought newspapers every day, read weekly and monthly magazines, followed the news on the radio and television, but he claims he had no idea sanitation workers were on strike in Memphis, or that Martin Luther King had arrived in the city that same morning.) The rain and the wind were roaring on the window when he heard the knocking on the door. It was Raoul. *Drenched*, he wrote, *in a trench coat. He looked like a Hollywood spy.*

•

Raoul looks around the room and sees the box with the rifle right away. Even though it is dark and pouring outside, he draws the curtains. He opens the box and pulls out the rifle. Sitting on the bed, with only the light from the nightstand, he checks the weapon carefully: the scope, the safety, the wooden stock, the trigger. He doesn't use gloves but his fingerprints will be nowhere on the weapon. He seems satisfied. He puts the rifle back in the box and gets ready to leave. Raoul tells him that the next day they will close the deal, at last. The twelve thousand dollars, the passport, he will get it then.

There is only one more thing he needs to do, says Raoul, handing him a piece of paper with something written on it: tomorrow at 3:00 p.m., rent a room in the boardinghouse located at 422 South Main Street, above a bar called Jim's Grill. Impossible to miss: the sign for Jim's Grill is always on. At this point Raoul disappears from the scene, as if he had walked away into that stormy night, beyond the lights of the New Rebel Motel. In some versions, he takes the rifle with him.

•

The narrative for the next day is just lazy. The morning is peaceful and clear. It had rained all night. He gets up slowly, pays the motel bill, and drives to downtown Memphis. No hurry. He still has a few hours to find the address Raoul indicated. There is plenty of time to familiarize himself with the layout of the city.

A turn west takes him to the banks of the Mississippi. He buys a newspaper, the Memphis *Commercial Appeal*, and reads it while eating breakfast on the sunny terrace of a cafe. He stares at the current of the river, the forests of Arkansas, the great iron bridge. Somehow he misses the story on the front page of the newspaper with the photo of Martin Luther King at the Lorraine Motel and the article with information about his visit to the city. The photo shows him leaning on a railing, in front of a door with an unmistakable number, 306.

He finds South Main Street and drives slowly, looking for the house number. As the numbers increase, the neighborhood gets more run-down. He goes inside a pub to ask directions and is surprised to see two men in suits and ties, completely out of place, staring at him. He drives around lost for some time. When he finally finds Jim's Grill and goes inside, he sees the same two men in suits. Those two figures go in and out of the successive versions, secondary details that are forgotten or that seemed promising and now prove irrelevant, or they're modified. Sometimes there's only one man; sometimes there are two but one of them is wearing some kind of uniform.

He parks the car in front and goes up a stairway that has the word

ROOMS painted in white on every step. He rents a room and pays for a week in advance, just as Raoul ordered. He uses the name John Willard.

When he comes down to Jim's Grill for a drink he sees Raoul at the bar. The two strange men are no longer there. Together they go up to the room. They sit. He doesn't know what they're waiting for. Raoul has a small radio or walkie-talkie in his jacket pocket. He says they might have to stay there for a few days. Perhaps he is waiting for the buyers or his Mexican contacts in the operation. He asks him to go to the armory and buy a pair of binoculars with infrared lenses.

It is 4:00 p.m. when he leaves and gets in the Mustang, glad to no longer be breathing the foul air of the boardinghouse. Everything is vague in the narration, threads that lead nowhere, false starts and gaps. He drives around for some time but can't find the armory. He goes back to ask Raoul for the address again. When he finally finds it, they tell him they don't carry infrared lenses. He buys a pair of regular binoculars on sale. He goes back to the room and Raoul is still there by himself.

Now Raoul says he won't need him for the next few hours. He's free to go walk around, see the sights, grab a drink. He could even go to the movies, Raoul says. He goes back to the car and sits inside for a while trying to decide what he is going to do. It's already afternoon. Once again, the account changes throughout the years. He went into Jim's Grill, ordered a burger and a Coke, then decided to go to a nearby gas station to change a tire. Or not, he did not go into Jim's Grill, he just drove by, following South Main, until he got to the Hotel Chisca, where he had an ice cream. He noticed that the young black waitress who served him was probably new, because she made mistakes and had to ask for help.

In other versions he buys a sandwich at a cheap restaurant called Chickasaw. He doesn't identify with certainty the gas station where he changed the tire or got it patched; sometimes he's helped by a mechanic, other times there are too many people in line and he leaves.

Around 6:00 p.m. he returns to the boardinghouse and parks in front of Jim's Grill. He's still sitting in the car when a loud noise, like a gunshot or a firecracker, startles him. Moments later, he sees Raoul approaching in the side mirror. He's walking fast and carries a bag and a bundle of things, a blanket or a quilt with the barrel of the rifle sticking out. Raoul drops the stuff on the sidewalk, quickly gets in the backseat and lies down, covers himself with a white bedsheet and orders him to drive. He drives off and begins to hear the sound of police sirens. Raoul tells him to stop at the next light, gets out of the car, slams the door, and walks away. His figure quickly disappears in the rearview mirror. He never sees him again.

•

In another version, he does not go back to Jim's Grill in the Mustang and does not see Raoul. The ending is even more abrupt, a draft that has been revised several times but it's never resolved. Around 6:00 p.m. he is driving down South Main. He's almost at the boardinghouse when he sees a police patrol with the flashing lights on.

Perhaps the appointment with the Mexican arms smugglers was a trap and Raoul is a snitch. Perhaps something went wrong with the transaction and there was a gunfight. He turns right on a residential road and drives out of the city. He's a fugitive and if they find him they'll lock him up again until the end of this sentence of twenty years. He is panicking. There are now police sirens sounding from all sides.

He drives south, along the river, trying to reach the state border as soon as possible. It is only when he turns on the radio that he learns about the crime, and it takes him a few minutes to understand the role he's been made to play. The key to the plot that's been woven around him for the last year finally turns. It's a sudden revelation, as in the final pages of a novel. The agitated voices on the radio repeat the alert every few minutes, announcing the target of the manhunt: a white man, thirty-five to forty years old, brown hair, dark suit, driving a white '66 Mustang with Alabama plates.

He will drive all night along local roads, heading toward Atlanta, stopping only once to get gas: in his story he's an innocent man who must now find those who framed him before the authorities find him. The next morning he gets on a bus in Atlanta and falls asleep with his sunglasses on. Around 1:30 a.m., the bus arrives in Cincinnati. The bus to Detroit will not leave for another two hours. The station is dark and desolate so he walks to a nearby pub.

Later on, as the bus drives off, he notices the distant glow of the fires in the city. Rows of military trucks are moving in the opposite direction. Young soldiers, numb with cold, stare at the passengers from the bus. There's fear in their faces. There are police checkpoints at the intersections, flashing lights, bulletproof vests, helmets, automatic rifles.

He falls asleep and a few hours later the first rays of sun wake him up with the alarming sensation of not knowing how long he slept or where he is. In the distance, he sees the smoke rising over Detroit. The city smells of wet ash and burnt tires. The same headline and the same face are on the front pages of every paper.

He goes into a barbershop that's just opened to get a haircut. The barber is old and has expert hands, albeit wobbly. The radio is on but the man does not seem to be paying attention. They're still looking for the driver of the white Mustang with Alabama plates. He will cross the Canadian border in a taxi and then take a train, where he will fall asleep again. At 5:00 or 6:00 p.m. on Saturday, April 6, he walks out of the Toronto station with his bag and a newspaper and wanders off. The farthest point on the map he will reach is a month and two days into the future. It is Lisbon. The story or the novel about Raoul is never completed.

24

I have searched for his trail in Lisbon and now I search for it in Memphis. I walk along a deserted street. I've just left the hotel, the room on the ninth floor with a view of a street corner and not a soul. There's an immense parking garage next to the hotel, and a Holiday Inn across the street. To the east, over the rooftops, the metallic blue sheet of the Mississippi River turns to gold as the sun sets and the orange disk melts away in the fog above the river. Beyond the forested horizon that marks the beginning of Arkansas.

I say aloud the names of the places I'm seeing for the first time, places that are now more than just glowing words in literature: Memphis, Tennessee, Mississippi, Arkansas. I have been watching the river and the city from the hotel window, my suitcase still unopened. I'm getting impatient to go out before it gets dark.

I read the word *Memphis* on the boarding pass and it still did not feel real. Then I saw it on the flight display monitor at Newark Airport and it began to dawn on me. Three hours later our plane was descending over the green forests and the mist and the pilot was making the announcement, "Welcome to Memphis, Tennessee."

The name appeared again as white letters on green signs along the highway, before the great river opened up before us and occupied the entire horizon, crowned in the distance by the double arch of an iron bridge. "The mighty Mississippi River," said the taxi driver with reverence, pointing to the current with his hand. His skin was dark and thin like paper. Gold rings and a watch adorned his left hand.

Among the green jungle, abandoned factories decay into rusted frames and broken windows, their brick walls covered in ivy. The taxi driver's voice was slow and deep. He said the U.S. government plotted the assassination of Dr. King, that F. D. Roosevelt had known in advance about the attack on Pearl Harbor, and that not a single Jewish person had gone to work at the Twin Towers the morning of September 11, 2001. He told us, proudly, that his name was Ulysses. Born and raised in Memphis. Lived there his entire life. He dressed with the elegance of a Cuban gentleman. His skin was the color of hard coal, accentuating the bushy white sideburns. He wore an impeccable light-brown Sahariana jacket; his pants were perfectly pressed, and his leather shoes were very polished. From the ninth floor of the hotel, Memphis was a deserted crossroads in the heat of the afternoon, Second Street and Union Avenue. There was no one on the sidewalks and the lights changed from green to red without any cars beneath them. Union Avenue stretched in a straight line to the west toward the river.

•

The stories we choose to tell borrow from what we have seen and lived. The writer who narrates a journey in the first person is a literary and lonely projection, a familiar figure in literature. I walk through Memphis one afternoon in May, searching for his trail, but I'm not alone. You're with me. We're walking together in these desolate streets and you were in the hotel room when I was watching the river in the distance and the yellow disk turned red in the violet haze above the water.

I asked the receptionist how far to the Lorraine Motel by foot and she seemed confused. "It's just five minutes by car," she said. She puts a map on the counter and traces the route with a pencil. It's almost a straight line south, parallel to the river.

•

It is very hot when we go out. There's an immediate desolation that is characteristic of certain American cities and it's accentuated the farther we get from the hotel. More parking garages, strip malls, stores with metal shutters down. There's barely anyone in the few commercial spaces that remain open. The ghost streets of the American city without open shops or people walking.

Life bursts suddenly in the parenthesis of Beale Street, with its neon signs and the sound of R&B coming from the bars. The oblique afternoon sun descends in a straight line and shines on the windows and redbrick walls. But time is of the essence. Soon it will be dark. We leave Beale Street and continue down the avenue. More empty buildings, more garages and parking lots with weeds growing through the cracks in the pavement. At the intersection of Second Street and Martin Luther King Jr. Avenue, the traffic lights swing from high cables in the wind. Not another soul on the street, just a passing car here and there.

There's a church with gothic towers to the east in the middle of a construction site. To the west, against the glare of the invisible river, we see a parking lot and the outlines of a structure of red bricks occupying the whole block. Rows of boarded-up windows line its side and ivy grows over the surfaces. A big metal framework must have held an electric sign that was once visible from very far away. The faded letters, at the height of the top floors, read: HOTEL CHISCA. The name sounds familiar, but I can't remember why. I have seen it somewhere, just one time.

Now we pass a long one-story building with door lintels and Art Deco window frames with broken glass. The interior is filled with heaps of trash, graffiti, and broken furniture from long ago. The front door is sealed with bricks and wood, and above, an old sign indicates that this was a supplier of equipment and food for cinemas. A young black woman is standing on the other side of the street looking at us. A small child holds her hand and she's pushing a stroller. Their long shadow is projected toward us.

•

It's easy to lose a sense of time and distance when walking through an empty city. We must be close to the Lorraine. A memory comes back: it was in the Hotel Chisca that James Earl Ray claimed to have eaten that ice cream on the afternoon of April 4. Thick vegetation has grown inside the abandoned buildings that line the street. Prodigious magnolias have occupied entirely what was probably a backyard once upon a time. The trunks have lifted the pavement around them and knocked down a few walls. A twisted trunk of ivy has fractured the stairway of another abandoned hotel and climbed all the way to the oxidized frame that once held its name. On a more recent ruin, there is a blue and pink sign that reads HOLLYWOOD DISCO.

An entire wall is painted with a Mexican mural that features skulls with hats and Virgin Marys and agaves and intensely colored sunsets. There's ranchera music coming from an open door. It leads to an internal courtyard filled with empty tables and two waiters standing at the far end. They see us peek in. They look bored, perhaps hopeful that we'll go in.

The sign suddenly appears as we turn the corner: Lorraine Motel. It is at the end of the street, high above the other rooftops. When the sun is finished setting, it will glow and flash its red neon arrow to attract drivers to this desolate corner of Memphis. The diverse typefaces in the sign allude to the world of a half century ago just like the light green of the metal poles that support it, the same color of the doors, a color from that time, the color of a faded modernity. What I have seen so many times in photographs and documentaries is now in front of me. As soon as we get to the end of the street I'll set foot in the place where I have lived in my imagination for the past few months. A few more steps and it will be like crossing a veil and entering the space and time of an old film, the interior of the unfinished book I left on hold in order to come here.

•

The Lorraine Motel is lower and longer and much less imposing than I expected. In the building annexed to it, a modern construction, the doors to the National Civil Rights Museum have already closed. I recognize the two rows of rooms, with their wide windows and doors facing the running railing. It was the rationalist architecture of back then; simple, open forms and light colors, in contrast to the dark brick of the rest of the neighborhood, with the soot of factories and coal locomotives. The Lorraine Motel could have been in Florida, in California, facing the ocean, with a background of palm trees. The courtyard in front of the parking lot was a pool fifty years ago. Room 306, toward the center, on the second floor, is distinguished by a wreath of white and red flowers hanging from the railing at the exact location where Martin Luther King was leaning when the shot was fired. Below the room two cars are parked, two models from the sixties, like the ones we see in the photos from that day, one of them is a long, white Cadillac with rear wings, identical to the one that the owner of a funeral home in Memphis made available for King when he was in town.

•

The museum has been closed for over an hour. It's just past seven in the evening, a day at the end of May. The light of this hour is the same as that of 6:00 p.m. in early April. Apart from two other visitors, who have wandered around taking photos and are now checking the museum hours before leaving, we're the only people in the forecourt of the Lorraine Motel, and the neighborhood it seems.

There's a profound stillness in this warm and humid afternoon. On April 4, 1968, the air would have been cooler and more transparent, due to the storm of the prior day. If I turn my back to the motel, I face the building where Bessie Brewer's boardinghouse used to be. It stands there, backlit, above a garden that was a garbage dump half a century ago. Now I can't distinguish the window where the barrel of that rifle stuck out that day at 6:00 p.m.

The distance between those back windows and the balconies of the Lorraine Motel is also smaller than I had imagined. If I hadn't come here, I would not have known that Martin Luther King's room was facing west. In just a few minutes there would not be enough light to make the shot from that distance. The most defining moments almost did not happen. We go up to South Main. I recognize the topography as if I had walked these streets in dreams, with a mixture of certainty and unreality. The corner, where the museum gift shop is now located, used to be Canipe Amusement Company. Here is the recessed entrance, between the store window and the corner, where he dropped the bag with the blanket and the rifle, and continued walking south toward the white Mustang, parked by the brick building that is still the firehouse.

Some things change and some do not. Jim's Grill does not exist anymore, but the facade is the same. Number 422. He crossed that doorstep and went up a stairway that perhaps is still there, with the word ROOMS painted on every step.

I recognize everything and yet nothing is exactly how I had imagined. Beyond the firehouse the street turns east and descends down a long hill to the train station and the road that leads to the state border. The landscape widens as you exit Memphis, the street becomes more open. It must have been a relief to see the city retract in the rearview mirror as the police sirens grew weaker, to step on the gas and feel that mixture of panic and incredulity at having accomplished the plan with only one shot and now be driving in silence through the countryside, moments before turning on the radio and hearing confirmation of the death and the sign that the hunt had begun.

•

The next morning the museum is open but the past seems to have receded, as the sea on a beach with a low tide. The esplanade in front of the Lorraine Motel is crowded with groups of tourists and students. People smile and pose for photos with Room 306 and the crown of white and red flowers in the background.

The museum was designed to give visitors an immediate and tactile impression of the past. In this space the past becomes practicable; it exists in the three dimensions of the present. You can read about the segregated buses of the South, but you can also get inside of one identical to where Rosa Parks once sat. You can touch the chrome surfaces, smell the plastic of back then, see the ads from 1954 lining the inside of the bus, above the windows. There's a sitting figure and she's a mannequin and a ghost, a woman with a hat and a coat and an air of righteousness and dignity.

The more effective the appearance of proximity, the more grave the inevitable lie. In a room with low lights, we see a burnt bus. This was one of the buses that carried Freedom Riders in May 1961, into some of the most racist cities of the South. Young women and men, black and white, committed to the mysterious heroism of doing ordinary and already legal things that could nevertheless cost them their lives, and not respond when violence rained upon them.

They arrived at stations where mobs of angry white men would be waiting with sticks, stones, and pipes. In pictures and in TV images on the monitors of the museum, we see those faces twisted by anger, by the intoxication of collective brutality and impunity, young faces for the most part, sometimes very young, almost all male, men with white shirts or overalls, surrounding a bus, breaking windows, trying to overturn it, retreating only when it's in flames, fierce and triumphant, exalted by revenge, by the fire that will burn alive all the people inside if they don't manage to get out.

I can touch the ribbed silver surface of the bus and I can step inside. I see the beautiful drawing of the greyhound that gives the company its name and the jubilant sign written along the side in blue letters against a white background: IT'S SUCH A COMFORT TO TRAVEL BY BUS. But who could experience the terror of arriving in Montgomery or Birmingham and see the innocuous spectacle of everyday life—the shops, the gas stations, the people on the sidewalks—and know that in a few minutes a mob will surround you, spit on you, beat you, perhaps even kill you, and not because you lifted a fist in protest or demanded equality or justice. No, they hate you because you dared to do what everyone else does: buy a soda and a sandwich at the lunch counter at the station, sit to read the newspaper in a waiting room without paying attention to the WHITES ONLY sign or the looks of the people around you.

•

The past can be visited at the museum not only to investigate what happened but to anoint oneself with its powerful alloy of heroism and suffering, unprecedented brutality and admirable rebellion. Fear, poverty, pain, are transmuted into martyrdom. The bursting abscess of hatred can no longer reach you. Black Americans with nothing but their dignity face water jets and police batons. The water jets are so strong they tear the bark of trees and send full-grown adults flying against the walls like rags.

The bodies of lynched men, with white shirts and broken necks, hang from trees in the South like burial mounds. Wooden churches burn in the night. On the silent video monitor, a group of young Freedom Riders—the women in dresses, the men in suits and ties—walks between two rows of thugs who spit at them, kick them, and push them. A white woman with a baby in her arms is seen opening her mouth widely. They will never forget what these mothers would yell: *Kill them niggers! Kill 'em all!* The intensity of the injury, the vehemence of hate and its mix of vulgarity and ignorance, cannot be translated.

Wiry black men march between lines of soldiers with rifles and bayonets, each carrying a sign with a single repeated phrase of words and letters that multiply silently into a unanimous affirmation, I AM A MAN I AM A MAN I AM A MAN.

In an exact replica of a lunch counter in the fifties, there are stools occupied by mannequins of men and women who dared challenge segregation, and empty stools for visitors to sit and join them and look at the menu and the sign over the bar that says WHITES ONLY.

Experience, both the verb and the noun, are inadequate terms. People in marketing like them so much they never stop repeating them. But that experience is largely a usurpation. You will get to sit on a metal stool and for a moment feel like you are in a segregated lunch counter in Birmingham, for instance, in 1961. But no one is going to come and pour the ketchup or a hot coffee on your head, or grab you by the shirt and try to break your jaw against the counter; there will be no fingernails trying to scratch your face and your eyeballs like a bird of prey.

The police officers will keep their distance, watching with indifference, waiting for the mob to satisfy their rage. After staring at the hate-filled faces of those white men, I realize the physical resemblance: Galt, Sneyd, Lowmeyr, Ray. He looks so much like them he could easily blend in; in fact, he could even pass for one of the police officers who watch and do nothing.

•

The museum is designed as a journey through time, an exemplary history that moves from darkness to light, from injustice to the full measure of citizenship, from the slave ships to the present, where at last we see what less than a half century ago would have seemed unheard-of in this country: black and white and brown children coming out of the same buses, obeying with difficulty their teacher who tells them to keep it low, using touch screens with ease and impatience, taking selfies with their phones.

The past is a theme park. You can pose next to the life-size figures that cover the wall as if you had been in one of those marches, walking right next to Martin Luther King. You can enter the cell where King was held in Birmingham, Alabama, sit on a bed identical to his, and read, projected on the wall, the letter that he wrote on loose sheets, in the margins of a newspaper, under the light that seeped through the bars, a light as weak in the darkness as the oil lamps that illuminated the prophets in their cells.

But who could know how that darkness felt, the sound of the bolts and the cries of the prisoners, who could know the insidious doubt in the middle of the night, the suspicion that all this sacrifice is in vain and that he has brought even more suffering to others, the thirst of the soul, the secret cowardice.

Who can imagine the fear of the approaching steps and the clacking sound of the batons on the metal bars announcing an imminent beating: the fear of the person who is locked in darkness and knows that the guards can beat him to a pulp, torture him, break his every bone, and nothing will happen to them, no consequences, not even a sanction. A group of children play, going in and out of the cell, putting their hands through the bars in a gesture of supplication. They snap photos of one another, their faces pressed against the metal, laughing.

•

The itinerary is an exemplary story and also a pilgrimage. Martin Luther King speaks in 1963 before a crowd of tens of thousands stretching from the Lincoln Memorial to the Washington Monument; in 1965 he leads the march from Selma to Montgomery; in March 1968, he advances, with a visible expression of vulnerability and anguish, in a protest march by striking Memphis sanitation workers, when police are already attacking and part of the march has turned into a riot.

The images from the speech on the night of April 3 in Memphis are in color. They are projected in a dark room that feels like a chapel, on a screen that is suspended from the ceiling in front of a few benches. The audience must look up in order to see them, like a crucifix on an altar. King's eyes are piercing. His face shines with perspiration and the skin around his temples and jaw tightens as he speaks.

We don't forget, not even for a second, that this man will never speak in public again and will die in less than twenty-four hours. The same voice and that same spoken music have been repeated in echoes multiplied through the rooms of the museum, a statement of condemnation and prophecy. After some metallic stairs and corridors with walls covered in photos, we come out to a space illuminated by the light of day. The last stop in the pilgrimage is a motel room.

The light of the present illuminates the last space of the past, preserved like a mausoleum, behind a glass wall. Beyond the windows of the Lorraine Motel is the pale blue sky over the city of Memphis.

Behind the glass wall, Room 306 is frozen in the evening of April 4, 1968. There are two beds. One of them is partially undone and there's an open newspaper on it. The bathroom door is open. On a low table there's a pack of cigarettes and a full ashtray. From the interior of the room the shot would have sounded like a firecracker. Perhaps one could have also heard the body thrown against the door by the bullet.

•

I see the bullet moments later. I've come out of an elevator and find myself in what used to be Bessie Brewer's boardinghouse. It takes a few moments for this to sink in. Just a few minutes before, we were in the museum. Now we see that history from the angle of a more somber and less visited room, a place beyond the reach of any spirit of celebration for the legacy of the civil rights movement. Here's where he hid, at the end of this dark hallway.

I see the bullet that pierced through the jaw and the spine of Martin Luther King: a deformed metal flower tucked in cotton inside one of the round little boxes the FBI used to collect evidence. I also see the rifle that fired it. It is smaller than I imagined and, without doubt, lighter than the one I had to carry during military service. There's the wooden stock and a scope, and the binoculars he bought for forty dollars.

I peek into room 5B and see the flimsy bed with the curved iron headboard and a green blanket, the dirty sofa, and the dusty Christmas ornaments on the mantelpiece. There is a dresser with a murky mirror that he moved in order to have a clear view of the window.

I see the shared bathroom at the end of the hall. The bathtub still stands against the left wall in the corner below the window, but the dirty footprints of where he stood, trying to keep his balance as he aimed, are no longer there. A glass wall prevents me from entering the bathroom and looking out that window, but there's a window in the next room with an almost identical view. It's hard to believe how close it is to the motel.

I can see the horizontal silhouette of the Lorraine Motel, the railing along the rooms with their green doors, and the crown of white and red flowers. Beyond the rooftop is the dark green of a thick forest and the light blue of the sky. It's the same landscape from the black-and-white photos that were taken then, but down below, instead of heaps of garbage, we see a garden with young trees. A gardener in overalls is cutting the grass and a powerful smell of sap enters through the open window.

•

It is then that I discover something unexpected: a vertical showcase in the center of a room, where all the objects I have read about and seen in photographs are on display. I have imagined them with such precision, it's hard to believe I'm now seeing them in real life. It's like staring at the barber's basin in *Don Quixote*, the vial of poison that Emma Bovary drank, the glasses and bandages of Wells's Invisible Man. I see the suitcase and everything else I've read in the typewritten lists of the FBI: the small shampoo bottle, the comb, the Schlitz beer cans, the quilt where the rifle was wrapped, the pocket radio he had when he escaped from prison. Everything is organized and tagged, like the fragmentary objects of those remote everyday lives preserved in the display cases of museums; material traces of a lost world.

I see the Liberty Chief revolver he had in his back pocket when they arrested him at the airport in London, the road maps of Mexico and Alabama and Georgia, the Canadian passport of Ramon George Sneyd, opened to the page with the faded photograph, the hint of a smile, the horn-rimmed glasses, the jacket and tie. There's also the other passport, identical except for the spelling of the last name, SNEYA; the birth certificate and the vaccination record; the jacket of the first suit he ever owned, the one that was made to measure in Montreal. I see the bill from the hotel, but I can't read what it says, not even the check-in and check-out dates, just the logo in blue capital letters on the header; it is one of those receipts that one puts in a pocket and ends up keeping for no reason, involuntary relics that register a moment in time with more precision than a memory.

•

I have come from so far away to see these objects up close. I peek inside the '66 Mustang, not the one he drove but otherwise identical, the most valuable thing he ever owned, the red leather interior, the ivory knobs on the radio, the silver silhouette of the bronco on the radiator, the gleaming chrome, the Alabama plates, the U.S.-Mexican border sticker on the windshield, dated October 1967.

I study every detail as closely as possible. I step back to look at something else but end up returning right away, leaning on the glass, making sure there is nothing I have missed, oblivious to all the people around me, including you.

I recognize everything and yet there is something in every one of these objects that feels inexplicably strange, the hint of a secret that I would have never guessed had I not seen them in person. There is something repulsive about them, perhaps the material unpleasantness of things cheaply made and worn from use. The pocket radio looks precarious. It is so small that sounds, voices, and music could have only come out weak and distorted. He would have had to press it hard against his ear to hear anything. The shampoo bottle is one of those tiny plastic containers that you find in cheap hotels; the bag is imitation leather and has a plastic zipper and handle; the synthetic blanket is filthy; the toothbrush has a clear plastic handle and yellowed bristles; the revolver is smaller than I imagined—a short barrel that looks like a tap with the grip crudely wrapped in dirty tape. Objects say what we don't; they reveal in public what we would prefer to keep secret. What they say without words makes fiction irrelevant.

•

But one still wants to imagine. Literature is the desire to dwell inside the mind of another person, like an intruder in a house, to see the world through someone else's eyes, from the interior of those windows where no one ever seems to peek out. It's impossible but one does not renounce the optical illusion. You walk past the tall and empty buildings of Lisbon or Memphis and want to know what they are like inside under the light that filters through the wooden planks covering the windows. You wake up in the middle of the night with the strange sensation of being inside the mind of another person, trapped or locked within it, a windowless solitary-confinement cell where you're serving a sentence for a crime that's unknown to you, but you also know you're not innocent.

It is easier to reach the mind through the senses. I had to know how that room smelled. I had to know what that bathroom looked like. The sound of the steps on the dark and narrow stairway as he went up and down: he went up, for the first time, around 3:00 p.m. to rent the room; he went back up later, with a bag but without the rifle, which was still in the trunk of the car; the bag had all the things he would need to spend at least a night in the boardinghouse, which provided nothing, not even toilet paper.

He went down at 4:00 p.m. and drove around in the Mustang looking for a store where he could buy the binoculars. When he returned half an hour later, there was another car parked in front of Jim's Grill and the boardinghouse, so he had to find another spot, not too far from there, but still less favorable, because now he would have to cover that distance carrying the box with the rifle, which was visible even with the blanket around it.

He turned off the car but remained inside. I imagine the smell of the red leather inside the hot car; the touch of the steering wheel, which must have been so familiar to him after having driven more than twelve thousand miles. He was going to get out but then he saw something behind a window. He always studied his surroundings before making any movement, before taking a single step between the bar and the sidewalk, or when he was entering a dimly lit room and waited for his eyes to adjust to the dark. He saw a woman looking out from a store window. He watched her sideways to avoid showing his full face. Both hands on the wheel, thinking through every step he would need to take to safely transport the box with the rifle to the room in the boardinghouse.

He stayed there for twenty minutes, doing nothing, watching, adjusting the rearview mirror to check different angles. He stayed still for so long that the woman at the store became curious as she waited for her husband's car to come pick her up.

•

But she did not see him get out. She became distracted with something else and when she turned around the white Mustang was empty. No one remembered him taking a big box from the trunk of the car or walking to the door that said ROOMS, next to the window of Jim's Grill.

He went up the steps and then down the hall to room 5B. He would have heard the voices of other guests behind the doors, the noise from radios and television programs.

In room 5B he removes the dresser that was in front of the window and puts a chair there instead, the only chair in the room. He is hesitant to touch anything. He needs to be careful not to leave any fingerprints. He places the box on the bed and takes out the rifle. He loads only one bullet. With the rifle on his lap, he looks out the window, slightly parting the dirty curtain.

The setting sun is shining on the windows of the Lorraine Motel. He looks through the binoculars. He can see room 306 clearly. Everything looks modern at the Lorraine Motel, everything looks new. Cream-color curtains protect the room interiors from the sun. Below the balcony, in the parking lot, he sees a group of elegant black men standing around a white Cadillac. The sun is reflected off their sunglasses and their gold rings. He adjusts the binoculars, magnifying the lens so he can see the faces more closely. But the face he's looking for is not there. He remains still, alert, isolated from the world despite its proximity, just as he was moments before, when he sat inside the Mustang waiting for the perfect time.

•

Room 306 is open. Just a moment ago it was closed. He got distracted watching the men around the Cadillac. A breeze lifts the curtain. He looks at his watch and it's now past 5:30 p.m. He moves the circle of the binoculars along the railing and then he sees him, so clearly, standing on the balcony, easily recognizable but at the same time different from any of the images he has seen of him.

He is adjusting the cuff links on his shirt and his face is slightly turned toward the interior of the room; his lips are moving, someone else must be inside the room. He keeps watching him, amazed that the man is there in the flesh. There's a feeling of numbness, as if he were in some kind of hypnotic trance and time had ceased to exist, but he knows the clock is ticking and he needs to act fast.

The image that was constructed so meticulously in the laboratory of his mind is now real. He lifts the rifle, slowly, but in order to aim he will have to hold it at an awkward angle and slightly out the window. The face in the lens is unbelievably close. His jaw shines as if he has just finished shaving. He can see him so clearly, it feels strange not to hear what he is saying.

•

But now he's gone. He made a sudden movement with the binoculars and lost him. The balcony is empty, although the door is still open and the curtain is flapping. Time has leaped forward. It is now fifteen minutes till six. The minute hand is moving faster in the sphere of his watch. He leans the rifle against the wall, opens the door, and peeks into the hallway. There is no one but he can hear a loud television. He sees the bathroom door is open. There's no one inside. He quickly steps out of his room with the rifle and into the bathroom. He carries the binoculars in his left hand. Fortunately, the door has a latch, though it would not be hard to break it with a strong push.

His hands are sweating. He should have taped his fingertips but there was no time. Perhaps the man already left the motel. Every second counts. In order to see room 306 he has to stand with his legs apart inside the tub. He has to maintain his balance and aim the rifle at the same time.

In the parking lot, two of the men are now getting inside a car that is not the white Cadillac. The only way to exit room 306 is to come out to the balcony. Keeping this difficult stance makes the knot of the tie feel even tighter. The jacket is also limiting his range of motion. His precarious stability depends on the fulcrum of the rifle barrel on the windowsill. Someone is now shaking the doorknob to the bathroom. Everything is oscillating from sharp to out of focus, from still to unstable. Beads of sweat are running down his forehead but he can't wipe it because both hands are occupied. The person outside the bathroom is now banging on the door and yelling.

The streetlights are beginning to turn on. In a few minutes it will be dark. If he can concentrate with enough energy, he can make him come back out. He blinks and suddenly the man is there, again, leaning on the railing, now wearing a suit jacket and a tie. He can see his eyes so clearly. They have a moist gleam.

He's shorter and stockier than he had imagined. There's an unlit cigarette in his left hand. For a moment, he seems to be staring intently across the street, toward the windows of the boardinghouse. He leans forward and puts his elbows on the railing as if about to speak to a person below. The knocks on the bathroom door have ceased. He barely had to pull the trigger.

25

It had been a hot day, but the air felt much cooler now as the sun began to set. It was the warm humid air of Memphis, emanating from the soaked ground and vegetation after the storm of the night before. There was a sudden perfection in his surroundings, a levity, a sweetness; it was something present and tangible and at the same time a promise; a certainty and a soothing sense of distance from it all.

He had noticed it only a few minutes ago, by surprise, when he came out to the balcony, securing his cuff links. He realized that for the first time that entire day he was breathing fresh air, and leaving the excessive refrigeration of the Lorraine. He was surprised by the warm touch of the breeze coming from the river, invisible and nearby, just beyond the rooftops of South Main, the walls surrounding abandoned sites, the collapse of the inner city in America, the crumbling neighborhoods where only the poor and black lived, the most trapped, the ones who ran to touch him as if he had stepped right out of the Gospel, hoping for some kind of miraculous cure; but also the ones who did not come, the ones who kept their distance, numbed by misery or alcohol or heroin, and the ones who now viewed him with suspicion, even hatred, no longer a brother, but a traitor, a sellout to the white man.

He had come out to the balcony because the smell of his shaving cream was too strong, almost repulsive, a running joke among his friends. He had applied the cream in front of the bathroom mirror, while Abernathy asked him to please close the bathroom door and crack open a window.

He also found the smell repugnant, almost as much as the feeling of that sticky substance on his skin, which was very sensitive and would get easily irritated if he used a regular razor blade. He cut the thin mustache very carefully. It was his secret flirtation, although he knew that it was now an outdated style, that it belonged to a time of ten or fifteen years ago, just like the hats that he still liked to wear. Nowadays all the men wore big mustaches and long sideburns, and almost nobody wanted to use a hat. Life can change rapidly around you and you won't even notice if you don't look up from your routine.

He washed his face with cold water and slapped on the aftershave. The clean ironed shirt was pleasant to the touch. He buttoned it halfway and went out to the balcony to get fresh air. He had plenty of time. They were going to a dinner with friends, nothing formal like those dinners in New York and Washington, which still made him nervous after all these years. It would be a simple feast, hearty food, and then some music, an event to honor the sanitation workers who were striking. He always asked Abernathy to do things he'd rather not do; this time, just a while ago, he had asked him to call the host of the dinner, Mrs. Kyles, to confirm that the menu did not have any strange dishes, any French sauces or steamed vegetables or pureed spinach with the consistency of his shaving cream. Eating and drinking with friends is one of life's great pleasures. For the Greeks, a feast was a banquet of love, the maximum expression of human harmony, the sweet intoxication of flesh and spirit.

Go thy way, eat thy bread with joy, and drink thy wine with a merry heart, says Ecclesiastes. He likes southern food, the plentiful servings of the restaurants in Memphis, fried catfish, barbecued ribs, smoked pork, pig's feet, sweet tea with ice, frosty cold beer, black beans and rice and creamy sweet potatoes, all the glory of God's creation.

•

It was a good sign to be thinking about food, to have an appetite again after so many days of darkness, the enormous and probably doomed effort of putting together the biggest march the world has seen, like the people of Israel marching toward the Promised Land, the great universal march of the poor to Washington, not just his people, because poverty and injustice are color-blind, but also Native American tribes, day laborers, immigrants, the Puerto Ricans of Spanish Harlem in New York, the Eskimos, the native Hawaiians, the white poor of Appalachia.

He and Abernathy had shared a big tray of fried catfish for lunch. The waiter of the Lorraine had made a mistake and brought just one huge plate. They almost preferred it that way. Like David and Jonathan, they had shared everything for many years. They were closer than brothers. There was no point in waiting for the extra plates or cutlery. They dug in with their hands and ate and talked and laughed; they even took the tray to the bedroom, where they continued eating and joking and even throwing food and napkins at each other.

The bedroom was a mess. Twenty-four hours since their arrival and the ashtrays had already overflowed; there were newspapers all over the floor and the beds, along with reports and drafts of sermons, beer bottles, the bottle of whiskey they had started the night before, a lone ice cube floating in a glass of lukewarm water.

•

Depression was a sin because it made you indifferent to the gifts of God, resentful against them. In those moments, the lines from Ecclesiastes would come to him as clearly as if someone were whispering them into his ear. *Therefore I hated life; because the work that is wrought under the sun is grievous unto me: for all is vanity and vexation of spirit.* Now that he was emerging from the darkness, he could see just how deep he had fallen in a secret and vindictive disappointment with everything and anger at himself. *I hated all my labour which I had taken under the sun: because I should leave it unto the man that shall be after me.*

While shaving, he had been able to look at himself in the mirror without shame, without seeing the face of an impostor, a sinner consumed by forbidden desires, the libertine who was the target of gossip and blackmailing by his enemies, the FBI agents who right now were probably sitting in an unmarked van nearby listening to the micro-phones they had planted in his room.

A sense of immunity to guilt and danger had filled him since the night before and it felt even stronger now. He was thankful for this in-ner calm because he knew how fragile it was.

As he exited onto the balcony, he felt the curtains and the breeze on his face, the stillness that filled that hour in these parts of Mem-phis, after people had left the factories for the day and were home getting ready for dinner. It was the sound of the daily sigh of relief in these fatigued lives. Faint sounds of ship sirens came from the invisible river. He remembered that mysterious passage in Genesis where God is *walking in the garden in the cool of the day*. He placed both hands on the railing. The metal still contained the heat of the day.

The sun had yet to set beyond the forests of Arkansas, on the other side of the river, but it was no longer within view from the bal-cony, only its golden shadow was visible across the sky, slowly back-lighting the row of buildings to the west. Time had slowed down just for those few moments, still without haste, before they called him from the parking lot and said it was time to go. It felt good to step out of the constant urgency to get somewhere, a meeting, a dinner, a march, an interview, a plane.

For thirteen years, his entire adult life, he had lived like that, al-ways in a hurry, each time with less energy and increasingly trapped by the anguish of obligations, the crowds who spent hours in the heat, waiting for his arrival to their church; the possible donors and power-ful benefactors who should never have to wait; his own children and his wife in the family home where he barely had time to stop nowa-days; the production assistants at the TV studios who were always rushing him through some backstage.

The more conscious he felt of his strength leaving him, the more daunting the task ahead, the more cruel the injustice, the more un-likely his success. In other times, when he was younger, everything had seemed possible. Now, unexpectedly, he was enjoying these few minutes in a parenthesis of calm. It was a gift, as tangible as the solid warmth of the metal under his hands or the way the clean shirt felt on his skin.

He went back to the room, flooded with the red glow of the afternoon and its lengthening shadows. He buttoned up the rest of the shirt. The last button gave him some difficulty. He had started to gain weight recently, and it was not for the pleasures of food and drink, but something darker. He lacked joy. He was eating from stress, drinking to appease his anguish, smoking until his lungs hurt, and waking up every morning in a hotel room that smelled of cigarettes, not knowing where he was, because all the rooms had started to look the same.

He fixed his tie, noticing the pressure of the shirt collar on his chin. He liked the feel of silk on his hands.

There were people in the movement, fervent fighters, who surrendered to asceticism as a perpetual penance, as if any delight was a frivolity, a betrayal to the cause of the oppressed. They would have liked to wear camel hair, like John the Baptist, with a leather belt around their waists. But Jesus Christ, on the very eve of the Passion, had thanked a woman in Bethany for pouring on his head *an alabaster box of very precious ointment*, and admonished the disciples, who had complained about wasting it when it could have been sold for money to help the poor.

He loved good cologne, the subtle blend of perfumes that emanated from attractive women, the elegance of high heels. He put his jacket on, delighted by the skill of the tailor who had known how to fit the suit to his new heft in a flattering way. People who met him for the first time were always surprised to see he wasn't tall.

He folded the linen handkerchief and slipped it into the breast pocket of the jacket, forming a small triangle. The black shoes were clean because he had not left the hotel all day, but he still gave them a quick polish. They were the elegant shoes of Sunday sermons and receptions, not the comfortable, rubber-soled ones of marches under the sun. Perhaps he had time to smoke a cigarette on the balcony, while Abernathy went back to the room to put on deodorant or cologne. Abernathy always scolded him when they were running late but he was the one who was always remembering things at the last minute and causing delay.

•

It was amazing that people could remain the same. It was good that way. To feel that you know a friend so well that you can predict his actions, that the good things happen according to a preexisting order, following the person's nature, like Genesis says, the particular and even whimsical nature of every creature. If he had to wait for Abernathy, he might as well do so on the balcony with a cigarette. He anticipated that small and guaranteed pleasure.

Below, around the cars, friends joked around and lit one another's cigarettes, playing pretend-fight, throwing hooks in the air and laughing. They wore dark suits, thin black ties, and hats and had an air of jazzmen and professors, which he liked, because it balanced out the propensity of Baptist pastors to look like funeral directors.

Jesse Jackson stood out with his leather jacket and turtleneck. But that was also according to his nature, and this time it did not annoy him. Jackson was younger, of course, though not as much as his style made him seem. That was the style of the day: to exhibit one's youth without shame and celebrate it, almost boastfully, imitating the jargon of pimps and drug dealers.

To be thirty-nine years old made you an old man and, according to some, inevitably reactionary. So solemn, with his "Dr." title always in front of the name, his Nobel Prize, his old-fashioned rhetoric. But beneath his tolerance for Jackson remained a sting of suspicion and that made him feel disloyal and ashamed of himself. He had never wished nor asked to be put on a pedestal, but they did it anyway; they elevated him to this earthly sainthood and then disowned him for not living up to their impossible expectations. They had turned him into a heroic statue only to throw stones at it. Shame was one of his most assiduous secret afflictions, throbbing deeper than the weight of his obligations, fed by the tension of public life, the gap between what others chose to see in him and who he really was. There is no public figure who is not an impostor.

Perhaps Judas Iscariot stood out among the other apostles; something made them mistrust him without a clear reason, and it was this unwarranted suspicion that pushed him to a place he would not have gone otherwise. But Jackson was not a traitor: he was just ambitious, anxious, impatient, and frustrated—as any veteran of the struggle would be—by the slow pace of change and the persistence of injustice. Perhaps he secretly wanted to put on a black jacket and a beret, wield a pistol or a rifle, and raise his clenched fist.

But Jackson also cared about being part of this circle of veterans of the struggle. Hadn't he forced a situation that afternoon in order to get invited? Just a while earlier he had told him, not entirely in jest, that he should wear a suit and a tie to visit the home of Reverend Kyles. Jackson quickly responded that the only requirement for going to someone's house for dinner is a good appetite. Now he was watching him from the balcony, the young man, strong, anxious, trying hard to joke with the others. He felt shame that he could not get over his unfounded suspicions despite the visible evidence of Jackson's love.

•

He could recognize all of them, match every voice with a name and a face, histories that went back to the beginning. But there was a voice that in his mind stood out more than all the others precisely because of its absence; a presence even more special because it was hidden, invisible yet so close to him. She was also waiting for the signal that it was time to go, and when that happened she would come out and get in the last car at the last minute, slipping out of a room on the ground floor, the room where she had been since the night before, when she arrived, exhausted but happy after the ten-hour journey, her lips freshly painted.

She had gotten used to making herself invisible, waiting for him in hotel rooms that were never under his name or apartments that belonged to people unknown to her. They could be photographed together from afar. Surely there were policemen with binoculars watching from a window or terrace in some building nearby. There could be microphones in the room, perhaps in the lamp on the bedside table, or behind the headboard. They don't bother protecting us from our enemies but they sure can keep a close watch on us, she had said, one of the first times, in another one of those secret meetings that always took place in the exact same way but were never immune to unleashed desire, the unbearable intensity of the wait, the gentle

knock on the door at a late hour, the precious time between hello and
goodbye, so short there was barely any time for a prelude, or the pleasant rest that came afterward, a cigarette in bed, the prolonged satisfaction of quenched desire.

They spoke in whispers. When he was about to moan she covered
his mouth. At the end, he would embrace her and fall asleep for a few
minutes wishing he could stay. Satiated love is the only sleeping pill
that works, it is the only thing stronger than guilt, the irrefutable
evidence of sin. *For the lips of a strange woman drop as a honeycomb, and her
mouth is smoother than oil.* A few minutes of rest and the weight of the
world came back, the restless man who was always in a hurry, the one
who had to look discreetly out the window before slipping out of her
room and walking down to his.

Now, one or two minutes to six, on the balcony, he realized that
he had dressed to look his best because she would be there and he
would look in her intelligent and beaming eyes for approval. Georgia
Davis, *Georgia on my mind*, he joked, whispering into her ear. No one
else knew that the tie he had chosen for the occasion was a gift from
her. They would sit very far from each other at the dinner table and
try not to look at each other too much, but that would make the few
glances they exchanged all the more exciting. He liked a line from a
poem by T. S. Eliot: *With private words I address you in public.*

He would let her know that tonight, when they were back at
the hotel, after the dinner and the assembly and the concert to honor
the strikers, he would come down to her room as he had the night before. He wouldn't even have to knock on the door because she would
leave it unlocked. *It is the voice of my beloved that knocketh,* says the Song
of Solomon. Lines that belonged not in sermons but in a whisper in
the dark. *Open to me, my sister, my love, my dove, my undefiled: for my head
is filled with dew, and my locks with the drops of the night.*

The curtains would be drawn, the lights turned off, but his silhouette would be visible against the lights of the parking lot, tinged with
the red, yellow, and blue of the hotel sign. He was the man whose
true self almost nobody, or nobody but her, could see. Undressing silently in the room, staring at each other, her body even more tempting
because it was no longer young, flattered by the strength of male desire,

a real man and not a photograph or a symbol or one of those images of a saint. *And they were both naked, the man and his wife, and were not ashamed.*

•

He had been so tired, yesterday evening, after an early morning and the flight from Atlanta and the lost hour at the airport due to a bomb threat, another one, and the arrival in Memphis, just a week after the previous trip, and the press conference, the malicious questions, the faces that had to be studied one by one in search of a look or expression that signaled immediate danger, the endless meetings, the rivers of unnecessary and worn-out words. Tired and depressed, exhausted to the bone, with no strength or desire for anything that wasn't his bed, listening to the wind howl against the window and then the downpour of rain or hail.

He had fainted the Sunday before as he was getting ready to deliver a sermon and then suddenly found himself making a public confession. In the motel in Memphis the Holy Spirit seemed to have abandoned him. He had a fever, or at least he touched his forehead and wanted to feel a fever so he would have an excuse. He often dreamed that he was at the pulpit about to deliver a sermon and had not prepared anything. He dreamed that he kept getting lost in stairways and corridors on his way to an auditorium or church where people were waiting for him. He told Abernathy, not without remorse, that he was not well, that he didn't even have the energy to get out of bed or light a cigarette. And his friend, who knew him so well, and was probably just as tired, told him not to worry, that he would speak on his behalf and apologize for his absence. And besides, who would even go out that night, with the storm that was already brewing, the repeated alerts on the radio and television about hurricane-like winds, torrential rains, and floods.

•

Not having to go anywhere that night had been an unspeakable blessing. Staying in bed while the storm raged outside, not having to see anyone for hours, doing nothing, perhaps watching a movie on TV for once; or just falling asleep, thinking about the woman who would be here in a few hours, all the way from Florida, because he had called her and said, almost in a whisper, breathing close to the receiver, that he had to see her, those were his words, I need you next to me.

It was a request for help that contained no promises. Neither was asking the future for anything more than what they already had. Secrecy, the brevity of each encounter, shaped the only world where they could or desired to be together. Every meeting was a mutual gift, but there was no heartbreak at the moment of saying goodbye. Her intelligence and sense of humor allowed her to see in him what few others could: a man, not the symbol, not the probable martyr, not the prophet.

The phone rang but he had fallen asleep so soundly that the rings repeated several times inside his dream before he woke up and reached for the bedside table. Perhaps it was her. Perhaps she was calling from the pay phone in a gas station to tell him the car had broken down and she would not be able to make it that night, or that she had changed her mind and had decided to stay with her husband.

But it was Abernathy. He could hear the storm in the phone, accompanied by a clamor that sounded like rain but was the crowd. They clapped and sang hymns and slogans. They repeated a name that was his. Abernathy stopped talking and raised the receiver so he could hear what was happening, all the people who had gathered despite the storm, wanting to hear him. How could he let them down. How could he stay in this room while their chants filled up the temple, thousands of men and women with their heads low, dressed in their Sunday best, black sanitation workers who did not even get gloves to do their jobs, much less health insurance or a day of rest; who lost days of wages if they got sick or if bad weather prevented the garbage trucks from going out; no pension, no workers' compensation, nothing for their wives and children should anything happen to them, like the two men who had been crushed to death when the compactor mechanism of a truck was accidentally triggered during a heavy rainstorm.

•

There was no limit to the horror and injustice. The cry of suffering never ceased. There could be no rest, no pause. *So I returned, and considered all the oppressions that are done under the sun: and behold the tears of such as were oppressed, and they had no comforter; and on the side of their oppressors there was power; but they had no comforter.* He hung up the phone and remained sitting on the edge of the bed, elbows on his knees, the loose tie hanging from his neck. Exhaustion was a stack of lead on his shoulders and a muddy swamp where every step sank and he no longer had the strength to keep moving.

As Job said, I was not in safety, neither had I rest, neither was I quiet; yet trouble came. But what could he give these people who had come out on a night like this to hear him, to see him from afar, to get close to him and touch him, to hope for some kind of revelation or miracle, something that no one could define, much less him, something that perhaps did not even exist.

They watched him with pleading eyes and he didn't know what they were seeing. Seeing the way they welcomed him into their homes without running water or electricity, he felt ashamed in his suit and polished shoes. They asked him to autograph books and photographs, magazines with his face on the cover, loose pieces of paper, printed prayers, drawings where sometimes he even had a halo around his head. They squeezed his hands and hugged him, and took photos as if trying to confirm that he was really there; they asked him to hold their babies, some asked for money, showed him medical bills, eviction letters, exorbitant rent and electricity bills.

At any moment, from any direction, close or far, a gunshot could end it all in a tenth of a second, in the flash of a camera, and the darkness that followed would be a relief. No warning, no time to be afraid: like the time Medgar Evers, a friend from many years in the struggle, was walking home at night and a bullet slammed him against his own door with keys in hand; or that time in Harlem, when he was signing books and a thin woman with glasses made her way through the crowd toward him. She had a drawn face and that expression of fearful shyness that was common on some of the people who were about to meet him for the first time and could not look him in the eyes. Her coat was buttoned all the way up, her purse held tightly against her chest. She seemed to be holding a pen. But that wasn't it. There was a glint and a sharp point.

The small hand suddenly tightened around the object and the pen became a knife. Now she was within arm's reach and the eyes behind her glasses were not shy but bloodshot, dilated, full of rage. No one but him seemed to notice her. It was as if the weapon were their mutual secret. The blade went into his chest and turned like a screwdriver. It penetrated so close to the aorta that had he taken a deep breath or sneezed in the hours that followed, the tip of the letter opener would have pierced right through the artery and he would have drowned in his own blood.

He stayed with the blade sunk in his chest, in shock, unable to move, a paused tape, as the ambulance sped through the streets of Harlem en route to the hospital. The blade had been so close to the aorta his whole chest had to be opened to remove it. After five hours, they succeeded. At first, upon waking in the hospital bed under the effects of the anesthesia, he could not remember anything, except the sweet pleasure of deep sleep.

•

He looked at the faces from the lectern where the Bible lay opened before him. He looked at the microphone and felt the heat of the spotlights. The concave depth of the auditorium in the Masonic Temple was so great that even with two or three thousand people in the stands, the place seemed almost empty. The vast space magnified the echoes of the crowd and the sound of thunder and rain pounding against the high windows.

It felt like a storm at the end of the world, the beginning of the Flood. As the applause and the screams began to wind down, he leaned in and grasped the sides of the lectern, an instinctive gesture that even he found theatrical, just another piece of the act. But that night he was holding on in order not to collapse, not from exhaustion, but from the monotony and lack of self-respect, which he saw reflected in the faces of his friends, the believers, the ones who were always there, Abernathy and the others, Andrew Young, Kyles, determined and capable but also tired, worn out by the fight that never seemed to end or accomplish an indisputable result, sometimes turned against one another by trivial administrations or pride.

If it were just a matter of marching with composure and courage through the rows of police officers and angry white people, or even going to jail, or delivering sermons and hearing the roaring approval of the crowd at the end of every sentence, then it would be bearable. But there was the organizing, the fund-raising, the schmoozing.

They were all, and he knew this well about himself, made of fragile materials, mud and dust from the earth, a mixture of gold and clay; noble and corruptible at the same time; heroes one moment and cowards the next; secret disbelievers, not for lack of faith but for the endless repetition of the same words, no matter how true or necessary they were, the whole routine that those closest to him could anticipate play by play, with resignation, cynicism, word for word, night after night, sometimes even several times the same day, like the assistants and technicians who follow a politician on the electoral trail.

•

But the cause of justice and equality had to remain sacred, the stubborn vindication of nonviolence, now that the ghettos in the cities were igniting with fury and the chemical fire of napalm was raining in Vietnam while people ran terrified and their homes, their crops, their jungles burned. How can anyone not decry the war in Vietnam while condemning segregation and exploitation in America? Three hundred thousand dollars to kill each alleged Vietnamese enemy; but not even fifty dollars a year invested in the life of a poor person in America.

He repeated these figures in his speeches and anticipated the reaction of the crowd. With his voice hoarse from fatigue, he announced, almost like a vision, the great march of biblical proportions that would descend on Washington before the summer; even more people than in 1963, with more immediate and unequivocal demands: work, livelihood, and dignity for all.

They would come by the thousands from all across the country. They would come by train and in caravans of buses, carrying backpacks and tents, ready to occupy the great lawns of Washington. There would be trucks filled with farmworkers, and even mule carts from the poorest cotton fields of the South.

They would come marching in compact columns and singing hymns, just as they had walked through the streets of Montgomery and on the road from Selma, a multitude that just kept on growing and multiplying beyond their wildest predictions, black and white marching together, rabbis, Catholic priests, nuns, university professors from the North, even stiff Episcopalian bishops, the sound of millions of steps in unison. The more his strength gave out, the more he lost confidence, the more urgent it was to keep getting up, with or without hope, with the help of the Holy Spirit or with a hunger of the soul that perhaps had no cure.

•

The prophets had been vulnerable to disillusion, but not to vanity or ambition. They had been called and they had obeyed, knowing that life would have been easier if somebody else had been tapped to lend their voice to those words.

Jehovah called on Jeremiah to preach next to the gate in Jerusalem where the king went in and out, and he was whipped and locked in a cell with his hands and feet and neck fastened in stocks. When God chose an envoy it was beyond appeal. The selection was terrifyingly arbitrary; there appeared to be no motive or any particular feature or capacity in the chosen one.

The simplicity of the call was frightening. God said the name of the chosen one two times. Abraham, Abraham, he said, and Abraham answered, Here I am. And God was calling on him to behead his son Isaac. God imposed and demanded human sacrifices without explanation. He himself recognized that Job's torment was for no reason. He welcomed Abel's offerings and disdained those of his brother Cain. He called Moses's name twice and ordered him to go before the pharaoh and demand the freedom of his people; but it was also He who hardened the heart of the pharaoh and thus brought upon the land of Egypt the plagues that He sent.

God broke the jaws of David's enemies and crushed their teeth.

God celebrated as the Babylonians sacrificed their children. God separated the waters of the Red Sea so his people could cross and then condemned them, as punishment for their ingratitude, to walk the desert for forty years before arriving at the Promised Land.

God allowed Moses to discern the Land of Canaan from the top of Mount Horeb, but He would have the prophet die before entering it. At the Garden of Gethsemane, in a night of terror and anticipation before the impending captivity, torture, and slow execution, Christ asked God if he could be spared his fate. But God remained silent, and a few moments before dying on the cross, Christ could not help but voice his doubt. Even the other two men who were being crucified insulted him. God was so often darkness and terror. In the place where Jacob wrestled an angel or a man till daybreak, the presence of God remained and it was a dreadful place.

•

And right now the wrath of God was descending over Memphis in all its terrifying magnificence. Lightning strikes the trees. The forests catch on fire. The wind tears the roofs of the poor, and rain floods the homes and roads around the delta. She would be driving on one of those roads at that very second, the windshield pounded by gusts of wind and rain, the woman he had begged to come be with him, to endure a long journey for a short and secret encounter, at most two hours. At first Job is caught between Satan's malevolence and God's whim, but then he is punished for the intellectual arrogance of demanding an explanation. Jonah wanted to escape the terrible fate of prophecy, so God led him to the sailors who would throw him overboard during a storm and then sent a whale to swallow him.

Deep in his heart, he had resisted going back to Memphis just as Jonah had resisted the divine order to preach at Nineveh. *Arise, go to Nineveh, that great city, and cry against it; for their wickedness is come up before me.* How many times he had wished to run away, like Jonah, to disappear overnight and abandon the exhausting and tyrannical mission that had fallen on his shoulders.

•

It had not been a call. The voice of God did not wake him in the middle of the night saying his name two times. He had not responded: Here I am. The patriarchs and the prophets heard voices, clear and unappealable orders. When he was blinded by the presence of Christ on the road to Damascus, Paul heard his voice. *Saul, Saul, why persecutest thou me?*

But schizophrenics also hear voices. And there was something very dangerous, very presumptuous, in considering yourself the recipient of a divine command. In his case, it could have been just a matter of chance, a series of misunderstandings. At the beginning, in Montgomery in '55, there was no voice from God at the top of a mountain or in a desert. It was an assembly in the early days of the boycott, tempestuous and disorderly, a vote to elect a provisional spokesperson for the nascent movement. He did not even volunteer as a candidate. He was younger and less experienced than most of the people there, a newcomer to the city, and was just getting used to being the pastor of a church. Someone nominated him and he was voted in. It could have been somebody else. He hadn't even met Mrs. Parks before she refused to give up her seat on the bus. He had never taken a bus in Montgomery, or Boston in any of the years during his doctorate in that unimaginable world of New England, where you quickly got used to using the same doors, the same park benches, the same classrooms, the same libraries. In Montgomery, as in Boston, he did not take the bus because he had his own car, a present from his father when he left for the doctorate.

How could his fate be determined when everything depended on so many coincidences, decisions taken at the last minute without much conviction. He had returned south so reluctantly, against his wife's preference and his own wishes, though he would not acknowledge this to her or even himself. The truth is that he came back because he did not want to go against his father's wishes again. The fact that he had decided to pursue the doctorate away from home after graduation, instead of staying with the congregation in Atlanta, had already been a source of tension. Why do you need to study theology and philosophy to be a Baptist pastor? his father had asked.

It had been difficult to stand by his decision, but not as much as he had anticipated. Eventually, his father agreed to it. It was this capitulation, and that of his mother, who was devastated that he was going so far, that made him doubt his purpose. He had always wanted to be a good son. Leaving them was much harder than he was willing to admit. How could a divine mandate to lead the poor and the persecuted fall on someone so privileged, someone raised in a loving family, a comfortable home, always protected by his parents and his older sister.

The church was an extension of the house. From the games with his siblings and their shared boredom during Sunday school, he had moved on to helping his father with the church. God was an invisible member of their house. He imagined God, who was both irascible and benevolent in the Bible, with the imposing presence and the deep voice of his father. What talent for resistance could someone who has been trained to revere his elders, and who is used to a comfortable life, possibly have? Tied to a fate he could no longer escape, even if he lived to be quite old, he imagined other possible futures and past decisions that could have taken him elsewhere.

He thought, most of all, of his time in Boston. He remembered the winter light that flooded the classrooms, the meditative hours in the library, the long halls with books and desks and small lamps, the drawers with blank paper and pencils, the white snow gently falling outside the window. Religion was not a sum of miraculous fantasies and terrible prejudices, it was a vast field of study ennobled by the intellectual rigor of philosophy and a wealth of historical scholarship, philology, archeology.

To make his parents happy, he wrote letters suggesting a longing for home he no longer felt. He enjoyed everything with spontaneity. He went to every seminar and spent Sunday evenings, and often entire nights, in the silence of the library.

The students attended class dressed as formally as the professors. For a time he took to smoking a pipe just like the others, and he also learned to conceal his southern accent and sound just like them. In their company, sometimes he forgot he was black.

In the chapel, during the Sunday morning service, the pastors delivered their sermons and read biblical passages with a distinguished accent and a sober intonation, as if they were reciting Emerson or Milton. No shouting, no arms waving, no eyes closed in ecstasy, no clapping, no stomping on the wooden floors until the whole place was shaking, no trance, no hysteria, no screaming, no spit flying over the audience.

He had come to feel secretly ashamed of his origins. In Boston, he came to prefer the Lutheran hymns, the choirs of men and women dressed in black robes, singing Bach cantatas. When they started dating, Coretta took him to see chamber music and piano recitals. She had straight hair and light skin. In church, she sang the soprano arias in the *St. Matthew Passion*. Dressed as if they were attending a religious service, they went to the opera to hear Donizetti, the sacred oratorios by Handel and Mendelssohn, Beethoven's *Missa Solemnis*, the Mass in B Minor by Bach.

•

They could have lived like that in New England. Coretta would have had the singing career she wanted, though he would have preferred that she put it to the side when the time came to raise a family. He could have accepted one of the job offers he started getting as soon as he finished the doctorate, as soon as he saw, for the first time, full of pride, his new full name, Dr. Martin Luther King, Jr., the distinction of the initials and abbreviations, "Ph.D." A professor of theology or philosophy, with a wool suit and leather elbow patches, white shirt, bow tie, pipe, a medieval dark gown and tam for official ceremonies, an office filled with books, academic journals, student papers, a window facing a lawn on campus, a house in a tree-lined suburb, not too far from the church that he would attend with his family on Sunday, and where he would preach every now and then as guest pastor.

Beneath the substrate of pure conviction was always the murmur of doubt, skepticism, remorse. The price of conformity was very high, but so was the price of rebellion, and the consequences of his action would affect others as well. Others would have raised their voices even if he did not. With more anger, more courage, more direct experience of the hardships he had not known. Others had risen in even darker times, and had paid the ultimate price without recognition or consequence

for their executioners, while he got to study at a university in Boston
and drive his own car to pick up his girlfriend and go to the classical
music concerts and the student dances; while he had the luxury of
traveling to Atlanta by plane during vacation and ordering his suits
made to measure.

•

Moses could have had a splendid life as an Egyptian prince. He indulged in these wonderings and then felt ashamed of them. *Nevertheless not my will, but thine, be done.* How arrogant to compare oneself to
a patriarch from the Old Testament; how insidious the suspicion that
all was in vain. Instead of progress the years seemed to bring new
possibilities for failure, new forms of bitterness. After every victory that
seemed certain and luminous, there had been rage and new cruelty.
Two weeks after the march in Washington, a bomb killed four little
girls in a church in Birmingham on a clear Sunday morning in
September. The tired crowd from the great march from Selma had
yet to disperse when that gang of murderers who never was punished
shot to death Viola Gregg Liuzzo, a blond woman, a mother of five, who
had driven all the way from Detroit by herself to help the organizers.
And after she was killed, the FBI lost no time spreading rumors about
her, saying that she was a bad mother, a bad wife, a promiscuous
woman who liked to sleep with black men.

Violence fueled more violence, and nonviolence. The righteous were
humiliated and the killers went unpunished. The clear sense of victory,
the intoxication of the struggle, the irrefutable virtue of self-sacrifice
and martyrdom, had abandoned him in the last few years. In the early
days of the movement, in Montgomery, in the incredulous joy of having resisted and prevailed in the boycott, he had believed that victories
were not only possible but also irreversible. Three hundred and eighty-
one days resisting, one after the other, walking on the sidewalks while
the empty buses drove by, giving one another rides, enduring with
dignity all the harassment by police.

Rise, take up thy bed, and walk. Black people in Montgomery had
risen up, as miraculously as the crippled man in the Gospel, after more
than three centuries of immobility and subjugation, and they had
started marching.

Confident steps heading in one direction; not dreams of paradise, but concrete achievements. The right to sit in a bus or go to school, the wonder of common things, ordering a sandwich and a soda in a cafeteria, drinking from a public fountain, taking a stroll in a park, registering to vote without fear of being harassed, beaten, or even killed. But a little time went by and what they had conquered was lost, or someone found a loophole in a law to frustrate or delay the reforms.

School integration was decreed and the governors from the southern states simply closed the schools, preferring no education to classes with black people. And what good was it to be able to sit in the same cafeteria with white people if you had no money to buy a sandwich and a coffee? You could send your children to the same public schools now, but white people had already taken their kids elsewhere and now the classrooms were as run-down as the old schools that had once been reserved for your people.

The segregation that was no longer allowed under the law was now more effectively enforced with money. They spent millions of dollars sending rockets to the moon but fought over cents for public schools and hospitals and soup kitchens. Gutted neighborhoods, ravaged by crime, by the simultaneous brutality of police and gangs, by misery and ignorance; neighborhoods torched by the self-destructive anger of the very same people who had no means of getting away.

And the young people were angry, drunk on violence, behaving like gangsters, filled with the same hate that white people had toward them, mocking him and those who were like him, hurling insults like any old white racist, Martin Lucifer King, Martin Loser King.

He had seen them just a few days before, right there in Memphis, and before they even started yelling and breaking streetlamps and windows, he had known what was coming, he had felt the swell of the terrified crowd pushing forward, the primitive fear of being knocked down and crushed. He saw the frightened faces of his friends, and the striking workers with their identical banners, vowels and simple consonants, like the sounds of a prayer or a work song, I AM A MAN I AM A MAN I AM A MAN. The workers with their sun-damaged faces, their rough hands, their Sunday clothes, surrounded him to protect him, while the commotion grew in the tail of the march, on the slope down Beale Street, the display windows exploding like hailstorms, and the police officers preparing their shields and batons and sounding their sirens, grinning widely under the visors of their helmets, waiting for the perfect moment to launch their attack and plant the seed of terror in the rest of the crowd.

And while the young, in perfect formation, tore the banners to use the masts as weapons and began to throw rocks, breaking streetlights and windows, the shards of glass fell on the faces of terrorized people, screaming in panic, bleeding, fainting, overtaken by a flood that dragged everything in its path, the blindness of someone who is drowning and can't get their head above water.

Later he saw his own face on the front page of the newspaper and felt ashamed by the public evidence of the fear he had felt: his body held by others, as if about to drown and not even trying to continue swimming, with his eyes wide open, a sheep or cow who has seen the glint of the blade that is coming for them.

•

He had never wished death more intensely than in those last few days, death because he knew he was too caught up in that world where there was no longer any other possible life for him. *Why died I not from the womb? Why did I not give up the ghost when I came out of the belly?* To close one's eyes and never have to open them again. To come home at night, very late, exhausted, after a long trip or an entire day of meetings; to get out of the car and look for the house keys under the dim streetlights, in the silence of a late hour; to have no time to even feel the impact, the bullet fired at close range from behind the honeysuckle tree; to die quickly and never know anything else. *For now should I have lain still and been quiet, I should have slept: then had I been at rest.*

To close one's eyes and be lost in sleep; to not wake up in anguish before the night is even over. *Wherefore I praised the dead which are already dead more than the living which are yet alive.* To die so you don't have to keep looking at the newspaper or at the television in anticipation of what they would be saying about you now.

The apostle of nonviolence was at the center of a riot caused by followers he could no longer control; he had left the scene cowardly, in a limousine that took him to the most luxurious hotel in Memphis, while his people burned the whole place down.

There was nothing they would not accuse him of. He was a communist and a traitor, a social climber who accepts money from white people. While he was safe at his luxury hotel, a cop was firing at a black boy at close range and then finishing him off on the ground with a bullet to the head. He preached evangelical poverty but had no trouble accepting gifts and treats from the millionaires of Park Avenue and Fifth Avenue, the docile black man who assured them there would be no revolution, the one who flew as a guest of honor in Nelson Rockefeller's private jet. While American soldiers were dying heroically in Vietnam, he was taking the side of the communists, the enemies.

•

He had wished to simply die. He had longed for that moment in Harlem when the letter opener sank into his chest and his white shirt was quickly soaked in blood, the sweet instant when he lost consciousness. *For now should I have lain still and been quiet, I should have slept: then had I been at rest.* He had secretly wished, with obsessive impatience, with a morbid desire for sacrifice and martyrdom, that one of the death threats finally came true, one of those anonymous letters or calls in the middle of the night.

One shot and everything would end. One shot and perhaps he would even be lucky enough to not hear or feel anything. No one knew that he wasn't brave: death was the only thing that no longer scared him. Much worse than dying is to never rest, always running late, always with the knowledge that somewhere else there's a crowd waiting for you, that you will have to get on a stage again, face the blinding lights, and gather all your strength to repeat words that remain true and just, but that you simply can't bear to hear yourself say again.

•

But this night, at the temple, after a few minutes of struggling to find his rhythm, the words began to flow on their own with a power that he had not anticipated or even thought he possessed anymore. They did not feel like his words. They did not flow from his tired repertoire. Their metallic echo filled and shook the room like the thunder outside. He felt overwhelmed by the words and hypnotized by the metal and cadence of his own voice, no longer governed by reason or will, and much less by the rhetorical devices of a preacher. Something similar had happened in those days of fear and solitude at the prison in Birmingham, the solitary confinement cell in a basement where only the sounds of boots, metal, and rats could be heard. A trance. *Then took they Jeremiah, and cast him into the dungeon of Malchiah the son of Hammelech, that was in the court of the prison: and they let down Jeremiah with cords. And in the dungeon there was no water, but mire: so Jeremiah sunk in the mire.*

Someone had left a newspaper in the cell. In the fold of a pocket, he found a pencil they missed during the pat-down. He began to write with the light that filtered through the bars, using the margins of the newspaper. There was barely any light and his eyes hurt from trying to focus on the small handwriting. He had to take advantage of every blank space. When steps approached, he hid the pencil and sat on the newspaper. At some point, he began to write so fast, the writing was running ahead of his thinking. The ecclesiastical formalities had given way to vindicated and outraged vehemence.

He would sharpen the pencil against the wall and continue filling margin after margin. When he ran out of space, a black prisoner who distributed food gave him some scraps of paper. It was so hot inside the cell, he had to keep wiping the sweat from his hands and forehead to protect the paper. He wrote without uncertainty, without turning back, with absolute conviction that he was right, that this was the truth and it was being dictated to him.

•

It was like that now, at the temple. He was speaking instead of writing, but the words flowed with the same urgency. He was at a pulpit in front of two thousand people instead of in a cell, but the fever was identical, the inner flood, the trance. The words swelled up as powerfully as the air that filled his lungs at every breath. He felt the blood rush through his body, his hands clutching the edges of the lectern as he leaned in.

He held up the Bible and there was no need to open it because he knew its every word, and the right passages came to his lips as he needed them. He held the book like a tool, a percussion instrument to strike against his palm, a hammer that sounded like thunder.

He no longer thought about the proximity of his friends or tried to see beyond the blinding lights and the TV cameras. He spoke into a darkness or an abyss of silence populated by a few voices. He challenged them and said things he had never said aloud before, only acknowledged to himself. He was alone at the top of the stage and far from the stands of the huge auditorium but he still perceived the unanimous response of the crowd as if he were singing the call of a work song. At thirty-nine years he felt as old as Moses and saw everything before him with a strange clarity that must only come after death.

There was angst pressing out against his chest, the sadness of a farewell but also a unique joy. The fever that unleashed his words was its own fuel and intensified.

Like a musician in a state of trance, he kept going deeper inside himself, while commanding with even greater control the attention and fervor of the crowd. All the darkness that had been germinating within him was suddenly bursting from his chest in a torrent of words. Fear became courage, despair became defiance, frustration became serenity. He defied whoever wanted to kill him or slander him. No man scared him; no lie, no humiliation, no extortion. He opened his eyes wide as if he were seeing events that did not yet exist, things that would only happen after he died.

He finished abruptly and could only stand with his hands clutching the lectern. Abernathy hugged him and led him to a chair. He was drenched in sweat as if they had just pulled him half-conscious from a river.

•

How strange that a night and almost a full day later, that lightness of being, that calm without guilt, was still with him. It remained like the warmth of the afternoon in Memphis, that suspended moment when the sky is an ember of light before dusk. The wind was picking up. Perhaps it was better to go back and get a coat.

Abernathy was still in the bathroom, although he had promised not to take long, just a moment to put on a bit of cologne. The driver of the Cadillac had turned on the engine. She would be in her room, downstairs, with the door half-open, attentive to the sounds outside, perhaps applying lipstick in the mirror, waiting to distinguish his voice among the many, so she could leave right at that moment and get in the other car. It was now too late to smoke that cigarette after all.

Next to the Cadillac he recognized one of the musicians who would play that night, the trumpeter. He had made him promise to play "Take My Hand, Precious Lord." God can take it all or give it all, more than you can dare ask, more than the poor imagination can desire. Leaning on the balcony, he counted all the gifts he had received on that trip, in just a few hours, the trip to Memphis that he had undertaken with such reluctance, with a taste of ashes in his mouth, so deep into that darkness of the soul that he never thought he would come out.

It was not that he had regained hope, but rather, he did not need to feel it, just as at this moment he did not feel fear, physical exhaustion, or even the passage of time. At dawn, in her room, as he was saying goodbye, he had said: "What little time we have." But he had said it without complaint, with gratitude that such little time could encompass so many gifts, secret lights in other people's rooms and in motels, minutes that were rescued from the whirlwind of obligations, the mandatory fate that he no longer saw any point in resisting, just as you can't rebel against chance, or the times you had to live, or the color of your skin.

•

But it was time to go. The more precious the time, the faster it runs. Below, his friends were getting in the cars and asking him to hurry. He caught a whiff of Abernathy's cologne and as his hands left the railing a shot he would not hear pierced through his jaw and his neck and his spine and lifted him up and threw him against the door of room 306 and then onto the concrete floor, where he remained with his eyes wide open and an expression of awe and wonder, a knee bent and a foot with a black shoe and a black sock sticking through the bars of the balcony, shaking.

26

I stop writing around 9:00 p.m. and take a shower before leaving. The room turns dark as I try to reconstruct a single minute forty-six years ago and imagine what took place in someone else's mind. But in the facade of the house right across the street, faint rays of the sun still shine on the balcony. It's an old stone building with chipped blue and white azulejo tiles. Sometimes I see in the interior a man in a T-shirt walking slowly from one end of the room to the other, as if looking for something. The balcony is filled with lush geraniums that perfume the sidewalk below.

The street is a cul-de-sac, resembling an old neighborhood courtyard. At the entrance, an Art Nouveau sign in blue and white tiles reads: VILA BERTA. Colorful pennant garlands that are starting to fade hang across the street, over the rooftops, along the cornices, and from balcony to balcony.

We can hear the voices of neighbors who lean out the windows to have conversations with those on the sidewalk. We hear the children play and cry, and the sound of brooms sweeping and mops splashing water on the floors. In the mornings, very early, the most clear sound is the whistling of the swallows.

When it's late, at three or four in the morning, and the intoxication of what I imagine and write no longer lets me sleep, I lean out the window and stare at the quiet shadows of the street.

Sometimes, through the open windows, the breeze carries the smell of stews or grilled sardines and people's conversations. Grass grows between the cobblestones. The only house on the block that stands out with a bit of opulence has one of those Lisbon rooftops that rise with the subtle curves of Chinese or Japanese architecture, a garden surrounded by grand trees, and bougainvilleas spilling over the wall.

•

I'm off for a walk but the satisfaction of having worked part of the morning and all afternoon does not clear my head. The shower, the wet hair in the warm afternoon, the cool breeze are not enough to take my mind from everything that has been occupying it for so long.

I have left the house but not the book where I have lived for so many months. We have returned to Lisbon so I can continue following his final episodes. I enjoy the anticipation of our meeting and a dinner in a different part of the city, but part of me remains hypnotized in front of the computer screen, the basements, the aisles of virtual files, reports, testimonies, confessions, newspaper clippings, forensic photographs, sketches of the bullet trajectory.

I have spent the entire afternoon exploring a few minutes in the afternoon of April 4, 1968. I step out of South Main and Mulberry Streets, the Lorraine Motel, Bessie Brewer's boardinghouse, and onto Vila Berta and Graça Street. A few steps take me from a distant dusk in April 1968 to this sunset today.

That afternoon someone heard the blast of a firecracker or the exhaust of a car. Someone else was certain it was a shot. But a car mechanic who was having a drink at Jim's Grill after work said the bar and the pinball machine were so loud he did not hear anything. In the music store next door, the owner had been playing music, and the two customers who had been looking through jazz records did not remember any alarming sound, just the police sirens wailing outside.

At the Lorraine Motel, in one of the ground-level rooms, Reverend A. D. King, the younger brother of Martin Luther King, Jr., slept so soundly from a hangover the shot did not wake him up. Georgia Davis, who hadn't seen King since he left her room before dawn, was applying her lipstick in the mirror. Ralph Abernathy was putting on cologne.

In Largo da Graça, most of the small shops have closed, but the bakeries and fruit stores are still open and the cafes are buzzing with people having dinner. I like this square, the stone, the trees, the benches where there are always people chatting or watching. The sound of the Lisbon tram reminds me of the trolleys in Memphis. But the ones in Memphis travel in straight lines, and are oftentimes empty, almost spectral, like the sidewalks where no one walks, the boarded-up buildings, and the stores with RENT signs in the windows.

•

Tram 28 turns the corner at the bottom of Graça Street. Seen from the front, it looks taller, narrower, almost weightless on the rails. It's still light out but its headlight is already on. Especially at night and dawn, the single headlight of the trams gives them an underwater quality.

At the jail in Memphis, Ray complained about the blinding light that stayed on day and night. But according to the police officers who kept watch, he slept most of the time, had an excellent appetite, and even joked with them. The guards brought him a sleeping mask so the lights would not bother him as much when he tried to sleep. He laughed as he put it on and asked them if he looked like Zorro.

I have seen photos of the prison wing that was reserved exclusively for him. It looks more like a hospital than a prison, with white surfaces and linoleum floors, and aseptic bars like a psychiatric ward. The first day, when they brought him from the airport in a caravan of armored cars, after removing the handcuffs, the waist chain, the leg shackles, and the bulletproof vest, they served him a big breakfast of scrambled eggs, sausages, white bread, and coffee. He ate to his heart's content and then slept deeply for six hours. For lunch, he had grilled meat, peas, roasted potatoes, beet salad, pudding, and iced tea. In the mornings wake-up time was at 6:30 a.m. for breakfast, but sometimes he wasn't hungry and kept sleeping until nine or ten, or had breakfast, read the paper for a bit, and went back to bed. On the website for the archives of the Memphis police, every minute of his life in pretrial custody is accounted for. He ends up escaping the electric chair by pleading guilty and accepting a sentence of ninety-nine years; then he recants his confession, pleads innocent, and demands a retrial that he will never get.

He wrote, of course, but only in stretches of half an hour or forty minutes. He read an entire paper in the morning and one in the afternoon. He asked for the weekly editions of *Newsweek* and *U.S. News & World Report*. He would walk for hours around the prison wing, walking fast, stopping only at the end of the corridor and turning around immediately, the way prisoners walk in the recreational yard. He took two aspirins every six hours for his headaches.

Sometimes he watched television and became furious when the news media painted him in a negative light, or when they talked about his miserable origins and his disastrous family. According to the logbook, he spent a lot of time reading, though the record does not state the titles. He would get tired of reading and start doing push-ups. He challenged the guards to push-up contests and always won. He told them stories about his time as a fugitive and the absurd calamities of his criminal career: the time he robbed a Chinese restaurant—for nothing, the loot was shit—and his military ID fell from his pocket as he ran out; the time he stole a car after a robbery but forgot to lock the door and almost fell out flying around a curve. He watched baseball on TV. The boarded-up windows and the permanent ceiling lights made him lose his sense of time but not his ability to sleep. Sometimes he slept for eight or ten hours at a time. He also took naps. Some nights he twisted and turned in bed, mumbling in his sleep.

•

Tram 28 brakes with the squeaking of metal and the gnashing of wood. I get in and scan my transport pass like any other passenger. You begin to know a city when you can walk quickly and use public transit without trouble. At this time of day, it's easy to get a seat. Staring out the window of a Lisbon tram is one of the great pleasures in life. The tram moves through the city in a very physical way, like walking, instead of the smooth speed of a car or a bus.

Every time I see a tram I imagine Ray sitting inside—though there's no evidence he ever took one—foreign and silent, blinking a lot or hiding his eyes behind sunglasses. From Figueira Square, just outside the Hotel Portugal, he could have taken the tram to the bars on Cais do Sodré.

I'm living in two worlds and two times, in the same city. I like the way that Tram 28 reaches the end of Largo da Graça and suddenly slopes down Voz do Operário Street in a straight line toward the Tagus River, where the golden sun is setting.

My gaze could be his. I'm watching the passengers in the tram climbing uphill toward us, and a pale man in sunglasses stares back at me. It could be him, it could have been him. I pretend, even with you and often without success, that I live in reality and in the present.

•

The tram continues its improbable journey through narrow winding streets, the wheels creak on the rails, and you can almost touch the walls of the houses. People get on the sidewalks and press their backs against the wall, so the tram can pass. A woman looks at me from behind the window of a small appliances shop. Above us the cables of the tram form a grid against the sky. It stops abruptly halfway up a slope and seems about to roll back. But it resumes with a jolt, a mechanical obstinacy, and continues its ascent with no apparent effort, passing within millimeters of dumpsters and parked cars, navigating around them with the prowess of a sea creature.

I'm lost in my thoughts and at the same time I perceive and take pleasure in everything around me. A baroque angel in the dusty window of an antiques shop. The profile of a foreign tourist standing next to the window on the other side, holding a guide to Lisbon. An enormous palace with all the drama of an impending collapse, with the stem of a tree growing through a crack in a balcony. A square opens up like a great outlook with bar terraces and an enormous statue of white stone that I now recognize as Saint Vincent.

The gradual knowledge organizes sights that had previously been unforeseen occurrences, situating them with certainty in a mental map of the city that with each visit becomes more dense and complete. I'm writing a novel at the same time that I'm discovering a city. In this square, which now has a name and an exact position in our daily routes, we arrived unexpectedly, the way one arrives somewhere in a dream, that night in December, during our walk with Paula and Arturo.

That night, the only voices, the only steps, were ours, and the only presence was the statue. But today, the square is buzzing with people eating outside, groups of tourists, street musicians and vendors, kids doing acrobatics to the sounds of hip-hop blasting from a boom box. I was listening to John Coltrane play "Alabama," with Elvin Jones on the drums, and I didn't know the terrible and hopeful resonance that this name could have for an African-American man in the early 1960s, or the fact that Coltrane had tried to re-create in that intense and mystical melody the cadence of the sermons of Martin Luther King.

•

Se escrevo o que sinto é porque assim diminuo a febre de sentir, says Fernando Pessoa. If I write what I feel, it's to reduce the fever of feeling. Feverish images and words proliferate like coral through the depths of insomnia. I feel I won't be able to sleep well until I know everything, until I have reviewed every detail and thread of the story. There isn't a blank space behind what could have been the final period of that fateful shot. And a shot does not exhaust and does not even summarize what happened in that instant, at six in the afternoon, six and one minute.

In the firehouse, just in front of the Lorraine Motel, the windows are covered with newspapers, as if painters were working on the place. But the newspaper sheets have small holes and behind, police officers and FBI agents keep watch, take photos of everyone who goes in and out of the hotel, and write down every license plate. One of the police officers hears the shot as he is watching King through his binoculars. At first, he does not believe what he has just seen and does not alert the others. But he looks at King again, now on the floor, as if he had missed a frame in the sequence; the knee is bent, a foot protruding from the balcony.

There isn't a fragment of information that under the magnifying lens of my insomnia does not become memorable. In the Lorraine Motel, at six and one minute, a maid is walking on the second floor and passing room 304. She was so busy she did not notice Dr. King standing by the railing two doors down. She only saw him as he fell back at the moment of the explosion, and she dropped everything.

At Bessie Brewer's boardinghouse, the deaf-mute from room 6B and the drunk from 4B (who had tried to open the bathroom door just minutes earlier) were watching television in her room and she did not understand why his face suddenly turned toward the window.

•

The novel simplifies life. It simplifies it and it tames it. It begets its own fever, especially when you intuit its end. I don't want to watch films, or listen to music that isn't spirituals, songs from the civil rights movement, and jazz from that time. I don't want to write articles, or give lectures, or plan trips, or see exhibits. All I need is a wooden desk and a laptop. If the laptop crashes or its battery dies, I would continue in a notebook. I don't read anything that doesn't have to do with what I'm writing.

The novel subjects life to its own limits and at the same time opens it up to an exploration of depths that are within and without you and that only you were meant to discover. You're writing even when you don't write. Narrative imagination does not feed on what is invented; it feeds on the past. Every minor or trivial event that one experiences or discovers in the course of an investigation can be valuable or even decisive for the novel, occupying a minimal but precise place within it, like an uneven cobblestone in a sidewalk in Lisbon.

I barely read the newspaper. I don't bother to open magazines or packages with books. I have deleted myself without difficulty, and to great relief, from social networks. I'm exercising my right to an ancient form of solitude, disconnected from everything; dedicating my time to one thing, and doing so because that's what I desire, for pleasure, for the satisfaction of the process in and of itself; free, for now, from all the anxiety that is sure to come, the uncertainty of the result, the fear of hostile reviews, the emptiness or silence that will overcome me when the book is published and I wait to hear from the first unknown readers.

The Internet is the gateway to a vast archive where every day I discover new information that feeds my writing. Admirers from all over the world write to Ray asking for his autograph. A firefighter said he did not remember the shot but he did remember the rattling of the windows. Ray wrote over four hundred letters during his time in prison and they have been preserved in the archives of Boston University. The store clerk who sold him the binoculars around 4:15 p.m. on April 4 was surprised to see him in a suit and with a loose tie. At the Canadian embassy in Lisbon, the person who helped him fill out the passport application said he held the pen and the forms as if he could not write or read.

When he was about to pay for something, he took money directly from his pockets, instead of a wallet. Several female witnesses noted with displeasure the excessive amounts of hair pomade he wore. After the shot, King's face looked as if it had been torn from front to back. At the jail in Memphis, he sang in the shower when he was in a good mood. The gush of blood from the wound reached the door of the room. Among the things that Ray left behind in the boardinghouse in Atlanta were maps of the southeastern United States, Texas, Oklahoma, Mexico, Louisiana, Los Angeles, California, Arizona, New Mexico, and Birmingham.

Some people thought he looked like an insurance agent, a door-to-door salesman, a preacher. In King's pockets, at the time of his death, there were two ten-dollar bills, a five, three ones, forty-five cents in change, a silver pen, various business cards, and an appointment book for the year 1968 with black covers.

The novel has developed on its own with the unlimited richness of reality and the blank spaces I haven't been tempted to fill, spaces in the shadows that cannot be illuminated, mostly because it has been too long, most of the witnesses have died, and memory is quite fragile.

The novel is what I write and also the room where I work. The novel is the fine-point pen that ran out of ink one day when I wrote for five or six hours without stopping and filled an entire notebook. The novel is made with everything I know and everything I don't know, and with the sensation of groping my way through this story but never finding a precise narrative outline. In 1977 James Earl Ray escaped from prison and remained on the run for fifty hours, chased by hundreds of armed officers, dogs, helicopters with searchlights, through a forest in the mountains of Tennessee. They found him hiding in a ditch, cold and starved, crouching under a layer of branches in an area infested with snakes.

The novel writes itself while I type away at the computer and also when I sit quietly and pensively with both hands on the edge of the table. It writes itself now as I travel in Tram 28 to meet with you at a pub you found on the corner of a sloping street, near the Bica Elevator and the viewpoint of Santa Catarina. After dinner, we're going to Cais do Sodré to see the lights of the bars and peek inside those doorways and stairways where he would have disappeared with women in tight skirts and high heels echoing on the stone steps.

Where does a story begin, where does it end? Don Quixote learns that Ginés de Pasamonte, one of the criminals he released with great folly, is writing his own autobiography. Don Quixote asks him if he has finished it, and Ginés responds: "How can it be finished, when my life is not yet finished?" We have been apart all afternoon and I'm dying to see you. Perhaps from the sidewalk, I will catch a glimpse of your face before you notice. To love the face is to love the soul.

Tram 28 rises and falls like a sailboat on the rolling waves of Lisbon's hills. Alone, in her room at the Lorraine Motel, her eyes wide open in the dark, stunned by the unreality of pain, hearing the sounds of police sirens and fire trucks in the distance, Memphis in flames, Georgia Davis notices a sound above her ceiling, a rubbing, a scraping. She comes out of her room and stands in the empty parking lot under the red, blue, and yellow glow of the motel sign. On the second floor, in front of room 306, custodians work quietly, scrubbing with sponges and rags the wall, the door, the floor to erase the traces of blood.